I0746061

THE MATCHLESS

by

Justin Robinson

A HellBound Books Publishing LLC Book
Houston TX

Justin Robinson

A HellBound Books LLC
Publication

Copyright © 2019 by HellBound Books Publishing LLC
All Rights Reserved

Cover and art design by
HellBound Books Publishing LLC

No part of this book may be reproduced, stored in a retrieval system, or transmitted by any means, electronic, mechanical, photocopying, recording or otherwise without written permission from the author This book is a work of fiction. Names, characters, places and incidents are entirely fictitious or are used fictitiously and any resemblance to actual persons, living or dead, events or locales is purely coincidental.

www.hellboundbookspublishing.com

Printed in the United States of America

THE MATCHLESS

The Kingdom

Nadia Eskandarian stood in the place her sister died. *Was murdered,* Nadia reminded herself. "Died" was too peaceful a word. It cut away the thorns drawing beads of crimson from the memory. She had to keep those, keep the stark reality of what happened by her heart. Never forget that Odette Eskandarian's life had ended in strange agony.

Had she been told, "Your sister has been murdered," at a younger age, she might have pictured a rolling moor from a Sherlock Holmes story. Somewhere cold and cruel, mysterious and dark. Even when she had been informed—she was away at her first year of Oberlin then—that Odette's body had been found in the Hollywood Hills, Nadia had the flash of those cold moors, before the hideous reminder that the Hills were home.

She had cried for three days. On the plane home, through the funeral. Inconsolable. Odette had been a good sister. Maybe looking at her, you wouldn't think it. She was the picture perfect Hollywood party girl: the painted-on dresses, the heavy makeup, the dangly gold earrings. She looked like expensive perfume and smelled like ivory. In those days, Nadia had still been her little bookworm imago, the skinny girl in baggy clothes who ran track and scored straight As.

But Odette knew her secret. It wasn't a secret now, but when it had been, Odette was the first on the inside. The first to know the true Nadia, and the first to love her with full knowledge of her being.

Nadia stood on the sun-kissed plateau overlooking Hollywood. The Hills were brown and gold, desiccated by the drought. The trees were cracked, their leaves like paper. Below, haze choked the city, making it look like something from a poison dream, disappearing into the smoke of awakening. All that was real was here. Close.

Six years ago. Six years gone by, and Nadia had only just gained the courage to come up here and see it for herself. She had been home, over breaks, from Oberlin. Then again while getting her master's at Berkeley. This site was an itch in her mind, an abscess she could not get to. It was there, waiting, but she could not go.

She still could not. Standing on this place—a patio, scorched by fire and cracked by sun, but a patio, recognizable and incurably mundane—she still could not go where Odette's body was found. That would be at the bottom of the swimming pool, calling to her with the horrible need of the restless. She was twenty feet away, trying not to look at the grimy lip, knowing that was where her sister died.

Was murdered.

She turned away from it. The plateau where this place stood was artificial, dug away and flattened a long time ago. A crumbling tiled wall kept the hill back, brown dirt spilling through in anthill piles. Near the pool, the tiles were in the pattern of a jellyfish, fish darting through its tentacles. The pattern was faded, but it would never be burned away entirely. When the dirt finally consumed it, the broken tiles would still have their puzzle pattern of the jellyfish, waiting for an archaeologist to unearth and wonder at the gods of the past.

Across the patio stood the scorched skeleton of an old Hollywood manor. These places dotted the Hills, some concealed by folds of land or explosions of brush, others exposed beneath the punishing sun. Some were perfectly preserved, still inhabited by someone clutching with white knuckles the fading glamor of the old city of dreams. Some were falling apart around the ears of a star or studio executive whose time was long past. Others were like this: abandoned, forgotten until something terrible gave them false life again.

It was the mansion of Eben Simcoe, a producer in the '20s, who was utterly broken by the Depression. Nadia only knew this because she had to know everything about this place where her sister was killed. Maybe knowledge would mean never having to face it.

She had been wrong.

The fire that destroyed the house was the only reason the police found Odette at all. Her boyfriend Tyrone's body had already surfaced, lying dead in their apartment—assumed killed by the same man who murdered her—and she was considered missing. Los Angeles was a big place, and no one would have ever looked here. Why would they? Only the dead knew it existed. Not until it shone bright orange against the purple hills, and firefighters made the awful discovery.

The burning house was filled with bodies. Some of them had been matched to missing persons, some remained unidentified. Most were men, though there was a little boy in there, and a woman as well. Other bodies lay on the patio, but unlike those who had been burned to death, these had been crushed. Mashed into a pulp somehow. Then there was her sister and the murderer, found together, entwined at the bottom of the pool.

Nadia liked to imagine this was Odette's last act of defiance. Somehow, she had turned the tables on her killer and taken him with her into death.

The Simcoe Killer was a mystery. He had no name. No record. No face even. That had been obliterated in whatever struggle had finally killed him. The only survivor of the attack, a lone woman, had been unable to identify him either. Nadia sometimes wished she could track this woman down, try to find anything else out about the man who killed Odette. She wouldn't get anything, but she would have liked to have known that for certain rather than just feeling it in her bones. The woman was a ghost. Her name would never be released, and any dream of finding her was just that.

The Simcoe Killer had turned into one of those weird news stories that occasionally made listicles of strange or terrifying crimes, but for most it passed out of consciousness. For Nadia, it had become everything.

It had to lead to here, a final exorcism. See the last place Odette was alive. Resolutely place the awful crime in the past.

Nadia could not face the pool. She was certain Odette would be in there. The six years wouldn't have completely stripped the flesh from her face, either. She would be horrible, rotting, her rage a harsh, undirected thing. At Nadia, at the world, at whoever was close. The Simcoe Killer was past her vengeance. Nadia was right there, and death would have robbed what remained of Odette's sanity. The bright sun of the drought-scrubbed skies should have banished the nightmares to their dank homes. Instead, it made Odette all too real. Nadia could hear her sister, the immaculate French tips scritching the pool's walls, trying to climb out.

Nadia turned to the remains of the house. It must have been something special before the fire claimed it, turned it to ash, and blew it into the sky. The area was huge, nearly as large as her parents' home on Mulholland. The walls were gone with only a few ribs still poking upward. A tree, nearly entirely consumed, looked to have been growing out of the side of the house. Now it was only a few shards of blackened wood.

Nadia paused at the threshold. The entire area was black and gray with soot and dust. The hills had only just begun to reclaim it, as though nature could sense that this was an unholy site.

Unholy.

The word felt right to Nadia, though not quite perfect. Holy. She rebelled against that as well, both her past, raised Christian like a good Armenian girl, and her present, this modern maybe-pagan maybe-atheist. The word was a tool of the old, a tool of the patriarchy, trying to pass ownership over something it could never understand. And yet, as she stepped over the threshold, between patio to ash, a tangible shiver passed through her body.

She stood in the burned-out mansion. The sounds of the hills—the slight breeze, the birds imitating car alarms, the distant grind of traffic—were muted. Maybe she was imagining the hallowed sensation drawing icy fingers up her spine. Maybe so many deaths could linger. That amount of pain and fear could leave a scar upon the world.

Nadia had not seen much more than the few pictures in the papers. They were on the LA Times website and could be found anywhere there was a fascination with true crime. The Simcoe Killer had quite the body count, and the most odd fact was that they all seemed to die that night. All of them, with lungs full of smoke and skin burnt crispy, had been slain in the same blaze.

Begged the question: what had he been doing with them until then?

The picture she had in mind was of the burned-out manor, from the other angle. A single shot over the scorched house, sheets covering indistinct lumps. They were all in one place, as though they had been sleeping in a giant lump when it had happened, and only had seconds to try to crawl to something approaching safety. It was a small mercy that Odette was not among them. Nadia wondered if it was because she had been taken relatively recently. She hoped it could be nothing else. That her sister had been spared the worst of the killer's evil.

There was another shot, and this was the one that continued to haunt her.

It was of the pool. That night, it had rained. Maybe the last good rain Los Angeles had before the drought. The shot was pointing down from the lip, and Nadia always imagined the photographer being pulled back and restrained by cops for breaking the crinkling yellow barrier of police tape. It showed the pool, partway filled with dark water, and two shapes, indistinct but horrible in the implication. Two grinning, shredded bodies. One was the Simcoe Killer.

The other was Odette.

Nadia swallowed, collecting herself.

In the middle of the burned-out house, a vibrant splash of green burst up from the ground. It wasn't the emerald of the jungle but rather the soft verdigris of the desert. It was something between a tree and a bush, a low, brown trunk with sharp branches like veins reaching upward. These were covered in brush-like leaves, and collections of red, ripe berries. The color of blood.

Nadia took a step forward. The bushes, and there were several, all grew in a copse. She frowned, taking another step. Her boot crunched on some fallen timber, not yet quite ground to dust. The plant fascinated her. She thought she had seen every kind of flora Southern California had. It looked somewhat like a mix between a manzanita and sagebrush, but not quite either. Those berries were like nothing she had ever seen, like tiny brains, blooming from a bed of delicate leaves.

The berries were ripe, but nothing fed upon them. The dirt and surrounding foliage were alive with brown grasshoppers and stained-glass beetles. Nothing came near the unfamiliar succulent fruit.

She took another step. Now she could smell the plant. She had expected it to bear the indistinct rosemary smell of most of the local plants, making everything outdoors carry the vague aroma of a spice rack. These had the undeniable meaty scent of fried fat. Not overpowering, just enough to make her recoil.

She hesitated as she reached for a berry. She had never been a squeamish person, but it felt like she was plucking a red ripe sore. She scolded herself; it was the location, Odette's death close enough to make her superstitious. The chiding rang hollow.

Still, she picked one from its bed of leaves.

The berry shivered. Nadia's fingers were long and slender, little more than bone and tendon. In them, the berry was stout. She allowed it to fall into her narrow palm. It lay there, still. Yet, the persistent hum worked its way through flesh, through her bones. She felt it in her teeth and jaw, like a sound she could feel, but could never hear. Some kind of life still animated it, hidden in the fleshy interior. Some kind of power.

She put it in the outer pocket of her satchel, a brown canvas messenger bag with leather belts securing it shut. She kept the berry without thinking, only knowing it would have felt weird, wrong even, to leave it.

The sun beat down on her head, sweat running in streams down the shaven sides. She stretched her shoulders, standing straighter in the hot day. She had the unshakeable sense that this place was somehow hers. These berries were her... food, property, tools. The words jumbled in her mind, but in the sun, in the burned-out place, it was true.

She opened her eyes and turned from the impossible plant. The sensation receded, but it did not vanish. It filled her with power. A frightening power. She was holding back a massive tide, and she did know if she could, or if it would engulf her. Like the dirt against the tiled wall, it would masticate her into shards, burying her with the rest of the ghosts.

She stepped out of the ring of ash, expecting the power to go with it. A momentary dream in the home of nightmares. It didn't; this entire place was holy.

She walked across the patio toward the pool. This was where police and firefighters found several bodies literally smashed flat. They looked to have been crushed by something heavy, but there was nothing close by that could have done it. Despite the hideous damage, they were the easiest to identify, since most of them had wallets on them. They turned out to be high-end security personnel, expensive bodyguards, hired by one of the victims. Police assumed they were attempting to rescue their employer when the Simcoe Killer somehow crushed them before being mangled and drowning in the pool. Most of the reports didn't acknowledge the holes in the official story, though these were leered over with pornographic glee whenever the tale found itself being rehashed.

The questions were not the worst part, but they had kept Nadia up at night. She was the little sister, the baby of the family. It was never her job to protect Odette from the big bad world. In fact, it had been Odette who had served that purpose for her, keeping a secret for Nadia and never once questioning it. There was no sense of justice, no desire for revenge. Odette had killed her killer somehow.

No. Nadia could not do it.

Her vision wobbled as her legs grew rigid. She could not approach this site. Not yet. There was too much here. Too much she might see.

She turned and fled. She did not run. She would not run. A flight of concrete stairs—another common sight on the hills of Los Angeles—led up to the patio, and she stumbled down these. Once, Simcoe Manor could be found off a side-street from Franklin Avenue, leading up into the hills. Now that place had been abandoned and grown over. When the murders had first been discovered, the path had been cleared. Time had passed, and even in the midst of the drought, hardy desert plants had reclaimed the pathway.

Finding it had been disturbingly easy. Directions right to it were on a website with the locations for all of LA's famous murders. Manson, Ramirez, Bugsy Siegel, and the newest entrant, the Simcoe Killer. It had given two separate sets of directions, one approaching through Griffith Park and the other up from Franklin. Nadia had chosen the latter, because it was closer to where her sister had lived. She thought that Odette might have taken that path—or been taken on it—and Nadia wanted to replicate her sister's route. She needed the connection.

She was thanking that impulse now, as she staggered down the path, mentally chastising herself for weakness. She knew Simcoe Manor was special, but she had thought it was for the violence that had stained it. She hadn't known it had become holy.

After the staircase, nearly hidden in a pergola of brambles, it was a relatively easy slope heading down to the street. Her legs were stiffened with fear, yet at the same time rubbery, ready to buckle underneath her at any moment.

She did not remember the entire walk. Later, she thought she must have blacked out and somehow her muscles kept puppeting her along the road. She was not there, and then suddenly she was, fumbling at the handle of the door of her car. It opened silently, and she collapsed in the driver's seat, breathing quickly trying to tell herself it was over. They were all dead. It was only the past, and the past could never touch her.

Her car was a late-model Audi, sleek and silver, a gift from her parents. She hadn't wanted it. Too flashy, too rich for who she was. They had insisted. They had an image to keep up, and if the youngest Eskandarian insisted on walking around looking like she looked, she at least would show the family took care of their own. So she accepted it, and tried to be thankful that at least she didn't have to worry about getting anywhere.

If they ever cut her off, the car would go with their goodwill.

She reached for a half-full bottle of water sitting in the drink holder, taking a mouthful and sloshing it around, cutting through the gummy mass of dirt and dried saliva.

Nadia started her car and made her way home.

The drive was easy, hugging the foothill as she headed west toward Laurel Canyon. Living at home was a hard thing to get used to after six years of school. There wasn't much choice. She had spent that time getting a Master's in English, and if she wanted to teach college, she was going to have to return for her PhD. She could not face the endless papers, the blue essay books, the casual sexism and homophobia of her professors. A year or two off might worry the edge off her anger, but in the meantime, no one was hiring

English majors. She felt she owed it to young women like her, who didn't have a voice they recognized analyzing literature, but a degree would have to wait.

She could have worked for her father's agency. Her brother Lex did, and was doing well for himself. They would have insisted she start presenting a little more femme, conform to the largely unwritten dress codes of the culture. Perhaps no skirts and blouses, but at least grow a full head of hair. You'd be so pretty if only you [fill in the blank], was her mother's favorite sentence, usually followed with a gruff nod from her father or at least a grunt of distant approval. She didn't have the energy to explain that she was all woman, but she preferred pants over skirts and felt like a fraud in makeup. When Odette had died—was murdered—they had given her clothes to Nadia. The ultra-femme designer stuff she could never wear. She had found refuge in the excuse that nothing fit. That, at least, had been factually true. Odette was all curves; Nadia was all angles.

It was hard enough dressing like herself. Telling them she was gay had been thus far impossible.

Part of her thought it was bizarre they hadn't figured it out, but Vartan and Siranush Eskandarian were old fashioned people in many ways. To them, she was still locked in some misguided teenaged rebellion. She never dated because she was a late bloomer, or because she insisted on making herself ugly. There were so many excuses to keep them from seeing what was in front of their faces.

So Nadia was stuck living at home until she could find a job of some kind. Poor little rich girl didn't get all her dreams, she thought in her more self-loathing moments. She hoped confronting Odette's death might push her to the next phase of existence, whatever that might be, but for the time being, she could only think of her defeat. She ran. She fled.

She pulled up into the driveway of her parents' house. The psychic self-flagellation could continue inside.

Lex's car was parked out front, a mirror image of hers. Vartan Eskandarian was many things, and one of those was predictable. Nadia wondered if he'd gotten a deal by buying cars in bulk. Two more identical Audis would be in the garage. His and hers.

The house looked to be a single story, Spanish-style hacienda. The bulk of it spilled out over the side of the canyon. There were three stories, two of which were invisible from the street, and a half-wild garden amongst the terraces. It was beautiful, and far larger than a family of five—no, four, she amended, feeling the splinter of loss anew—needed.

She got out of the car, her limbs rebelling over any kind of movement. She wanted to sink into a hot bath and maybe sleep for a week. Marshal her strength for another attempt. She unlocked the front door and opened it up into the wide, airy living room. The large doors on the other side leading to one of the terraces, were open, the silky drapes pushed aside, but still filling with the breeze from the canyon. Outside, servers were setting up a bar and a banquet at the outside table, overseen by Nadia's parents. Lex leaned against the wall, nursing a bottle of beer, and gazing out over the canyon.

Vartan Eskandarian was a large man. In the old pictures of him, when he was playing football for Hollywood High, he was a lean and muscled athlete. Now, everything had thickened. He looked like a studio head, and probably cultivated that image to put it in the brains of executives to gain the advantage in negotiations. His hair was graying, but it was the gray of a silverback. He was out on the patio, sitting at the head of a table, scotch and soda in one hand, thick cigar in the other, barking orders from time to time.

Nadia's mother, Siranush, was the perfect Armenian beauty. Her hair was styled, dyed burgundy with an ostentatious blonde streak. Her features were strong, including a prominent, hooked nose that she had given to Nadia. While that nose was far from the tiny buttons so valued in the culture at large, it bestowed an exoticism to Siranush's formidable loveliness. Like Odette, Siranush was never less than immaculately dressed in designer brands. Her charm dovetailed with her husband's force. They were the image of the Hollywood power couple.

Lex took after Vartan. Put Lex's high school photo next to Vartan's, and they could be the same person. He was the prince, the presumptive heir. This was true even when Odette, the eldest child, was still alive. He was the boy, after all. Unlike his father's linen suits, Lex favored complicated t-shirts and designer jeans, maybe the one trait he had gotten from his mother.

"Who's here?" Siranush said, peering into the house. "Nadia!" Siranush's accent was thicker than the rest of the family's. She hadn't left Armenia until the age of nine. "I thought you were going out?"

Nadia remembered the conversation, though the events at Simcoe Manor had effectively pushed it from her mind. They had mentioned they were hosting a small party, clearly concerned that their weird daughter would be there. Nadia had assumed that after facing Odette's... even now, she had trouble thinking it. After being there, she assumed she was going to have a drink or three, and the prospect of navigating a party with her parents' friends would have driven her out of her mind.

"Nadia?" Vartan rumbled from the patio.

Lex blinked and peered through the curtains, then raised his beer absently to Nadia in a toast.

Siranush bustled into the house, her smile dying on her lips. "Nadia! What happened to you?" There was no one around but the family and hired help. She could be as loud as she liked.

"I'm fine. I just went hiking."

"Hiking? You brought back half the dirt in the hills."

Nadia looked down, and her black boots were in fact tan with a thin layer of road dust. She was about to protest when Siranush kept talking.

"I don't know why you have to go hiking anyway. You're home in time for the party. Are you going to get yourself cleaned up?"

"Actually, mom. I'm kind of bushed."

"You look terrible. Are you sick?"

"Maybe," she said, latching onto that. "I probably just need a nap or something."

Siranush shook her head. "Go to your room and get some rest." Nadia saw the relief in her eyes. She didn't want to explain Nadia's new look. They liked the old one, before school, with her long hair and more feminine clothes. Couldn't get a skirt or makeup on her even then, but she was still hiding. College had made her stop hiding. Now she wondered if she had to retreat into her hole.

"Thanks mom."

Siranush gave her a kiss and put the back of her hand over Nadia's forehead. "I don't feel a fever. If you need anything, call okay?"

"I will."

Siranush nodded and returned to Vartan, acting as interpreter. "Nadia isn't feeling well. She's going to get some rest."

Vartan wouldn't ask for elaboration. Though he was not as outwardly critical of Nadia's transformation, he was not much more a fan than his wife.

Nadia went into her room and closed the door. The space was a time capsule to her high school days. She'd only updated it in the brief windows when she'd been home, but that barely touched the surface. She found it faintly embarrassing and funny now. The posters of pop music stars whose music she hated, but who were the only way to have beautiful women on her wall without raising any questions. Her old stuffed animals. Pictures of her friends. Track trophies. Academic honors. An overflowing huge bookcase of paperbacks, tracing her love of literature from the fantasy and science fiction of her youth, to the literature of high school and early college, and the final melding of genre literature that had become her specialty in school. Her parents never understood her desire for books and had given her an e-reader to help replace them. She still loved the feel of pages, and it was that love that made her spend six years understanding the written word.

She closed the door and looked at herself in the mirror. A punk looked back at her, tired and dusty from a day in the sun. Gillian had said like a member of the Clash.

Gillian.

Nadia closed her eyes. That was almost a full day without thinking about Gillian. That was at least a record. Hope she loved Portland. Probably still couldn't understand why Nadia hadn't gone with her. Nadia didn't quite understand either, only that she couldn't move ahead with Odette still behind.

Her pants, ragged at the cuffs from where she had snipped a few inches, were dusty and sticking to her legs with sweat. Her shirt was grimy. She took it off, revealing the wifebeater underneath. She pulled that over her head and threw it into the hamper, following that with the sportsbra she barely needed. Her mother had wanted her to wear the silly, frilly stuff Odette favored. Something pretty, something soft, something feminine. Nadia fought for the simple sportsbras, pointing out that her time on the track team necessitated them. Siranush relented, probably assuring herself she would eventually get Nadia in something lacy. She never did.

Nadia took off her high boots, socks, pants, and underwear. She looked herself over, as though the trip up to Simcoe Manor had infected her. Her skin was smooth, damp with sweat, and curdling with salt and dirt.

Nadia took the straight razor from the hidden pocket in her boot and went into her bathroom, directly connected to her bedroom. She sat on the rim of the tub as she filled it, running the razor over a strap of leather hanging from a hook on the sink cabinet. The act was not necessary but she did it to empty her mind.

The razor itself was an antique. She had found it in a shop down on Melrose that no longer existed. The handle was inlaid abalone shell, shining like oil made out of moonlight. The blade had been replaced, and she kept it as sharp as obsidian. Sometimes it drove her crazy that she could never get it down to a single molecule edge, and so it would remain inexcusably blunt. Yet it would slice flesh like paper were she so inclined.

When the tub was full, she climbed in. The aches in her muscles began to bleed away. She lay there for a time, then investigated her body once again. Her legs were still bare, but tiny hairs had begun to sprout from her arms.

She found her pot of lather on the side of the tub. She had it mixed special, each batch being far more expensive than she could really justify. Crafting the scent had been important to her, and she finally settled on one smelling as close to night-blooming jasmine as she could. It was a clean aroma of night, secret and comforting, growing wild in her city.

She mixed the lather with a brush—horsehair and bone handled, cared for meticulously—and applied it. She addressed each part in turn, whether or not she found hair. It didn't matter to her ritual. All that mattered was that she be utterly denuded, with only eyebrows and the top of her head covered. At times, she thought of removing these last two vestiges. It felt like the one thing keeping her back from what she truly was, whatever that might be. But it was too big a step, the thought filling her blood with moths. Only when she was bare once again, when the glittering razor had passed over every inch of her, only then could she completely relax.

Her habit of shaving was unusual in her circle. Her friends, Gillian especially, had teased her for it. "Bowing to the patriarchal obsession for jailbait," they said. She told them it was because she ran track; it stripped away a tiny bit of drag, letting her go fractions of a second faster. The lie was easier than the truth. For Nadia, it always was.

She had been in the 4th grade and fighting tears on the long ride home from school. She fled to her room the instant the front door opened, and the tears came out of her in a torrent. Only Odette had stayed long enough to find out what the matter was. Nadia pointed to her arms, covered in a thin, downy, but undeniably black coating of hair.

"They were teasing me," she told Odette.

"That's easy enough to fix."

Odette taught Nadia to shave her arms. Nadia expanded from there. Wherever she found hair, she excised it. Soon, it was no longer about being mocked. It was her. And the more of her flesh she bared, the better she felt. She was never supposed to have this vulgar, mammalian cover. She was a creature far older, far closer to the earth.

She dried herself off and put on another undershirt and pair of boxer briefs, then picked up an old Tiptree novel, *Up the Walls of the World,* to keep her company, and climbed into bed. She was pleasantly overheated as she started to read the words she knew so well.

A soft knock came at the door a few hours later. "Yeah, mom?" she said.

"It's Lex."

"Oh. Come in." She hadn't been expecting her brother. If it didn't involve lifting weights, the business, or fucking club girls, Lex didn't care. Being dad's heir was the culmination of an expected life, and he was content. She was just curious enough to see what he wanted to let him in.

He opened up the door. He held a plate in one hand and shut the door with his other. "Mom said you weren't feeling well. Thought you might want something to eat."

Nadia sat up in bed, frowning. "Thanks, Lex."

"Yeah, no problem." He put it down in her lap. Garlic chicken, hummus, bread, grape leaves, the usual spread at one of her parents' parties. He ruffled her hair. "Eat up. Maybe put some curves on those bones."

"Yeah, what I've been dying for."

"Goodnight, Shorty."

Nadia, in gentle confusion, watched her brother leave the room. The food helped the odd feelings that permeated her since Simcoe Manor. She felt as though she had been exsanguinated and was only now regaining her heart's blood. She cleaned her plate and put it aside. Sleep, heavy and black, claimed her quickly.

***

I heard ur back in town

Nadia stared at her phone in mute incomprehension. The text was from Angie Alcala, who she hadn't seen in years. They had last hung out the summer after Nadia's Frosh year, before the transformation. Before Modern Nadia. Nadia erectus. Angie only knew Nadia habilis. Nadia sapiens was still another metamorphosis away, though close enough to frighten her.

Still, Angie Alcala. Her best friend from back when that term meant everything. No matter how long had passed, the memory of Angie filled Nadia with warmth. There had never been anything romantic between the two of them. They had met before those things mattered, and Angie had always been the safe place. She had known Nadia's secret, back when it was one, and apart from a fleeting, momentary worry, had never been anything less than supportive.

Yah. Home on the range

It was a week after the failure at Simcoe Manor. That strange day should have receded like a dream. It had been so bizarre; it should have been unbelievable in the daylight. It was not. The burned out house and its jellyfish pool lingered in her consciousness. Calling. Only a matter of time until she went back up, though for what reason she could not be entirely sure.

Want to have lunch?

Nadia typed an agreement and was pleased to find an eager smile on her face. Angie Alcala, after all this time. Nadia was out on the patio with the remains of her breakfast, watching the still rising sun turn the foliage gold. She took her dishes inside, put them in the sink, and spent a leisurely morning getting ready.

She was meeting Angie over on the other side of the canyon in the Valley, not far from the Warner Brothers lot. The restaurant was an upscale place serving a kind of Baja-Cuban fusion, which looked like a favored destination for executives looking for a casual lunch. Nadia found Angie sitting at a window table, looking up from her phone every minute or so to scan the restaurant. She still looked exactly like herself, though refined and professionalized: Angie was short and curvy, a few acne scars on her olive cheeks, her black hair cut in a short and fashionable shag. Angie's gaze slid right off Nadia with no spark of recognition. She smirked and marched over to Angie's table.

"What, no hug?"

"Nadia?" Angie was incredulous. Then she saw it, the smile blooming over her face like a sunrise. "Nadia! Oh my god!"

Angie hopped up from her chair and embraced her friend. Nadia hugged the shorter woman back. "I know I look a little different and all."

"Different? You look like a whole other person." Angie pulled back to look at her. "I like it," she decided.

"Me too."

They sat.

"You used to look so uncomfortable in your own skin."

"Guess I shed it."

"Guess so!"

A charm bracelet jingled on Angie's wrist. It had been there since they were little, and she had added something to it in each phase of her life. There was a microphone for when she was singing in choir, a cross from her mild faith, a movie camera for her current career, and many others, all jingling like tiny wind chimes. Nadia's hand darted out, catching Angie's wrist gently, and turning it over. One of the charms sparkled in the light.

A tiny rabbit.

"You still have this?" Nadia asked with undisguised pleasure.

"Yeah, of course. You don't get rid of gifts from your best friend, even if you haven't seen each other in a while."

Nadia sat back, a smile spreading over her face. "No, you don't."

Despite the time, the two of them fell into the rhythms easily. Nadia had been mousey with other people, but not Angie. No need. Lunch ended long after both plates had been taken back to the kitchen, and the rush abated. Angie checked the time on her phone. "Oh, crap. Well, let's hope no one noticed the long lunch."

"We have to do this again."

"Like you even have to say it."

Angie insisted on paying the check, saying she was making good money doing administration work at Warners. She was on track for producing her dream since she was old enough to know that such a job existed. Nadia could not have been more happy for her friend, and even happier knowing that they could pick up right where they had left off with none of the time in between.

***

Nadia was not sleepwalking. Not exactly. She had risen from her bed, sometime well after midnight. An hour existing between the ones on the clock, when only one person in a city might be awake. She had moved in a haze, and now she was outside, among the trees. Her parents' house was behind her, invisible in the darkness and leaves.

She was in her undershirt and shorts, the breeze carrying an unseasonable chill. She stared east, toward Simcoe Manor, imagining she could see it, lingering on the strange mysteries there. She thought that if she started walking, she would make it there, and the numbers on the clock would never advance. She was something else now, some integral part of the night, able to travel the same secret corridors of the shadows.

The pool was calling. It wanted to spill its secrets. It had so much to show. She reached one hand out, silver here in this goblin light and the phantom brush of its fingers over her brow. Odette.

A place her sister had been murdered, carrying such wonder.

An awful, yet tantalizing thought: it was her sister's murder that had sanctified it. Profaned it. These words were the same at their marrow.

She was dressed and driving east before she could consciously stop herself. Her satchel was in the passenger seat, and resting on it, the single berry she had taken from the odd bush at Simcoe Manor. She found it when she grabbed the bag, the soft mass tumbling around in one pocket. She winced, cursing herself for forgetting, and fished it out, expecting to find a rotten and shriveled lump.

The berry was alive. It sang with the bloody meat smell. It trilled its pleasure between her fingers. Tendrils of warmth and bliss crept up through her arms. It wanted her. Needed her.

She parked on the empty road, going up the hills in the dark. The moon hung low in the sky. The light blooming up from the night city made a distinct barrier between the material and the ethereal. Nadia was hiking to the penumbra between, where the skeletal mansion marked the halfway point. She followed the path effortlessly, every step on the road toward Simcoe Manor calling her home.

She stopped at the staircase emerging from the dirt. Twisted branches enclosed it. In a wetter time, there would be leaves on them, but the drought had stripped them clean of everything but thorns. They formed a natural ceiling in the tunnel leading to the manor, a portal into another world.

She took the stairs one at a time. With each step, she shed her clothing. She could not be certain why she did this, but she knew facing this holy place clad in anything but moonlight was wrong. She was not in her proper skin—a clean thought, though one she did not yet understand—but this was as close as she could come. Now.

Her bare feet were soft against the flagstones of the patio. The burned ribs of the manor poked into the bruised sky. The pool yawned out in front of her. She hesitated, poised, ready to flee once again down the stairs.

No.

The berry was whole. Not rotted. Not eaten. Not diminished. This single detail stuck in her mind. A sign, that this place was hers. Waiting. She had only to push through the final caul of birth, shed the final bit of pain, and claim what was rightfully hers.

She stepped closer to the lip of the pool. The walls were grimy, and mostly dry. In places it appeared as though there were still rivulets of moisture going down the concrete, or perhaps the saliva of an inanimate object given life by pain. Odette was not down there. Odette was in the family plot at Forest Lawn. The Simcoe Killer was wherever they buried serial killers whose names they never knew. The pool had been empty for six years. There was nothing to see.

She took another step, her bare toes gripping the rough lip of the pool. She took a deep breath and looked down, knowing she would see her sister and knowing she would not.

Odette was not in the pool. What was, however, still made her gasp.

Water.

In the midst of the worst drought her state had seen, there was standing water at the bottom of the pool. A couple of feet of it, grimy and black, and it should not be there. There was nothing else. No bodies, none of the random collection of items the police had fished from the pool: a phone, an action figure, a necklace, a ring of keys. Another bizarre note in a bizarre case. Gone now, leaving only the water. She kept staring. Something would breach the surface, proving the pool was far deeper than it appeared. Showing a portal elsewhere. There was no ghastly flesh. No pale bones.

But something moved beneath the oily surface.

She thought it was her imagination at first. It had to be. The presence of water in itself was unlikely enough, but something living within it beggared belief. Her mind, expecting something awful, had provided the sense of movement.

Then she saw it again. A slender shape flitting through the black water. Not her imagination. No insect was large enough to be what she saw, and no fish could live in such a shallow, silty puddle for long. She walked down the steps at the shallow end of the pool, where it was dry. As she approached, the dark movement grew quicker, more violent.

Were the things in the black water angry? Resentful of the death they had seen? Closer now, and she could make out a little more. The shapes within were long and lean. In the few glimpses she caught of them, they looked like eels. There were no eels in Los Angeles, especially not in some stagnant water at the bottom of an otherwise dry pool.

Nadia backed away from the water. This place was haunted. She did not feel a consciousness, as she would have expected, but there was something. No mind, no direction. Emotion. Memory. Power. Too much had happened here, and in the happening had been change. Reshaped by a malign will for unguessable reasons. The residue of terrible acts given form.

She kept her eyes on the black water, dim serpentine shapes slithering within.

The clatter pulled her head around. It sounded like a strip of rough plastic yanked through a bag of finger bones.

A rattlesnake.

It had been piled by the edge of the patio, concealed against the brambles steadily consuming the borders of the property. As it uncoiled itself, tasting the air as it went, Nadia gasped. It was huge. She could not get a good estimate in the dim light, but it stretched forever, revealing foot after foot of muscled length as it unraveled itself. Twelve feet? Eighteen? Could such a beast even be measured in human terms?

It was beautiful in its way. Its scales were a tawny, vibrant amber and mahogany, a pattern of diamonds picked over its back. Its arrow-shaped head was raised an inch over the stones of the patio, its ancient eyes fixed on Nadia. She had the sense that this creature, though it was literally sliding through the dust, as low as any being could be, was some kind of dragon, held over from the end of the previous world.

It was also shaking the rattle at the end of its tail.

Nadia froze on the stairs. Rattlesnakes used their rattles as a warning. *Stop doing what you're doing*, they said, *or I bite*. They didn't do it while advancing. They didn't do it in discrete, lazy shakes, heralding inevitable movement. Nadia was only too happy to stay motionless, but this monster was headed right for her.

As it came to the edge of the pool, it gathered itself, drawing its long coils into a heavy, meaty ball. The slightest kiss of a breeze chilled her. The reptile was still focused, its rattle, bigger than her hand, quivering at the end of his muscular tail.

His. She knew this beast was a he without knowing why. She knew it in the same place she knew that this site was holy.

The serpent flicked his tongue out, over and over, tasting her on the air. His eyes were like mercury, glinting in the moonlight, only the slitted pupil providing any feature. It was the eye of a creature from a time before human beings profaned the earth. She had no doubt that this creature, this dragon, had lived for millions of years. Now he was in front of her, deciding if she was a meal or not. A god, deciding if such a sacrifice was worthy.

She could not move. She was not a fearful person by nature, but this snake awakened a terror within her deeper than her human roots. This was a predator who could have consumed one of her tiny, arboreal ancestors. Not a predator of his kind, but this precise individual might have hunted her family tree for generations. The mad thought felt right and correct in this place between worlds.

He watched her, tasting her, the workings of his ancient mind a riddle.

He opened his mouth slowly, showing off an expanse of fleshy pink. His tongue fluttered out from a sheathe on the floor of his mouth. His teeth were like glass, all facing backwards to the bottomless gullet. Then the fangs unfolded from the roof of the mouth. They were huge, curved scimitars, perfected for the single goal of death. They shined, either with saliva or poison.

Nadia had never heard of a snake doing this. He wanted her to see the killing tools. Wanted to show her what he could do if he so chose. That was entirely too mammalian motive, yet she could not escape the sensation of communion.

The serpent closed his mouth, the fangs once again flattening. He shook his rattle once more, a single undulation. You're spared, it said. Nadia's heart began to beat again. She let out a breath in preparation for the creature to return to the brown hills, to hunt whatever was large enough to satisfy its appetite. Coyotes probably. No, mountain lions.

It struck faster than her eye could follow. It felt like a spear had been jabbed into her throat. Her blood thundered in her neck, pushing against the snake's shuddering mouth. Then the pressure was gone, leaving behind twin points of molten flesh.

Nadia blinked, staring at the snake, now placidly coiled, no longer rattling, merely watching her. Her hand went to her neck, her carotid pulsing jets of hot agony into her body. Her fingers were wet. Bloody, but the blood was suspended in a clear, yellowish liquid, like oil. *Venom*, she reminded herself. *Dripping with venom.*

From her throat.

Her legs wobbled. Her hand was shaking. The only thing she could see was the dragon, her eyes meeting his impassive gaze. He tumbled, falling upward, and no, that was her, collapsing to the bottom of the pool. The venom raced through her body, burning her blood to ash, just like the house at her back.

She was dying, in the same spot as her sister. She fell backward, rolling down the slope of the pool. The black water was cold against her skin, reaching up to devour her, but it would never douse the pyre of the venom inside. One of the eel-like shapes brushed against her, and she wanted to flinch, but her limbs were crystal.

This is how I die? The last coherent thought that went through her mind as her brain boiled itself on the flames of poison. She felt herself coughing, body shaking, muscles burning, bones crumbling, and she fell, fell far back into the abyss. The water pulled at her with hands now. It wasn't a puddle. It was a pool, a lake, an ocean. He was there. The Simcoe Killer. pulling her down to drown her in the endless void. No, it was Odette, welcoming her sweet baby sister home.

No, it was the water, the filthy water alive with creatures that should not be, forcing its way into her eyes, ears, nose, throat, pores, vagina, the punctures in her throat, joining venom and blood, and birthing something new.

Foundation

Nadia had expected there to be nothing after death. The lights go off, done now, see your own way home. Though she was not precisely surprised when the images tumbled through her mind's eye. An overheated brain grasping at the dim electricity keeping it alive was nothing remarkable. That the images did not belong to her was strange. A life flashed before her eyes, but not her own.

It belonged to the pool. An inanimate object. A mere feature. She had a dim memory of falling into the black water collected in the deep end, and the serpent, coiled at the lip. While everything else was washed out and faded like ash, the snake, the dragon, was vibrant and solid in his diamond-leather colors. She reached for him, but the water took her again.

She saw a man, a little nothing of a man. She could have passed him a hundred times and never known it. Yet, he was not a nothing man. He only appeared to be one. He did not exactly shine; it was almost the opposite. He was a hungry void, a human black hole.

Nadia wanted to recognize him as someone she had known for her entire life, yet her mind rebelled against the impulse. He wasn't that. He was Nobody, the personification of nothingness in identity. He was a parasite, but a parasite greater than any one person. He had power. He was power. His entire form hummed with it.

He was both mortal and divine. Born of flesh, but a spark within made him evolve. From nobody to Nobody.

He stood in the pool, and it was night, and rain was falling in freezing sheets. He bled from a hundred wounds while bloated flesh-colored insects tore him apart. Something the size of a crocodile burst from the black waters behind the Nobody. A great beast whose outline conformed to nothing of the earth. It clamped a hideous, almost human mouth around his hips, and tried to drag the parasite beneath the sucking water.

Then she recognized what her mind begged not to comprehend: the insects were not insects at all. They were swatches of human flesh with fingernails and teeth, taking revenge on their creator for their half-lives. The parasite had made these somehow, though Nadia could not imagine anything other than an accidental birth. The worst of the foul children was the monster eating the Nobody from the feet up. A terrible, stunted wormlike creature, with strips of olive skin over strips of silvery wrapping, a distended maw at one end. Its teeth were gigantic, yet disturbingly human, chewing the parasite apart as it swallowed him.

She watched the Nobody die, half-swallowed by this monster he had somehow made. As his life bled away into the black water, the insects and the beast fell away, their half-lives tied to their creator's. The flesh came away in swatches from the creatures, revealing the plastic and metal skins of the inanimate. They were the random assortment of objects found in the pool later by baffled investigators: a phone, a necklace, an action figure, and so forth. Mundane things. When the worm-monster lost its skin, it revealed Odette, cocooned in duct tape, muddy rain pooling in her sightless eyes.

Nadia knew, for certain, that the Nobody was gone, but his power had lingered. Bled into the location of his death.

She had no time to reflect; the vision, on its wings of venom, sang through her veins. She was looking at herself now. Sitting on a throne, a crown on her head, surrounded by velvet pools of shadow. The crown and throne were made of living snakes, slithering over one another, their scales shining in the night. Her crown was another one of these, moving over her brow, consuming its own tail. This other Nadia, the queen, looked up, and she had the same quicksilver eyes as the dragon.

In the shadows, there were others, arrayed behind her, half glimpsed in the consuming shadow. Allies perhaps? Advisors? Assassins? A pale woman whose hands were twisted into claws. A stunted, ape-like silhouette. A slender girl with skin of lumpy gray. A short man glistening wetly in orange and white.

She awoke with a gasp, staring upward into the sky. Another vision, because the sky over Los Angeles was never that full of stars. Never that deep and black and bright. No, it was covered in a perpetual cloak of light and haze.

She was breathing. Her legs were cold. A weight sat on her chest, smooth against her bare flesh.

Nadia blinked. Her muscles were on fire, but she was alive. She was fairly certain of that. She would not be shivering otherwise. She craned her head to see what the weight was.

The snake was coiled on her chest, watching her. The tongue fluttered out and went back into his mouth. He was much smaller now; she estimated maybe six feet were hidden in his heavy coils. His solidity, his presence, had not diminished in the slightest. He was still the dragon, ruler of this holy place.

Nadia swallowed, waiting to see if the beast was going to take another taste of her. His rattle was still. He regarded her, then uncoiled, in the languorous, inevitable way of geology, and slithered off her chest. Her nipples trilled as he brushed over them. He didn't carry the stinging scent of reptile that she associated with snakes, but rather the same rosemary as the surrounding hills. He was a part of them, some kind of scaled sovereign.

She stayed still as he moved over and off her, the scales kissing her cheek as they went, and finally the rattle, held up off the ground. She turned over and watched the snake slither up over the lip of the pool at the shallow end.

Nadia got to her feet, pulling her legs from the water, trembling with the damp and the vision.

The serpent was already gone, back into whatever dream of dragons he had slithered from. Nadia was alone in on the holy site. She was soaked and filthy, yet somehow she was clean. She glanced at the water, but in the dark, she saw nothing moving. She shivered in the night air.

She looked out over the city, now lights stretching into the distance, and wondered how long she had been unconscious. It was still night, deep and quiet in its depths. As she stood, her nakedness against the city, she felt potent. With her skinny, muscled body, partly-shaved head, and hooked nose, she was called ugly in every creeping stare. Dismissed. Now she was something so much more.

She touched her neck, hissing as she contacted the punctures. Her skin was dry and rough—no, covered with dried blood. Dried blood was preferable to wet.

She staggered from the pool, her limbs still brittle from whatever the venom had done to her. She took one last look at the Jellyfish Pool, at the burned corpse of Simcoe Manor, and stumbled down the hidden concrete steps that led to this place, collecting her clothing as she went. At the bottom of the stairs, she once again felt bound by the rules of the world. She pulled the clothes on over her damp skin and was diminished.

The walk down to her car was quick, and she was grateful for it. Moving was hard. The venom scorched her veins and arteries as it flowed through her body. When she unlocked the door, she nearly collapsed, taking time to catch her breath. Her satchel waited on the passenger seat. On top was the berry.

We are yours, its presence seemed to say. She had to smile and put it in safely in the pocket where she had initially found it. Abruptly she was concerned it should be out, when it was so valuable. Somehow, it was valuable. The most precious thing she owned.

She took a few deep breaths and sat up to check herself in the rearview. She looked ghastly. Her skin, normally ranging from a deep olive to downright brown in the summers, was washed out. Two lines of dried blood ran down her neck. She moved the collar of her checked work shirt aside. The blood trailed to a stop just above her left breast. It looked like a vampire had taken a bite out of her. The mop of hair she grew on the top of her head had fallen forward, and she brushed it away to look at her tawny brown eyes. The rings she found underneath were a tortured purple.

Nadia slumped back into her seat. Simcoe Manor had coughed up its last secret. She did not understand it, or all of it, but she knew it was true. The manor had given her an even greater gift: the power of the nothing man, the Nobody, the parasite who was the Simcoe Killer. He had lived and had abilities far beyond anything a human should be able to do. And he had left some of these behind in the spot where he had been killed.

As she thought of this, her heart warmed. Her sister had killed him, as she had hoped. Justice.

The clock on the dash said it was just after four in the morning. Nadia couldn't remember when it was she had left. She felt like she had been unconscious for an instant, or perhaps for several days. She shuddered. She knew she should be worried about the snake venom causing some kind of lasting damage. Should go to the hospital for the antivenin. The thought brought back the paralyzed fear she'd had when she first saw the dragon. That the venom should be neutralized, cured, turned her stomach. It was spitting in the face of the holy-unholy site, and the gift from the serpent.

No, the venom had to be allowed to circulate. Join her blood. Help her become.

The dragon had judged her or was judging her now. This was a test. The punctures throbbed against her neck, not with pain, but with bliss. She shuddered, the pleasure wracking her body in delirious waves. The serpent wanted her. Needed her.

And she needed him.

She tore her hand away with a bolt of physical pain and collapsed into the seat. The tears were hot on her face. The explanation, terrible and sure, calcified in her vision.

She was going insane.

***

The Midway was a shock. Angie had simply said it was a speakeasy in Hollywood, and they were going. Part of some Angie initiative to get Nadia out of the house, and Nadia needed it. Stewing in her old room was a good way to put down roots, both physical and emotional, in a place she did not need.

Angie had picked her up and said her hellos to Vartan and Siranush, who had seemed almost relieved to see her. Angie was as girly as she had always been, and Nadia's parents were fond of her. Nadia suspected that some of it was due to Angie being able to pass as Armenian—her family was in fact predominantly Salvadoran—but most of it, now, had to do with what no one was discussing. They probably hoped she would rub off on who they considered to be their little tomboy.

Angie took them down into Hollywood proper in her little black Jetta, parking it in an expensive lot.

"Where is this place?" Nadia asked as they walked down a side street.

"It's hidden. I told you, it's a speakeasy."

"You know we don't need those anymore. Alcohol has been legal for like eighty years or so."

"Are you going to complain all night?"

"Not all night."

Angie turned to Nadia, her eyes flashing. "There's this woman there who tells your fortune."

Nadia wanted to laugh, but something in Angie's expression stopped her. "You believe in that stuff?" That sentence spilled out of her and she immediately felt like a fraud. Considering what she had experienced at Simcoe Manor, she had a lot of nerve judging anyone.

Angie didn't pick up on it. "Well, I didn't. I heard about it, the same as anyone else. Alyssa, who I work with, she told me all about the fortuneteller. You go, she plays poker with you—she always has a game there— and she tells your fortune. So I went, and she won about forty bucks off me, then she just looks up at me, and says my boss is going to get in a car accident. Hit a Coke truck. Going to break his ankle and total his new Mercedes. Guess what? A week later, it happened."

"That's not really your fortune, is it?"

"Well, no. But it came true. All of it, right down to the Coke truck and the new Mercedes."

"You paid forty bucks to hear about your boss?"

Angie deflated. "Come on, Nadia."

"Right, I'm sorry. Maybe I'll hear Lex's fortune."

Angie touched her temple. "He will petition Affliction to start making business suits."

Nadia laughed.

The entrance to the Midway was in an alley between a sports bar and a gastropub. A narrow brick passage led back to a wire-framed staircase. The sports bar had developed a hunchback, taking over much of the end and an entire second story. No doorman marked it, but Angie scampered up the stairs with the eagerness of an excited kid. She opened the unadorned metal door and waved Nadia in.

The room was made up like a train station. It was not large, barely the size of a bedroom. The walls were paneled in dark wood with a few brass fixings. A man leaned against one wall, dressed in a flamboyant red suit. He looked like a ringmaster, Nadia decided, from his top hat to his high-heeled boots. He rubbed a wax mustache as they entered, regarded them with bored semi-interest.

"Yeah?" he said.

"I'm running away," Angie said. It sounded rehearsed.

"Oh? And where to?"

"To the circus."

The ringmaster stood up straight and swept his hat off in a bow. "Then take your friend past the door and enjoy yourselves." He kicked a panel behind him, and a door swung open. The babble of conversation spilled out on a haze of popcorn aroma. The light inside was the gold of the past century, and Nadia could almost imagine that whale oil was burning in those lamps.

She followed Angie through the door and was promptly overwhelmed. The walls were coated in multicolored canvas, gathered at the ceilings to resemble tents. The first room was dominated by the bar, crowded with hipsters. The bartenders and the waitresses were made up like clowns, the bartenders in old-style uniforms with arm garters, the waitresses in the high-waisted shorts and halter tops of cigarette girls. Nadia was having a hard time not watching their long legs, all in fishnets. As she looked away, she saw a bartender take a mouthful from a bottle, lift up a burning brand, and puff out a ball of fire. The patrons cheered.

Behind the bar, a huge antique poster advertised firebreathers. It could not have been vintage, but it certainly looked it. A popcorn machine took up one corner, and people just helped themselves to a bag whenever it took them. The pot was continually boiling over with fresh, golden kernels.

"What do you think?" Angie asked over the din of conversation.

A clown waitress brushed past Nadia. She felt the fishnets against the back of her hand. "It's... it's something."

"It is! What are you drinking?"

"Sazerac."

"Be right back."

Nadia was left in the middle of this insanity. The bartender continued his fire breathing act, and the waitresses continued bustling about. One stopped, her green hair piled high in a Marie Antoinette wig. "Can I get you something?"

Nadia could not quite tell if her face was beautiful, or if the simple geometry and unspoiled planes had eased away imperfections. Her gaze fell to the woman's slender neck. Her carotid artery pulsed, and utterly enchanting Nadia with the motion. She opened her mouth, wondering if she was really going to try her luck by hitting on a waitress.

Angie pressed a drink into Nadia's hand.

"Oh, good," the waitress said, and might have smiled. She was gone through the crowd before Nadia could say anything else.

"Got a thing for clowns, huh?" Angie asked. "You're blushing."

"Great, I'm fucking blushing."

"Come on. This will be fun."

Angie moved toward one of the open doorways. Nadia glanced through the one across the way. A poster advertising the fat lady was on the wall, overlooking a section of small cafe-style wooden tables. People ate at these; the meals looked to be gourmet versions of carnival fare.

They passed through this open doorway, into a room with a poster featuring an elephant, a lion, and a monkey. The center was cleared out for a dance floor, but no music was playing at the moment. The walls were covered in framed pictures, most in black and white, or in the odd washed-out colors of the '60s and '70s, of circus animals. A DJ booth was presently empty, and the majority of those in the room were engaged in conversation.

Other doorways led from there. It was a maze in this place, each room labeled with a different exhibit of the circus, and every one of them covered in the multicolored canvas. Nadia followed in delirium, her senses entirely overwhelmed. She could not decide if she loved this place or not, but she had never seen anything like it. Trust Angie to find it.

Finally, they arrived at their destination. The room was one of the smallest, the sound muffled by heavy curtains on the way in. It was as close to private as anyplace in the Midway got. Shadows grew strong here, with the intimidating intimacy of a fortune-teller's tent. The circular table was wooden, and inlaid with ornate symbols along the edge, a lit crystal ball in the center.

Four people sat around the table, all holding hands of cards. Three of them looked like the usual hipsters and low-level industry people who frequented this place. The last stole Nadia's breath.

The woman was maybe in her early thirties, of middling height, and curvy. Her skin was pale, though her features had the cast of Spanish or Italian. Her hair was curly, dark brown and thick, gathered beneath a snood embroidered with pearls. Her dress, what Nadia could see, was cream-colored and vintage. The neck was scooped, and revealed impressive, and distracting, cleavage. When the woman looked up, her brown eyes were large, liquid, and rimmed in heavy black makeup, like the kohl on a silent movie starlet. Her face and body had the proportions of a Botticelli model, as though this were a Medici princess somehow traveled through time.

"Would you like to be dealt in?"

Nadia nodded, suddenly mute.

"I'll leave you to it," Angie whispered in her ear.

Nadia sat, and the woman finished her hand with those she already had. She locked eyes with a thin man wearing thick horn-rimmed glasses and sporting a ginger beard. "Tomorrow, at lunch, you're going to be at a sandwich shop. The kind of place that sells subs. You'll see a young woman there. You'll want to talk to her, and you will. You'll remember me saying this, but you'll think it's nothing. You will date her. She will cheat on you with your cousin Adrian."

The man blinked. "How did you know I had a cousin?"

The fortuneteller put her cards down on the table, calling the bet. She beat everyone there, the man worst of all. He had stayed in the hand with a king high. "You came here because I know these things." She brought the money to her side of the table, and her quick, clever hands secreted away. Her nails were trimmed, rounded, and subtly polished. "Now go drink and ignore what I've told you."

The man blinked and staggered away like he'd been hit. The fortuneteller gestured to his seat without looking up at Nadia. "There you are, newcomer. Each hand is five dollars, and it takes a couple for me to read your future. Sit down if you dare."

The other two—a young woman with a blunt, stylish haircut, and a chubby man with a goatee—gave Nadia a nervous smile. She nodded to them and sat down. The fortuneteller flipped the cards across the table. Her control was astounding. They slid to a stop in front of each player ready to be picked up, and all of this without any apparent concentration.

Nadia picked up her cards and saw that she had a pair of queens—Spades and Hearts—and watched the others. She wasn't sure if she was supposed to win or not. Looking out over the flop, she saw another queen: Clubs. She mentally shrugged, and decided if she won, she won.

The fortuneteller barely looked up from her game. Nadia watched the chubby man deflate as the last two cards were dealt into the center, and the subtle gasp from the woman when the Three of Diamonds was revealed on the turn. Nadia was silent when the last queen turned up on fifth street. When the fortuneteller put her cards down, she had a respectable full house, easily beating the other two. Not Nadia's queens.

The fortuneteller was already reflexively reaching for the pot when she paused. "Oh. You won." She settled back and looked at Nadia's cards, then Nadia's face. The sharp intake of breath was impossible to miss.

Nadia looked up and found that the fortuneteller was staring. Her pale cheeks were flushed, eyes filmy and wide, made more so by the dark makeup around them. Her chest was heaving, and Nadia did her best to stay eye to eye. It was difficult, because she was looking into desire itself. The fortuneteller had the expression of amazed ecstasy on her face, an expression Nadia had not seen in a long time. Even before she and Gillian had split.

Nadia collected the money and barely noted the other two throwing glares her way. Over the next few hands, the fortuneteller keyed back into the game, playing smart. Before it looked like she had been effortlessly fleecing the new arrivals. Now she had to try. She won a few more hands and sent the others on their way with fortunes.

More people came in and replaced those who left. Nadia did not get up from her seat. She could not. She never even considered it, as whenever the fortuneteller looked up, it was with that raw need. Nadia felt it too, a burgeoning heat below her belly, melting her from the inside out.

The fortuneteller did not read her, either. Periodically, she would start, "And you—" and catch herself. Turning to someone else and rattling off a prediction that never failed to chill them. They were seldom truly helpful, but there were just enough details to make them real. The fortuneteller wasn't hiding behind cold reading techniques, pawning events off on initials. She named names. She was specific enough to awaken a delicious chill in Nadia's spine.

Nadia barely noticed when Angie came back. Just a whisper in her ear about going home with someone. Nadia nodded and muttered she could find her own way home. She had no idea how, and no real care either. All that mattered was the fortuneteller at the other side of the table.

"Where are you going?" the fortuneteller asked.

"What?"

"Tonight. Where are you going?"

"Nowhere. I'm here."

"It's four in the morning. We're closed."

"Four in the—" Nadia glanced about. She was alone.

"Do you want to come home with me?"

Nadia nodded, her neck working without her consciously wanting it to.

"Good," the fortuneteller said. She rose from her side of the table, her cream-colored gown dripping over her bountiful curves. Nadia was fascinated by this woman's ostentatious femininity. She really was some kind of avatar of the past, when lovely women had heavy breasts and fat hips and arsenic-pale flesh. Nadia wanted her with the intensity of a drug, wanted to see what was underneath the dress. She checked her own pants, suddenly worried she had soaked them right through.

"I'm Nadia."

"Milena," the fortuneteller said, offering her secret smile. Nadia had to resist the urge to kiss her. Instead, Milena took Nadia's hand in hers, fingers twining through each other, and led her out. This was a back exit, and the other employees barely gave them a second glance. Milena guided her down a back staircase to a waiting car. Nadia had been expecting some kind of classic, maybe a vintage Beetle. It was distressingly mundane, a late-model hybrid.

The music came on, soft indie crooning, just a woman with a heartbreaking voice and a few instruments behind her, and drove east. They did not speak, because they did not precisely know each other. Milena had seen something, but she kept it behind her lips. Instead, she periodically glanced at the passenger seat, as though to make certain Nadia was still there.

Nadia put a hand on the other woman's soft thigh. A bold gesture, but it felt right. Milena gasped, and put a hand over it, driving one-handed.

Milena's perfume somehow smelled like an old movie.

They sped through the darkened city. The streets were almost bare at that time of night. Only the few night dwellers like them were out, all of them racing for home. Dawn would dispel the voluptuous night, and they could not wait that long. Milena pulled into Echo Park, a community of old Victorians on crumbling streets, going up a long driveway bordered by desert plants. The headlights splashed against a small guest house, utterly hidden from all sides by foliage. The beams caught a family of raccoons crossing the open expanse of the driveway. They paused, some rearing up on hind legs, their eyes throwing back the light as silver and gold. They fell to all fours and waddled quickly to disappear in the thick plant life by the side of the guest house.

Milena guided the nearly silent car to the end of the driveway, turned off the engine, and got out.

Nadia followed. Milena opened the front door, glanced back, suddenly coquettish, innocent, then disappeared inside. This hidden house was a magical place, away from a city she knew. She felt an echo of Simcoe Manor, but it was different here. This was the home of life.

She looked up the driveway and had the inescapable sense that if she walked up the cracked concrete, by the time she got to the mouth, it would be morning. Back here, it would be night forever. She tried to remember the clock in the car, how long it had taken, but she found she had no memory of that at all.

She went inside. The central area was the largest room in the house, a combination living room and kitchen. It was cluttered with the kinds of antique kitsch Nadia had expected, the kinds of things that would have been common in Milena's time. Handmade afghans draped over a well-worn sofa. Vintage board games sat on a shelf next to thick hardbacks. An entire collection of wooden animals were displayed under a glass case. More full bookcases made Nadia feel at home; she was thrilled to learn the gorgeous fortuneteller was an avid reader.

Milena had paused at a doorway on the left, past this living area. A single lamp was on, to guide Nadia's steps. Milena shrugged out of her dress. It caught on her breasts, bunching up in creamy waves. She made another graceful movement and it fell to her hips. Another, and it was gone. Nadia's breath stuck in her throat again. Revealed now, even as her body was turned modestly away, she could have been a painting. Nadia had never wanted anyone more. There was no one to compare her to. No one else in the world.

Nadia took a step into the room and shut the door behind her. She unbuttoned her work shirt and dropped it. Took another step. Her undershirt joined it, then the bra. She enjoyed the hungry look on Milena's face as she looked at Nadia's bare torso. She had a reedy, muscled body from her years as a distance runner. Her abs were there for the counting, her breasts weren't worth the name. She was lithe, sinew and tendon, and when Milena beheld this, her teeth dimpled Renaissance lips.

Milena disappeared into the room. Nadia removed her boots, padding in behind on bare feet. She paused now in the doorway. Was this too far? Too insane? The questions were there, but she could only answer them with blinding need.

The bedroom was only lit with a dim carnival glass lamp. Milena was on the bed, nude now. She was on her side, turned toward the door. She had to know what she looked like, because she was posing again. And yet, there did not seem to be any artifice beyond seduction. Her copious curves were there to be appreciated, and she was enticing Nadia with every fair slope. Her neck was graceful, her eyes like embers. Her pubic hair was black, a small patch breaking up the pale expanse of her soft belly and thighs. Nadia wanted to drop to her knees in worship. She didn't think women like this existed, never even knew she wanted one. Here she was, given.

She paused, slipping out of her pants. Underwear followed those, and she was nude before the other woman. No, Milena did not pose. She was merely there, powerful. Strong. Constant. Yes, constant, Nadia thought. She had no idea why the word stuck in her mind, but it did.

She fell into bed and found Milena as soft and pliable as she hoped. Their first kiss was not tentative, as first kisses always had been with Nadia in the past. No, she needed Milena too much, and the other woman was just as eager. They kissed like old lovers, their tongues knowing intimately the pathways of the other. Nadia had to part periodically to experience Milena, to concentrate on the smell of her—like pigment on canvas, like expensive brandy, like sparkling wit. To concentrate on the sight of her—the billowing curves, the gentle arch of her back, the wanton spread of her thighs. To concentrate on the feel of her—soft, yet beneath a core of taut strength. Nadia found that Milena was doing the same thing. Their eyes met, and they grinned, offering a breathy chuckle as each saw amazement in the eyes of the other. Neither one could quite believe they were exploring anyone quite so beautiful.

Nadia could not spend another moment on the earth without tasting Milena. Eager, perhaps, but the other woman gave a ghost of a nod as Nadia crept down her body. Nadia teased first, licks and nibbles over Milena's inner thighs, spiraling ever closer to her lovely vulva. Milena's hips were desperate, chasing Nadia's clever tongue.

When Nadia finally dipped her head, and tasted, she tore a moan, ragged and wounded, from Milena's throat. She was like liquor, musky, mysterious, intoxicating. She did not allow herself simply to lap. No, she chased the sounds Milena made, exploring every part of her, exulting in her.

The heat had grown in Nadia's belly, and her insides were molten gold, running down her legs. She felt herself moving without meaning to, a sinuous dance in the rhythm of Milena's cries. The act of pleasing her had ignited the nerves, like a string of firecrackers, along Nadia's tongue, through her spine, down into the spark of her clitoris. She was no longer a separate organism but connected to this other woman.

And Nadia's tongue grew. She could not say how—or even if—it was happening. She had gone beyond questioning, not with the gorgeous woman writhing at the end of her. She was inside her, alternating with delicate circles and strong beckons, and then, she was tasting another part of Milena. She felt the hard nubbin of her cervix. Then that opened, and she was in Milena's womb, then entwined around the Christmas lights of her spine, igniting the glow of sentience to her mind.

Milena's moans grew louder, sharper, an edge to them bordering on panic. Still, Nadia's tongue moved deeper inside, winding serpentine up the jingling spine. She felt the hole at the base of Milena's skull and pushed through that, into her mind, behind her eyes, to the crown of her head. All around, in dazzling pops and explosions, Milena's brain frantically firing stuttered thoughts into the ether.

Nadia dimly saw Milena's hands balled up in the sheets, her knuckles white. Her thighs were apart, knees high. Then, with a broken cry, she unspooled. In that moment of ecstatic connection, Nadia saw through Milena's eyes, and she too found herself shuddering in helpless abandon. Another vision, like the one at Simcoe Manor, but this was not death. This was life. A new kind, like nothing Nadia could have imagined. She saw a strange house, the walls covered in bloody symbols and hanging with ribbons. She saw a woman made of glass, who had taken Milena inside. That moment had dropped the scales from her eyes, and Milena could see everything. Nadia could see everything.

Nadia did not remember climbing up her lover's body, but she was there, holding a shivering Milena in the dark until sleep claimed them both.

***

Nadia opened her eyes. The scent of night-blooming jasmine was strong. For a moment, she thought she was at home, the smells of the hills wafting through her window. But the other aromas, of bliss, brought it back to her. She and Milena were still interlaced, though a sheet had been thrown over them. She did not know if it was she or Milena who had done this in the middle of the night.

It was still dark. Even the window glowed only with the faintly bluish fairy light of the time when morning was still night. Nadia watched it, smelling the jasmine, and only then came to a realization. It had been four when they left the Midway. Then the drive home. Then the sex—and that put a smile on her face as she remembered it—and they had slept. She felt rested, though not from a full night.

It should be morning. There should be sunlight.

There was not even the first golden hints. What had transpired between them had done so between the borders of time.

Milena stirred in her sleep. Nadia leaned over and brushed a kiss over the older woman's forehead. Milena smiled, and thickly said, "You're here?"

"Shh. It's still late."

Milena reached out and drew Nadia to her. "You'll be here when I wake up?"

"Of course."

Nadia did not know if Milena heard it, because she was already asleep. Nadia pulled the sheets up around them, and only then noticed where the smell had been coming from.

Night blooming jasmine grew over the sheet.

At first, she thought it was some kind of prank. Someone had thrown in branches while they were asleep. By the dim light she saw that, no, it was growing from the sheets themselves, sprouting as though from fertile soil. In this half-waking world, it felt normal. Right.

Nadia snuggled close to Milena and once again sleep found her.

***

Nadia woke again, and this time the sun was streaming through the window, casting a box of white on the bed. The jasmine was gone, but it lingered as a scent. The stronger aroma was coffee.

Nadia blinked and sat up in bed, the sheets falling to her waist.

Milena walked through the door. She was wrapped in a Victorian robe and holding two steaming mugs. "You're up," she said, smiling. "I didn't know how you take it, so I figured cream and two sugars?"

"Sure," Nadia said, holding her hand out.

Milena handed over the coffee. "Good morning," she said, sitting down on the bed.

A moment of awkwardness stretched between them. Nadia couldn't stop thinking about the sex the night before. Not just that it had been the best she'd ever had, but the connection she experienced with Milena. In four years with Gillian, she had never gotten close.

Milena chuckled, smiling over her coffee like a cat. "Okay, I'll say it. I want to see you again."

"Yeah! Yeah, I mean. Of course. I don't... generally do that."

"Then the world is poorer for it."

"Oh, I mean, that..."

Milena patted Nadia's leg. "I'm just teasing. It was wonderful, and I believe I owe you a little something."

"You don't owe me anything. It was fun for me too."

"Fine. I won't eat your pussy."

"Oh."

"Teasing again. Sorry, I'm being terrible. I'm just not used to... liking someone this much? Is that stupid?"

"Not at all," Nadia said. "I like you too." She did, but there was more. She wanted to know more of what she'd seen during their connection. The woman made of glass. The house of blood. How Milena had become the fortuneteller.

"Good." Milena sipped. "My name is Milena Franco."

"Nadia Eskandarian."

"It's very nice to meet you, Nadia," Milena said, shaking her hand.

Nadia shook it and had to smile, feeling the sun in her cheeks. "It's nice to meet you too."

"When can I see you again?"

"For this?"

"I was thinking I'd like to take you on an actual date."

Nadia didn't bother to hide her smile as the two of them scheduled a date and exchanged numbers. Milena offered her a ride home, but Nadia demurred. She wanted the cab ride to give her time to think. It arrived when Milena was in the shower. Nadia said goodbye, but the shower turned off, and Milena came out long enough to give her a kiss.

"You're getting water all over everything," Nadia protested.

"Worth it," she said, giving her ample ass a playful slap as she went back into the bathroom.

Nadia shook her head, laughing to herself, as she went up the long driveway. Watching the mischief in Milena's eyes as she stole that final kiss told Nadia that the other woman was just as smitten as she was. It was a nice feeling.

The sex had been something else entirely. Beyond the mere physical, she had felt consecrated. The connection to what she had experienced at Simcoe Manor was not direct, but the similarity was unmistakable, beyond even the visions. As she watched the city go by out the windows, she connected to the task.

The task of determining how and why Simcoe Manor was holy, unholy, some word meaning both that had never been invented. Milena Franco was holy as well, and sex had been much like a prayer. Nadia could not have sex with a place, but she could look at the lingering power left by the Nobody. She could harvest them.

The word, harvest, plucked a string in her mind. The note was pure and good. As right as settling between Milena's thighs. The need took Nadia once again, and she would not be denied.

The cab driver dropped her off at home, and Nadia paid him. A credit card whose bills went to her parents. It was difficult not to rankle under that, but there was precious little other money, and none coming in. The mundane concerns of living were quiet compared to the insistence of the mystery she had found. She had the time, had the indulgence. She would use it.

She went inside, and into the kitchen. With the buzzing in her fingers, so like the sensation of handling the berries, she assumed she would want to leave immediately. She did not know why but going up there in the daytime would not be quite right. Odette had died at night; so perhaps that was the genesis of the link in Nadia's mind. Or perhaps night was when mysteries wrapped their coils most tightly.

Maybe she would go that night. Maybe another night. Milena's mystery had been sweet. This one still carried the thorns of Odette's death.

But she could prepare.

Nadia looked through the fridge. She found several jars nearly scraped clean of their contents. Her mother hated to throw any food out, even if it was only food residue. Nadia cleaned these out, washing the labels off of them.

Siranush came into the kitchen, and Nadia instantly froze. She realized she hadn't yet showered and imagined that Milena's brandy-scent was coming off of her in waves.

"Nadia! You didn't come home last night."

"Sorry, mom. I slept over at Angie's. On her sofa," she added at the end, and mentally cursed herself for that extra little bit of deception.

"That's fine. How is Angie?" The tension went out of Siranush's voice, but nothing signaled her calm faster than the way she switched to Armenian.

"She's good. It's been nice to see her." Nadia responded in Armenian as well. She was a little out of practice, but the skills would never completely go away.

"Invite her over. I would like to see her."

"I'll do that."

"Why are you washing jars?"

"Just cleaning out the refrigerator, mom."

Siranush kissed her on the cheek. "Such a good girl." Then, in English. "Are you wearing perfume?"

Nadia's face got hot. She hoped she wasn't bright red. "Uh... yeah. I borrowed some from Angie."

"That's good," Siranush said in Armenian. She ran a hand over the shaved side of Nadia's head, up into the short mop at the top. "Maybe she can get you to grow your hair again. You look so nice with pretty, long hair."

"Yeah, maybe," Nadia said in English.

***

Milena could not quite believe what happened. When Nadia Eskandarian sat at the table, her first thought wasn't, "I'm taking this girl home and having mad, roof-rattling sex with her." It wasn't until she won the first hand. No one won the first hand.

Milena had been playing poker professionally for nearly ten years. In the old days, most of her games had been in places like Griffith Park and she had gotten very, very good matching wits with the chiselers. She had the skill to go after larger pots and bigger games, but she never could put a decent stake together. Real life always intruded. A car repair, an emergency, a medical bill. Something always reared its head and she was back to playing for singles.

Until her visit to the house of wonders and the meeting with the glass woman. She had been changed. Somehow it had attached to her skill at cards. She always had the ability to size someone up, but now, as long as the cards were flapping and the money was moving, she could follow her impressions down certain avenues of time. It was frustrating because she could sense there was so much more she could not see. Looming perpetually out of view.

The glass woman—the Celestial, that was her name—was powerful, but she was the creation of someone more powerful. A man who had been broken by his own brush with the divine inside of him.

When Nadia won the hand, Milena gained a glimpse inside the young woman, and it nearly blinded her.

Nadia was power. Her future was far too bright to see, and Milena knew that touching her was dangerous. Yet she could not resist. Pick your metaphor, she thought, knowing there was nothing that could take her from the other woman.

Milena checked the clock. An hour until work. She wasn't playing cards at the Midway tonight. It was her other job, the one she wished she could leave behind, but couldn't. So few clients these days, fewer with every year that went by. She hoped there would be a time when she had aged out of them entirely. Until then, she could not leave. Not when she was still partially owned and there was value to be gained from her.

Milena put on her work makeup. Heavier. Gaudier. There was little style to it, but it hid the markers of age. Made her look younger, innocent, surprised. Put on her work clothes. The vintage style was still there—it was too ingrained in her to go away entirely–but these were smaller, shorter, tighter. She never liked how she looked, but the clients did.

And the customer was never wrong.

***

Nadia felt ridiculous. She was wearing her swimming outfit: a pair of baggy trunks and a tank top. Her mind turned to Simcoe Manor and Milena at turns. She had a date with Milena in a couple days, and one with the Jellyfish Pool whenever she wanted it.

Angie drove the car, sitting as stiff and straight as a mannequin. They were passing into Malibu, where the houses of the rich and famous lined up facing the rising ocean. Nadia was not looking forward to this party, of not knowing a single person other than Angie. But Angie had begged, and Nadia could not say no. Now, looking at Angie, Nadia was beginning to wonder who was dreading this party more. Angie had stressed she was only there for business, and while Nadia believed her for the most part, she knew "only" was inaccurate.

"When you see Devin, tell me how you think he looks."

"I'm gay, Ang," Nadia said, peering out the passenger side window at the olive-green hills.

"Not that. I mean, how he looks. Like, is he weird?"

"I have no frame of reference." She caught Angie's exasperated sigh. "I'll do my best." Nadia had never met Devin Kassir. He had been dating Angie for about a year until they broke up suddenly a month before. Angie had thought there had been a future, but then he started to hang out with the host of the party. Now, he was her boyfriend, or something, Angie had said. Nadia would have expected that to be delivered with an eyeroll, but there was fear beneath it. Something was very wrong.

The entire situation was surreal. Nadia had never wanted to meet Jason or China Jennings. Jason Jennings made the kinds of movies she forgot fairly quickly after seeing them, the big actioners she enjoyed as long as she could mentally edit out just how aggressively heteronormative they were. Lex would freak out if he knew she was going to Jason Jennings's place. He had grown up on those movies and still saw any new one on opening day.

She had no idea what Lex thought about China, Jason's daughter. She was half a celebutante in a time when that concept was out of fashion. Angie mentioned, with derision, that China considered herself a writer-director-star, but any career she would have would be thanks to her superstar father. Nadia was tempted to dismiss China for this but reminded herself that she was almost as blessed.

Then, China wasn't completely blessed, or so the story went. The car accident that had killed her mother had nearly done the same to China. Cutting-edge plastic surgery had restored her, and when she made her first public appearances afterwards, the gossip press gushed over her. Called her inspirational, courageous, a party-girl who had seen hell and come back from it.

This was her party, for the lower rungs of the Hollywood establishment to network in bathing suits while sipping daiquiris.

The house was huge, white, and open. Glass walls looked out over a wide beach. A gate, now standing open, welcomed guests. A variety of cars parked in the big driveway and out on the sandy shoulder of the road. Palm trees and other tropical plants formed organic walls to the closest neighbors. They would probably be other actors, or musicians, or producers—people as desirous of privacy as the Jenningses.

Angie pulled over behind a Lexus and got out. She took a deep breath.

"It's going to be fine," Nadia said.

"Just going to make some contacts. Then we can go." Angie did look nice, in white shorts and a clingy top. She carried a few beach items in a wicker purse.

"So, am I your girlfriend or your friend in here?"

Angie laughed, the bark of tension at the beginning telling Nadia just how much her friend needed that. "We'll call that a game time decision. Just roll with it."

"You got it, chief."

They went up the road toward the house. Nadia tried not to let the anxiety take her. She concentrated on Angie. She was there for Angie.

Evidence of the party was obvious as soon as they got out of the car. A few towels and blankets were visible on the beach, and both young men and women were playing out there. Most, though, were in the house. The glass walls showed rooms utterly packed with young Hollywood. Nadia wouldn't recognize faces, though she would not be shocked if one or more of the beautiful people were represented by her family. They wouldn't know her, though. She was the invisible Eskandarian.

They went inside, and conversation and music formed into a muddy swirl.

"'Scuse me, bro," said a big guy as he bumped past Nadia.

She flinched, mentally scolding herself for showing weakness. No matter how often she got mistaken for a man, she never quite got used to it. That one bump made her look forward to leaving, her noble intentions gone.

"There he is," Angie said.

Nadia followed her gaze and spotted who Angie must be talking about. Looking at Devin Kassir, she wondered if he hadn't originally come in a six pack of men. All with the same dark eyes and hair, the same punished gym bodies, the same practiced indifference to fashion. Nadia wondered if Angie's taste had gotten worse since high school, or if this was some evidence of the change she alluded to.

Nadia barely had time to consider when the crowd shifted like a school of fish, revealing China Jennings. Nadia had never thought very much of her. She was blonde and pretty and in her own way just as generic and uninteresting as Devin. As it turned out, China looked very different through the lens of a camera.

The plastic surgery that had stitched her back together was just fine, when hidden behind makeup and large sunglasses and Photoshop. China Jennings was drinking and laughing at the center of her generic boys, looking like she was wearing a plastic mask of herself, and it was in danger of falling off at any moment. Nadia's own skin crawled as she pictured the mask tumbling off China's head, revealing the tortured flesh beneath. Worse than the urge to flee was the conflicting emotion: she wanted to touch China. It was not a sexual urge—the tight white dress over her tight white body did not stir Nadia in the slightest—but a rank fascination with the grotesque.

When China turned in their direction, a laugh on her lips, Nadia saw that one eye was entirely dead. It appeared human, detailed like flesh, but it might as well have been a sliver of flint, put in the woman's skull and forced to come to life. It failed in this. Her other eye wasn't much better, though it at least possessed a hooded semblance of vitality.

"Holy shit," Nadia breathed.

"Yeah," Angie said.

Nadia hadn't realized she'd spoken. She tried to think of anything to say, but she saw everything in Angie's eyes. The same combination of fear and revulsion. What she didn't see was the fascination. There was no conflict, no desire there. Angie just wanted to stay the hell away from China Jennings.

"Oh god," Angie whispered. Nadia read the words on her lips. It was too loud to hear.

She turned, thinking China would be coming this way. Nadia had the urge to slip the razor from her boot and cut the mask off China and see what was underneath. She imagined a collection of machinery, of glass lenses throwing back a muted and sick light. She realized then she was wearing her flip-flops. The razor was at home. An electric shock ran through her body. Defenseless in this place.

Devin advanced on the crowd. He was a tall man, and though Nadia wasn't precisely short, he was a good head taller than she.

"I can't right now," Angie said. "Can you run interference?"

"Yeah, of course."

"Thanks." Angie squeezed Nadia's shoulder and pushed through the gathering.

Nadia turned around, and intercepted Devin. He was nearly on top of her. Nadia felt naked without her razor. "Hey, Devin, right? Devin Kassir?"

Devin looked down at her. There was no blink of confusion. No adjustment to a new stimulus. Devin simply stopped and moved his head. Nadia noticed that his eyes did not move—only his neck. "Yes?"

"I'm a friend of Angie's. I've heard a lot about you."

"Where is Angie?"

"What do you want with Angie? I heard you guys broke up."

"We never broke up." From Angie's story, this was technically accurate.

"Yeah, you ghosted her."

"I was busy." Devin's answers didn't sound rehearsed, precisely. They did not have any ring of repetition. They were just absent of any consideration, hedging, or stuttering. He began to move, Nadia no longer a factor.

She stopped him with a hand on his chest. The way he looked at it put more electricity in her veins. Though he was not animated, not angry, she felt the violence in him boiling over. She swallowed, wishing she had worn her boots, and with them, her razor.

"Just a second there. I was wondering how you were doing."

"Fine," he said, brushing Nadia's hand away, and moving into the crowd behind her.

Nadia sighed. Angie was nowhere to be seen. Hopefully she had gotten enough time to get away and was networking or whatever she intended to do.

Nadia turned back around and caught China Jennings staring at her with that dead flint-eye. Nadia was transfixed, and though the eye was dead, recognition sparked within it. As suddenly, the moment was over as China looked to her companion and laughed, another of the genericons like Devin.

Nadia slipped away and out, trying to shed the sick obsession. She followed the hallways toward the back of the house, slipping between the people at the party. The walls were covered with black and white photos, most of which were close-ups of praying mantises. The odd insects stared from their homes in the frames, selecting their prey from the party guests.

Nadia found the back door, emerged out onto the deck, and from there went down sandy wooden stairs to the beach itself. The waves licked the shore, and the seagulls cried out from where they coasted on the winds. The weirdness was behind her and in the house. Nadia would remain outside until Angie came to collect her.

A few of the partygoers played in the surf, and some others were lying out on towels, soaking in the sun. Nadia settled into the sand and watched the waves, occasionally checking out one of the prettier guests out of the corner of her eyes.

She was not sure how long she watched the water. The sea and the sky lulled her into waking sleep. She thought of Milena Franco and Simcoe Manor and occasionally of China Jennings.

"Not big on parties either?" The voice was a contralto, friendly but cautious.

Nadia turned and saw the speaker. He had a narrow, feminine face, a slender jaw, and clever green eyes. His hair was cut short and indifferently spiked. He was dressed in shorts and a sleeveless t-shirt cut to show off his arms. It wasn't the muscle on display but the ink. His shoulders were a line of sea anemones, orange-and-white clownfish chasing one another up and down his arms. The tattoos were so real, so vibrant, they were alive.

"Not really."

"Me neither. Mind if I sit down, or did you want to stare at the ocean?"

"Pull up some sand."

The young man, who could not have been much older than Nadia's own twenty-four years, settled down. He stuck a delicate hand out. "Zach Gold."

"Nadia Eskandarian."

They shook.

"Sorry about this. I technically have friends here, but I never fit in at these things. I see you out here, and I think to myself maybe you have the same problem."

"Pretty close. I came here with a friend. Angie Alcala?"

Zach frowned. "Devin's girlfriend, right?"

"Ex. You know Devin?"

"Yeah. I mean, not well. He's nice enough. Or was." Nadia heard the same fear in Zach's voice that had been in Angie's.

"What do you mean 'was'?"

Zach sighed. "I'm going to need a beer for this. Want one?"

Nadia nodded.

"Be right back." Zach jogged up the beach, leaving his flip-flops behind as though to mark his place. They were tiny. He returned in a few minutes carrying two sweaty cold bottles of a cheap import. He handed one over to Nadia. The bottle cap was still on. She appreciated that.

Zach popped the top off his with an opener on his keychain and handed it over to Nadia as he sat back down. She opened her beer, and the two of them took long pulls, squinting out to the ocean. She could sense Zach's need to get to it on his own time.

"Okay. Devin." Zach sighed. "Like I said, we were friends. Not close or anything, but he was always cool. Didn't bat an eye when I came out. When he and Angie got together, he was pretty happy. I met her a few times at parties. Seemed like they were good for each other."

Zach drank. "And then he met China Jennings. I mean, we all know her a little. We live in LA. We're starfuckers the lot of us, and say what you will, but she's a star."

"Angie said she's an auteur or something."

"That's the word China would use. I mean, there are a lot of kids of famous people in this town, and not all of them have careers, so give I her that."

"She has a career?"

"I might be overstating it. She has a movie. She's supposedly making movies all the time, but no one's ever seen them."

Nadia frowned. "No one?"

"Not no one. She finished one about a year ago. *Lights Out*. She was buzzing about it all over the place. Online, parties, you name it. This was her big movie, the thing that was going to make her from Jason Jennings's daughter into an honest-to-god artist in her own right. It showed at one festival, and then that was it. No release, no studios knocking. Nothing. She stopped mentioning it in public. Might have been the reviews."

"They were bad?"

"Not exactly. There were only a couple critics who made the showing, and the number of them keeps changing. Some who most people think were there swear up and down they weren't. Others who definitely were there say no. Anyway, the reviews were... weird."

"What does that mean?"

"I'm not really a hundred percent sure." Zach gestured, growing more animated, but still looking out at the ocean. "Still, *Lights Out* still gets mentioned at stuff like this, the parties, the gallery openings, the indie premieres. The larger social circle of celebrity kids, bit players, young execs, and people like us. There were those who had seen it—or seen part of it—at those festivals. They walked out, said it was disgusting, turned their stomachs. Some puked their guts out. So there was this kind of fascination."

He sighed then, his voice growing rougher. "It turned into this almost urban legend. Almost. The thing is, China would occasionally fixate on someone. Always one of those guys like Devin. Handsome, fit, that type. She would cozy up to them. And sure, she's a little strange after the accident, but she can still turn them on. Every one of those guys roughed up the suspect to her at least once. I just stayed the hell away—I'm so not her type, but still, you know? Better safe than sorry. Then she sets her sights on Devin."

Zach rubbed his forehead. Minute gold freckles dotted his skin. "Some party, she wraps him around her finger. Angie wasn't there. I don't know why. Maybe working, maybe sick, maybe who knows? The point is, she gets Devin, and they go off. Some people were talking that he was cheating on her."

Nadia remembered this. When Angie told the story, that was the reason she gave for the breakup, even though it sounded like the real reason was he never called again.

"That wasn't it. Devin was going off to see the movie. He saw it, and when he came back... he was like that. Not as bad, but something had changed. Like he's just a suit, and whoever was wearing him, the real Devin, was gone. Now there's just enough left to make him move around and act like a person. And every time I see him, he's a little worse." Zach chuckled and took another pull. "So, now that you think I'm crazy..."

"I don't think you're crazy."

Zach turned his head, probing her with his dark green eyes. "You don't, do you?" he decided. "Lucky me. I guess I picked my new friend well."

"That you did." Nadia drank, and despite the conversation, she liked being with Zach. There was no bullshit in him, and no intimation he wanted anything beyond conversation.

They turned to idle talk after that, leaving the revelation about China and Devin to hang there. Zach revealed that he was a tattoo artist, and though he had designed the work on his arms, they had been inked by his teacher. He laughed when Nadia told him she had a Master's in English, and she had to do the same. He had heard of her family, or specifically their agency, and confirmed her suspicion that there were several clients inside.

"Maybe you could sign China," Zach said.

"Yeah, right. Or I could just stick my face in a jellyfish." The word summoned Simcoe Manor, and though she laughed, it was brittle.

"There you are!" Angie, coming from behind, ragged with unshed tears.

Nadia turned around to see Angie doing her best not to stumble over the uneven sands. She was a mess, her hair hanging over a face red and puffy.

"Oh god," Nadia said, getting up. "What happened?"

Angie sniffed. "Can we go?"

Zach stood up. "Hey, Angie. Are you okay?"

Angie shook her head. A tear escaped her, and she clamped down on it. "Hi. No."

"Devin?"

Angie nodded, and the sobs were quiet. Nadia hugged her friend, and Angie held on through the minor attack. Nadia looked around. They were as alone as they were likely to be, and none of the few others on the beach were looking at them. "Do you want to talk about it? We're pretty much alone."

Angie sniffed again and verified for herself. "Yeah... yeah, I think that'd be best."

She settled down between Nadia and Zach, who put a hand on Angie's shoulder.

"It was weird," Angie said. "Devin... found me, I guess. I was doing my best to stay away from him, but he still found me. And... and I can't explain exactly what was so wrong. He was acting like we were still together, but not like he cared one way or the other. Like he was going to kiss me, but not because he wanted to." Angie shrugged helplessly.

"I was telling Nadia about... the changes."

Angie looked from Zach to Nadia. "I didn't know you two knew each other."

"Just the weirdo magnets hanging out," Nadia said.

Angie gave a chuckle broken with a sob. "Glad you found each other then."

Nadia put her arm around Angie's shoulder, and Zach rubbed her back. "It's okay. You'll be okay."

"I just... I wish that I wasn't still hurt by this. I wish I knew what happened to him."

Nadia hugged her friend closer. She wondered if she would be able to find out what happened to Devin. If this was some kind of echo of Odette, caught soon enough to prevent the tragic end.

They got up soon after, Angie hugging Zach goodbye. Nadia and Zach exchanged info, and she knew she would be seeing the young tattoo artist again. She had none herself, but the quality of ink on him was intoxicating. She had always been tempted, and maybe this was the final change. Or at least part of it.

***

Milena hadn't been so nervous about a date in a long time. She felt silly, especially after what the two of them had already shared. That didn't stop the prey-quick hammering of her heart, or the sharp breaths sucked between her teeth.

She had arrived early to the coffee place in Los Feliz. They'd chosen it after a bit of haggling, both willing to meet in the other's neighborhood, but neither one wanting to impose on the other. So they picked a place roughly in the middle, in the unspoken social agreement that if everyone was inconvenienced, no one was.

The coffee place had a few tables and chairs on the sidewalk, set up like a European cafe, but on the side of the undeniably grimy urban area of Los Angeles. She liked the juxtaposition. She was dressed casually, for her, in a brown and cream wave dress and matching Oxford comment heels. She topped it off with a straw Edith hat and faux-vintage sunglasses. She needed them to hide her darting eyes.

She sipped at her sugary iced coffee, wondering if her stomach was going to stop with the backflips anytime soon. When she saw Nadia coming up the street, she saw this wasn't going to be the case.

Nadia looked, even in the harsh light of day, like a badass. Her hipster-punk style might have made Milena roll her eyes on another woman, but not on Nadia. The harsh haircut, now slicked back with a slight pompadour in front, the shortened pants, the heavy boots, and work shirt opened to reveal a wifebeater over a slimly muscled chest, fit her. Nadia was unconventional, yes, and gorgeous in her way.

Today, she hid her tawny brown eyes—eyes that turned bright amber when the light hit them, or when they were turned on Milena—behind simple black Ray-Bans. She carried a battered messenger bag over one shoulder.

"Hi," she said, sitting down across from Milena.

"Hi." Milena had no idea what to say. Seeing Nadia here, in so mundane a setting, was jarring after how they'd met. The bond was there, but in the sun, it was not secret.

Fortunately a waiter came by, and Nadia ordered an iced chai, and the two of them started talking. Part of the process of becoming an Angeleno was learning to recognize Armenian names, and Milena knew that part already. Nadia was second generation, and spoke the language, which she self-consciously demonstrated, to Milena's delight. Milena wasn't so connected to her heritage: the little Spanish and French she spoke weren't about her blood, but for her adopted city and ill-advised flirtation with avant-garde cinema.

Nadia let it drop that she'd just got back from getting her master's degree.

"In what?"

"English Literature," Nadia said, blushing. "Focusing specifically on feminist genre fiction. It might be the single most useless degree anyone has ever earned."

Milena lit up, leaning forward. "Feminist genre fiction?"

Nadia explained that it started with a love of James Tiptree, Jr., which was the penname of Alice Bradley Shelton, forced to hide her identity to make it as a sci-fi writer. It bloomed into a love of LeGuin, Atwood, Connie Willis, Charles Stross, Tamora Pierce, and so on. Nadia threw so many names at Milena, she felt like she should be writing them down.

"Are you okay?" Nadia asked.

"Yeah, of course. Why?"

"Usually when I start rattling off authors I like, people sort of glaze over."

"Stupid people, sure."

Nadia laughed. "I saw the books in your place, but I didn't get a look at the titles. Are you a big sci-fi fan?"

"Excuse me?"

Milena turned in her seat, unable to comprehend an interruption. The world only held Nadia; there was no more room for anyone else. The speaker was a handsome man, fit and bearded, showing off strong legs in a pair of checkered shorts, and gym-strong arms in an ironic *Jurassic Park* shirt. Milena blinked at him, nonplussed. "Yes?"

"Sorry to interrupt. I know you're here with your friend, but I had to introduce myself. I'm Keith, you're gorgeous, and I was wondering if it was okay if I called you sometime."

Milena turned to Nadia. Though the younger woman's face was an impassive mask, she saw the seething anger in the clench of her jaw and the subtle way she was angled away from Keith.

"Well, Keith. I'm actually not here with my friend. I'm on a date."

Keith's eyes widened. "Oh, shit. I am so sorry." He turned to Nadia. "Really, I'm sorry. I had no idea. My bad, ladies."

Keith left them.

"I'm sorry," Milena said.

"It's not your fault," Nadia said, her voice brittle. "Not the first time it's happened. They don't see us as a romantic couple."

"I don't know how romantic we are."

"Give me time," Nadia said, warming up.

"You've got as long as you like," Milena said, and meant it.

"Well, okay then."

Milena desperately wanted to get the date back on track, heal it from the young man's thoughtless interruption. "We were talking about books?"

"Yeah, right. Sorry. Who do you like?"

"Well, I was pretty into Anne Rice and Clive Barker for a long time."

"Nothing wrong with Barker."

"And Rice?"

"Can you take the Fifth on a date?" A grin pulled at Nadia's slender lips.

Milena chuckled. "I'll allow it, but only because you're cute."

"Who else?"

"I love Patricia Highsmith."

Nadia nodded eagerly. "Good taste."

"I've read *Gatsby* probably as many times as you think I have considering how I dress."

Nadia smiled. Milena listed off a few more authors, then: "What would you recommend for me? Something to get a former horror girl into this world of... what was it? Feminist genre literature?"

"I should just give you my dissertation," Nadia said.

"Okay," Milena said, eager to see the workings of this fascinating woman's mind.

"Seriously?"

"If you give it to me, I'll read it."

"That's pretty much the best thing anyone has ever said."

They ended up staying at their table for hours, the conversation simmering between them.

***

Nadia knew it would be that evening she would return to Simcoe Manor. She had preparations to make. First were the practical elements: her collection of jars, her satchel, and cloth to pack the glass in. She had a flashlight as well, but she was not certain she would need it. Waiting for a full moon had its advantages.

There were other preparations as well. Not practical, but spiritual somehow. They were not tied to any religion but were instead the cult of the self. Nadia understood that to return to Simcoe Manor, she would have to do so as the clearest representation of Nadia Eskandarian. She would begin her rites until well after sundown, wanting to arrive as close to midnight as she could.

In the meantime, she wandered her house filled with jittery energy. She thought of texting Milena, but it felt desperate. They had seen each other briefly the day before. Nadia had been faintly amused that they were apparently dating in reverse. They spent the afternoon talking about all the things one should discuss on a date.

Nadia was ready to follow Milena home, but Milena had demurred. She had an appointment. Nadia had only nodded. Probably a card game—Milena had talked extensively about making her money at cards.

So Nadia was left to her own devices. She read but was too keyed up to make any headway. She couldn't sleep, and TV was hard to concentrate on. She ran, and that helped a little. As she jogged up to her house, she heard her father cursing loudly in Armenian.

She rounded the corner, removing her earbuds. Vartan Eskandarian stood by the side of the house, staring down into the grass, with a half-frightened, half-surprised look on her face.

"Dad?"

"Nadia! Be careful. I was just walking, and there was a goddamn snake!" He pointed at the ground where winding vines from a bush gave some shade.

Nadia's mind conjured the image of the dragon who ruled Simcoe Manor. Had he followed her down? It was a silly, juvenile thought, and gone as soon as she thought it. Curious, she took a step toward the patch of ground her father was staring at.

"Nadia!"

She ignored him and moved closer. There, coiled up under some of the vines, a baby rattlesnake. It was so small, it only had a single bead on the end of its tail, which it couldn't even shake as a warning. It watched father and daughter with metallic eyes.

"I'm going to get a shovel and kill this thing."

"Dad!" Nadia scolded. "It's not doing anything."

"It could bite someone. Hurt someone."

"You're not killing it."

"Nadia, let your father do this."

"I'm going to move it out of the yard."

"It could bite you."

"It won't bite me." She said this with the calm surety of fact, no more remarkable than if she had informed him that she had brown eyes.

He did not open his mouth to protest. Later, he might wonder why. Now, in the still air, the heat of the afternoon pressing in on them, there was no argument. Nadia knelt by the tiny snake. The sweat of her run drying on her skin, she pushed her sunglasses to the top of her head. The serpent had transferred its attention to her from her father. It wiggled the tip of its tail in pantomime of what it could do as an adult. The diamonds picked out against its back shimmered in the dappled sun.

"It's okay," she whispered, now in English. "You're safe."

The snake's coils loosened. Nadia continued to whisper comfort to it, less concerned by the words themselves as she was by their meaning. It slithered out from cover, now unable to strike even if it wanted to. Nadia stood, without knowing why, and flung her arm out. A stinging, jarring pain lanced up it. Vartan cursed.

Nadia stood. The baby rattlesnake was between her legs, heading for the bushes away from the house and the slope down into the canyon. Vartan's eyes were wide, not looking at his daughter's face, but at her arm.

"I told you, dad," she told him in measured Armenian. "Don't hurt him."

"Nadia, I'm sorry. I didn't think you would—"

She frowned and followed his gaze. Her arm was ripped open, the blood running down her forearm. The blade of the shovel had given her a nasty cut, but it looked that fortunately Vartan had pulled the blow as soon as he saw his daughter in the way.

"I'll get the first aid kit," Vartan said, chastened by what he had seen. He ran off, still holding the shovel.

Nadia knelt. The rattlesnake was off the flagstone sidewalk and into the bushes. "Go on," she said. Drops of her blood tapped the earth. She liked the looks of it.

The snake was gone when Vartan returned. The cut wasn't nearly as bad as it looked initially and had already clotted by the time they got a bandage on it.

He felt so guilty about it that he didn't even tell the story about the snake to Siranush. Nadia was many things, but she would always be the baby of the family. Vartan spent the evening doting on his daughter.

Nadia was just passing time now. It was impossible to see the appearance of a rattlesnake as anything but what it was. A sign. An invitation. The dragon knew she would be returning, and it was welcoming her to Simcoe Manor.

Her parents were only night owls when they were hosting parties. On a normal evening, Vartan and Siranush were in bed by ten, Vartan reading *Variety* and Siranush watching a reality show with her headphones. Nadia knew that after ten, she was completely alone.

She stripped first, taking her razor into the bathroom with her. As she ran a bath, she removed the bandage. The cut was much smaller than she remembered; there didn't even seem to be a way that much blood could have come out of her. She turned it over to look from another angle. No, she was fine. The ragged tips of her skin the spade had torn were dead and flaking off. The scab was fresh and dry.

Nadia knelt by the tub, mixed up the lather and scraped a few minute hairs from her body. She was clean again. Herself. She emerged from the bath rejuvenated. There would be no new bandage for her. She wanted it exposed to the air. She dressed quickly, grabbed her satchel, and slipped out of the sliding door on the patio—quieter than the front door. Soon, she was driving back toward the place her sister was murdered.

Nadia parked on the side street, and hiked up the slope, past the broken gates. The landscape was bright, both from the lights billowing up from the city, and streaming down from the full moon. The hills sang with the yips of coyotes, always out of sight. Warning those who approached, this place is ours now.

No, it's not, Nadia thought to them.

Nadia found the staircase easily, the shield of brambles now obvious to her eyes. She passed through and up, emerging on the patio. Her breath came quicker now, and she knew she was still wrong. She set her satchel down at the top of the cement staircase. She disrobed respectfully, folding her clothing in a neat stack.

She picked up her satchel and took a step on the patio. It was cold under her bare feet, but she felt right. This was the correct way to do things. The holy place welcomed her. Wanted her. She found that though it was relatively dark, she could pick everything out with complete clarity, even down to the colors. In her preparation, she had synced her personal rhythms to the vibrations of this place, and now the secrets were revealed.

The items must be gathered in order of escalating holiness. She did not know why, but this fact was clear in her mind. She padded across the patio. There was no fear in her of being seen out here, nude under the night sky. There was only the slight worry she could not truly understand this magical place.

She stepped over the side of the house and made her way to the plant. She opened a jar and filled it with berries, their meaty, bloody scent flooding her senses. She filled two more jars, wrapped them in cloth, and placed them in her satchel.

Then it was time. She shivered, though it was not the air against her bare skin that did it. She looked through the burned out remains of the house toward the pool. Her sister had died in there. No matter what she had found, there was still the simple truth. Nadia needed it.

She stepped out of the house's burned borders, and made her way toward the pool, descending the steps. She knelt at the edge of the grimy water. The sense of movement within was even stronger now, though she still could not see what was causing it. She filled a jar with the water and held it up to the moonlight. Something was moving around in there, but she didn't remember catching anything. The other two jars she filled had the same sense. She would investigate more thoroughly when she brought them home.

Satisfied, she stood. She gave thanks to her sister. Not to the parasite, the Nobody, the Simcoe Killer, who had been the one to sanctify this place. He could rot. Odette's sacrifice, though unwilling, was far more important, as it drew Nadia to this place. She knew her sister was extinguished, and could not hear her, but for a moment she would pretend. *Thank you, Odette. I love you.*

Nadia stepped out of the pool and to the stairs. She was on the second one when she noticed the dragon coiled at the top. He was huge, and utterly silent. His rattle held up as a threat, but he did not so much as twitch it. His antediluvian head, in the center of his powerful coils, watched her.

Azhdahak, she thought, a dragon she'd read about in a book of children's stories. This was him, reincarnated into a form suitable for the modern day. His power was apparent in the ancient muscles beneath the diamonds on his skin. He was pleased, or so he said by the silent rattle and the sheathed fangs. She had saved one of his children today. A final test? Or could this creature have such human motives? Was trying to anthropomorphize it a way to utterly misunderstand its terrible will?

She shrugged the satchel to the floor. Then, she bent over, reaching out deliberately, placing her hand on the patio in front of the great serpent.

The dragon tasted her through the air. She remained in her position, not supplicate, but not dominant. She and he were one and the same. She knew that if he were to strike again, that would be it. His poison before had been a test, perhaps, or a warning. The second bite would be fatal.

She was utterly still, breathing in the clean hillside scent of the creature. Was she worthy? What did that even mean?

The serpent uncoiled himself. It took years. Its movement revealed more strong, ropy sections of body, shining like jewels under the moonlight. He slithered forward, coming closer to Nadia's hand. With every foot he traveled, he grew smaller, though not diminished; no matter his physical size, he carried the potency of the age of reptiles in him. Then, his tongue flickered against her fingers. It was little more than a flutter, but a sting was beneath it, carrying the ghost of his powerful venom.

Then, the dragon coiled around her arm. She felt his muscles, undulating against her bare flesh, as he climbed her like a trellis. When he was entirely off the ground, she stood straight. The serpent was wrapped all around her arm, her torso, up by her neck. The dragon—Azh, she decided, his name was Azh—had made his decision. The covenant was formed.

She and the serpent were one.

Splendor

In the few isolated moments she surfaced from her task, Nadia dimly understood the passage of time. As close as she could determine, it had been a little over a week since she locked herself away in her room. She was not really sleeping, and meals happened whenever her mother insisted. And though she had spent her days without bathing, she smelled of jasmine. She had since the night with Milena.

A week was as close as she could come to an estimate. A week looking into her treasures, and she still did not truly understand them.

She had avoided texts from everyone, including Milena, in this time. She wouldn't be worthy company for anyone. There was too much to understand, too many mysteries to solve.

She learned fairly quickly that the water was far more powerful than the berries. She did not quite understand what this truly meant, or even how she knew it. The berries buzzed a little less, didn't make her bones ache quite as much, didn't provoke the same primal need of a junkie for her needle.

The water had the closest connection to Odette's killer, and it fairly glittered with his masking residue. The berries were distanced, though Nadia could not understand precisely how. Through a filter was as close as she could come. Removed by one step from the Nobody's humanistically divine glory.

The water was black and grimy. The shapes inside were eel-like, rubbery strips of black moving at the edges of her vision. Soon, she determined they were nothing at all. Stretching and contracting shadows. Ephemera, a mark upon the water of supernature. Marking it as special.

She attempted to plant some of the berries in pots by her window. Though she hoped to grow more, she felt as though she were wasting them by putting them into the soil. Wasting the persistent hum within. The power. When she thought of it in raw terms, of power, her blood quickened. Her fingers tingled, and her body slicked in arousal.

Her only companion in this time was Azh, but he was far from reliable. He would vanish, and Nadia could turn her room upside-down trying to find him. It was fruitless; he was simply gone. Then he would return, coiled neatly in the center of her bed, tasting the air. He was small in these times, barely more than four feet, an unremarkable example of his apparent species, the western diamondback. *Crotalus atrox*, Nadia noted with some pleasure, savoring the romantic taste of the words. She knew Azh was no mere diamondback, but he had chosen a form pleasing to him.

She had received texts and emails from Milena, Angie, and Zach. All asking the same thing. Where are you? What are you up to? Nadia did not think she could go anywhere until she knew more. And she knew she could not make them understand.

Zach's email had been the one thing to get through her self-made shield. It had reminded her of what she wanted, and she paused in her work. She was dressed in an undershirt and pair of shorts, the same ones for several days. Five minutes after the email chimed on her phone, she had the left leg of her shorts hiked up to her hip, and she was carefully drawing the diamondback pattern of Azh on her thigh. It felt like she was drawing her real skin rather than defacing what she had. Show the world your scales. The words in her mind came in her voice, but it was not her speaking. It was Azh.

The knock surprised her. She blinked at the clock. It wasn't time for dinner, the one meal her mother consistently notified her about, whether Nadia emerged or not.

"Yes?"

"It's me." Lex.

"What do you want?"

"Can I come in?"

She frowned. "Uh... okay?"

The door opened and Lex came in on a cloud of cologne. He was in his usual uniform of designer t-shirts, jeans, and gold jewelry, his hair and beard barely a fuzzy layer over his skin. His face said he was feeling a little ill. He sat down on Nadia's bed, and her heart stopped for a moment, as she imagined him sitting on Azh. The dragon wouldn't brook that level of disrespect. She exhaled when Lex wasn't instantly bitten.

"What are you doing?" he asked her.

"I'm in my room."

"Yeah, for like three weeks. Mom and dad are worried."

"Oh. I'm okay."

"You sure?"

"What's going on, Lex?" Her suspicion shone through in a flat tone.

"I don't know. It's just... after Odette... I thought maybe I should keep an eye on you is all."

She stared at the filthy pool water lined up in its trio of jars, the afternoon sun lighting the grimy depths. The elastic worm-like shapes cruised through the muddy gloom. Could Lex see them? Or were they only revealed for her eyes, because she had taken the dragon's venom inside her?

"It's okay," she said, her voice softer now. "I'm not Odette."

"I know. I know. I thought she was the tough one, right? Then you come back looking like some gutterpunk and I think maybe I had it all backwards."

"You never looked out for me when I wasn't looking like this."

"Yeah. I know."

"Odette always did."

"I know that too." He sighed.

She turned away from the things on her desk. Lex did not so much as glance at the jars containing the wonders. She could hear them snapping with the Nobody's energy. Lex, if he saw them as anything, would be odds and ends put in jars by his strange sister. Something gnawed at his mind. She watched it working on his small forehead, furrowing his brow again and again. His hair up top was beginning to thin. Isolated strands of gray threaded his beard.

"What's going on?" she asked him.

"Oh, you know. Working with dad."

"Not what you wanted?"

"It is... just, you know. It's dad."

She knew exactly what he meant. Their dad had never expected as much out of her as he did from his only son. Nadia had a job at the agency if she wanted it. She would never have the one waiting for Lex, though. She settled back and allowed him to speak, for the time being forgetting about her studies. Her brother needed her.

***

Zach's apartment in Highland Park was tiny. The centerpiece was a saltwater aquarium far too large for the space. The fluorescent light made the gravel and the tank glow. The tank was filled with an artificial coral reef, covered with vibrant organisms somewhere between animal and plant. Brightly-colored shrimp wandered over the underwater ridge while clownfish hid amongst the waving tentacles of sea anemones.

"Beautiful," Nadia said.

"Thanks. It's too expensive, but I couldn't imagine living without it."

They were sitting in the combination living and dining room. A kitchen, barely big enough for one person, opened off it, as did a small bedroom and a bathroom the size of a closet.

"I'd like to get some seahorses, but you can't put them in a tank with anemones."

"That's too bad."

"Okay, so what am I looking at?"

Nadia stood up and set the beer aside on the table. She began unbuckling her belt and paused.

"It's okay," Zach said. "This isn't some ploy to get you naked. I'm your tattoo artist. Besides, you're a little manly for me."

Nadia smiled. "I was going to say the same thing about you."

"Drop trou. You're the one who had to draw it on her thigh."

"It was right there," she said, pulling her pants down and hiking her boxers up. The drawing was crude by Zach's standards, if the reef on his shoulders was any indicator, but it got the point across. She'd drawn in the scales, and the diamond pattern up her thigh. Zach leaned close, peering at it. "I'd want you to, you know, do better than I did."

"Sure. I'd like to get some pictures. Did you have a specific species in mind?"

She had a specific animal in mind, but she couldn't very well show him the dragon. It was too close to disrespect. "Yeah. I can get you some pictures."

"Okay, good. I can see what you want. The question is, how much of it do you want on your skin?"

"Cover the big muscle," Nadia said, demonstrating on her leg. "I also want my arms, but those I want as snakes. Several of them."

"Coiling around your arms, like?"

"Exactly. I also want a strip of snakeskin along my spine."

"That's a pretty big commitment. You sure?"

"I'm sure."

"How detailed?"

"As detailed as you can make it."

"Well, it'll take some time. You'll get the friends discount, but it could get expensive."

"It's okay," she said. Her parents wouldn't be crazy about her using the money they gave her for this. She needed it though, for no reason she could name. Azh had revealed himself where Odette had died, and Nadia knew she had to honor him for it. As the drawing had spread over her left thigh, her breathing had slowed, and her heartbeat became as regular as a metronome. She needed to be marked as soon as possible.

"You can sit down now," Zach said, leaning back and picking his beer up. "Unless you want to lounge around my place without your pants on."

Nadia shot him the finger and pulled her pants back up, buckling her belt. She sat, watching the fish flutter through the underwater environment.

"Ever think about getting an eel?" she asked.

"Nah. It'd eat all my clownfish."

***

The temptation to withdraw completely beckoned from the dark, to do nothing but delve into the mysteries of the objects retrieved from Simcoe Manor. Seeing Lex, and then Zach, was good for her, despite the distraction. She reminded herself that there was a life to be lived, and it existed outside of her room.

Milena returned her text nearly instantaneously. Good to know Nadia had not been imagining the connection. Nadia picked her satchel up reflexively— even the idea of a simple date without the objects was unthinkable. She carried only one of each, a jar of the pool water and a collection of the berries. These were packed in cloth and hidden amongst other, mundane things: a book, her wallet, a bottle of water, some protein bars. She tucked the razor into her boot.

She headed for the Midway. Milena gave her the go ahead to use the service entrance, and Nadia was grateful. While she would have to get through some of the crowd, the back rooms were always far more sparsely populated than the front rooms.

She nodded to the security guard, a thickset man with olive skin, a shaved head, and an LA Dodger logo tattooed below and to the side of his left eye like a tear. "Milena said—"

"Her girlfriend, yeah," the man said in his faint Chicano accent. "Go on in."

Nadia felt her face grow hot. Girlfriend. She had been wanting to go in that direction, but she hadn't broached it. Had thought her past week or so of hermitage would require some smoothing over. It had to be rationalized—Milena had only used girlfriend because "woman I'm fucking," while accurate, wasn't the kind of thing that got too many doors opened. She'd said it, though. And maybe it was enough.

The internal staircase was covered in beaten down old carpeting, worn flat by the tromp of feet. The paint back here was peeling, and there was nothing on the walls save for a few tags scratched indifferently into the wood. Nadia took the stairs two at a time, desperate to get a read on Milena.

She passed from the hall through the door into the elephant man room. The poster greeting visitors was of a man in a loincloth reclining on a bed of nails, and the walls were decorated with pictures of elephants and performers subjecting their bodies to gruesome procedures they did not seem to feel. A low stage, lit in lurid reds, took up one end of the room. Two pretty young women in small, yet vintage lingerie were allowing audience members to staple dollar bills to their skin, while a hootchie-koo track featuring a muted trumpet leered in the background.

Nadia lingered on the women for a moment. Both were lovely in that slender wood nymph kind of way. Occasionally, a line of blood ran below one of the dollar bills, bright and scarlet against their pale flesh. Though the staples were all over their skin, the two women showed no sense of pain, dancing with each other like lovers, before one would break off, get stapled, and return to her partner.

Despite herself, Nadia wanted to stay. She felt like she should be offended by this geek show. Instead, she watched the energy between the two, the way the eyes of one flashed when the other ran her hand over a new dollar bill. As their performance continued, they were becoming steadily more covered, and yet with each addition, they were more bare.

Nadia ducked out of there and went up the short hall to find Milena's fortuneteller room. The game was full up. Two of the players looked distinctly out of place, like bros who had somehow gotten lost. The women on the other side of the table had scooted over, giving them the widest possible berth. Milena was wearing a black-and-white striped dress and looked like a Tim Burton character.

Milena glanced up as Nadia parted the curtains, and her face exploded into a smile. She dropped the stony fortuneteller act and her cards at the same time, and got up, meeting Nadia halfway across the room. Milena took Nadia in her arms and planted a lingering kiss on her mouth. "Hey, gorgeous. Thanks for coming."

One of the bros hooted. Nadia tensed. She hated this bullshit, and even if she wasn't going to cut him with the razor in her boot, she didn't want to put on a show. Milena broke contact, brushed a kiss over Nadia's nose, and turned to the bro, sliding an arm around Nadia's waist. "Someone took pictures of you and Craig. They're already online, and they're getting found next week."

The bro went white as a sheet and fled the room, leaving his cards and money behind.

"I still have an hour or so until my break, so if you want to get a drink, I'll join you when I'm done?" Milena said to Nadia.

"Sure."

"Tell Dave—the bartender—that you're with me. I warned him you'd be coming."

"Your girlfriend?"

"I might have used those words," said Milena, teasing, challenging.

"Good to know." Nadia kissed her girlfriend, and this time the players were silent. Milena returned to her seat as Nadia left for the fire-eaters room and the bar.

The Midway was packed that night. If it had been more open, she would not have been so surprised. She pushed her way through the crowd to the bar, ready to announce to Dave and whoever was listening, that she was Milena's girlfriend. She was struck silent when she saw who was at the bar.

China Jennings, surrounded by her band of dead-eyed men, held court at the Midway. Nadia felt a stab of offense. This was Milena's place. This wasn't for China and her brand of TMZ celebrity.

China sat at the bar, her dress hugging curves sculpted at the gym and the surgeon's scalpel. Her back was to the bar, one hand languorously out by a half-empty cosmo. Her boys, and that was what they were, hemmed her in. They were all standing, and though their expressions were that of rapturous interest, of ill-concealed erotic attention, their eyes were flinty. They had a variety of drinks, amber cocktails or beer in bottles, bringing them to their lips in even intervals.

Devin was at China's right shoulder, closest in the ring to Nadia. He had what looked like a whiskey on the rocks, setting it on the bar, waiting a minute, laughing, then sipping. She bet each movement was done in perfect increments of time, as constant as an atomic clock.

Nadia saw Angie's helpless crying. Remembered Zach's words. One look at China and Nadia knew something was wrong, but what that was couldn't be solved here.

An idea wheedled into Nadia's mind. Once it was there, it could not go, becoming as strong, as persistent as the desire to see Simcoe Manor. As much part of her as the desire to have her skin show scales.

The items called to her. Use us. She reached into her satchel and withdrew the jelly jar filled with pool water. The image of Scooby-Doo smiled back at her from the glass surface. Beneath him, one of the phantom worms stretched out, elastic, then vanished into the silt.

Devin pushed off from the bar, heading in the direction of the men's room. He left his drink, half full of whiskey and melted ice, on the bar. Nadia slinked through the crowd, using her thin frame to her advantage. She cradled the jelly jar in hand, unscrewing the lid but keeping it tamped down over the sloshing contents.

China and her boys were caught in their world, yet there was nothing stopping them from turning around and seeing Nadia. The whole thing was madness, really, but Nadia could not stop herself. It was not an outer force compelling her on this path. It was the true her, the woman of the scales, Nadia sapiens. She would listen to this exemplar of herself and obey the blasphemous song.

She snatched the glass off the bar and turned in one motion, heading toward the men's room. Her back to China, Nadia held up the glass. The imprint of his lips was a smudge on the rim. She dumped a bit of the pool water into the drink, screwed the lid back on, and returned it to the satchel. She glanced at the liquid. The whiskey was dirty, the phantom worms crawling through their new environment, as alive or as dead as they had always been.

Devin emerged from the men's room. He didn't even look at Nadia; China utterly consumed his attention and all his effort was on returning to her side.

Nadia didn't hesitate in her impulse. She brought the glass up and tipped the contents entirely into her mouth. She felt the movement of the eels, gone in the moments she tried to isolate them with a questing tongue. The acrid and sour taste burned her mouth. It did not stay for long. She spat the entire mouthful of whiskey and gritty pool water into Devin's face.

The liquid ran in rivers, leaving only small streaks of black dirt. Devin blinked in confusion, only then noticing Nadia standing in front of him. He reared back to punch, but a big guy standing nearby caught his shoulder. Nadia dropped the glass where it shattered on the floor. Devin turned, staggered the Samaritan with a haymaker, and lunged for Nadia again. The bouncers were quick, wading in and yanking everyone apart. They had Devin by a handful of lapel and another had Nadia by the collar of her shirt.

"Okay, you've all had enough."

Nadia didn't struggle. There wasn't much she could do against someone who fought professionally. The guy was a mountain. Devin didn't have any such prohibition. He uncorked a swing at one of the bouncers and got a fist in the gut for his trouble.

Nadia, Devin, the good Samaritan, and another man who had barely been involved were getting the bum's rush, when China stepped in front of them. Her face was like a mask, a literal one. Her skin was a single golden tanned tone, stretched taut over her skull. Though she was young, she had none of the pleasing curves of youth. She was beautiful, but it was the beauty of an off-brand Barbie.

"Excuse me," she said, though what she meant was "Stop."

The bouncers did. They might have recognized her, or else they recognized the stink of privilege oozing off of her in palpable waves.

"I don't think you need to do that to my friend," China said. The real message was a lot shorter and more forceful.

Nadia sagged. She had no idea why she was listening to insane urges like spitting old pool water into someone's face. Then China went to Nadia and slipped her skinny arm around Nadia's waist. "You can take the rest of the trash out now."

The bouncers, released from whatever hypnotic hold she'd had them under, started moving again, hauling the large men out the side exit. China turned to Nadia, "What was that all about?"

Nadia stammered, "I... I don't know." China was gazing at her with recognition, holding her with ease. Nadia's skin crawled at the contact. With less than a foot between them, China looked even more artificial, from the crepe-thin flesh around her too-blue eyes, to the lines on her neck like plastic seams.

China shook her head. Her blonde hair barely moved. "It looked like that girl spit on you."

Nadia coughed. She remembered the parasite, the shifting face, the things eating him. He was the Nobody. The power, the glass, the face. What she had done. What this had all been telling her. His abilities, momentarily gifted to her in the ritual act.

"Yeah. It was weird."

A momentary frown rippled over China's face, though it was hard to see how it would change her features much as they were hermetically incapable of such. "Okay, Devin. Let's go."

China swept out of the Midway like a princess, Nadia caught in her wake. The dead-eyed men surrounded her. She felt like one of Zach's clownfish, the tentacles of the anemone waving about her. If it just realized the fish was meat, it would draw it into the horrible mouth to be consumed whole.

She was no fish. She could bite.

As they left, piling into several late model sportscars, Nadia felt a pang. She was sitting shotgun with two nearly identical men in the car, one driving, one in the back, both staring straight ahead. Neither were fidgeting the way modern people did, no fiddling with the car radio or checking their phones. She pulled out her phone, watching the men out of the corner of her eyes. Seeing if this was somehow a breach of pod person etiquette. If they came for her, the razor was her only hope. The razor, the most obvious fang of this particular snake.

But she wasn't going to leave without texting Milena.

Sorry. Had to go.

The text came back quickly. *Too bad. Can I see you later?*

I'll call when I'm finished.

She couldn't tell Milena what she was up to. Not when she wasn't sure herself. This was rank madness. She saw that and felt the slick ice of fear up her limbs. The way she crept in here, keeping the anemone's tentacles from recognizing her through the gummy sheen of dream over everything. She felt powerful, even as she prepared herself for the man in back lunging.

He did not. The car, along with the other two—China's and another load of her boys—pulled into a cramped parking lot beside a neon dance club. This was the kind of place Nadia would imagine China Jennings would frequent. The people were the rich, young, and beautiful. She half expected to see Lex there, flirting with someone barely out of high school. On a normal night, they never would have let someone looking like Nadia in, unless they somehow saw her last name and made the connection.

Yet she went right in, amongst the boys, in China's wake. They did not speak to one another, and only made noise if China addressed one directly, or to, en masse, laugh at one of her jokes, murmur encouragement, or pay her a preening compliment.

Nadia, from her position in the midst of them, watched the crowd of people as she went by. There were recognizable faces—not stars exactly, but the children of stars who had a movie or two under their belts and would never go anywhere else. There were agents too, and some younger executives and creative types, and of course the hangers-on, those beautiful enough to be invited in.

Nadia was alone in this room full of people.

They watched China Jennings as she came in with her entourage. Some openly gawked. Most hid their attention with furtive glances or kept her clocked at the corners of their eyes. China was something unique, and she knew it. Some combination of her status as true Hollywood royalty, the accident, and the bizarre creature she had become, had elevated her beyond anyone in the club. She was the rarest of birds: the public enigma. Nadia wondered if everyone had the same reaction she did, of repulsed fascination, an unshakeable need to get closer, and the inescapable grip of fear whenever China's one dead doll eye focused on them for too long. Or maybe China was a simple oddity to them, and the same ability that fooled her had given Nadia the power to recognize the strange other lurking within.

China had a corner reserved. A big looping couch where they could sit and glow under the faint blue lighting. They spread out, and Nadia was poised for the far end, so she could bolt if she had to.

"Devin!" China called over the music. When Nadia turned her head, China patted the cushion next to her.

None of the others reacted to this, though Nadia could swear the closest one showed the barest flicker of anger in his eyes. Nadia could not disobey. Using her phone had been one thing, but there was no gainsaying whatever China demanded. Nadia went to China and settled in next to her. China leaned over, and once again a frown barely crinkled her plasticky skin.

Nadia smiled at her. China's eyes moved somewhat independently. The right was alive, and moved in normal, jittery twitches. The left was stony and cold, staring through whatever she had focused on. Nadia had assumed it was glass, and that it had been put out in the accident. Though now, barely a foot from China's face, and she could see the eye was biologically alive. The soul was missing.

Nadia fought the urge to swallow on her dry throat. Fought the urge to go for the razor or just to run. She had to stay confident. Hope whatever power had put the illusion in China's head would hold strong.

China only looked away when one of her boys returned with a tray holding a bottle of vodka, the glass frosty from the freezer, a pitcher of cranberry juice, a bucket of ice, and a collection of tumblers. He set it on the low table in the middle of them and mixed drinks without being asked. All drank from them, though Nadia did her best to drink as little as possible. When the time came to mix more cocktails, and it came at the same time as all finished them at once, Nadia got up to do so. Even with the vodka clouding her mind, she mixed hers with mostly cranberry juice and ice, while everyone else got an extra shot of vodka.

They went through two bottles this way, while China kept up an unending stream of conversation. "A place like this is basically a void. No one likes it, not the people here, not the owners, not the employees. But we're all here because it makes money—our money— and if we aren't here, then we aren't seen. We aren't real. An empty place makes us empty, but also keeps us from being empty." She laughed. It wasn't precisely a joke, but the men laughed around her. Nadia fought out a fake chuckle. She actually agreed with China a little bit, but there was no talking to her. Not without the mask falling away.

Maybe from the both of her. Nadia's stomach turned over, and the acid rose in her throat like venom. She concentrated on her drink, forcing it down with the gorge.

After the second bottle, China rose from her seat. "I think it's time for a movie, don't you?"

Nadia murmured assent with all the others, though when she glanced around, she could swear she saw fear ghosting past their eyes.

She did not have time to reflect. They were sweeping from this club and to the valet, who retrieved the three cars for whatever bills one of China's boys passed him. Nadia felt a momentary pang as she got into the car with the boys. They had been drinking, after all. That would be ironic. Creep into the social circle of one of the oddest fixtures of Hollywood, a woman Nadia was almost certain was extremely dangerous, and done so with some fantastic power defying explanation, only to die in a mundane drunk driving accident.

The three cars formed a low, swift caravan, getting onto the freeway and heading west to the manor. China's green Porsche was at the head, dancing in and out of traffic with near suicidal ease. The others followed, their movements jerky and uncertain compared to the smooth way their odd mistress handled her vehicle.

The drive was fast only because they regularly exceeded ninety. Not a single cop stopped them or even whooped his siren. Nadia wondered how common a sight this was, the green Porsche Cayman, trailed by a Jaguar and a Corvette. The cops either ignored the heiress or just mailed the tickets directly to her place.

When they hit Malibu, the ocean stretched out blue-black like a fresh bruise. All three cars pulled up in front of the house Nadia remembered from the party. They got out, the salt wind howling off the Pacific buffeting them. China threw Nadia a smile, which Nadia did her best to return, even as the frigid gusts cut into her bones. She looked up and down the street. There wasn't really anywhere to run. The far side of the street was just a hill. The neighbors on either side of the property were not close. She had been a distance runner, and while she had no doubt she could run all of these gym rats into the ground given time, a sprint would favor their longer legs.

China looked away without raising the alarm. Nadia sighed, and caught herself, fighting the urge to be too demonstrative with her relief. She had to be one of the boys. Hide amongst them. Not be noticed. She felt the anemone's tentacles brushing her, the barbs of the stingers refusing to fire on one of their own.

China opened the door and flung it wide. Nadia imagined Jason Jennings, still lean and fit after fifty, wandering into the living room to find his daughter returning with eight men. Well, seven men and an impostor. Nadia wasn't the biggest Jason Jennings fan, but she'd seen his movies, watched him on the red carpet, and she couldn't imagine anything quite so surreal as running into him tonight.

He was not there. The house was clearly empty, silent and dark, waiting for China's return. Nadia wanted to know why. She also knew asking was entirely out of the question.

The house was clean and white, the splashes of color coming from the pictures on the walls. Directly across from the door was one of the largest, a close up of the face of a praying mantis. The green insect's mandibles were wide, its alien eyes perhaps focused on the camera, wondering what sort of creature this was intruding on its hunt.

China unbuckled her heels and kicked them off upon entering. None of the boys removed their shoes. Nadia was relieved. She couldn't leave her razor behind. Not now. She was too close to the danger, come too far. Though her nerves were jangling like wind chimes, she had to know what this woman was. What she had done. What she had become.

China's body language had changed. She was still wrapped in her white dress, but she was looser, her limbs relaxed. With her dolly face and plastic eye, she looked like a toy that was done being played with, cast away on the floor, limbs carelessly splayed.

"Up to the screening room, everyone. I have a new cut I'm dying for you to see."

The boys filed into the hall and up an open staircase. Nadia fell into line with them. China was right at her back, nearly skipping along. On a night when Nadia had thought she was done being frightened, this was most chilling of all. China was like a child, even singing softly under her breath. Nadia could not get a tune, let alone lyrics, but had the strange idea the song was somehow fragmented, broken and stitched together with a hundred other tunes. She was oddly grateful she couldn't hear the whole thing, as though in completed form it would carry some kind of terrible, maddening strength.

The top of the staircase was a landing, opening onto an airy second floor. Right ahead was a large double door, and the men headed inside into a small movie theater built into the house. Nadia had seen more than one of these, though this one was more lavish than most. It could quite easily seat fifty people, with the kinds of large, comfy chairs they had only just started adding in the upscale commercial theaters. A small projection room stood in the back, the various cameras and players visible through the open door.

The boys fanned out, each one going to a specific seat in the theater. It was not the block of military seating she expected. Not a test, but one she couldn't help but fail. It was up to whatever power she had invoked at the Midway. Still, she sat close to the exit, though not directly by it.

China emerged from the projection room with a remote. She looked over the audience with a plastic smile on her face. Nadia waited for her to pause on Nadia's choice of seat, but China did not. She went to the front of the room.

"Thank you all for coming. Again." She laughed, and so did they, even though she was laughing at them. "I had a lot to think about. I ended up cutting a good chunk of the second act, where I thought it was sagging. But I put the flashback back in. The one in France? I don't think the story works without it. So let's all settle in and we'll discuss afterwards."

China clicked the remote, and the huge screen behind her showed a DVD menu. The image was gray and white, thin graffiti scratched into a cement wall. Or perhaps those were natural water cracks, sculpted by pareidolia into a saturnine face. The image flanked China, placing her as more real than everything around her.

"The larger themes have not changed, and I know they speak to all of you. Thank you all for coming and I trust you will enjoy this."

Then, without another word, she plucked the shoulders of her dress and pushed it down her body. She was not wearing any sort of undergarment, but she would not need it. Nadia saw why, with mounting horror, as the body beneath the dress was revealed into the light.

The surgeons could only do so much. The skin on China's face, neck, shoulders, arms and legs was all she had left. Everything covered by the dress, from most of her breasts to the tops of her thighs, was nothing but a mass of undifferentiated scar tissue. Lumps and whorls of mortified flesh spread out over her torso. Slices from wreckage, livid burns, and other, more unidentifiable marks created a hideous landscape. The lumpy, raw scars consumed her breasts, nipples, and vulva. Outside, she was the vision of a plastic woman, but there was only a single layer of white cloth between perfection and horror.

China held her arms out, and cocked her hip, displaying the aberration her body had become. "What do you think? Am I beautiful?"

The seven men all broke into applause, their clapping in perfect, four-four time.

Nadia could not think of anything but what was in front of her. She no longer hid, no longer had the brainpower to remember what she was in the midst of.

"Thank you," she said, curtsying in a ghastly parody of gamine youth.

The brief performance over, China raised the remote to start the movie. Nadia blew out the breath she hadn't realized she'd been holding. China paused.

"Oh, before we start, we have a new convert."

The sentence alighted in the black water of Nadia's mind before she translated it. By then, all of the boys were staring at her.

"This is not Devin. It looks like him... unless you look at him out of the corner of your eye. He's so much smaller. I'm wondering how that could be, but I suppose I'll ask him. Grab him, will you boys?"

The boys did not hesitate. Their faces did not contort in animal rage. Worse, they maintained the faintly blank expressions as they scrambled over seats, sprinting for her. Nadia hesitated—too long, she knew it was too long—and bolted to her feet. The jars in the satchel rang as they were jostled about. She ran for the door of the theater, hoping she could make it before her long-legged pursuers. Knowing she would not.

She did not know what China would do to her. Something, whatever had turned these men into husks. The movie, Nadia's mind whispered. Power in the movie. Even with her life in danger, she wanted to know if this hunch was correct. Wanted to know if this was another source, like the objects in her satchel. Could she even watch it? Would that be enough to burn her mind to ash?

She pounded up the carpeted aisle. The door ahead was open. She thought she could get through it, maybe fling it shut, maybe throw something in the way. So close, and she could get out of there. She was at the portal, almost through, almost to the stairs.

A hand closed over her shoulder, fingers biting into her muscle. It spun her around, and she was face-to-face with one of the empty boys. His blank expression uttered no threats and carried no hatred. He merely grabbed her and was pulling her down toward the others.

Nadia kicked him between the legs. Her boots were heavy. No steel toe on them, but bulky and hard enough to cause damage. He didn't react. Nadia reached for the razor, ready to carve him up. He was too strong and yanked her back into the room. Over his shoulder, she saw the others closing in. In seconds, she would be surrounded, held by too many to fight.

A rattle twisted through her ears. Assumed it was her mind panicking, firing off electrical impulses in a doomed attempt to stay alive. It sounded again, the quick, spinning rattle. Azh warning her at the pool. *Thanks, Azh, I know I'm in trouble.* The last time she saw the dragon he was coiled on her desk, watching her get ready to see Milena at the Midway.

Oh, god. Milena. That was the last time she'd see her, really see her, as herself. The last kiss. Disappearing, then coming back as a distaff husk.

Nadia felt a muscle in her left thigh shudder. It was no muscle she'd ever had, a sudden, jellying tremor rocked through her leg. Azh, two feet of Azh, jutted from her thigh, the very spot where she had drawn her scales. The serpent had half-emerged, and the end of him was stuck in the leg of the man holding her, pumping thick yellow venom directly into his femoral artery.

The empty boy's grip came loose, and he staggered back, hands going helplessly to the new wound between his legs. Nadia did not bother to see where Azh went—she was not even certain he was there at all, as she saw him only in the fractions of a second between heartbeats—but turned and ran down the staircase. There was no angry stew of voices above, and that was somehow worse. There was only China's strident tones, urging her boys to grab "Devin."

China verbally added the air quotes, an absurd detail that threatened to pull a mad giggle from Nadia.

The lower floor was empty, the rooms large and open. The velvet Pacific was huge through the floor-to-ceiling windows. The walls and furniture were as white as China's dress, now in a puddle below her ruined body. The floors were slate tiles. No way Nadia could camouflage herself, even if she knew what they were seeing.

The footsteps thundered on the stairs. She couldn't outrun them. She hatched the plan and made the decision. She ran to the sliding door on the patio, tried to throw it open. It didn't budge. She mentally cursed, the footsteps growing closer, flipped the lock, and slid the door open on its runner.

She threw herself sideways, behind the large, curving sofa running along a section of wall. From the outside, she'd be totally visible, crammed between white sofa and glass so clean it was nearly invisible. From the living room, though, she would be invisible. If it worked, she would be safe, and it had better, because there was no way to run now.

She folded her arms over the satchel on her chest, hugging the glassy lumps of her treasures, making herself as small as she could. Only because her body was so narrow could she even fit. She listened as the boys ran downstairs and fanned out. Then, China's even tone: "The back door is open. Follow her."

Nadia watched them run by her, one by one, all except the one bitten by Azh. The question was there—where had the dragon come from?—but she had no time to ponder. Scales beget scales, her mind lectured making the insane sound tantalizingly reasonable, and she felt another giggle of hysteria boiling in her throat.

China followed, once again wearing her tight white dress. Barefoot, she moved with a dainty kind of grace. If any of them looked to their left or turned around—if China issued an order from the patio—they would see Nadia, trapped in her hiding place.

They did not. China followed her boys down and onto the beach, no doubt looking for tracks in the morning-wet sand. They would not find any, and as soon as they realized that, they would turn around. Nadia was going to have to move. She pulled herself out of the hiding place and reflexively checked the satchel. Both jars were there and intact. Azh was gone. She thought of going for him upstairs, if even he was there, but he had followed somehow already. Trust in him to find his way home.

Nadia ran to the door, hand on the knob.

And paused.

China was something else. Something akin to the Simcoe Killer. A parasite, like him, but somehow different. A new species. One who didn't feed on identity, but on art, on fame, on the language of film. She would have objects collecting her unique power, mysterious as the scars across her body. Nadia let the doorknob go, knowing this was insanity. China and her husks would be returning any second.

Nadia could not leave when the promise was whispering in her ears. She felt it humming in the big pictures along the wall. China had taken them. She knew that with a bolt of inspiration. Only China's eye could be so good.

Eye.

Nadia went down a hallway, away from the front, and to the door at the end. She opened it and found a bedroom. Everything in white, the only decoration more of the photos. Some of the mantis, others black-and-white shots of nothing Nadia could quite identify, and the more she looked, the more a blade worked into her forehead.

A door opened off of it, leading into a palatial bathroom, everything in immaculate white tile. Nadia gagged when she stepped inside. A smell, like burned plastic, permeated the room. The rain shower, a glass box larger than Milena's bedroom, was the source. Nadia opened the door, holding her hand over her nose. The scent was bad, worse than plastic, worming its way into her senses, throwing her off balance.

It was unnatural.

Or perhaps more than natural.

The shower was spotless. Cleaner than anything should be. Not a single smudge, not from water, soap, or a handprint, marred the glass box. There was no soap, either, or shampoo or any of the many fancy grooming products Nadia was expecting. Odette had always kept a chemistry lab in her bathroom, a huge assortment of soaps, lathers, lotions, haircare products, and so on, the purposes of which Nadia could barely guess.

The only feature was the black drain. The location of the smell.

Nadia approached the drain, the stench growing stronger. The burned plastic was overwhelming, but it brought with it subtle hints of more awfulness. Of sewage, of filth, of disease.

She reached for the drain without knowing quite why she did. When she touched it, her fingers probing the slimy surface, she made a realization: the drain was silver, not black.

She drew her fingers back, a strand of ooze clinging to it, bridging the gap between her and the drain. It was like nothing Nadia had ever seen, but she knew it had come from China. Some new kind of effluvium extruded from this hopelessly deformed new body.

Nadia recoiled, wiping her fingers on her pants and moving back into the bedroom. There would be treasures there, not this cast-off gunk.

On the nightstand, Nadia found a camera, a long lens jutting from it. She hefted the object. Heavy. The power was far more specific, too. This was not precisely China's eye, but it represented the same thing. Her eye in the artistic sense, in the way she wanted the world to perceive as she did. In many ways a truer eye than the flinty orb in her head. Nadia unscrewed the precious lens and dropped the useless camera on the floor.

Yes, the lens was buzzing. More powerful than the berries. No, this was the equal of the water, as important to China's life as the water was to the Simcoe Killer's death. Nadia peered through it. The room was not as the lens displayed it, dyed in stripes of electric color. Motion, not quite shapes and not quite shadows, writhed in the periphery. She shoved it into the satchel and crept to the door.

At the end of the hall stood one of the empty boys. He saw her at the instant she saw him and sprinted for her. Nadia slammed the door and threw the lock. A heavy thud made the door shudder. Wouldn't keep them out for long. Maybe long enough. She ran to the window, tore it open. Below were wooden stairs, weathered from salt and water, leading up to the driveway. Nadia jumped the five feet, stumbled, and ran up. Fleeing to the beach was a mistake. She needed to match her endurance against their speed, while giving herself somewhere to go. That meant uphill.

She dashed out onto the driveway and was through the gate when the front door burst open. The husks came out in a wave, China sauntering along behind. She probably had not discovered the theft, or she would be angry. Now, she was still faintly amused and curious at this impostor who had somehow gained entry to her home.

A car whispered by on the salty road in front of Nadia. She didn't have time to flag it down, nor did she think anyone would stop for her. This was a rich neighborhood, and she was just brown enough, just odd enough, to trigger the danger impulse. Though the thought of getting into an unfamiliar car triggered another wave of panic, she'd take it when the other choice was China and her empty boys.

The hill was almost vertical, formed of crumbling yellowish dirt. The plants on the surface were made hard and crunchy by drought. The beginning was a climb, then the slope grew easier. She hauled herself up as the boys tore after her, yanking herself to her feet. She hissed in pain as the plants ripped into her palm, but she made it. Her muscles bunched up and flung her vertical. A narrow game trail led up and away, heading for the top of the ridge. She began to run, her body falling into the rhythms she had drilled into it over the course of a decade, her breath even, her feet sure.

She glanced back. A few had made it up and were struggling to maintain balance on the thin flat areas. Another way her smaller frame would be an advantage.

She continued to run. She wasn't even moving particularly fast. It was more important to keep her feet underneath her; never sacrifice speed for balance, something she'd learned running the Hollywood Hills. As the boys scrambled, they pitched over headlong. Some rolled down the hill. Others tripped, steadied themselves and pushed upward. She was sure, slow, steady. Nadia could run them into the ground.

The satchel clinked beside her, and she thought of glasses kissed in toasts. To me, she thought.

She stopped running a half hour later. A warm sweat sheathed her body, and the scent of jasmine came stronger, but underneath, something ancient and reptilian. The breeze off the Pacific raised icy beads on her skin. She thanked Azh, murmuring it into the wind, as she paused. Distantly, she could see the boys along the ridge, still following her. They would do so until they dropped dead.

She needed a breather. Needed a way out. She took her phone out and dialed Milena.

The phone buzzed several times, then, Milena's voice, soft. "Nadia?"

"Milena?" Just hearing her voice made the fear flood back into her. Something to lose. Someone too precious. She watched the boys scramble over the uneven terrain, occasionally tumbling down the hill. It was nearly funny, and that made it worse.

"You don't sound good. Where are you?"

"I need you to pick me up. I'm in Malibu."

"Where?"

Nadia looked around. She gave Milena a location a few miles away and hoped she would meet her there.

"Okay. I'm on my way. Stay safe."

The call clicked to end. Nadia almost wished Milena would stay on the line, but it was foolish. She had to save her wind for running. Run until her veins pumped thunder. She could not give up because they would not. She dropped the phone into her satchel and continued along the serpentine game trail. It widened, going from a place for the local rabbits to small deer and coyotes. Now she was the deer and the coyotes were the men behind her. She had no doubt they would tear her apart and consume her, but it would not be the pure and natural death dance of predator and prey.

So she ran.

Her breath had razors in it. Her heart pounded against her sternum. Her joints begged for rest. The husks behind her never slowed, continuing their clumsy and yet animalistic pursuit. Now it was her willpower against whatever hold China had. One was absolute. The other was not.

Nadia kept Milena's face in mind. The kohl-rimmed eyes, the Botticelli features, the flour-fair skin. Nadia had to see her again. That would keep her feet moving, keep the breath going in and out. Nadia came to a trail leading down to the road, hidden partly by a fold in the terrain. She would not be silhouetted, just a dim shape headed downward. Good enough. Speed was no longer a concern, now it was endurance, and she could use flat ground. That counted as rest.

She went down the trail, quickly, but taking care not to go ass over kettle. There was the temptation, gravity really, calling her to the asphalt. Follow it, and she'd go tumbling. Unlike her pursuers, she couldn't ignore a broken limb.

She took the last five feet with a leap, the clatter of dirt and rocks tumbling after her. As she hit the asphalt, she put on a burst of speed, going around the curved corner of the hill. Her soles scraped along the rough road. The balls of her feet were a mass of pain. Boots were well and good, but they couldn't touch her running shoes. She'd run until they fell off her feet, if that's what it took.

Nadia was not certain when she lost them, or even if. She found herself on the corner she told Milena to meet her, entirely alone, the only light coming from a nearby gas station. Not a single person was on the street. No husks dogged her tracks, and China was probably miles behind. Nadia's own body wanted to collapse, her breath coming in on ragged sheets. She sat, promising herself she'd get up as soon as she saw them. Knew this was a lie as soon as her ass hit the concrete. She wasn't running anywhere.

Milena's car was a relief. It was the third set of headlights she saw, spaced out in ten minute intervals. Nadia split her time watching for the arriving cars, and for the mad silhouettes of her pursuers. She was certain they would appear at any time, and now she had nothing left to put into her legs.

When Milena's car came into view, the fear dumped back into Nadia's body like ice water. Now would be the time she'd get grabbed. When salvation was here. She stood, fighting the urge to cry, waving Milena over. The Prius looped around in a U-turn and pulled up to the curb.

Milena's door opened and she stepped out. "Nadia?"

Nadia threw herself into Milena's arms, shuddering, the horrors of the night bleeding back into her body. Milena held her, stroking her back, breath warm on her neck.

"What happened?"

"Not yet. Let's go."

"Okay, no problem. We can go."

Nadia opened the door and was buckled in and tapping her feet by the time Milena was behind the wheel. Any moment, she knew she would see them, jogging over the lip of the hill, only to pick up speed when they saw their quarry. They never came, though. The car started and moved off, and only then did Nadia sigh in relief. The music was soft on the stereo. The dust of the hills, clinging to sweat, began to dry and cake on her skin.

Milena spoke again when they made it to the freeway, going east toward both of their homes. "What happened?"

Nadia told her. She edited a little bit. The most obviously weird parts, the ones that made her sound insane. These she danced around, left vague. Something happened, she said. They didn't get a good look at me. Her story would fall apart like crepe in the rain, but Milena didn't tear.

As she told the story, Nadia's senses returned to her. Milena looked wrong. She was heavily made up, but it was not the vintage style she normally favored. The lipstick was more modern, the wet kind Odette had always liked. Her dress was tight and lacked the flirty, '30s style that hid, and tantalized, more. Her perfume was overpowering and common. Milena was playing dress up.

"Where were you?" Nadia asked. She hated asking the question and wished she could swallow it as soon as she did.

"I was on a date."

Nadia's heart fell into her stomach. She swallowed on a suddenly swollen throat. "Oh. I thought... I don't know what I thought."

"It wasn't like that. It was work."

"Work?"

Milena watched the road, and Nadia watched the story play out on her face. The other woman didn't want to say what it was, but knew she had to. "I'm a sex worker." The word was so clinical, so precise.

"I didn't know."

"I didn't tell you."

"It's... it's okay," Nadia said.

"Really?"

No. "Yes." She put a hand on Milena's thigh. Milena smiled, weary, relieved, exhausted.

"I'm sorry you had to find out like this."

"I get it. You're... safe?"

"Yeah. Very. I don't have as many clients as I used to."

"Oh."

"Where do you want to go?" Milena asked.

"Your place," Nadia said. Regardless of everything, she needed to be with Milena.

"I was really hoping you would say that."

Twenty minutes later, Nadia was in the shower, washing off the trail dirt. She was trying not to think of what Milena had told her. She knew intellectually sex work was just work, but it was difficult to wrap her heart around the truth. She wanted Milena all to herself. She wouldn't press it. This was where ideas became principles.

She turned off the shower and dabbed herself dry. She stepped out into Milena's dark apartment naked, faintly amused at how comfortable she was. Milena got up as she did so. She had already stripped off her work clothes and was wrapped in a robe.

Milena paused to kiss her but hesitated. Then, "I'll be right back."

Nadia read it in her. She wanted to wash off the makeup, the perfume, the client. Didn't want to mix them both. Nadia stretched out on the bed and fell into a fitful doze.

***

Milena stood beneath the spray of the shower, the night swirling down the drain between her legs. The date had been a disaster, her hustling out of the old man's apartment, stammering apologies the whole way. Him, ridiculous, his now-useless Viagra-granted erection swaying as he protested. She felt terrible; Henry was a sweet guy, all things considered, and he was a loyal client and a good tipper. She hated doing that to him, but she could not ignore the fear in Nadia's voice.

Milena shouldn't have even looked at her phone. But she felt it, as sure as she knew when the flop was going to put the hand together she needed to win. She knew it was Nadia, and when she glanced at the screen, saw Nadia's name, she had answered, even though that broke every rule of etiquette.

Nadia had been trying to hide the terror in her voice. Little punk girl, too tough to get scared. It was there, fighting the calm and measured tone. A wasp in the apple, and Milena found it as soon as she took a bite. She could not ignore it, no matter the hell she was going to catch the next day. Nadia was too important.

That solved that.

She turned off the shower, dried herself, and cleaned her work makeup from her face. She stared into the mirror, at her face, clean and vulnerable now. The crow's feet at the corners of her eyes. The deepening lines by her nose and mouth. *When I start going gray,* she thought, *then this is all over.*

It should already be over. She would have stopped years ago, if such a thing were possible. Fun for a time. Now she was finished. But she wasn't going to be done until the last bit of money had been squeezed from her. She sighed into the mirror, knowing tomorrow she was going to have to make it up. Beg for a job she no longer wanted.

She left the bathroom and returned to the bedroom. Nadia was curled up, facing away, nearly in the fetal position. Her spine poked up in regular intervals between her muscled back. So vulnerable, but Milena knew the vulnerability was one piece in an extraordinary puzzle.

Nadia was somehow like a man Milena knew once years ago. He had vanished—died, probably—consumed by the wonders he'd made. She'd seen them once, and they had changed her. Now Nadia was here, and the power to make more wonders. Milena had to know what was within the other woman. Wanted to be near her for as long as she could.

Milena climbed into bed behind her and cuddled close, the slender Nadia fitting easily into Milena's soft curves. She held Nadia until sleep came for them both.

***

Milena rose first. She wanted to get this part of her day over with as quickly as she could. She didn't bother to bathe, but reapplied her work makeup, although more lightly than if she were seeing a client. Karo preferred a slightly more subtle look, though he was thoroughly a modernist. She usually looked like a porn star for her clients, with the caked on foundation and huge false eyelashes. With Karo, it was all about metallics: gold on the eyelids, strong eyeliner, a more natural lipstick. Closer to her real look, but still a costume.

She came back into the bedroom and Nadia had stirred. She looked at Milena, her eyes dying when she saw the makeup. Milena turned away, dropping her towel and beginning to dress. Like everything, it was closer to her style, but a little tighter, a little shorter, a little less.

"Do you need a ride home?" she asked.

"Yeah. No, I'm parked at the Midway." The pause following was gravid. Finally: "Where are you going?"

"I need to see my booker."

"Your pimp."

Milena swallowed. She'd always hated the word, even back when she enjoyed the work. "Yeah, my pimp."

"Why?"

"Because I ran out on a good client last night, and I need to apologize."

"Apologize?"

"Yeah, make things right."

The discomfort in Nadia's voice was worse than a blow. "Yeah. Yeah, I could use a ride."

The two of them got dressed in silence and went out to Milena's car. They backed out and drove without speaking into Hollywood. "You picked an all night lot," Milena said.

"Got lucky, I guess."

Nadia went to open the door. Milena put her hand on Nadia's arm. "Can I call you later?"

Nadia swallowed. "Yeah, of course." Milena couldn't hear the meaning in it. Couldn't tell if it was the eagerness of new love fighting disappointment, or if it was the flat effect of a breakup. The three syllables merely hung there, devoid of meaning.

After Nadia got out, Milena drove away. Nadia stood at the edge of the parking lot, watching the car go down the street. Milena saw her once again on the bed, alone, vulnerable, and hoped it wasn't the last time.

***

As soon as Milena's car was through the first light, Nadia was sprinting to hers. She paid at the gate, hoping she hadn't already lost Milena. It was stupid, what she was doing. After the previous night, she couldn't look at any plan as being truly moronic.

She was hoping the light of day would have burned the immediacy away from it. Made it diffuse and smoky, a dream. There was no denying the reality of China Jennings. She was out there in Malibu with her cult of husks, probably stewing over the mystery person's escape.

No time to worry about that now. There was only Milena. Nadia guided her car onto the road and caught sight of Milena's little Prius a few lights up. Nadia covered the distance quickly, keeping a buffer of several cars between them. She thought of what little she knew of tailing from various spy shows. Milena couldn't be looking for someone following her.

She went off the main strips and into the residential areas pressed up against the hills. She pulled up on a narrow street and got out of her car. Nadia parked a block away and waited. Milena walked to a house that looked like two cubes stacked atop one other, each one the color of a sunset. It reminded Nadia a bit of China's place, though smaller, cheaper, more colorful. The inhabitant would aspire to, but never get, the Jennings House.

The fence was stained wood, packed close with horizontal slats. More tasteful than Nadia would expect from a pimp. She wasn't sure what to expect. Her experience with pimps had been movies, the mass culture image of a man dressed like a clown headed for the disco. This couldn't be accurate. She couldn't imagine Milena working for someone like that, but then, she couldn't imagine Milena doing sex work.

Milena stopped by a callbox. After a moment, the gate slid open automatically.

Nadia followed along the street, keeping close to the hedges and fences marking the boundaries of these properties. She had no idea what she was going to do, either. Her satchel sat on the floor of the passenger side of her car. The razor waited in her boot.

At the fence, Nadia found it effectively blocked the view into the windows. She crept to the corner, where a tree hung over from a neighbor's yard, giving a little bit of cover. Nadia hopped, caught the edge of the fence and hauled herself up and over. The yard was small, with only a few patches of wood chips and cactus, the perfect drought lawn.

She was ridiculously exposed here, as both stories sported floor-to-ceiling glass windows looking out onto the street. Fortunately, no one was looking out.

Milena was on the floor above, talking to a short, fire hydrant of an Armenian man. He had thick, beetling brows, and dark patches of hair over his bulging forearms. His head was shaved to poorly conceal a spreading bald spot, his beard a manicured chin strap. He could have been one of Lex's friends.

Lex never would have hung out with anyone who raised a hand to a woman. This man did that, and Milena flinched, but the hand did not fall. Milena went into a seductive act, and the man softened. And then she was on her knees in front of him. Nadia could not see much more. The tears blinded her, and she too was on her knees, vomiting into the corner of the garden.

Nadia did not remember getting back over the fence. She came to reality weaving to her car, promising she would find a way to get revenge on this man.

***

Milena brushed her teeth again. It usually took twice to get the taste out of her mouth. She washed the costume off her face and laid out her clothes for her shift at the Midway again. She wished that hadn't been the only time. Karo was used to getting what he wanted, even from girls who weren't earning what they used to. When she'd suggested this could be the end, his hand had nearly come down on her.

She rubbed her eyes. If she hadn't gotten so deep with him, none of this would matter. There would be no great, thorny patch between her and Nadia. The money would be less, but it would be easier to look herself in the mirror. Fewer nights wearing a costume.

She began to apply the dark eyeliner. Just like Theda Bara, she thought with a wan smile. She'd always wanted to look like one of the starlets of those days. Now she no longer felt like them; she felt like her. The one who had emerged from the glass woman, with a bit of the wonder still clinging to her.

Karo was a relic of the old life. Although, as he reminded her, he owned her. And he would keep her until there was nothing left.

Victory

Nadia did not precisely have a plan, but she was confident in her goal. If Milena's arrangement was a matter of a debt, Nadia had money. This guy was a businessman. Those kinds always said they were, so she would take him at his presumed word.

She arrived at the house early in the morning, even though she knew there was no way he was getting up before noon. When he did rise, at two in the afternoon, and headed for his car two hours later, Nadia was jittery with boredom, nerves, and a persistent need for a bathroom.

She followed his BMW to a strip club on the edges of Little Armenia. She pulled into the mostly empty lot and went across the street to a coffee place to use the bathroom before returning to her car to wait. She was not certain how long she sat, but the parking lot moved around her, cars arriving, cars departing. All except the BMW, which stayed still. By the time she stepped outside, it was dark. She left her razor behind; she didn't want to try to sneak it past the bouncer and run the risk of losing it. She kept the satchel with her, a jar of pool water, a jar of berries, and the camera lens giving her comfort with their occult power.

The bouncer stopped her. "Twenty bucks cover."

"Oh," she said, and reached into the satchel.

"Sorry. Females get in free," he said.

Nadia was too jagged with nerves to roll her eyes. She went inside. The music was loud and bad. The main stage was in the center of the club, while topless women writhed for the men seated around; a sterile business transaction between the dancers and the customers. The right strip club could be great. She and Gillian would go from time to time. The dancers, both straight and queer, loved them. Probably for the big tips, but she and Gillian never got handsy, either. This place, though, wasn't her scene. No taste, all neon and caught in the bad parts of the '80s. Good thing too. She didn't need the distraction.

Today she had business.

The man she was looking for was in the corner of the club with a commanding view. A goon lurked by his side, leaning against the wall. While the boss mostly watched the dancers, it was the goon who clocked Nadia as soon as she headed resolutely for the corner table.

He took two steps to meet her, cutting her off from access.

"What do you want?" he asked.

"I want to talk to him."

"Do you know who he is?"

"It's about Milena Franco," Nadia said, loud enough for the man to hear.

"Pat her down. Then let her past," the boss said.

The goon patted her, and she was thankful she had left the razor in the car. He pawed through her satchel, frowning when he found the arcane collection. He did not have the eyes to see what he held and returned them without comment. She looked over at the boss, raising an eyebrow. He caught the question in her look. "I know to be careful around crazy bitches." Then he laughed, like this was an inside joke only he got.

The goon finished and gave an affirmative nod. The boss gestured and Nadia slid into the booth opposite him. The goon loomed behind her.

"So, what do you want?" he asked her in Armenian. A miasma of Drakkar Noir cologne surrounded him and stuck to her tongue.

"Milena Franco."

"You run girls too? You don't look like it."

"No."

"What do you want from her?"

"How much?"

He laughed. "All of this, you haven't given me a name."

"Nadia."

"Karo. It's nice to meet you, Nadia. Now what do you want with Milena? You understand, she has been with me a long time. Made me good money."

Nadia swallowed, and hated what came out of her next. "Milena is a little old for sex work, isn't she?"

Karo laughed. "That's good, yes. With age comes experience, and Milena has loyal clientele. People who put money in my pocket."

"How much?"

"Milena's debt isn't for sale, tsavd tanem." She burned at the term of endearment. It didn't quite translate into English but meant "Let me take your pain away from you." Nadia's mother used it from time to time, though mostly with Odette.

"Everything's for sale," she said through gritted teeth.

"You're funny, little Nadia. Come into my club and tell me how things are. Because you made me laugh, I'll let you walk out the door."

"Name a price."

"There is no price. And my patience is running out."

"Look, you greasy cocksucker," Nadia growled, this time in English, "you name—"

She caught Karo nodding, and the goon behind her slammed her head into the table.

"Like I said. I'm used to crazy bitches now," Karo said, getting up.

Nadia's head swam. Black creeped in from the edges of her vision.

"So I need to convince you this was a mistake. A bad mistake. Whatever you want Milena for? You don't get her. You get nothing at all. Now, you might forget this, but I'll give you a way to remember."

Nadia felt the goon's thick fingers curving up under her armpits and hoisting her from the booth. The club was lurching around, the music thudding through her tissues in a ragged heartbeat. They hustled her through a back door, and the music was muted now, like they had thrown a blanket over her head. Some kind of backstage area, a few faces, some frightened, some curious, looming out of the dizziness. Nadia had no clear knowledge of anything until she was hurled, bodily, onto the dry concrete. She heard a shatter, and felt points of burning agony, under her body, abruptly wet.

The jar, maybe both, had shattered under her. The pool water was gone, soaking the bag, the promise of what it contained lost. Nadia shrieked, a wordless, horrible sound of despair and rolled off the bag, turning over, desperately trying to save what she could. She dimly saw she was in an alley, trash forming a thick rind along either side.

Pop

The pain, white and hot exploded in her middle. Then again. She tried to roll from it, and this time it caught her ribs. She looked up through the haze of anguish and saw Karo above her. His face contorted in rage, he brought his foot up and stomped her again. And again. Again.

She wanted to tell him to stop. Let her try to save the water. Maybe the berries. She didn't know how much was being destroyed. Her body was weak. Flesh. The objects he was callously, ignorantly crushing were eternal.

He wants me to cry out. She realized this somewhere in the beating. She had not done so, biting her lip until she tasted blood. She wasn't going to scream for him. She was going to take whatever he gave.

She merely flopped over, giving him a perfect target, her body rolling up around the satchel like a doomed pillbug. The stench of Drakkar Noir worked into her nostrils, hardening this memory. Much later, a whiff of the cologne would put her in the alley, Karo's boots rising and falling in her mind.

Finally, Karo paused, breathing heavily. He addressed his goon, now leaning against the wall and watching the mouth of the alley impassively. "This used to be easier," Karo said with good humor.

The goon smiled.

Karo looked down at Nadia. "Do you understand what you did is wrong?" he asked. "Do you understand why you made me do this?"

"Fuck you," she said.

"I think you do not. Yet."

He raised his foot. She knew this would be the last of them. The worst of them.

"Maybe you do now."

He brought his foot down on her right calf. She felt the crack rather than heard it. The agony had tendrils, covered in glass, ripping up and outward from her leg. She screamed then, sobbing as every successive moment send another tsunami through her.

"I think you do now," was the last thing Karo said as he left her writhing there.

***

The water was gone. A thin dampness and a layer of black grit at the bottom of her bag was all that remained. The berries had been crushed as well, their power seeping away in bloody lines of juice. Only the lens remained intact. Not as a functioning camera lens, but the true value lingered in the parts left behind. Nadia took inventory of this while lying in the alley. Before she investigated her battered body.

Only then had she dragged herself to the mouth of the alley. A young guy spotted her on his way into the club. He broke off, running to her. "Holy shit," he said. "Are you okay? Should I call an ambulance?"

She convinced him not to, though she had no idea how. He helped her to her car, hemmed and hawed about calling an ambulance again, but left her alone. She drove with her left leg, crying out again when the bones of her right ground together. She imagined the broken ends slicing into her muscle tissue.

The raw ache was nearly worse than the blinding agony of the initial break. Her body telling her something was very, very wrong. She should go to a hospital. She needed one. There would be questions. Ones that would lead back to Milena.

Ones that would lead to her when her revenge on Karo was complete.

The thought, clear as a shard of diamond, sliced through the burning pain. Karo had his chance. He hadn't taken it.

She got out of the car with difficulty, hopping and bracing herself on any nearby surface. She made it inside and to her room, where Azh awaited her. The ancient reptile watched her curiously from his coils.

She bit back another scream as she lifted her leg and braced it on a chair. Removing her boot and rolling up her pants had to be done in stages. The slightest jostle and she was ready to cry out again.

Broken. There was no doubt. The bruise was a livid wash of colors over her shin.

She was staring at it when the knock came. "Not now," she said, hoping the pain didn't sound through her voice, and knowing it did.

"Nadia? You okay?" Lex.

"I'm fine, Lex. Just fine."

"Bullshit." He opened the door. "Holy fuck, Nadia what happened to your leg?"

"Shut the fuck up and get in here."

"Nadia, what—"

"A guy broke it, now come in and shut the goddamn door."

He obeyed, nearly slamming the door. "What guy? Where is he?"

"Lex, calm down."

"Fuck calm. Someone breaks my little sister's leg? I'm gonna break his face!"

"Please, Lex, don't." Now the tears were coming, all the worse because she fought them. Tears were weakness. Tears at her helplessness, at what Karo did, at what Lex was going to do. The world coming apart, leaving behind only raw frustration.

"Oh. Oh, no. No, don't cry. I'm sorry, I don't..." he trailed off, kneeling by her leg. "Tell me what you want."

"I don't know."

"I have to take you to a hospital at least."

"No, Lex. Not right now."

"You're in pain."

"You think that's news to me?"

"You think mom and dad aren't going to notice you can't walk?"

"Lex, please! Just one day. One day."

He finally nodded. "Okay. But if you change your mind, you call me. I'll bring you some food later, check on you." He got up. "This is stupid. I am the worst brother there is."

She shook her head. "You're the best brother, Lex. Please, just trust me."

"Okay. Okay." He was still muttering and shaking his head as he left the room.

Nadia's phone buzzed. Milena Franco. Nadia shut her eyes. If it wasn't one thing, it was another.

"Nadia? What happened?"

"You tell me."

"I had to talk Karo down."

"You just talked?"

The pause was taut.

"I'm not going to answer that," Milena said finally.

"What did he want?"

"Hurt me. Hurt you. The way he was talking, he said he hurt you already. Are you okay? Can I see you? Do you need me to take care of you?"

"No," Nadia said.

"No?"

"What about tomorrow? I can come over tomorrow."

"No."

"No now? Or no ever?"

Nadia swallowed. "No ever." She regretted the words as soon as they were out, but there was no way to take them back.

"All right," Milena said. Nadia heard the tears in the other woman's voice, and there was no attempt at all to conceal them.

"Goodbye," Nadia whispering, wishing she could say anything else.

*****

When Lex returned in an hour, carrying a plate of food and questions from their parents, Nadia asked him to get as many bandages as there were in the house. "You need a doctor," he grumbled, but did it anyway. He showed up with everything from gauze pads to tape to the linens used to wrap sprains.

Nadia went to work. There was logic to what she did, but it was warped, dream logic. She could not quite explain it if asked. When she tasted the berries for the first time they had the flavor of blood. Bright, arterial blood. She considered this a sign.

She popped the first into her mouth and chewed it, then when it was thick and red, she spat it onto a bandage. She worked the stained saliva into the fabric with her thumbs, coating it as she went. As she ran out, she chewed another berry, and another, as many as it took. When she had enough, she gingerly wrapped the injured part of her leg in the sticky bandage.

Her leg grew hot, but it no longer felt like swallowed glass.

The pain momentarily addressed, she picked up the plate of food, now cold, and began to eat. Everything carried the bloody aftertaste of the berries.

Azh stirred from his place on the bed, his tongue tasting the air. He slithered toward Nadia, and when he reached her, he moved toward the leg. She sucked in breath, dreading the snake's weight on her. It was bad, but not blindingly so. He continued to move, slithering around and around, wrapping leg, bandage, and break in his coils. Then he was still.

Nadia blinked, and realized by the light streaming through her window, it was daytime. She had slept in her chair, plate of food in her lap, leg propped up on another chair. Her neck was stiff, her shoulders worse. She dreaded moving, expecting the sudden, stabbing pain of an injury neglected.

Azh was gone, leaving only the bandages wrapped around her. She carefully moved her leg off the chair. The pain was more of an ache, flaring as soon as she placed it on the floor. Fine, no weight, she said, making a deal with it. Broken, but healing. She hopped to the bathroom as best she could, supporting herself along the walls.

Lex came in later and was astounded when she showed him the range of movement. "Maybe it was just a bad bone bruise," he said uncertainly.

"Maybe," she agreed.

He gave her the same deal as before, pledging to take her to the hospital as soon as she admitted she needed one.

Nadia didn't need a hospital. Over a week, the leg healed. She gained the courage to look at it on the second day. As soon as she unwrapped the bandages, the agony, fresh and fire-bright, flared again. She kept herself unwrapped only long enough to investigate. The bruise was gone, covered in a leafy wrapper of dead skin. She rewrapped the injury.

She told her mother she was sick. Siranush believed it and proceeded to baby her.

By day three, Nadia could walk with a cane.

By day seven, she could walk. She had a limp, a small hitch in her step, and it would be with her the rest of her life, but her leg was no longer broken.

She removed the bandage on day seven. There was no pain, only a twinge every now and again. The place over her broken shin was bright with new skin, the edges still ragged from what she'd shed.

She did not spend her time idle. She went back to her research.

The berries would not grow. She planted them, watered them. Tried to get the conditions as close as she could to the burned out manor, even adding a layer of ash over the soil. Nothing. When she unearthed the planted berries, she found they had not rotted in the slightest, and still gave their bloody juice.

China's lens went on the shelf next to the pool water. Nadia sifted through the fragments of it, keeping what retained the buzz of the misshapen auteur, discarding what did not. The bits and pieces made it into their own jar.

Once she could walk without difficulty, she returned to Simcoe Manor and collected. Her suspicions were confirmed. The places she picked the berries from were withered and dead. It was difficult to tell if the pool water had diminished at all, but she had to assume it had. This was a finite resource, and once it was exhausted, that was it. The harvest would be barren.

She cursed Karo for wasting bits of her precious supply. Something else he would have to answer for. Though she had a great deal left, she still felt they were dwindling, and the thought of being without them filled her with bright panic. One source was not tapped. One source was still producing items of power: China Jennings.

Even after her flight through the hills, her near death or whatever it was, she could not get the scarred woman from her mind. Unlike her normal fascination with specific women—Milena, oh god, don't think of Milena—she was drawn to China like a scientist to an experiment. Like one of those old oil barons to a spouting well. China had to be altering everything around her.

Nadia was not certain how long she would stay away. Not long. Not long enough.

***

Two weeks after Nadia's broken leg, Angie sent her a text. Within an hour, they were out by their secret spot, looking out over the shimmering haze baking the canyon floor. Both of them had full glasses of lemonade, the vodka invisible underneath.

Their secret spot was a table and some chairs Nadia scavenged when Siranush replaced the old set for what they had. These were wood, weathered, and often used by the local animals. They were also the exclusive property of Nadia and Angie, used whenever they had something serious to discuss. Nadia had been sitting in this very spot when she'd told Angie she was gay.

Not every conversation there was so momentous.

The spot was down the slope from the house, hidden by trees and terrain, and only approachable by small game trails. No one else knew about it, so far as either of them knew, and this helped make it perfect.

Angie sipped her lemonade, the charm bracelet on her wrist jingling.

"Are you okay?" Nadia asked. "About Devin, I mean?"

"Yeah," Angie said. "I think I am. I think that party was sort of like the last kick I needed, you know? Now I know it's not really him anymore."

"It isn't."

"China. Whoever enters her orbit gets turned into whatever she wants. I wish it hadn't happened to Devin, but there's not a lot I can do."

"I know," Nadia said.

That was when she saw the eyes out in the grass. Hundreds of them, all around. Surrounding them. Snakes, all coiled, watching, their ancient attention on the two women. Nadia did not panic. She knew she should feel fear, but the snakes wouldn't move. Wouldn't harm her. Maybe even couldn't.

***

Milena was barely concentrating on the cards. She hadn't bothered to read them either. She was too angry, too distracted. Nadia tumbled through her mind. She couldn't believe it was already over when it had barely begun. She felt a little silly lamenting such a new relationship, but that hadn't stopped her.

None of those in the room had asked for their fortune, so she was content to fleece them. It was their own fault for playing against a professional. She didn't even have to cheat; none of these had the faintest idea of what they were doing.

Milena registered someone sitting down across from her only vaguely. The slight thump-scrape of the chair, followed by the faint whiff of perfume. It didn't matter. Another wallet to empty. If someone asked to be read, or if she couldn't help herself, then she'd look along the avenues of the cards. It was hard to concentrate with Nadia on the other side of her eyes.

It was the second hand when Milena glanced at the hand from the new woman. Nothing remarkable. A three and a five, leading up to a pair. She didn't even win. No, Milena saw between the cards, though the wobbling haze of the glass woman.

This new arrival was like Nadia.

Milena gaped at the message the cards conveyed, and then looked up.

The woman across from her was gold. Her hair was an ash blonde. Her skin shone in a golden tan. She wore a slinky blue dress, hugging a gym-hard body. She was clearly in her late forties, and wearing it quite well, with only the lines in her neck betraying her. Her jewelry was tasteful, modern, delicate. Her eyes were a bright feline green, watching Milena with interest.

Milena fought the urge to gawk. She was generally a little more interested in men than women, but the preference was slight. She had never had quite as strong a reaction to a woman until Nadia, and now this mysterious older woman at the other side of the table.

"Milena Franco?" the woman said, her voice strong, smoky.

"Yes?"

"Can I buy you a drink?"

"Sure. That sounds good."

Milena ignored the game and got up. The other players made sounds of protest, but Milena scarcely heard. A tingle spread up and out from her, and Milena abruptly felt entirely naked as the other woman escorted her to the bar.

"What are you drinking?"

"Old fashioned," Milena croaked.

The woman ordered, adding a Manhattan for herself. "My name is Dagmar Eichel. I'm pleased to meet you."

Milena took her hand. The jolt she felt was similar to Nadia's touch, but this one had a barb in it. Milena's mind whisked her to Dagmar's car, taken to one of the rich houses she would sometimes go when she was younger and tighter. She imagined the two of them falling into bed together, feeling those places only Nadia had managed to find, lost in a razored bliss.

"Are you all right?" Dagmar asked.

"Hmm? Oh yes, I'm fine." The drinks came and Dave the bartender raised an obnoxious eyebrow at

Milena. She took a sip, trying to banish the thoughts from her mind. She could not.

"I've heard a lot about you."

"Huh? How?" Milena couldn't even imagine the scenario, not with the other images crowding it out. In her mind, Dagmar's hand was pressed between Milena's pillowy thighs, her other arm cradling Milena's head, and whispering sweet and filthy things into her ear.

"Stories. I suspect the same ones that draw so many to your games. The woman who can see the future."

In her mind, Milena was shuddering, curling around Dagmar's hand, helpless against her. The older woman was pulling her, bodily through herself, turning her flesh to fire.

"It's not... it's a trick. A carny trick."

Dagmar smirked. "No, it's not."

It took real willpower not to lean over and kiss Dagmar's lips. In her mind, they were doing that and more, speaking in some whispering, secret language to one another. Milena was past caring, only wanting the pleasure Dagmar could bring.

"Do you want a reading? We have to play cards."

"Why is that? I would think you could do it anywhere."

Then, Milena came apart like a zipper. The mind-Dagmar drew her fingers up from Milena, through her womb, belly, chest. The fire hurt now, continuing to burn through her, carrying the same bliss. Dagmar held up her hand in front of Milena's face, the fingers dripping blood—Milena's blood. Dagmar's fingers were no longer fingers, but curved claws, white as bone and dripping with gore. And yet Milena could not stop her body's helpless shuddering, the extreme ecstasy wracking her.

"I'm sorry, I have to go." Milena hopped up, hoping she wasn't as wet as she felt, hoping it was in fact arousal and not some bleeding reached through the membrane of her dreams. She hustled away, never looking back. Because if she did, she just might invite Dagmar home.

***

Nadia had done it twice. Spells, hexes, curses, whatever they were, she had altered reality in some way twice. Figuring out how became a matter of reverse engineering. She believed she was close. There was a formula, she thought, though it was far bigger and more nebulous than so precise a word implied. To create her wishes, she needed three things.

The first was power. This came from objects like the water, the berries, and the lens. Something linked to semi-divine people she did not quite understand. She believed researching them was the next step in truly understanding what she was doing. Now, it was a small triumph just to realize their importance to these metaphysics.

These items though, were not raw power. They were not mere batteries ready to be slotted into any device and expected to perform. No, the items, the juice, had desires of their own. The berries had empowered her healing, but she did not think the pool water would have, nor the lens. They were mindless, but how they were created, and who had created them—accidentally, she believed—mattered.

The second was effect. She needed to link the power with what she wished to do. Tell it how to change the world. To heal her leg she needed bandages. Not because they would help on their own, but to inform the power on its task. Spitting the mixed water and whiskey on Devin had accomplished much the same thing. An act in lieu of an object. She wondered if she had added an actual mask, if her ruse would have lasted longer, been harder for China to pierce.

The last was the target. She did not believe she could have targeted Devin with anyone's drink. It had to be his, and she had to drink over the imprint of his lips on the glass. She believed other links would be possible, ones much less direct. She would not have to confront someone she cursed in the future. Not if she had their fingernails, or hair, or blood.

Nadia was thinking about these things because it was time to destroy Karo.

She had to spend a few sleepless nights staring at the ceiling, thinking about what she had, and what she could do. She believed she had the perfect recipe for it. She was lacking one small thing. One thing she did not believe she could get on her own. For now, she would use what she had.

The package arrived in the mail a few days later. A bottle of Drakkar Noir. Karo's brand of cologne. She knew because more than one of her relatives wore the same stuff. The stench of it brought a vision of Karo's foot rising over her prostrate form, ready to administer the blinding agony of the break. She held onto the pain, promising herself that soon, it would fuel the hatred she would visit upon him.

She took a glass down to her secret place and filled it with the pungent stuff. Her eyes watered, and she was grateful she hadn't done this inside. In the grass, the rattlesnakes watched her, never once twitching their rattles.

She had fashioned a crude doll out of leather. Good enough to pass, she thought. She hoped. She dunked this into the cologne and left it there for a few days.

Persuading Azh to bite her was not as difficult as she'd hoped. The serpent was waiting for her, coiled up on the bed, tail poking up from his muscled folds. She reached for him, and the snake struck, burying his fangs in her leg, just above the wound he had healed. She yelped, and felt the noxious poisons pumping into her limb. Then he let go.

Nadia watched him slither away to wherever he went and wondered how much control over him she truly had. The venom spread its aching way out; she didn't have much time. She opened her razor—she knew it had to be the razor—and sliced an X into her skin by the two bloody puncture marks. Her skin opened up like butter. No pain on the slices, but as she peeled the flesh back, the burning, black pain seared into her.

She held the wound over a cup—a mug with a cartoon snake on it her father had found in some Arizona gift shop. The choice of the mug mattered too, somehow. Every step had to be pregnant with symbolic import. She was changing the fabric of the real, and imprecision could mean disaster.

The venom dripped from the wound in syrupy amber drops. Her blood came with it, inky stains spreading out through the killing liquid. She let herself bleed and burn until the venom was gone and the blood flowed dark and red. She wrapped a bandage around herself. She did not use one of the berry-treated ones. That would remove the price of her magic. It needed a price.

She dropped two berries into the mug of venom and blood, marinating them. These she also left for several days.

The last bit could not be accomplished on her own. That was why, late one night, she went to Milena's. Nadia couldn't face her at the Midway. Not in front of her friends and co-workers who probably already heard about the heartless bitch who dumped her. She parked, and made her way up the driveway, into the small and secret house in the back, its windows dark and lonely.

Nadia knocked anyway, and when no response came, she settled down on the stoop. Her snakebite was sore, but she kept from rubbing it. The bandage, seen when she hiked up the leg of her pants, was bloody, though not leaking. She stayed in place and flipped her razor open and closed, occasionally catching silver light on the blade.

A raccoon waddled over the neighbor's fence and across the driveway. When Nadia shifted in her seat, the creature jumped. It peered at her through its mask, decided she was not a threat, and continued on its way. In a few minutes, she could hear it one yard over rummaging through the garbage.

Not long afterwards Milena's car hummed up the driveway. Nadia stood, haloed in the light. The car stopped for a moment, then continued to move forward. Nadia stepped aside, and let the car slide up to the side of the house. Milena got out, looking flushed and lovely in the dim light.

"Nadia?"

"Hi."

They stood a few feet from one another. Nadia couldn't find any of the words she wanted to say. There was too much between them, and added onto it, an apology.

"Do you want to come inside?" Milena asked.

Nadia nodded.

In moments, they were in bed together, and it was like she had never left. She found Milena warm and wet, and the things she whispered were sweet, the wordless sounds she made even sweeter. The two of them cuddled close in the aftermath, Nadia wrapped around Milena, her head on Milena's chest, hand over her gentle heartbeat.

"I'm sorry," Nadia said finally.

Milena's fingers stroked Nadia's smooth temple. "Sorry?"

"I lied to you. I couldn't handle it." It. Nadia knew the other woman understood what it was. It could only be one thing.

"But you can handle it now?"

"No."

Milena sighed, her head tipping back, her fingers going still. "Nadia, I don't want to do this. I'm not some pity fuck you can have whenever the mood strikes you."

"That's not what this is." Nadia lifted her head up, and Milena did as well, their eyes meeting.

"Then what is this?"

"I want you to get something from Karo."

"Karo, oh shit. Just stay away from him, sweetie. Pretend he doesn't exist."

"I can't do that. He told me he owns you."

Milena shut her eyes, freeing a tear. Nadia leaned over and kissed it away, wishing she could take all of Milena's pain so easily.

"I'm in debt to him. When I was starting out as a card player. He staked me, I lost it, and he... bought me. He does that. He puts people in his pocket, and then he takes whatever he wants out of them. Since I was already... tricking... it didn't really matter. I thought."

"I can get you away from him."

"How?" Now Milena's eyes were open, wide, innocent.

"I need something of him."

"Of him? What does that mean?"

"Hair. Fingernails. Blood." Nadia swallowed, looked away. "Semen."

"What are you going to do with that? Frame him or something? It isn't like it is on TV. They don't have everyone's DNA on file—"

Nadia waved it away. "Just trust me. Can you get me one of those things?"

"I don't understand."

"I know. I just need you to trust me... I'll explain everything. Just not now. Not right now."

Milena watched her, and Nadia hoped she looked sincere. Hoped Milena saw the meaning in her words. "Yes. I think I can." She paused. "Then what?"

"Then we're free of them."

"We?"

"You heard me."

***

It was not butterflies in Milena's stomach as she went to see Karo Minasian. It was hummingbirds. Frantic, suffocating hummingbirds battering themselves against the walls of her insides. Stealing from Karo, even something so innocuous, rebelled against years of thinking of him as all-powerful.

I don't have to steal, she thought. Nadia had said semen, and Milena knew she could get that from him without trouble. The thought nauseated her. The last time had been the last time. She would do something else. Hair, fingernails. Something, anything else. She clutched her purse closer. Inside was an old tin that used to contain breath mints. Soon it would hold a piece of Karo.

She leaned over by the intercom and hit a button. After a moment, she heard Karo, "Yes?"

"It's Milena."

"Come in."

The gate slid open on its automatic track. Milena tried to calm her breathing. She was not doing anything wrong. She was seeing Karo. It was abnormal. She never came over to his place except on the few occasions she'd had to make things right. He would know she was up to something. He would sniff it out. Know she was on this mad errand she barely understood.

He opened the front door. It was still early for him—just after noon—and he was wearing an undershirt and pajama pants. "Milena. I wasn't expecting you."

She smiled and curtsied. "That's why it's a surprise."

Karo chuckled. "Well, come in. You want some coffee?"

"Sure."

She followed him inside. The house was airy and open, so strange to think this was the lair of a career criminal. She was never certain how plugged in Karo was to the Armenian mafia. He made comments implying a close one, but it could have just been boisterous talk. Don't fuck with me or else. Then again, it could have been entirely true. What would they do to a whore who betrayed one of them?

Milena followed Karo into the kitchen. Rich coffee billowed throughout. He poured her a cup and passed over the sugar and a pitcher of half and half. Milena concentrated on fixing her coffee.

He had to hear her heart. It was thundering across the room.

"So what do I owe the pleasure?" he asked.

"Nadia," she blurted.

Karo frowned, then the recognition dawned over his face. "She came out of the ground. I was beginning to think no one would see her again."

"I saw her around. At the Midway."

"Do you know where she lives?"

Milena shook her head.

"Find out. Next time she comes around, try to find where she lives. Then you tell me."

"I will." She sipped at her coffee. He had to know. The lie was too transparent. She must look white as a sheet, breathing like a sled dog. "Can I use the bathroom?"

"Yeah, of course. You know where it is."

Milena nodded and put her coffee down. She tried not to run from the kitchen. Her blood stuttered through her veins. The downstairs bathroom was just off the living room. Karo's bathroom, where she would find what she needed, was upstairs, off his bedroom. He would not want her up there. Or worse, he might.

She moved quickly. Had to get it done before he noticed she had gone to the wrong one. She went up the stairs, thanking Karo for covering them in thick carpeting. Then, upstairs, she stepped as lightly as she could. One creak, and he would know.

Karo's house was aggressively minimalist. She had never asked him the reasoning behind this. He seemed to find bare walls and empty shelves to be comfortable. Now she thought she knew; nothing to swallow the echoes. Every step was broadcast.

The bed was unmade, the single comforter twisted into a helix. Milena moved past this and into his bathroom and shut the door. She looked around, wondering where to start. The trashcan?

She poked through it, wincing whenever her hand touched a used tissue. Fingernails might be in the bottom. Hope he'd clipped them recently. The bag was mostly empty. There was nothing of the sort. She looked at the tissue, searching for a spot of blood from a shaving nick. No such luck.

She was running out of time. Karo never left anyone alone for long. He would be checking soon, and when he saw the downstairs bathroom was unoccupied, he would know she was snooping.

For something she didn't even understand. And didn't look to be here.

Her heart was pounding so loudly, she imagined it reverberating off Karo's bare walls and finding him downstairs. She cast about the room, looking for anything. The shower drain? She found it entirely clean. The same for his bar of soap. She had never been so upset over a man's cleanliness.

"Milena?" His voice, on the stairs.

"In the bathroom!" she called back and cursed to herself. What was left? What hadn't she looked for?

"What are you doing up there?" He was growing closer.

She opened up the drawers. His footsteps approached. He was still talking, but Milena did not respond. She was too busy rummaging and praying the clatter of his possessions wasn't too loud. She pulled out his electric shaver, looking at it in mute incomprehension.

Then she remembered seeing a client clean one once. They opened. And behind the screen was a gray dust formed of dead skin cells and hair ground into a rancid powder. She fumbled in her purse, put the mint tin on the counter, and opened up the shaver over it.

"Milena?" He knocked.

"Yes?" She shook out as much of the dust into the tin and put the lid back on.

"What are you doing up here?"

"I had to go to the bathroom," she said, like it was the most normal thing in the world. Meanwhile, she was putting his shaver back together, and wincing as the head clicked into place. Too loud, she thought.

"You know I have one downstairs."

"This one is more comfortable," she said, realizing how lame that response was.

"Come out, Milena."

She flushed the toilet, using the sound to cover the closing of the drawer. She washed her hands and nearly opened the door when she saw the tin on the counter. She shoved it into her purse as she planted what she hoped was a casual smile on her face and opened the door.

"Hi," she said.

He moved closer, sliding an arm around her waist. "You sure you like this bathroom, or did you just want to get a little closer to my bed?"

She groaned. "I'd love to stay, but I can't."

"Why not?"

"The Midway. I want to make sure I'm there next time Nadia's there. I want to bring her to you."

"Good girl," he said, patting her ass with one hand. "I knew she was a crazy bitch. You'd never want to leave me, would you?"

"Of course not." She brushed her lips over his. "But I have to go."

"Okay, you can go. But you come back, you hear me? You come back to me."

"You couldn't keep me away," Milena purred.

Karo stepped aside. Milena wanted to scurry out, to get to her car where Nadia was waiting. She couldn't. She had to keep selling. Keep him thinking this was his loyal girl doing what he wanted. So she waved her hips at him, giving him plenty to look at. He let her go, and only when she was on the street did she run.

"What, what is it? What happened?" Nadia was panicked.

Milena handed over the tin. "Got what you wanted."

***

Nadia prepared the rest of her curse. She pulled the berries from the venom, the liquid stinging her fingers.

She rolled the berries in the dust Milena had brought. It didn't look like much, almost like sand, but it betrayed its link in its cloying, fleshy stink. Then she extracted the leather doll man from the cologne, her gorge rising as the strong stench hit her. She opened up his belly with the razor and placed the berries within it, then sewed up the hole. Lastly, she put the whole thing in a glass jar, the lid of which she painted like a sunset.

She stuck this into the satchel, where it found a home next to other jars filled with her odds and ends.

There was only one thing left to do.

She took her things to the car. Azh was already there, coiled in the passenger seat. The other hexes had been impulsive, or else they had been private. This was the first truly conscious attempt. Azh watched her with eternal eyes, overseeing this next step. This change from who Nadia was to what she could be.

She drove down the hill and east toward Karo's house. She knew the route well. A road leading to death, dark and brilliant.

Nadia pulled over and got out. She made it over the fence easily. The shadows were wide, pregnant things, swallowing everything. A blessing maybe? Somehow Azh was marking her steps. Or pure luck? It did not matter.

The windows were lit, Karo wandering around within. It made her want to hide, but light inside and dark outside meant she was little more than a ghost. He checked his phone periodically, pacing in his large antiseptic home.

Nadia went to the corner of the house and plunged her fingers into the dirt. She tore a hole open in the earth and planted the jar within. She spat once, on the top of it, then pushed the dirt over it, patting it down and into place. Goodbye, Karo, she thought at him, and slipped over the gate again.

There was no indecision. She never considered going to her parents' house. She drove to Echo Park, and Milena let her in without a word. As Milena insistently pulled her toward the bed, Nadia realized she had come home.

***

Angie Alcala was home alone, and happy that way. It was a wonderful feeling, and knowing she actually meant it, was even better. While Nadia had been acting a little strange over the past several weeks, overall she had been great to reconnect with. It wasn't like old times; it was better. Devin was firmly in the rearview mirror and Angie could find someone else, or not. Wasn't like she couldn't use the time to turn herself into a powerful executive.

She was enjoying her night off, lounging on her sofa and watching trash TV when she heard the knock at her door. She lived in a bungalow court tucked away off the main drag in Los Feliz. No one came to her door who didn't mean to be there. She had friends, lots of them, but very few would drop by without at least a text.

She went to her door. The chain was over it, and the deadbolt was flipped. Whoever was outside could see the lights on. No need to pretend she wasn't home. "Who's there?"

"Angie?" It was Devin.

"Oh god, Devin. Fuck off, okay? It's over."

"Angie, we need to talk."

"I don't have anything to say to you."

"Angie. I'm not with China anymore. I'm trying to tell you, I'm me."

Angie went to the peephole, angry with herself at the hope welling up within her. The hope turned to ashes. Through the fisheye, she saw not just Devin but five other big guys, with China at the center. Devin must have seen the shadow pass in front, because he kicked the door.

The wood cracked like thunder, and Angie staggered backward as though she was hit. The door held, the chain rattled. "Fuck off, all of you! I'm calling the cops!" she shrieked.

The door boomed again, the cracking louder. It was ready to buckle.

She turned and ran for her phone, sitting on the coffee table. On the TV, a wide-eyed *celebutante* complained about a mundane annoyance. Absurd, especially now, with one outside Angie's apartment.

The door cracked inward. From the sound, Angie imagined it had broken in half. Devin lunged into the room, his eyes dead. She screamed as she reached for her phone. He leapt on her and clamped a hand over her mouth. Two more of the identical men helped pick her up. China Jennings wandered into the bungalow, looking around with patrician disdain. "Nice place," she lied. "Kind of small."

Angie tried to scream, but Devin's palm was a perfect, meaty seal over her lips. She searched his eyes, and spotted the barest flash, almost a ghost, of the man he was. Sorry for what he was doing. Drowned by the waves of indifference. He did not let go.

"Get her up and out," China said. "Before anyone thinks to call the police. If they still come to this neighborhood."

The comment was bizarre. Los Feliz was a perfectly nice neighborhood, and the weirdness of it all caught Angie off guard. When the men carried her up and out, she woke up from her momentary lapse and began to struggle. For all the good it did. They shoved her into the backseat of an Escalade, one on either side, Devin in the front, and China driving. The other two climbed into a green Porsche and followed.

As the cars moved onto the road, Angie stopped struggling. She knew she was going to have to save her strength. Being between these two, she was effectively trapped. No one would hear her. There was no getting away. Instead, her fear sharpened into defiance.

"Story time!" China said. She was barely paying attention to the road, periodically leaning around to address Angie directly. Her eyes looked like plastic in the neon Los Angeles night.

"Fuck your stories," Angie said.

China didn't hear her. "About a month ago, something really weird happened to me. We were all hanging at the Midway. Do you know it? I bet you do. Your friend Devin almost gets in a fistfight because someone spat a drink in his face. Strange, right? I mean, who does that? Well, I get Devin out of the Midway and take him home. When we get there, I realized it wasn't Devin at all. Looked like Devin, smelled like Devin, sounded like Devin, and not Devin!"

China paused as though she was waiting for some kind of acknowledgement. Angie did not give it to her. "I don't really know when I realized it either. I mean, I kind of always knew. There was something... off about fake Devin. Can't really put my finger on it, either. Turns out, I was right."

China laughed, and the boys joined in obediently in a joyless babble. "It gets even stranger. I start thinking back on it, and Devin looks less and less like Devin. In fact, when I think back on that night, I don't even see a man. I see a little mannish girl! Skinny, brown, big nose, nearly bald hipster hair? Oh, you know. You know because she's your friend."

Angie's mouth was bone dry. That was an accurate, if unflattering, description of Nadia. What had happened? What had Nadia got herself into?

"So, what I'm asking, Angie, is who is your friend?"

"I don't know what you're talking about."

China laughed. "This is such a cliché! I mean, if I saw this in a movie, I would fucking hate it. Another scene where someone gets tortured and spits out the information, right? The kind of garbage where people say things like 'intel' and 'rendition.'"

Angie felt her stomach trying to turn inside out.

"Oh, god. I would never forgive myself if I did something so trite. There's no way I'll torture you, Angie. No, you're going to tell me everything out of your own free will."

"The hell I will," Angie said, the shake in her voice betraying just how hollow her protestation was.

"You don't know what you're saying," China told her. "I understand. If I met me and was like you, I wouldn't know either."

The Escalade pulled up in front of China's place in Malibu. Angie looked around in confusion. There was no way they could have covered that distance. They hadn't been moving nearly fast or long enough.

"I'm different, Angie. I'm better."

"What?"

"You'll get it in a second. You'll understand all of what I mean, and it's going to be so very interesting for you. The boys here might have doubted me once. Not anymore."

Angie screamed and lunged for the door. The boys held her easily, two carrying her from the car, then Devin grabbing her legs in a tight hold. He was so strong. He had been very proud of his physique when they were together, and back then, she had loved it too.

Now it was holding her fast, as she flopped like a tuna, unable to get away.

China led the way into her house, and up the stairs into a screening room. "I don't think we need any ceremony tonight, do we?" she asked, as she dropped the skintight dress to the floor. She was nude beneath it. No, not nude, raw. That was a far better word. Her skin was burned, slashed, ruined. A swirling mass of inhuman agony. No recognizable features could be found on its twisted surface. Her ass was a block of tissue. When she turned, Angie saw no nipples, no navel. Even worse, there was nothing like a vulva, just a twisted mound of broken flesh. The accident had rendered her sexless.

China smiled with her emotionless doll face. "You see? Different."

"Beautiful," the boys all murmured.

"Yes, beautiful," China preened. "Still beautiful."

The boys clamped down on Angie's arms, sitting her in the middle of the theater. They surrounded her in a beefy cordon.

China strode out to the front of the screen as a DVD menu appeared behind her. "All right, boys. Keep our new convert in place. Enjoy the film, everyone. But especially you, Angie. I really think you'll like it. It's been too long since I've had a feminine perspective."

China sat down on the floor in front of the screen, cross legged, like a child lingering too close to the television. Then the movie started.

The images were black and white. The dialogue was stilted, the acting amateurish. It should have been the most film-school collection of nonsense, the bullshit pretension a thousand student directors send to the studios every day thinking it would be their big break. It was the clichéd depiction of a soul made empty by wealth.

And yet, there was something to it Angie could not identify. The trite images, the labored dialogue, the stock characters, all collapsed in on themselves into a kind of singularity. The longer Angie watched, the less she understood, but the deeper she fell.

The movie filled her body with its emptiness, like a balloon inflated inside her. Her tissues tingled with the revelations she should have already known. Soon, there was little room in her mind for anything except the sublime images of *Lights Out*, and its creator, China Jennings, elevated to the great genius of the medium.

She remembered very little beyond that. Flashes, surfacing only rarely. Moments when her mind screamed at her to do something, but her body was far too heavy a stone to lift. She saw the bizarre rites on the beach, the group of them worshiping China as a pagan goddess. The last thing she felt, before her mind took mercy on her and snapped, was her body changing. Warping. Not her anymore.

Beauty

The needle sent sparks of white-hot agony through her body, pulling minute drops of blood to then pool in the creases between her muscles. Nadia was stretched out on Zach's chair in his shop. He leaned over her back, drawing the first of her scales up her spine. Despite her supplicate pose, she felt powerful. *Closer,* she thought. *Closer to what I truly am.*

The ink would eventually stretch from the nape of her neck to the crack of her ass, a line of reptilian diamonds marking her as blessed. The work would take a few days. Zach kept stopping, asking if she had enough for the day. Usually the pain was too much, especially for a newly marked person. Nadia never minded, tasting the pain as a delicious shivering, as it remade her, matching outside to in.

Only when the needle was away, when her tortured flesh caught up, did she feel the burning. Zach covered it with gauze and Saran wrap. Nadia wouldn't unwrap it until the next day, when Milena would coat the great line of inflamed tissue with sticky Neosporin.

Nadia thought she should lay down on her belly and relax. Let her body heal. Adjust to its true appearance. She found she could not.

Then, returning to Zach to get more work done. He lectured her the first time about proper care for her tattoos. Covered for the first day, then gently washed with antibacterial soap—something Milena had only been too happy to help with—pat dry, and covered in coconut oil. The abrasions would kill for a few days, so Nadia went topless when she was home, only putting on a shirt to visit Zach.

Two days later, when she returned for her next session, he stretched her out on the chair and looked over his work, his light fingers tracing over her spine. "The abrasions are already gone."

Of course, she wanted to say: *You're not marking me. You're unmarking me.* But she did not. She only smiled and said, "I have a very good tattooist."

"Flatterer," he said, smirking. "Now let's get to work." She disappeared beneath the buzzing needle for another stretch of snakeskin to be revealed on her.

Even as she was calmed, becoming more herself, trouble preoccupied her.

Danger lurked on the horizon. Two enemies already: China and Karo. There could only be more as she learned more of her own secrets. Someone would come. Someone would try to hurt her or Milena. Someone would want something.

The dreams only enhanced the vague sensation of menace. In them, she was up at Simcoe Manor in the middle of the kind of rainstorm Los Angeles hadn't seen since the night Odette was murdered. Nadia stood at the lip of the pool, in the greedy dark. Smashed corpses littered the patio. The house burned behind sheets of rain. Where there should have been a pile of corpses, claimed by the fire, there was instead a gargantuan shape, flames running up its flanks. It was almost human, but elephantine, huge and terrifying, thrashing about as the fire consumed it.

Below her, Odette was a monster. The thing with the distended mouth, covered in strips of silver and flesh, devouring the divine parasite. The Simcoe Killer screamed in terrified agony as the slug like monstrosity that had been Nadia's sister ate her murderer. The rain filled the pool around them, slicking off both forms claiming from them the residue of power and imbuing it into the water itself.

Nadia would awaken in the still room, Milena warm beside her, snoring softly. A dream. A dream far too real for her liking. Though it showed madness, it carried the clear scent of truth.

The parasite was dead. There were others like him out there. China was one, and there must be others. Creatures like the Simcoe Killer or China Jennings would eventually catch sight of Nadia, perceiving her as predator or prey. How they would strike her was a mystery, but they would strike. And she would be ready.

The time had come to tell Milena. Nadia had been putting it off, but she saw the question simmering behind Milena's eyes. Ever since the errand to Karo's that made no sense. Yet it had worked; the pimp had not contacted Milena once. The errand, as pointless as it had seemed, had borne fruit. Milena wanted to know why.

She deserved to know why. She never asked, and Nadia was certain it was for much the same reasons she hadn't offered the truth. They were both afraid of what a new revelation would mean to them. They were too good together. Neither wanted anything spoiling it.

But Milena needed to know. If there were others coming, she had to know what, and why, even if Nadia did not quite understand herself. She had to know of the danger facing them, and that Nadia had some unconventional ways to keep them safe. Nadia had some ideas on the matter, and she would need blood from them both. She could harvest her own without squeamishness: bleeding herself had become a simple method of survival. Milena was not going to allow Nadia to painlessly open a vein with the razor. Not without an explanation.

Nadia started with the simple, sitting Milena down and explaining what she was. Milena tensed first, no doubt thinking this was a prelude to a break up. Then she relaxed as Nadia explained the past few months of her life. Nadia expected more disbelief, but then remembered what she had glimpsed through Milena when they were together.

"You're saying you're a witch," Milena said. Her tone was nearly casual.

"I never said that word."

"What word would you use?"

Nadia shrugged. Milena's neutral tone was far more interesting in what it did not reveal.

"It sounds like you believe me."

Milena shrugged. "I've seen a few things."

The glass woman. The house of blood and wonder. These memories tantalized Nadia. There would be so many more things in that house like the water, like the camera lens. So many things carrying the energy of inspiration, chief among them the glass woman herself. So many hexes waited to be sculpted from such transcendent material.

Milena did not elaborate on what she had seen, nor did she agree to submit to the razor. The compromise was menstrual, and Nadia privately wondered if this weren't more powerful. She mixed their blood with mashed berries, and soaked threads in the meaty paste. These she strung about the guest house on the angles of approach. Milena did not look like she quite understood, and wrinkled her nose when Nadia was making them, but allowed her to do so.

As Nadia moved around the perimeter of the ivy-covered chain link fence at the back of the property, she heard a rattle. She looked down, freezing. A rattlesnake lay coiled in the grass. She took a step away, and another rattle sounded behind her.

Snakes covered the ground. Watching.

She stepped over and around, going back into the house. Then, her hand was moving, faster than she could think. Something twisted and flexed in her fist, and her mind had to put together what happened through the flashbulbs of memory. One of the snakes struck. She had caught it.

Nadia stared at the white mouth, the fangs unsheathed and dripping death. The snake struggled in her hand, but it could not go anywhere. The other snakes watched with their tongues.

Nadia gave the serpent a single sharp shake. The creature's spine snapped, and it died. The other snakes, as one, uncoiled, and slithered away, some into the deeper shrubs at the edges of the yard, or away through the fence. She wondered if they were still there at all, or if they had come into being for this.

The sacrifice they gave her was precious. The fangs and venom went into her growing supply of interesting odds and ends. The skin she turned into a belt. The meat she ate.

***

Angie lived in a nightmare. Mercifully, her mind had broken, and most of the abuse she endured was little more than a viscous haze clogging her eyes, ears, nose, and throat. On the isolated moments she surfaced from this muck, gasping for air, she would see such oddities.

The worship continued. Mad ceremonies elevating China to a demigoddess, or a kind of spirit for the spiritless time and place. The celebration of her beauty was at the center of it, both her old, innocent natural loveliness as the gamine daughter of a movie star and fashion model, then the monstrous creature she had become, plastic and melted at turns.

There were movie shoots as well. These were almost quaint, but the things China filmed were like nothing anyone would ever watch. She put her troupe of actors through the motions, and now they had a leading lady. China did not even have to force them into their performances. No, Angie went as willingly as they, even as she was screaming inside.

There were so many finished films. China had a vault of them. Angie could not imagine what sort of horrors were there. The ones she knew about were awful enough.

The worst moments, though, was during a scene when she would look into Devin's eyes, and she would see the old Devin, the one she very nearly loved. She could see him, screaming, crying, as terrified as she was, locked within China's crystal prison.

Angie's mind was so gone that by the time she noticed the changes, the flaps of flesh swallowing up her features, she felt comfort.

Death would set her free soon.

***

The nightmare threw Nadia into the silver place between waking and sleep. The room around her was merely a collection of mountainous silhouettes. She saw the beast of her sister eating the Nobody, and she was reaching, but there was something else, warm and soft holding her. She struggled, a cry building in her throat.

"Shh. Shh. You're having a nightmare," Milena whispered, her voice husky. Low.

The words penetrated the blind prey panic of Nadia's mind, and she collapsed into Milena's gentle embrace. She felt the other woman's fingers playing along her temple, followed by the soft brush of her lips.

"I'm sorry I woke you," Nadia whispered. Any louder and she might have woken the world, and this moment might end.

"You can always wake me."

Nadia turned her head, and she found Milena's lips. She had only been intending the soft kiss of thanks, but the feel of Milena, the taste, pressed the kiss for an instant longer. Her tongue traced the edges of Milena's mouth.

"What was that for?"

"You know."

"Careful. You're liable to get me going."

"Maybe I want to," Nadia challenged. The nightmare still gripped her in its slimy claws, and it would drag her back down as soon as she surrendered to sleep. The only one who would keep her was Milena, safe and warm and loved.

Milena did not respond with a quip. She clutched Nadia's head, stroking her jaw, and found her lips. Nadia groped for Milena's short nightgown, pulling it up over her head and dropping it on the floor. Milena was just as swift, divesting Nadia of her underwear. Nadia was already kissing down Milena's body when Milena stopped her with a hand on her chest, pushing her back into the pillows.

"Lie back, gorgeous," she whispered in the dark.

Nadia could only track where Milena was by the sultry feel of her breath and tongue against her skin. Down her neck, tracing the twin lifelines of carotid and jugular, to the frame of her clavicles, then to her breasts and nipples. Milena stopped there, teasing, tasting, exploring. She ran her hands over Nadia's belly, uttering a throaty laugh as her fingers dipped into the creases of Nadia's muscles. A smile like the sun pulled at Nadia's lips.

Milena took her time at Nadia's legs and thighs. Nadia felt electric snaps: Milena's teeth gently tugging at the taut flesh. Tiny bolts of pain burrowing beneath into her belly, joining in a steadily growing ball, beating, wet, warm.

Nadia felt her eyes rolling up as she desperately spread her legs, willing Milena to finish her. When Milena finally dipped her head, opening Nadia up gently, Nadia let out a low groan of frustration. But Milena was not content merely to drag her to the edge and throw her over. No, she was relentless. Milena explored her, though she knew Nadia's body as well as anyone. She knew the sensitive places, knew where Nadia needed to be touched to bring her to quick, shuddering climax.

She danced around these. An errant brush of her tongue, a soft puff of breath from a low chuckle. The ball within Nadia only grew, the sensations merging within her body. She opened up to Milena, trusting her to do what she must.

She felt the first of Milena's fingers inside of her. She had never been terribly fond of being penetrated before, but this felt right. More than right. Something she needed, craved. Something she wanted to give to Milena, wanted Milena to give to her. To be the only woman who ever made her feel thus.

She made a little noise of assent, and even that small grunt spurred that great red place within her to grow.

Milena added a second finger. The place behind Nadia's eyes brightened. The black light of the room was silver now, everything wreathed in it. She was full, and yet she wanted more of this bliss, wanted more of Milena inside of her. Wanted everything she could give.

Milena's lips were on her now, on her lower belly, on her thighs, on her clitoris. Gently bringing her along, coaxing her to bloom.

The third finger was not a surprise. Nadia gave a choked cry. Tears welled in her eyes, but there was no pain. The sob in her throat came from that blessed sensation of being full, of being full with Milena, as it would be with no one else. The redness within her threatened to explode, yet somehow it swelled, beating like a second heart, glistening and secret.

Milena added a fourth finger, and Nadia could feel the thumb at the gates of her body. She tried to nod, to make any sound, she wanted to tell Milena, *Yes, more all of it, I need you*, but she could do nothing. Her body was rigid, pinioned to the spot with the ecstasy inside her. She gripped the sheets. Otherwise, she would fall. Milena was all through her, a connection she had never experienced. As close to two ever becoming a single entity.

There would be no way Milena could fit. Nadia felt the hand moving, shifting, but there was no way. Her body was entirely full.

There was no teetering on the edge. She could not conceive of anything beyond being full, a great light behind her eyes. Then Nadia's body opened. Somehow, it bloomed, and Milena was inside her.

Nadia's vision went white. The only sound she could hear was the frantic rushing of blood. Every nerve ending burned in delicious flame. She had found a place beyond pleasure, beyond the mere experience of being human. Milena filled every tissue of her. She felt her in her legs, in her arms, in her heart, lungs, mind. In her joy and in her fear. Milena was in every part of her.

The red ball inside her belly was no ball at all. It was a seed. It split open, hatching, giving birth to a great tree. The tree's roots found sustenance in Nadia's womb, the branches stretching through her limbs, the trunk up her spine to the crown of her head. Winding around the tree, his powerful, diamond coils on the branches and trunk, was the dragon.

The tears ran down Nadia's cheeks in rivers. Her mouth was open, maybe breathing, maybe nothing. Milena breathed for them both. Milena's pulse, through her wrist, into Nadia's vagina, to her heart, and they were beating in time. One with the other.

She did not know how long they were united. Days, maybe. Seconds. The difference was meaningless in this wonderful place. Then, Milena's hand moved within her, fingers curling, stretching, filling. Nadia cried out, and then she was shuddering helplessly, electricity crackling from her center through her body.

She felt Milena gently leave her, and she was cold and alone for a moment, but then Milena crawled up the bed, cradling her, stroking her hair and whispering sweet words of love. Nadia clutched at Milena desperately, the blissful tears continuing to fall. She pulled Milena into a kiss, soft and trembling. They would not be apart.

***

The only light in the bedroom came from a few candles. Milena was sitting back against a makeshift throne of pillows. She had never seen a woman come like Nadia had, and had herself never connected with anyone quite so intensely. The sheets were hopelessly twisted after their lovemaking, but they were barely using them. In the shimmering heat, sheets were unnecessary. Nadia was on her stomach, stretched out on the bed beside her. Milena was enchanted.

Milena was always enchanted.

Nadia had recovered and luxuriated in the cathartic afterglow. Her muscles coiled and uncoiled as she shifted. Her lean arms pillowed her head, and her eyes were sweetly closed, though she was still awake. The line of snakeskin was finished, from the soft and downy place at the back of her neck down to the cleft of her ass. The tattoo was lustrous, fascinating, alive. Nadia was already talking about adding more to her arms and legs.

Milena ran a playful finger down Nadia's spine, and as the other woman giggled and rolled on her side, Milena felt the heat returning to her. Watching Nadia stretch out now once again, her muscles clearly outlined over taut skin, the expression of bliss still on her pretty face, Milena realized she was in love. A bolt of realization at once shocking as it was painfully obvious.

"What?" Nadia asked. She had one eye open. In the dim light, it looked black. Milena found the other woman's eyes incredible. A deep brown, they could appear every color from black to amber, depending on light and mood.

"I didn't say anything."

"You're staring," Nadia said, stretching out her vowels.

"I didn't mean to."

"It's okay. I like it when it's you."

The warmth spread upward through Milena's belly, to her chest, and face. "Would you like to move in?"

Nadia's other eye opened. "Here?"

"I know it's not what you're used to." Milena had seen Nadia's house once while dropping her off. Milena had solidly middle-class, American mutt roots. The kind of wealth she saw from the front of Nadia's house, the way she thought it stopped, only to see it continuing through the trees, and nestled in some of the prime real estate in Southern California, told her Nadia was used to a level of space, of wealth, Milena could not provide. The guest house was fine for one person, but two?

And yet, she had to ask. She already felt stupid, bracing for Nadia's rejection.

She felt Nadia's graceful fingers on her thigh. "Yeah, I'd love to. Not to ruin the romance, but were you thinking like a fifty-fifty split on rent, or what?"

Milena's full laugh was more about the tension than the joke. She rolled over, trapping Nadia on the bed and kissing the shaved side of her head.

"Smothering me!" Nadia managed.

Milena rolled back, still smiling. "You weren't complaining before."

"Those talented hands forgive a lot."

Milena held up her right hand, as though inspecting her nails. "Talented, huh?"

"I have never been fucked like that."

Milena smiled. "You're so crass."

"You're getting Nadia uncut now. We're living together."

"I'm already regretting this."

Nadia turned over, staring at the ceiling, her olive skin glowed gold under the candlelight. Milena did not bother looking away now.

Finally, Nadia said, "What happened to you?"

Milena knew what she was asking. It was not some meatheaded jealous question about Karo. He was in the past, and nothing proved it more than the utter silence from his phone number. No calls for clients, no checking in. Milena hadn't realized how free she would feel until he was gone.

No, Nadia was asking about the House of Wonders.

"You remind me of someone I used to know," Milena said. "I met him around six or seven years ago."

"Was? Is he dead?"

"I don't know. He must be, I guess."

"Was he your friend?"

"Yes. Sort of. I don't think he had friends the way normal people would. He wasn't normal. He was... very, very far from it."

Nadia turned on her side, propping her head up on one hand. "What was he?" The way she asked the question made it sound like she knew the answer, but it filled her with fascination.

"He was beautiful, but oh god, was he delicate. Skin and bones, but these bright blue eyes you'd swear were a piece of the sky. I met him through another friend." Milena fumbled, thinking about Tyler Kunitsugu, a dear friend and client of hers. He had died, somehow of thirst, in his own bedroom. Another mystery she would never solve but helped prepare her for accepting Nadia. Sometimes she wondered if her whole life hadn't been preparing her for the strange and lovely woman in her bed. "He had started playing cards to earn money, and unlike most people who try that, he was good. Not because he had a talent. It was more that he was brilliant. His mind was... intimidating. He needed more money than he could get from the games, so I referred him to Karo for a loan."

Milena smiled. "The next time I saw Karo after that, he had a thick bandage on his arm. One of his guys had an arm in a sling as well. He never said what happened."

Milena faltered. The candle flames in the room, though they were set in different corners, were all pulling toward the bed. No, not to the bed. To Nadia.

Of course. Wouldn't fire want to be near the spark?

"I finally went to my friend's place one time when he hadn't been around in awhile. He lived in this mansion out in Pasadena. Real old. Huge. Big wall all around it. When I went in there, the house wasn't like anyplace a person could live. It had been made beautiful for someone whose mind wasn't human. I found him upstairs, and he was dying. I think he might have already been dead, the important parts anyway, but he was breathing. It was like every part of him had been used up, and what was left was only living through reflex. Because nothing taught it to die."

Milena swallowed, trying to separate the horror of what she'd seen with the fantastic truths. "The house was full, though. Of women. Women who were not... flesh and blood. Somehow, he had made real women, thinking and feeling women, out of the inanimate. One of them had my face. She was made of interlocking pieces of glass, and she and I were... together."

It was an inadequate description. The glass woman had enveloped Milena. It was not precisely sex, but something far more intimate. The glass woman had been a lens, and Milena, the light through it, intensified, strengthened.

"She changed me. I knew something had happened but wasn't sure quite what. I left the house, and I never went back... I knew that was it. I was allowed in once, to meet the woman with my face, but if I stayed, she would not continue my protection. The others might do something unguessable to me. Anyway, I was at a game a week later, and in the middle of it, I looked into the face of my opponent and saw him, in my mind, clutching his heart and gasping."

Milena turned away, picking up a deck of cards from the side of the bed. "A week after that, and he was dead of a heart attack."

She reflexively shuffled, her clever hands turning the deck into a blur. Nadia was focused on the deck, unblinking.

"What?" Milena asked.

"The cards."

"What about them?"

"There's power in them."

Milena recognized this tone. When Nadia told her about the curse she'd leveled on Karo, she had used the same tone to describe the berries. Berries she'd used for her cat's cradle of tripwires outside.

She offered the cards to Nadia.

"Are you sure?" Nadia asked.

"It's like one deck. Do you know how many cards I have lying around?"

Nadia accepted them, flipping through them with the attitude of someone who had never seen a deck in her life. "There is power here," she said in confirmation, then hesitated.

"What were you going to say?"

"Not as much as the pool water," she said apologetically, referring to the jars of disgusting dirty water she treated with reverence. "Or the berries."

"What does that mean? You say it, and... I know there is something about you. I've seen it, but I don't..."

"People like your friend, or like you. They reshape the world, and when they do, they leave behind marks. In these marks, there is a bit of their power. When the glass woman changed you, you became something else too. I think."

She offered the cards to Milena.

"Keep them," Milena said. "Not as good as pool water, but maybe you'll find a use for them."

Nadia crawled over Milena as she set the cards on the night table and punctuated it with a kiss. Milena's eyes closed and her hands automatically went to Nadia's face. "We should probably celebrate this whole moving in thing," Nadia murmured.

Milena reached hungrily for Nadia's lips again.

***

Milena was still happily buzzing the next night at the Midway. Reading on a night like that was easy, easier even than the cards themselves. She was making plans already for Nadia moving in, mentally shifting some of her things around to make way for Nadia's. It was quick to be moving in, but Milena knew one didn't meet a woman like Nadia every day.

She was thinking of very little else but the straight she was working on and how to tell the young man across from her his mother's lung cancer had returned. She hoped she might see something else, something happy for him, but she kept seeing the same image, of him on the phone, getting the news, and trying not to cry.

She was not ready for Dagmar Eichel. The older woman settled in one of the empty seats with a languid smile. This night her dress was amber, a gold necklace pooling in her cleavage. Milena looked up into this, fumbled, and met Dagmar's smiling green eyes. She'd seen Milena checking her out and kept the power firmly in hand.

"Hello, Miss Franco," Dagmar said.

"Ms. Eichel," Milena managed, her voice rusty.

"You ran out the other night. I was worried I had offended you."

Milena saw herself in Dagmar's lap, a nipple in the other woman's mouth, Dagmar's skilled hand working between her legs. She was already inches from exploding, holding onto Dagmar desperately, praying she would not stop, even as she was devoured.

"No, nothing like that. I had an appointment."

"I imagine a woman like you has exactly as many appointments as she likes."

"Sometimes more."

Dagmar chuckled. There were still other people around the table, but they had ceased to matter. Milena saw the young man exchange a look with the hipster girl at the other side of it, their expressions saying, *What's going on here?*

"I'm glad to hear there was no offense taken."

"None. I take it you're here to be read?"

"I was here to make one of those appointments."

Milena's eyebrows shot up. She kept a rein on the stutter threatening to develop. She might have been used to being hired for her body, but that didn't stop this intense, physical desire for this woman. "An appointment?"

"I'd like to be the person you're rushing outside for," Dagmar said with a smile.

Milena felt the response on her lips. *I'd like that too.* She would like it, even if she was in love. Even if she had just invited Nadia to move in. The commitment didn't quell the desire. She nearly spoke it, but the curtain parted, and Nadia walked in.

Milena blinked, trying to process both avatars of desire in one place. "Nadia!" she said too loudly and got up from her seat. She watched Dagmar out of the corner of her eyes, seeing the older woman looking at them with naked interest. Milena kissed Nadia. "I'm sorry. I'm still working."

"It's fine. I wanted to say hi before I got Dave to give me free booze."

Dagmar, now fascinated, also stood. She spoke to Nadia. "Hello, I'm a friend of Milena's. Dagmar Eichel."

"Nadia Eskandarian," Nadia said, shaking her hand.

"Since Milena's busy, how about you and I have a drink? I think we have a thing or two to discuss."

"Okay." Nadia glanced at Milena, offered a cute lopsided smile. "Join us when you're done."

"Um, yeah. Yeah, sure."

Milena sat down, shaken. As the other two left, she burned. She loathed the jealousy within her, but it didn't stop. Nadia with Dagmar. Milena left behind.

Inevitable.

***

Nadia followed this odd older woman toward the bar. Dagmar was beautiful, but it was a very traditional sort of beauty Nadia only appreciated on an abstract level. She had the blonde hair, the green eyes, the tanned skin, the toned body, the expensive tastes the culture assured Nadia were what was desired. As far from her own prominent nose, brown eyes, olive skin, and flat chest as possible. Far away from Milena's antique beauty, pale complexion, ample curves, and soft body as well.

The prevailing culture was wrong a lot of the time.

Dagmar Eichel did not look like the sort of person who would be in the Midway. Most were Hollywood kids. Hipsters, hangers-on, low-level executives, working actors, and the odd model. Not this woman who should be the savvy and connected bride of a political shark.

Yet Dagmar did not appear to have any self-consciousness about being out of place. Of course not. When one is the avatar of traditional beauty, one goes where one likes. Nadia wondered what that was like. She was used to distrusting stares and double-takes. The only question she had was why people were reacting to her strangely: because she was brown or because she was butch.

To her credit, Dagmar was not giving off any sort of judgey vibe about either, so Nadia planned to listen to her.

They arrived at the bar, and a pair of seats were magically cleared just as they approached. Dave blew a jet of fire over the heads of the cheering bar, then stopped by to take orders. Dagmar ordered a Manhattan and offered Nadia a drink as well.

"Sazerac," she said to Dave, even though he already knew her drink well. She had been spending a lot of time there, drinking with Milena when she could.

"I just want to start by apologizing," Dagmar said, when Dave left to build their drinks. "I had no idea she was taken."

"No worries," Nadia said, "it's a new thing." That Dagmar might be gay was not even remotely surprising considering the way she looked at Milena.

Dagmar frowned. "She was Kissed recently?"

Nadia already knew she wasn't talking about the kiss at the table. It was too obvious, and then there was the way Dagmar said "Kissed." The capital letter, the reverence, shone clear and plain.

Dave set the drinks in front of them, and Nadia mouthed a thank you at him. Dagmar slid a folded twenty to the other side of the bar without looking. Dave picked it up and tucked it in his arm garter in a single motion.

"I think we should start at the beginning," Nadia said.

"Yes, I think you could be right." Dagmar's eyes flashed, and for the first time, Nadia saw the implacable will beneath the other woman. Something very much like China Jennings.

Nadia was in a certain amount of danger.

"Don't you know what you are?" Dagmar asked.

"What am I?"

Dagmar's smile had no humor in it. "A test? I think you know exactly what you are, especially if you've claimed Miss Franco as your own."

"Milena is my girlfriend."

"Of course, of course. But you know what's in her past. You know she's been Kissed."

The image of Milena's story, told between their bouts of lovemaking, flashed to mind. She saw the glass woman and Milena together, locked in an inhuman embrace. "I didn't know the word."

Now the smile lit her eyes. "You are new at this."

"Yes."

"We all have to start somewhere. The Kissed are those who have some minor power, gained from lingering close to the sun. When I heard the story of the woman who sees the future in her card games, I had to see what I was dealing with. I had hoped she was single, but I will respect your claim. She belongs to you and I will make no further overtures."

"Thanks," Nadia said. She didn't like the terminology, but she wasn't going to kick. Not when there was something to be learned. Not when the teller was quite this dangerous.

"After all, there's plenty for everyone."

"Everyone? Are there more like us?"

"I am certain there are. You're the first I've met, and I must admit to some curiosity."

"Glad I'm not the only one."

"Not at all, Miss Eskandarian."

"Nadia."

"Then make it Dagmar." She offered her Manhattan for a clink.

Nadia touched the glass and sipped her Sazerac.

"Tell me, Nadia, what have you done thus far?"

"You first."

"Of course." Dagmar took a thoughtful sip, bringing up a memory. "A man who shall remain nameless assaulted a friend of mine. He's dead now. I had him coughing up glass until he bled out."

Nadia's eyebrows went up. Then she remembered what she intended to do to Karo. "I, uh, impersonated, I guess you'd say. I impersonated a man."

"Oh," Dagmar said, trying to cover disappointment, and not well.

"No, he's like six-three, six-four, and over two hundred pounds. I'm five-six. Maybe one ten, one twenty."

"Impressive. And did you fool his friends?"

"For a little while. Then they saw through it somehow and there was..." she shrugged.

"If they hurt you, you can already get back at them. Have you thought about stealing their faces? Or perhaps reversing them? Making everyone see them as something hated?"

"No," Nadia said, swallowing her shock.

"Your limits are your imagination," Dagmar said. "And what talismans you can find."

"Talismans?"

"You know what I mean. The objects that power your hexes. They likely appear mundane, with tells. Grave dirt, perhaps, that produces its own worms? A movie whose story takes on reality of its own?"

Nadia nodded. "Yeah, something like that."

"What have you found?" Dagmar leaned forward, eagerly.

Nadia knew right then and there she would never show the pool water. Nothing so powerful. The cards, though. Those could be seen, and Dagmar likely suspected them already. Nadia fished into the satchel and removed the deck by touch and set it on the bar.

"Cards. From Miss Franco, I am guessing."

Nadia nodded.

Dagmar leaned close, not putting her hands on the pack. Nadia wondered if this was part of the rules Dagmar was alluding to earlier with who Milena "belonged" to. Or if this was simply what two powerful people did to keep from killing one another.

"Remarkable," Dagmar breathed. "Have you used these?"

"Nope. Not yet."

"Linked to chance, perhaps. Or the future. As though there is a difference."

"So they do have their own desires."

"Of course. The price of those who made them."

"What do you mean?"

"We have a lot to discuss, Nadia. Can I invite you to dinner?"

"Sure."

Dagmar handed over a card with practiced elegance. "Please call or email your details and we'll plan. Oh, Nadia, I am so glad to have met you. Even if I couldn't claim Miss Franco, an ally, a friend, is so much more precious." She finished her cocktail and stood. "Thank you, my dear."

Dagmar leaned in and before Nadia could move, kissed her on the mouth. It was not quite the kiss of a friend, but it was more chaste than that of a lover.

"I'll see you soon," Dagmar said, and she glided from the club.

Milena joined her at the bar as Nadia finished her drink, still wondering what she had gotten into. "Where's Dagmar?" Milena asked, her tone light, but Nadia caught the nails underneath.

"She left."

"What did she want?"

"Say hi, mostly." Nadia watched Milena, watched the spike of jealousy dancing in her eyes, and found there was a twin in her own mind. "She wanted to meet someone like her."

"You two aren't really alike."

"We're both... what we are."

Milena nodded. The jealousy was at bay now, tempered by fear and perhaps interest. "I guess I kind of knew."

"She's very interested in you," Nadia said.

Milena blushed. "What for?"

"I think these." Nadia gestured at the deck of cards on the bar, humming with the power Milena had unintentionally imbued them.

"How did she know about the cards?"

"She didn't. Not exactly. But she knows about talismans—stuff like this, and the pool water, and so on—and she thought you would have created some."

"How would she think that?"

"The same way I found you. The woman who can see your future if you play cards against her."

"Oh." Nadia could not help but take pleasure in watching Milena deflate. She scolded herself. This was stupid. They were together for such a short time, and that didn't mean Milena's eyes stopped working. She was a bit surprised Milena's tastes would be so average, but different strokes and all that.

Nadia leaned over and set her hands on Milena's thighs, looking into her face. "If that's all she wanted, she's setting her sights low. You're worth a hell of a lot more than that to me."

Milena blushed, quite prettily. "You know, I thought I was through blushing. But you give me that look, and it's tough."

"You want to get out of here?"

"I'd love to, but I have half a shift and rent doesn't make itself."

"Right." Nadia felt a stab of guilt. She was paying her way with money from her parents. There was no need for a job.

"I'll see you at home later." Milena leaned in for a kiss and signaled Dave for another round, then returned to her game.

Nadia was alone at the bar. She had been so wrapped up in Milena, she had been neglecting nearly everyone else. Perhaps it was time to change that. She texted Angie, inviting her down to the Midway, or being open to go elsewhere. She sipped her Sazerac and waited for a response. She didn't get one. She might chalk up the absence of an answer to Angie being busy or her phone being dead. Angie was far too conscientious, her phone much too important to her job. Nadia checked Angie's various social networks. There were status updates, but nothing descriptive, nothing clear.

Nadia texted Zach. His response came fairly quickly. He hadn't seen Angie. He had not known she wasn't talking to Nadia either, and finished the conversation with a simple, chilling, *I'm worried.*

Nadia was too.

***

The trip to the Midway had been an unexpected joy. Dagmar found herself jangly and loose on the drive home, nearly drumming on the steering wheel of her BMW. She drove west, to the rich hills of Brentwood. Her street was fairly quiet, the homes spaced apart far enough that they were never bothering one another. Her home was much more than she needed, one of Frank Lloyd Wright's textile block mansions. More than she needed, but not more than she wanted.

She never could have dreamed of it when she was younger. Now it was hers. All because she understood the true nature of power.

She parked her car in the garage and entered her home. While the high ceilings and long hallways gave an impression of endless space, Dagmar was certain to decorate with art and antiques. Not quite cozy, but enough to look at. Things to impress any who entered. Easy to see who the truly important were. Enchanted by the Winslow Homer original on the wall? No one important. Obsessed with the half-destroyed VHS tape she kept in her ritual room? Someone to treat with gravity.

Nadia Eskandarian was one such person. Dagmar smelled it on the young woman as soon as she saw her. It was madness to carry around so much in a satchel—Dagmar could hear the jars clinking together, promising more secrets—but perhaps Nadia was ready for a fight. She would be formidable.

Dagmar passed through the upstairs, pleased her maid was gone for the evening. She did not know what lurked in this place. She only knew the man Dagmar lived with was strange and awful. She was not wrong in this assessment.

Dagmar heard him well before she saw him. The clank of his weights on the bar as he worked out. He was always lifting weights, sculpting his body into a perfect engine. Dagmar certainly appreciated the results, and there were times when she wanted to appreciate them more closely. Neither of them was consumed in desire for the other, but the lingering attraction helped unite them in the few ways their past did not.

Hernán Gaff was bench pressing six hundred pounds without too much effort. He was dressed only in a pair of black boxer-briefs, contrasting sharply with his stark white skin. Between that, and his massive muscles, he looked almost like a Michelangelo statue. If he was, it was a mutilated one. What at first looked like irregular scales dimpling his hairless flesh, were in fact shards of glass embedded in his skin. His fingernails were of clear glass; his teeth were shards of mirror. Even his eyes were beneath a layer of glass, rendering them distant, cloudy, inhuman.

Gaff sat up as she entered. His head was bald. His eyebrows were tattooed on, too thin and feminine for his titan frame. Dagmar's gaze crawled over the sloping muscles, swollen with exercise, but what looked like desire was actually a keen urge to harvest.

"Was she everything you'd hoped?" Gaff had a soft accent, muddled and unplaceable.

"She was merely Kissed, but she already has a patron."

Gaff stood. He was a mountain of a man, and with the glimmer of glass and the ghost-white skin, a mountain covered in fresh snow. "Am I to pay this patron a visit?"

Dagmar smiled. She appreciated Gaff's loyalty, though she had bought it in blood. "No, you're not to touch this one. I have another errand in mind." A dangerous errand, she thought. But Gaff wouldn't poke around where he wasn't supposed to. He would do as she said, and nothing more.

"Anything."

"Dr. Richard Vorspan," she said. Gaff nodded. While they had never formally met—Dagmar had good reason to keep them out of conversation with one another—Gaff had seen the good doctor around.

"He runs the asylum."

"The mental hospital," Dagmar corrected gently.

"What's he done?" That would be the dangerous question.

"Displeased me."

Gaff nodded. "And what do you wish done?"

"Bring him to me."

"In what condition?"

"Relatively unharmed."

Gaff took a step to the door. Dagmar stopped him with a soft hand on his chest. The scales of glass were hard under her fingers, embedded in the spongy tissue. "Not at the moment. Watch him. Take him when he's alone. Off his guard."

"Of course."

"And before you go..." she stroked his chest, then his shoulders and arms, fingers playing off the smooth glass. She found a hard piece, grown large and strong over his shoulder. With her fingernails, she pulled it out of him. Blood ran down the fresh wound in his arm. Gaff did not react. Dagmar plucked a few more bloody pieces from her man, placing them in her palm.

"Now you can go," she told him.

Gaff nodded and set off for his room. Traveling outside, he would bundle up. It was no longer possible to completely hide his inhumanity, but he could pass a casual inspection with enough on him.

Dagmar did her best to suppress her worry. Any interaction between Vorspan and Gaff could be quite dangerous. She didn't have much choice. After the argument she and Vorspan had, it was clear he would be alert for her. Possibly hiring bodyguards to keep her away. She could kill Vorspan fairly easily; she had long ago taken a lock of hair from him for just this eventuality. Their long association had made him useful, more than a replacement could be. He needed to be brought back to heel. To be turned into an instrument better suited to her will.

The bits of glass jingled in her hands, the wet blood pooling in her palm. The ritual room was upstairs, just off her bedroom. The inner sanctum of the house. Her bedroom was enormous, opening out onto the upper balcony. Below the patio running around three sides of the house made an elegant walkway for her guests. This place was just for her and the few she invited.

The ritual room was hidden. A door in the back of the walk-in closet led to this relatively small space. She lit the candles in the corner—electric light felt crass. A large antique glass cabinet dominated one side of the room, displaying her collection of talismans.

Between two bookends, a collection of VHS tapes. The one on the far left was as close to an original she could find, the label partly scratched off. The others were increasingly degraded copies she had made for quick use. They were of a cartoon from the '30s, *Fill Me with Moonlight*, a phantasmagorical descent into the underworld. With every copy, the original lost some quality, some power. She was dreading losing it entirely. In many ways it was the crown jewel of her collection. She had tried to have it uploaded online, but it crashed every computer she tried it on. She was forced to make the degraded copies, or else use the original and exhaust every last bit of energy in the cartoon.

A box of thick soil alive with earthworms was next to it. That had taken a trip to a graveyard to harvest, the last little bit of it she had left. The power left in his grave was no longer strong enough. That dirt was brown, carrying none of the life or the ripe smell of the talismanic version.

There were other things: the few remaining scraps of a bandanna, a couple locks of hair each tied with a crusty and stained ribbon, a half-cannibalized electric guitar, several knuckle-sized leather cylinders, a few jars filled with ephemeral shadowy spiders. The bloody glass went into a jewelry box already brimming with it.

Then there was a closed cigar box filled with things that could kill her. The old syringes and tubes would not themselves harm her, not beyond the truly impressive power they contained, but if Gaff saw them, the bonds between them would likely be shattered.

She stared at her collection. It was incredible how quickly her supplies dwindled. Some of it was the fault of those she had to harvest; how quickly these types burned themselves out, until all that was left was to loot their graves. It was why she needed those like Gaff or even Milena. They were more rational, easier to keep alive.

Dagmar sighed. She did need Milena Franco. Needed another source of easily-harvested talismans. At least until she could take another of her big fish alive. Stella Mortimer had proven how difficult that could be.

The Matchless did not often like captivity.

***

It was a bright morning, with Milena in the kitchen area cooking breakfast. Nadia went into the bathroom and began drawing a bath. It had been too long since she shaved, since just before she had been tattooed, and she felt dirty. She pulled her shirt over her head and threw it in the corner. She inspected first her arms, the places she had always been most sensitive about, the places she'd been first teased for.

They were bare. She frowned. There should have been stubble. She stripped out of her pants and checked her calves. They were partly covered in the beginnings of her tattoos, the serpents Zach sketched first. She leaned into the mirror. The sides and back of her head were utterly smooth.

She stared. Her hair was thinner than it had been. She could easily see her scalp through the top of her head. And her eyebrows were patchy.

She passed the razor over her skin anyway. The silvery feeling had too much of an association for her. A comfort.

She jumped when Milena screamed.

Nadia hopped out of the tub and ran into the main room, her razor unfolded, ready to use it.

Milena was staring into the frying pan with horror, a broken eggshell in one nerveless hand.

"What is it?" Nadia asked.

"Come here."

Nadia left wet footprints as she approached, not wanting to see what had so horrified Milena, but having to. She leaned over, and her eyes widened.

"When I cracked this egg, there was a snake inside," Milena said.

A snake now sitting in the frying pan. Dead. Nadia dumped the snake in the garbage, then took Milena in her arms. Milena held on. "Sorry, I'm being stupid," she said.

"No, it's okay. Probably a bit of a shock."

"I didn't think. Snake eggs?"

Nadia parted from her and took the broken shell, looking it over. It was not a snake egg. "Yeah. That is weird." She threw that away as well.

"Breakfast out?" Milena asked.

"I think so."

They stayed in the kitchen for a moment, and Nadia began to realize she was still naked and holding a razor. "I should... I'll be right back."

She went into the bedroom and pulled on a clean set of clothes. As she dressed, she looked over at Milena's purse, open on a chair by the door. "Hey, sweetie? The cards you used last night, are they in your purse?"

"Yes," Milena called back. "You can have them if you want."

Nadia was glad she'd said it, because she was already pulling them from the purse. They buzzed with power, though not as much as the others had. She returned them to the purse. Milena was valuable. She was producing talismans—Dagmar's word, she thought—and Milena would produce as many as they wanted.

Nadia shivered. She could farm her girlfriend.

***

Angie had never been more exhausted. Her ruined body had no strength left. She had been devoured alive, inch by burning inch. China watched through the black eye of her camera lens, a grin lighting up her plastic face. Devin's body blocked her from time to time, and when Angie looked up into his face, she saw the man he was inside. Crying. Begging her forgiveness. But there was nothing left of her to grant it.

Angie Alcala died two hours later. Though it was much more comforting to think she had died weeks ago, the last little bit of her left with the rattling of breath.

Strength

The needle filled in the scales on Nadia's left arm. Zach's work was incredible, managing to capture the inhuman life of the diamondbacks' scales. They shone the way real scales did, and even reacted to the ambient light, the gleaming as though wet. As she moved her arm, it appeared as though the snakes themselves were writhing, straining toward her slender fingers. The more scales went down over smooth flesh, the more she was at peace.

Her legs were entirely done, going from the tops of her feet all the way to her hips. More serpents. More signs that she was touched by the dragon, but also that she carried him within her. The commitment, in time and pain, had been substantial, but Nadia didn't care. Far more important was that her change be made complete. Now Zach worked on her arms. Another week or two of these sessions, luxuriating under the sweet agony of the needle until she could take no more, and her arms would be covered in complete sleeves.

Milena watched with interest.

"You like?" Nadia asked.

"Oh, very much. I've never had the courage to get one."

"I can draw you something," Zach said without looking up. He was in the zone, jeweler's glasses over his eyes.

Nadia felt the needle not just in her arm but through her body. Peeling back the skin, showing what was underneath.

Milena flinched as Zach dabbed a bit of blood from Nadia's arm. "No, I'm good."

Zach sat back. "Might be for the best." He flipped the glasses to his forehead and wiped his eyes.

"What?" Nadia said.

"Look at you. Look at your body."

Nadia looked her scales over. They were everything she could have wanted. When her muscles moved under her skin, they gave the faint sense of a knot of snakes uncoiling. "They're perfect."

"They're better than perfect," Zach said. "I'm not that good. Or I didn't used to be."

"What do you mean?"

"I don't mean to sound full of myself here, but since we started, my tattoos are almost alive. Yours are the best I've done, but I'm better across the board. I drew a dolphin on a woman the other day that looked like it was diving up and down through the waves." He paused. "This might sound stupid, but you're changing me."

Nadia watched him.

"And you know exactly what I'm talking about," he said. It was not a question.

She nodded. "It's okay, Zach." She touched his hand, where he held the gun. It fairly hummed with power.

"You'll be fine," Milena told him.

"But if someone ever comes here, asking about it, especially a skinny blonde woman in her forties, you call me."

"Who is that?" Zach asked, trembling.

"Just call me. I'll deal with it."

"Fine." He put the glasses over his face. His eyes were distorted, only half-visible. "I don't know if I want an explanation or not."

"Enjoy your newfound skills," Nadia said, and the needle went back to buzzing.

***

Dr. Richard Vorspan returned home well after dark. There were never easy days, but there were hard ones. This was one of those. It didn't help that he could not stop replaying his confrontation with Dagmar Eichel over and over in his head.

She had wanted to see Stella Mortimer. Mortimer, who wasn't even supposed to be in the hospital. Mortimer, staying under a false name. Mrs. Louisa Starr, so said the paperwork. She wasn't supposed to be in there because Stella Mortimer was dead.

It had said so in the paper.

Now, it would be in the online archives, there for anyone to see. CAR ACCIDENT REVEALS ANGEL OF DEATH. Below would be the initial dry description of the car accident, accompanied by a picture of twisted metal and unidentifiable stains on the asphalt. Those cars had it out for Stella Mortimer. She'd somehow managed to be rear-ended, sandwiched between two cars, then t-boned by cross traffic. Her trunk came open when they separated the masses of metal, revealing its nauseating cargo.

Her small house near USC was a chamber of horrors. She had been operating largely unchecked, because she hunted those who were nearly invisible to the police in places they scarcely went. Sure, her hospital had a higher-than-average mortality rate, but it was also the poorest one in the city. They were lucky to get any medical care at all.

After the initial discovery, the article would dip into Mortimer's entire horrifying biography. It might point out she was a local Angeleno, born and raised in Watts. There might even be an undercurrent of racism, couched in comforting euphemisms like "urban." They would all point out there was no way to know what had turned her into a monster, but then it would cite the crime statistics in her neighborhood. Abuse would be hypothesized, but nothing could be confirmed.

Then it would move into her more lurid deeds. Her first victims were her patients, and the article never failed to note with ghoulish glee, how she'd been a nurse on the maternity floor for years. When she no longer got a thrill from poisoning her charges, she began to hunt, and her true body count could only be estimated.

When she was alive, Stella Mortimer had been a shadow of a shadow.

All of the articles ended the same way; how lucky we all were that the pileup had taken such a dangerous person out of circulation. Her gravesite was kept out of the papers to prevent the curious from clogging one of the local cemeteries.

This was a lie, but only two people in the world knew it. Dr. Vorspan was one. Dagmar Eichel was the other.

He had no idea what Dagmar wanted with the notorious killer. Just after the accident, Dagmar offered Vorspan a deal: he could conceal this woman for her and be rewarded. Or he could cross her. She never said what she would do if he did, and for fifteen years, the unspoken promise had kept him cowed. The way she said it was disturbing enough. Not even a threat. No lowering of her voice, no ominous cackle. She stated it as one possible way he could go and watched him with her unblinking green gaze and waited. Vorspan had never truly known fear until he found it in Dagmar's eyes.

She had rewarded him. She had always been one of the largest private contributors to the hospital and used the influence she bought to put Vorspan in charge. As far as the staff knew, Louisa Starr, held in the highest-security wing in the basement, was dangerous but not famous for it. Vorspan handled her care personally.

There was no care. Dagmar had been abundantly clear that there would be none. He wasn't supposed to talk to Stella Mortimer. Wasn't supposed to medicate what had gone wrong in her brain. Wasn't even supposed to learn what that was. The way Dagmar talked about the serial killer was the way someone might refer to an avant-garde artist who would be spoiled by any immersion into the world. Mortimer was to be kept in restraints, physical and chemical, for twenty-four hours a day, and fed personally by Vorspan himself.

He should have killed her. Some extra morphine in her drip, and that would be the end. Carried off in a cloud. But that would mean crossing Dagmar. Whenever his thoughts brushed up against that conclusion, his bowels turned to ice. What she had done to Mortimer was worse than death. What she would do to Vorspan would be somehow even worse than that.

Dagmar had some kind of need for the killer. Once a month, she would arrive at the hospital, and take a trip to the basement to see Mortimer. Vorspan would open the door, and Dagmar, completely unafraid, would go inside. A little while later, she would come out, tucking a jar into her purse. She would smile at Vorspan and say, "Same time next month."

Until last time when Vorspan told her no.

She had stared at him, her face an expressionless mask. He might as well have been speaking Greek. He scratched nervously at his beard and repeated the single syllable into the silence.

"I heard you," Dagmar said. "I just can't fathom why you would be saying it."

He didn't tell her the truth. Couldn't. Fifteen years of his conscience worrying at him. At first, he had been able to dismiss Mortimer. She was a monster. A killer. Whatever they had been doing to her was entirely deserved. She was far too dangerous to release.

The guilt grew. It pushed away his now ex-wife, and she took their friends with her, all convinced he had been unfaithful with Dagmar. He could not speak to his colleagues, either. He knew they could see through his mask. They would know he was a fraud. There was no one except Dagmar. His rock, his conscience, his patron. And everything she whispered in his ear was wrong.

The voice inside him grew more persistent over the years. At first it was a murmur, steadily growing in volume. It was shouting now. Everyone deserves help. Everyone.

Everyone included Stella Mortimer.

His mind worried at the edges of the problem. Outlining a treatment plan. Trying to come up with a way to allow Mortimer some kind of existence. Some sort of respite after spending fifteen years in purgatory.

Stupid, stupid. He should have just killed her. Should have called it an accident. But no matter what else happened, he didn't have the stomach. Whatever Stella and Dagmar had within them, whatever steel that allowed them to step so far outside morality, was not within him.

He did not say this. Instead he tried to bull ahead, "I am the head administrator of this facility, Ms. Eichel. We all appreciate your contributions, but not when they come at the expense of a patient."

Dagmar finally smiled. A chill worked its way through Vorspan. "You'll change your mind." Then she turned and walked away.

"I'm afraid not, Ms. Eichel," he called after her, his voice weak and small.

She didn't bother to respond, returning to her rich car to drive away. He had shaken the rest of the day and hadn't slept. But it had been two weeks and Dagmar had not done anything. He was not even certain of what she would do. She had a strange way about her, almost otherworldly. She was almost like a movie star, in her nearly ageless looks, in her elegance and grace. She was also like Mortimer herself: cold, knowing, aloof, and above. Even when Mortimer was in full restraints, she looked at Vorspan like he was an insect.

She shouldn't have been able to focus at all, not with the medication she was taking. Vorspan tried to pretend he was imagining it, but he could not. Mortimer knew him. And hated him.

Four weeks after the threat, and Dagmar had not done anything. Maybe she saw it was time to stop. Whatever tortures she had been visiting on Stella Mortimer were finished. He had long speculated that Dagmar must be extracting some kind of revenge for someone, but he couldn't reconcile Mortimer's working class, mostly black and hispanic victims with the coldly patrician and extremely white Dagmar Eichel.

He walked up to his door. Fatigue weighed his bones down. This would be the first good night's sleep in a week. He could feel it. He was trying to think up some kind of treatment plan for Stella Mortimer, his conscious mind finding that his subconscious had already industriously been working. There might not be one. Fifteen years of relative isolation had not done anything good for her. Perhaps he could settle for as little as keeping her comfortable and shielded from whatever weird torments she had been subjected to.

He pulled his keys from his pocket and gripped the doorknob. It swung open into his darkened house. Already ajar.

Vorspan stared into the black hallway. His home was abruptly not really his. Someone was inside, someone who didn't belong. In the distance, a neighbor's dog barked at nothing. The street was quiet.

Vorspan reached into his briefcase and withdrew a .38 snubnose revolver. He'd bought it three years ago, back when he first had the impulse to stand up to Dagmar. Three years from that day to this one. He had gone to shooting ranges and everything, and even had a permit. It had been the secret source of his strength for some time, and now he was going to use it.

Killing someone who broke in wasn't a crime at all.

He stepped into the house, his foot creaking off the board. He winced, then scolded himself. *She knows you're here. She knew the minute your door opened.*

He cleared his throat, trying to affect the courage he did not feel. "Whoever's in there, I have a gun. Get out now, or I will shoot you."

He paused. There was no echo. The gloom had swallowed it up.

He fancied he could hear it breathe.

He took another step, the revolver glinting silver in the dim light. He reached over and clicked the light switch in the hall. He thought it would have returned mundanity to his home, banishing the shapes dancing just out of sight. It did not. The light felt even stranger, and he had the unshakeable feeling, only for a moment, that he was in someone else's home.

He shut the door. "Last chance," he said.

No answer. The dark continued to breathe, unconcerned with this intruder.

He walked down the hallway, past the closet, to where it opened into his living room. He reached over to turn on the light.

"Leave it off," a voice said. He did not recognize it. Masculine, and with a faint and unfamiliar accent, like nothing Vorspan had heard.

"Who's there?"

"A friend."

Vorspan squinted into the gloom of the living room. He finally saw the silhouette. He was in a chair, his left side facing Vorspan. The shape had not turned his head. He was stark white, his skin shimmering like water in the sunlight.

"I have a gun," Vorspan said, his voice quavering.

"I know."

"What do you want? Why did you break in?"

"Do you know how lucky we are?"

"I'm sorry?" Vorspan faltered, his gun no longer pointing at the strange invader.

"We walk in her grace, you and I. We feel her favor."

"Dagmar?"

"I dislike using her name so flippantly. There's another name for her. A title. I wish I knew it, but it only comes to me just before I sleep, and in the morning I never remember."

"Dagmar knows the deal. She has to live with it."

The shape stood. He was massive. He had the frame of a wrestler, a body builder, an action star. The light from the hallway caught his face, and it glittered like no flesh ever could. Like jewels embedded in his skin.

Vorspan brought up the gun. "Stay right where you are."

He didn't. Vorspan got off one shot before the massive man was on top of him. He could have sworn he caught the other man in the center of mass, just like the targets at the range. He should be down, bleeding out. He could have at least stumbled.

The massive shape lifted Vorspan off the ground like a child. He drove a left into Vorspan's gut, then across his jaw. The doctor saw a great explosion, and then nothing.

***

Nadia's phone buzzed while she was out running, interrupting the podcast she was listening to. She was in the midst of slowly exploring Milena's—our, she reminded herself—neighborhood, trying to map out a good run for herself. The leg Karo had broken was stuttering every third or fourth step, but she could ignore the twinges of pain. She took the phone from its sheath on her upper arm, then checked the name on the screen. SILVIA. She didn't recognize it but answered anyway.

"Nadia? It's Silvia. Silvia Alcala."

Oh shit. "Silvia. Hi. How are you?"

"Have you seen Angie?"

"Not lately. You haven't either?"

"I'm sorry to be calling you like this." Silvia had the traces of a Mexican accent, even though she was born and raised in east LA.

"It's no bother."

"Angie mentioned to me that you two were spending time together again."

"Yeah." Nadia felt the but coming, when the parent would be concerned the lesbian was going to corrupt their precious little girl.

"Do you know where she is? Who she is spending time with?"

"I'm sorry, Silvia, I don't. Have you checked with anyone else? Or looked at her social media?"

"I have. She's updating it, but no pictures. And she hasn't been to work in three weeks. She doesn't have a job there anymore."

"Want me to ask around?"

"I couldn't ask you to."

"I'm offering, Silvia. I'm happy to." *I should have been all along. I've just been lost inside a new relationship, and oh yeah, I'm a witch or something.*

"Thank you, Nadia."

"I'll call you if I find anything."

"Bless you, *mija*."

Nadia felt the warmth through her chest at the term of endearment. Silvia had only called her that a few times, and mostly when she and Angie had been very young. There were times she liked to pass them off as sisters. Many years ago, it had been possible.

Nadia sprinted home, ignoring the pain shooting from the supernaturally repaired bone. She slowed at Milena's driveway, her limp coming back in a big way. She stumbled into the house, her left leg wringing out bolts of agony, and grabbed her laptop. She did the obvious first, checking up on Angie's social networks. The updates were as vague as ever but fairly consistent. A day or two of nothing, then up to three in a day, then another short fallow period.

They did not sound like Angie. Angie was one of the new breed of people who liked to live in public. Her joys were an inspiration to all, and her heartbreaks were rallies for all of her friends. She was never the type to name names when it came to the negative parts of life but reading between the lines was simple.

At a certain point in her feed, a little over a month before, she went from Angie the Oversharer to Angie the Shallow. Lots of laughing, mentions of going to clubs with "new friends," lots of dancing, and lots of men, but no names. Never names. Angie would always bring up names when she was talking about a good time. She liked people to know where she was and who she was with because that meant more people could join her. It baffled Nadia, who found anything more than four people to be uncomfortably stifling.

Nadia cleaned up and waited for dark to head to the Midway. Angie had introduced her and had frequented it on occasion. Unfortunately, Milena was not working there that night; she'd found another game she could make rent from, farming money from those who were willing to give it up. Perhaps it was better to focus.

The bouncers waved Nadia past. She was known: the regular girlfriend of the fortuneteller. The staff gave her smiles and nods. Somehow, Nadia belonged. A circus-themed speakeasy in Hollywood. If that's what it took to find a safe place, that's what it took. And it was safe. She was not given a second look. Even something as simple as the bathrooms, where someone like her could go without causing frightened women to scurry out or angry women to yell at her for using the "wrong one" was a blessing.

She went through, asking the various employees she knew. No luck. It wasn't until she was backstage, behind the Elephant Girls show, that she found anything. Keegan sat on a steamer trunk, plucking staples and dollars from her body. The staple remover was a tiny jade elephant, which she used by hooking the tusks under the metal and working the hinge at the back of the head. Her dyed silver-gray hair was done up in the fancier version of what Nadia had, a buzz cut all around, and a high pompadour in the front, a modern style contrasting with her burlesque lingerie. She pulled the metal from her skin with businesslike comportment, with no wincing, no hissing, no indication she felt any pain at all. She expressed only a faint interest in the denominations of the bills.

Keegan didn't know Angie by name, but after Nadia showed her Angie's profile pic on her phone, Keegan nodded. "Oh yeah. I've seen her around a couple times." She wrinkled her face in the first disgust she'd shown. "She was hanging out with China Jennings when she was here, the Wednesday before last. You know, that vapid whore." Keegan pulled a twenty from where it was stapled on her inner thigh. She made a small noise of approval and added it to the stack.

"How do you remember?"

Keegan tapped her temple absently. "Photographic memory. Worst superpower ever. Most people love to forget. I can't."

Nadia filed that bit of information away. "Angie was here with China? What does that mean exactly?"

Keegan gestured with the staple remover. The elephant's mouth opened and shut, hungry for more staples. "Well, she comes in here with her cult, you know? They act like they own the place, and they don't tip for shit. Ask Dave. They've stiffed his ass every single time they've been in here. They came to see our show one time, and China wanted to put the bill on Bekah's ass, right? She flashes a fifty, and Bekah turns around and gives her the full moon. When we took the bill off after the show, it's a one. Fucking cunt switched it."

"That sucks, but Angie?"

"Oh yeah. Normally it's China and her Manazons, right? Only this time, there's this short Latina chick with them, which was weird. She was acting like all the others, too. Vacant expression, laughing at whatever stupid shit came out of China's mouth." Keegan frowned, a bloody staple in the elephant's jaws. "Why, what's up, Nadia?"

"No, it's okay. I was looking for Angie."

"She's fallen to the dark side. I'm sorry to say it."

The anger freezing Nadia's insides said more. She had danced around China for long enough. Now she was fucking with Angie, and Nadia was going to show her just what a bad idea that was.

"What?" Keegan said, leaning back in confusion and fear. "You got this look on your face."

"It's nothing," Nadia said, forcing a smile. "Thanks, Keegan."

"No problem. One tip. When you're that pissed, don't smile. It's creepy as fuck."

Nadia had to chuckle. "Got it."

"I'd hate to be that bitch right now," Keegan said.

Nadia left, neither confirming or denying. She returned to the home she shared with Milena. Moving out had been a production. Neither her mother nor her father had wanted it, but Nadia had insisted. She wanted to be on her own, and Siranush challenged her. If she really wanted to be on her own, she would cut up her family credit cards.

Siranush relented right afterwards, asking where she was going. Nadia told the truth, though she did not mention Milena. That would be the bridge too far, and that would cut off financial support. Support she needed for the time being.

"Going to write your novel," Siranush said, nodding.

"Yeah, mom." It was a pointless clarification to make. Siranush was convinced Nadia was a novelist. Why else would someone spend so much time on literature? Writing was a career; she and Vartan had more than one screenwriter as a client. What they never understood was that the true meaning was found only when the author was finished. Interpretation was the home of wisdom.

She moved as much of her stuff as she thought would fit, merging her impressive library with Milena's. Now stacks of books bolstered nearly every wall of the guest house. Nadia thought she should clear a few out, but the thought of losing any of her treasured words made her stomach spin in loops.

Her work area, a repurposed antique sewing table Milena found at a rummage sale, was in the middle of a fort made entirely by paperbacks, the bulk of which were from second hand stories, with lurid painted covers from the 1970s. Nadia's treasures covered the surface, organized in vague groups. Jars of pool water stayed with the pieces of lens in the middle. The jars of berries were in alcoves on the right; a few decks of cards on the left. Her hand played over the talismans as she thought of how she might like to combine them to craft a curse for China.

She quickly came to an unsettling realization: she had no way to target China. She could power it with anything on the table, craft whatever she liked as long as she was creative enough, but she had nothing to tell the malice where to latch. No way to point the path to China's jugular. The only thing of China's she owned was the lens, and Nadia felt in her bones this was a bad idea, like strapping a nuke to another nuke. No, she would need something else. Hair or blood would be perfect. Another possession, one China had not filtered her own power through, would also do, though it might not be as precise or cruel.

Nadia looked up to the window, still lost in thought. The view looked out over the back of a hill, over a selection of Victorian houses that had been in the neighborhood for over a hundred years. She could not see anything. Vibrant green leaves covered the glass.

One of the leaves grabbed a neighbor, and snicker-snacked its head off. They were not leaves. It was a swarm of praying mantises.

***

Milena was surprised to see the name on her phone. Karo Minasian. It had been such a long time, she assumed whatever Nadia had done had frightened him off. Her ringtone sounded.

She was alone in their home. Nadia had gone to some secret place. She had spoken about it thus far only vaguely, and when she did, she stared off at nothing. Milena didn't want to press. Wherever it was, it was the source of two of her "talismans," and there would soon be new jars over on her worktable. There were other things there now too, though they had not been placed with the same reverence. A jug with a few praying mantises on branches. A bloody dollar bill. An empty bottle of scotch. These were gathered toward one end, almost an afterthought, while the talismans were given space to breathe.

"Milena?" Karo's voice was quavering, soft.

"Yes, Karo. I don't work for you anymore."

"I have to see you," he said. His voice was so needy, so desperate. He sounded nothing like the blustery alpha male he had always been.

"If this is some kind of way to get me back..."

"No! No, I promise you. Please, you have to come and see me."

"I don't have to do anything you say. Ever again."

"No, just... please. Please, Milena." The tone was one she had never heard in his aggressively masculine voice. He was no longer a figure of control and strength. He was shriveled and pitiable, pathetic in a way she could never have imagined. She needed to see him. Needed to see what had brought him so low.

"Okay. Okay, fine. I'll be right over."

Milena ended the call and checked herself in the mirror. Her weakness had always been vanity, though it was not always recognizable to those who were slaves to the modern. She had her own aesthetic, and never wanted to be any less than that. Despite the sound of him over the phone, despite her fascination, she wanted to show him just how much he wasn't needed.

She didn't anticipate physical force. Karo seldom liked to resort to it. He could be violent when it suited him, but he was at his core a businessman. Violence never filled a single wallet. Intimidation, though, he had mastered. She had been on the other end enough times to have no illusions about that. But in his voice she heard herself. When he had her at her most cowed, that was what she sounded like inside, and now Karo was speaking that way to her. He wasn't empathetic enough to use it as a lure.

He used his physicality as a blunt instrument. He was a gym rat, in large part because his job depended on him having a large, scary physique. He cultivated a level of bravado, the subtle way men dominate one another with loud laughs, pervasive physical contact, and one-upmanship. He took up as much space as he could, both physical and emotional, underlying how important he was in the lives of those around him.

He would remind her of her debt to him, most likely. No matter that she had long ago paid it off, back when the work appealed to her. By Karo's reckoning the debt would be paid when he could wring no more money out of her. Then, and only then, would she be free. She looked forward to explaining that time was now.

She drove to Karo's house, doing her best to ignore her roiling stomach. She felt like she might want to throw up, but even that was weakness. She wasn't going to show any.

She buzzed him on the intercom and expected to hear him checking to see who was there. In his home, he could be slightly paranoid, though he did have his reasons. Instead, the gate simply rolled open on its automatic track. Milena went to the front door and found it open.

"Karo?" she called out, her voice echoing through the house.

She saw herself the last time she was here. Creeping past the front door to go upstairs and get the hair from his shaver. She had been the one quivering in fear.

"Milena?" The voice was whispery, weak. Coming from upstairs.

Milena moved into the living room and paused. A line small, red splatters pockmarked the hardwood. Drops. Brown drops of something. Leading upstairs, where Karo's voice emanated from. She followed it, and finding another, larger collection of drops. Dry now, but they shone like burned sugar.

The stairs were another matter. Now she could see they were definitely bloodstains. Some older than others, browned, flaking. A smear across the wall. Someone had been bleeding. Badly.

"Karo?" she said again.

"I'm in my bedroom. Don't be afraid. Don't..." The rest disappeared.

Milena climbed the staircase, half-expecting some bloody knife-wielding killer to leap out and attack her. Karo, gone mad.

The top floor was even worse. Blood was everywhere, on the white carpet, the bare walls. She did not know how anyone could bleed so much and still be alive.

She nearly screamed when she stepped into the doorway of Karo's bedroom. She clapped a hand over her mouth, and still, a squeak escaped.

Karo lay in bed, though there was not much left of him. He was skeletal, his bones pushed up through a layer of flesh hanging lank and loose. The blood on the bed at least wasn't wet. It spread out from his crotch in a wide circle.

As Milena entered, Karo uttered a whispering laugh. "I guess that answers how I look."

His body was covered in sores, open and weeping blood and pus, some illness eating him alive. Milena took a step back, in horror realizing she was breathing the same air as he.

"Don't be afraid. The doctors say it's not contagious. That's all they can tell me. They don't know what it is."

"Karo, I—"

"Please, Milena, I need you to hear me." He sat up, the sores leaving streaks of tacky blood along the sheets. He was exhausted and diminished, but his gaze was clear. Too clear, perhaps, dancing close to madness. "You are free. Your debt is paid in full."

"Is that why you called me here?"

"Yes!" It was nearly a sob. She had never heard anything so soft, so weak, coming from this man's mouth, though there was little to be seen of the old Karo in this hemorrhaging skeleton.

Nadia. Nadia did this. The thought was insane, but it had weight. Nadia had said she was going to free Milena from Karo, and this was what she meant. How could anyone have this kind of power? Milena felt something almost like reverence, an awe born of religious revelation. She said she would. Confident, even as the errand had been insane.

"Please, Milena. I know your friend is some kind of witch. She came to me, I say no, and this happens. I know she hates me for hurting her. Tell her I understand now. Tell her you are hers. Just please, make her take this curse off of me."

"I can't make her do anything."

"Yes you can! She was willing to do anything for you. She came to me and I said no. Tell her I'm sorry. Tell her your debts are forgiven. Tell her I will never come after her. I will never even think her name, just tell her she has to fix me."

"I will." Milena was not certain if she meant it or not.

Karo leaned back in his bed. "Will she listen?"

Nadia had called this plague from somewhere else. Created it. Let there be death, she said, and there was.

"I don't know."

***

Dagmar was pleased when she saw what Gaff had prepared for her. The house, as it was in Los Angeles, had no basement. She had foreseen the need for a place no one would find, where no one could escape, however, and had one of the rooms downstairs converted. She'd installed a heavy door that locked from the outside, soundproofed the walls, and had the few pieces of furniture inside securely bolted to the floor. The soundproofing was more for her benefit than anything; even if Vorspan started to rant, Gaff would hear none of it.

Gaff fetched her in the morning, after her daily run through the hills and her breakfast of fruit and egg whites. She, alone in the kitchen, eating primly at the counter, browsing the news on her phone, would have been such a normal sight. A wealthy woman enjoying the morning of the relentless work it took to look as she did. The illusion was shattered when Gaff lumbered into the room. He would never have a place in the normal world.

As he was when home alone, he was stripped to the waist, showing off the regularly-spaced glass scales embedded in his flesh. Even now, after having reduced him to little more than a milk cow, she was fascinated. Installed back when he had been fully human, now they grew from him like scales, and yet agonized the skin as they did so. His tattooed eyebrows, thin and delicately arched, made him look almost like a drag queen.

A ragged hole in Gaff's abdominals wept a tiny rivulet of blood.

"Dr. Vorspan is downstairs, Ms. Eichel."

"Thank you," she said, popping the last piece of honeydew into her mouth, and placing the plate in the sink. "He's bound?"

"Securely. The door is locked as well."

"Good. What happened?" she asked, gesturing at the hole.

"He had a gun."

"I see. Wait for me outside the door. I need to prepare."

The huge, pale man sucked in a breath and nodded. She suspected he might flush, but there was not enough blood in him for that. Most of it had been taken away by his creator.

Dagmar went upstairs, quickly showered the run off of her, put on some subtle makeup, a little perfume, and her clothes. She would not be seen in anything less than her best. She finished with an elegant pair of heels. She went into the ritual room and assembled the kit of what she would need, placing it all in an old doctor's bag. Then she came down the stairs to her makeshift prison.

Gaff waited by the door, his arms folded in front of him, those weird glassy eyes staring straight ahead. As she approached, he opened the door and let her into the small chamber. The room was barely fifteen feet on a side. The light came from a single lamp bolted to the dresser. At the center of the room was Dr. Richard Vorspan, attached to a chair with leather restraints, a ball gag in his mouth. Drying blood ran from both nostrils and a cut at the bridge of his nose. One eye was blackened, but other than that, he was fine.

Gaff stepped in the room behind her and the door closed with a sepulchral thud. Vorspan flinched.

Dagmar took the gag off him. It was dangerous, with Gaff so close, but she needed the both of them in the palm of her hand. Needed them to see what she was capable of.

She set the gag beneath the lamp, the light glittering on the spit-soaked ball and regarded Vorspan. She refused to speak, fixing him instead with an unblinking gaze, willing him to speak first. Let fear supplicate him.

"Please, Ms. Eichel, we can work this out. Just let me go. I won't call the cops. I won't do anything. You can see—"

She cut him off. No way was she letting him finish that sentence around Gaff. "You think I plan to kill you?"

Vorspan furrowed his brow, glancing over her shoulder at the pale, ghostlike man in the corner. There was only one thing anyone would use a creature like Gaff for. Yet Vorspan wouldn't speak it for the terror of having it confirmed.

"I have no plans to kill you, Richard. You and I have had far too profitable a relationship for so many years without throwing it away over one foolish decision."

"Thank you, Ms. Eichel! I promise, you won't be disappointed!"

"But you do have to be punished."

Gaff's breath was heavy in the tiny room, now coming faster. She had heard that sound before, on the few times she had taken him for her own. He always sounded more excited by displays of her power than her body.

"What? No, please don't."

"I am afraid so, doctor." Of course, Vorspan couldn't know what she was about to do to him. He had no way of understanding. She removed a syringe from the bag. Vorspan wouldn't have recognized it, beyond that age had given the plastic bag a sepia tinge. It was slightly over fifteen years old and had been used multiple times by Stella Mortimer to inject her killing cocktail. The needle had taken many lives. Made more precious with every murder.

She tied Vorspan's arm off with a belt, brown leather, embroidered with beads. Droplets of dried blood freckled it, from the boy mauled by one of the mountain lions that occasionally haunted the mountains around Los Angeles. She slapped his forearm and got a vein, then brought the syringe closer.

Vorspan struggled. "No!"

"Either stop struggling or I ask Mr. Gaff to hold you down."

"Please, Ms. Eichel, don't."

"The needle is clean, doctor. I wouldn't hurt you with something so mundane."

He frowned, which disappeared in a hiss as she buried the needle in him. She drew a bit of his blood and stopped. "See? Frightened over nothing."

She removed a second item from the doctor's bag. This was the most important, and the most difficult to obtain. "I have been looking for an excuse to bestow this on someone for a time, Dr. Vorspan. Then you choose to defy me. It was fortuitous timing. From my perspective, of course."

The object was about the size of a man's thumb, and it was wrapped in a white cotton handkerchief. She unfolded the cloth, and revealed the cargo, resting on a stain of blood. Her blood. It was a cocoon, fat and white. The caterpillar was still inside, long dead. What was also inside was the claw of a mountain lion, which she had to buy illegally from a poacher. It would be worth it.

She injected Vorspan's blood into the cocoon. He watched, uncomprehending, terrified, his mind incapable of making sense of the insanity. She stepped closer, swaying her hips, crossing her ankles in front of her in her delicate society stride. Behind her, Gaff heaved and huffed.

"Tilt your head back?" she murmured.

"What?"

She grabbed his thinning hair and yanked his head where she wanted it. With the other hand, she jammed the cocoon into his mouth. He coughed and gasped, his body trying to expel the foul thing. She scooped the ball gag off the dresser and slammed it into place, gripping the leather straps in one hand, bunched behind his bald spot. His eyes were wide, tearing. His throat worked against the awful thing.

"That's it," she murmured to him. "Swallow it. As soon as you swallow it, this is all over." She continued to whisper, until she saw the terrible bulge sliding inexorably down his throat.

Then she backed off, casting the ball gag into the corner. The red ball glistened in the dim light.

He tried to speak, but his tortured throat could give no more than choked gagging. Saliva, suddenly freed, ran from his lips and into his beard.

Gaff chuckled. She wondered if she looked over, would he be stroking himself?

Vorspan watched them, frightened and angry. Words were almost returning, the sounds in his throat nearly recognizable.

Then the curse took hold. It started in his left hand, the fingers contorting in a rictus, the tendons reaching for new anchor points. He stared in terror, but there was only a moment to do that before the curse spread. It wracked his body, drawing him bodily into a seizure. His mouth foamed. His muscles strained. She wondered if he was truly secure in his chair. If not, this could become quite dangerous. The thought only made her heart pound faster, her breath coming as quick and jagged as Gaff's.

The horrible, crimson squishing sounds of his organs, muscle, and skeleton rearranging themselves echoed in the small room. His muscles slithered through him like living things. His clothes split and fell about him in rags. His skin grew golden blond fur. His eyes reshaped, turned green, catlike. His teeth sank into his gums or grew dramatically to fangs.

Then he was a mountain lion, hissing and spitting, awkwardly restrained in the chair.

She watched her triumph. A part of her had not believed she could enact the change. She had the power of legend on her side. He would be human by the following morning, and, bound to her, he would change on her schedule. She wondered what might happen when menopause hit her. No matter, Vorspan would likely be dead by then, used up by her whims.

She removed the last ingredient from the doctor's bag. Two silver bracelets, purified in her blood, saliva, and urine. She approached the angry cat. It—he, it was Vorspan, buried under animal aggression—snapped at her, hissing and snarling. She placed the bracelets on the wrists above its forepaws. Manacles from master to servant.

Gaff watched her with naked worship. He opened the door for her, and the two of them left the changed

Vorspan in the prison. He would be let out in the morning.

When he was human.

***

Nadia was only waiting for nightfall. Her satchel was packed. She was going after China Jennings that night. The thought was bright and clear, like her razor. And like the razor, it could cut her.

Taking out Karo was one thing. He was powerful, but he was strictly mundane. China was something else entirely. A far more dangerous enemy. Truly deadly prey.

At night, China was likely to be gone. Out at one of her clubs, seeing and being seen. Nadia could get in, get enough to target China—and take a few more talismans, though she did her best not to dwell on this venal motive—and leave. China would be destroyed, and Angie would be freed from whatever hold the other woman had on her.

Milena came through the door, returning home after a day out. Nadia barely saw her.

"What's up?" Milena asked. "You're thinking of doing something."

Nadia told her.

"You're sure?"

"I have to."

Milena nodded. "I wanted to talk to you about Karo?"

The mention of him might have shocked Nadia or awakened a serpent of jealousy in her. He was already on her mind, though, an example of one of the vanquished. "What about him?"

"He called me, wanting to see me. I went over there. He's... sick, Nadia. It's awful. He's bleeding from every part of him. He's dying, I think. Or he's close enough that dying would be a blessing."

Heat bloomed from Nadia's chest, radiating into her limbs. "And?"

"And... I don't know. He knows you did it. He begged me to ask you to lift it. The curse." Milena shook her head, chuckling. "It sounds insane, but I know you did it. I know you somehow put a curse on Karo and now he's bleeding his life away."

Nadia took a step forward, placing a hand on Milena's hip. The other woman's eyelids fluttered at the sudden contact, sucking a soft breath into suddenly starved lungs. Her cheeks flushed.

"If you're asking me to, I'll do it," Nadia said.

"I know." Milena's lips reflexively reached for Nadia's.

"And?" Nadia whispered into Milena's mouth.

"And I'm only a messenger." Milena's hands went up and around Nadia's head, pulling her into the kiss. Nadia pulled Milena close, relishing the small grunt of surprise she made. When they parted, Nadia nodded. "I'll think about it."

"Can I talk you out of going to China's?"

"Tempting, but this is something I have to do. For Angie."

"I guess this was good timing, then." She reluctantly disengaged, fetching a small bag from her purse, and extracting a ring from it. She handed it over. "I got this for you."

The ring was silver, a tiny snake to coil around Nadia's finger. Its eyes glittered black.

"I love it."

"I figured with the tattoos, and everything, you like snakes."

Nadia slipped it over the middle finger of her left hand and hugged her girlfriend. "Thank you."

"Call me when you're done."

Nadia drew Milena into an embrace. It felt final. She prayed it was not.

"I'll see you when I'm finished," Nadia said. *"Srtid mernem."*

"What was that?" Milena whispered in her ear.

"Armenian. It means, like, 'Let me die for your heart.'"

"That's lovely. I'd rather you didn't die."

Nadia kissed Milena's forehead. "She's not going to be there. I'll be fine."

The drive to China's was as easy as it ever got from Echo Park into Malibu. Nadia kept her mind on the task at hand. Get in, get out. She would head directly for the bathroom off of China's bedroom. She would find a hair, nail clippings, something to link the curse to China herself. It was around ten when Nadia rolled to a stop on the winding, coastal street. China's house was still a half mile away, but Nadia didn't want to have her car associated with it. She didn't want a trail.

She left her phone in the car. She wasn't going to use it inside, and if worst came to it, giving away her presence with a buzz. She grabbed her satchel, though, filled with her talismans and enough items to craft her curse if she so chose. As she hefted the bag, she felt Azh's comforting weight within, bestowing his antediluvian blessing on her agenda.

She got out of the car and used a narrow wooden staircase between some of the houses to make her way to the beach. It was not technically a private beach, but she knew the locals would hide behind private security and a neighborhood watch to make it that way. For a brown girl who looked like her, that could be dangerous in a white bread place. It was more dangerous, she thought, to be on the street. So she approached, keeping down to where the water could no longer reach the sand, doing her best to look like a beachcomber just passing through.

She was not bothered. She avoided glancing around as she made the hard turn toward China's house. She was not stopped with shouts or any security. The beach was deserted. A few lights beckoned from some of the houses, but China's, thankfully, was dark.

When Nadia reached the stairs around the side of China's place, she relaxed a bit. A screen of trees and bushes hid her from the neighbors. She went to China's window, leapt up, and pulled herself until her elbow was resting on the ledge, supporting her weight. She tried the window. It was locked.

She hadn't figured on being quite that lucky.

She dropped down and made her way around the back of the house. The wide deck was up on stilts, reachable from a wooden staircase. She went to the sliding glass door at the back quickly. She felt completely exposed, now silhouetted against the darkened sky.

The deck was so large she could have fit several copies of hers and Milena's house on it. Nadia had never realized just how much space she had taken up before. China's house was only a little larger than her parents' place, after all. And Jason Jennings owned properties all across the world; this was just his Malibu home.

Nadia was ready to test one of the sliding doors when she saw it was open. Not just unlocked, but open, a crack wide enough for someone with Nadia's slender frame to slither in.

Her eyes adjusted to the darkness. This was the same room she had hidden in to avoid China the last time. The space behind the couch was still there, a reminder of how close she'd been. Nadia had left as a fugitive, but she had returned as a conqueror.

She moved quickly down the hall toward China's bedroom. The bathroom was just off it. Find a hairbrush or even the shower drain, and she would be fine. The thought of pulling up a clog of China's weird slimy discharge turned her stomach, but there was a jar waiting for it in the satchel. Then go beneath the house and craft the curse, ready to plant in the cool sand below China's bedroom.

She paused, halfway down the hallway. She wasn't going to get another chance at this. She could attempt to return after the curse had done its work. Try to loot as much as she could, before the precious items vanished to wherever the possessions of the dead go. China's things would go to her father, but would he hang onto them or auction them off?

Nadia couldn't risk it. When she had someone like China at her mercy in this way, she had to exploit it. There would be talismans here somewhere. Something China had placed her skill, her trust, in. Something Nadia could use.

For what?

She ignored this voice. It mattered more to have talismans to use than a purpose to use them for. Find the talisman, and the purpose would present itself. She turned away from the bedroom, knowing she could return later, and began to look through the house. She thought she should be able to sniff this stuff out, and though when she held a talisman or was looking at it closely, she could tell it was special. She couldn't detect it like a dowsing rod.

Not yet anyway.

She considered this. Some sort of talisman detector would have been a useful thing to have with her now, but she had yet to create one. Soon she would, for later. There would be other times like this. Nadia knew that already.

Being in the home gave her nearly the same feeling as holding a talisman. Her skin was alive with a lovely tingle, the feeling of Milena blowing softly across her neck. It was power, being in this place she should not be. She was, in essence, taking it from the owner just by virtue of her presence.

Nadia went upstairs. The screening room felt to be an area of strength for China. Nadia shuddered as she looked at the screening room doors. Whatever went on behind them was plainly unnatural. A place for talismans.

Nadia looked down the airy hallway leading in either direction, harboring a dim hope there would be something there. Something calling to her as the obvious location of what she sought. There was not.

She opened the screening room door.

It was empty, dead without China and her husks, the site of a massacre after the bodies have been buried and the blood all washed away. The menace carried within was dormant, but ready to rise. Nadia made her way down the aisle between the seats, passing by the chair she had occupied briefly. She went to the door by the screen, listened, and opened it.

She did not scream. The sense of dread building in her the whole way had steeled her somewhat to the probabilities of what she would find. She had expected something; she had not expected this.

Angie's body, lying nude on a table. She was not the only one. Three others, two men and a woman, lay on a series of tables. The other woman was farthest from the door, Angie the closest. The tables were covered in white cloth, embroidery along the edges. The room was lit with colored neon along the walls in squiggled patterns. Each one had a collection of jewelry piled by their heads. For the men, it was a watch and perhaps a ring. For the two women, it was a slightly larger pile including necklaces, earrings, and bracelets.

Nadia did not want to believe Angie was dead. She did not look dead. Her skin was not discolored. There was no stench of decay. She looked perfectly healthy, her eyes open and staring sightlessly at the ceiling, and her chest motionless. She'll get up. She's just playing, her mind told her, knowing it was a lie. She needed reassurance, needed to know this wasn't her fault, needed to know her friend hadn't been killed.

As Nadia got closer, step by tiny step, she began to see the imperfections. Or, more accurately, the perfections. Angie no longer looked quite like herself. The shallow acne scars on her cheeks were smoothed over. The large mole on her arm, likewise gone. Her skin was hairless and plasticky, her eyes dry and glassy. She looked less like Angie and more like a high-end sex doll commissioned by some rich and disgusting admirer. Yet even that was a bad comparison, as Angie's vulva had been partially sealed by new skin, her nipples sinking into the matte flesh.

Nadia turned away, trying to hold down her gorge. She wanted to tell herself this could not be Angie. It really was some kind of doll. A prop, her mind said, supplying the word to make this all make sense. It was not. She knew this was the expression of what China had become, though it did not answer what that was.

And the worst, that brought chunks of burning food into Nadia's throat: Angie was power now. Angie's body was a talisman. Nadia turned away, blinking back tears. Not just for her friend, but because of the need in her to cut Angie apart. Use her. Nadia staggered back from the body, knowing if she was around it for too much longer, she would begin to harvest. Treat her friend the way China had. A collection of meat for her own purposes.

Nadia tried to focus on the nature of her enemy. Somehow China had done this to Angie—and the others, Nadia found as she investigated, no longer able to look at her friend. The men had also been changed, in both cases, their penises, scrotums, and nipples looked to be the process of being reabsorbed into their bodies.

Four people. China had killed four people.

More than four. These were just the ones she saved. Just the ones she killed after she knew what she was doing. When she had her methodology down. When she knew what she had to do, when she understood the sick requirements of her madness.

Without Nadia, there was no doubt China would continue. This room would be stacked to the ceiling. She would need a larger place to keep all her bodies. All to some unguessable purpose. Or were the bodies even the goal? Or mere mementos of another journey?

Nadia wondered what Jason Jennings thought about of his daughter's proclivities. She found it unlikely he knew nothing. He probably had an inkling, but turned a blind eye, and even had unofficially ceded this house to China. She was staying off the gossip sites with it, so it wasn't a problem. He couldn't understand what a monster she really was. Who could?

Nadia found herself standing by the corpse of the woman. She knew what she was doing before she did it. She wanted to leave, put her body on autopilot and go somewhere else while it happened. She could not. She needed to be there for this.

She placed an empty jar on the table next to the body. The jar used to have peanut butter, some artisanal hippie kind Milena preferred, and Nadia had washed off the label and cleaned the last dregs from it. She unscrewed it and paused. *Am I doing this?*

She unfolded the razor.

Yes.

She did not feel ill. Perhaps that was worst. She felt only the silver clarity in the mirrored blade. She leaned over the woman's head. She was pretty in a very normative way, one of those brunettes that stocked every casting room. Nadia bet she could look back and find this young woman's name in old gossip pieces, or perhaps as Coed #2 in some VOD comedy. She was probably a friend of China's from around the time of the accident. Helped the battered victim through trauma, and this was her reward.

Nadia cut around the young woman's eye with the razor. The skin separated bloodlessly. Nadia gouged the eye from the socket, slicing through the optic nerve with care. The eye was nearly the consistency of glass. Some give, but when she dropped it into the jar, it jingled.

She took the other eye from the woman, several fingers severed between the bone—these had a rubbery consistency. There was so much more to this woman. Her internal organs were treasures. There was no way to get at the heart with a mere razor and coming back wasn't possible.

Nadia screwed the top on the jar and held it up, letting the neon light flow over the two eyeballs and severed fingers. A grin pulled at her lips, and her stomach tried to turn inside out. She turned around, holding a hand over her mouth. A burning column of refuse worked its way up her throat. Her eyes watered. She forced herself to swallow. She felt like her insides were bleeding.

She put the jar with the others in the satchel, secure in Azh's powerful coils, and left the corpses where they were, unable to harvest more. She paused at Angie's head, unable to look at her friend for fear of what she might do. She reached over, and her hands blindly found the charm bracelet. There was no power in it, but Nadia took the rabbit from the chain, the first gift she had ever given Angie. Her friend was within the tiny slip of metal, a memory of a time when they had been close. I'm sorry, Angie, she thought. But you will be the last one China hurts.

Nadia's purpose called. Get the hair, get the nails, get something to link her curse with the doll-murderess. She left, pausing at the Blu-ray player, and hitting eject. An unadorned disc came out, but the way it tingled under her fingertips, she knew it was valuable. More talismans, no link yet.

Nadia made her way downstairs, ready to turn down the hallway and go to China's bathroom.

Until the front doorknob moved. Nadia barely had time to throw herself behind a wall—one of the free-standing semi-barriers separating the living area from the open kitchen and bar area—before the door opened. Nadia heard the clack of high heels on stone floors, followed by the scuffle of men's dress shoes. She didn't have to look to know China was home with the others.

There was no conversation. While the husks had little of interest to say, it didn't stop them from saying it. China was always surrounded by an aura of inane babble, some of it empty responses to something she said, the rest little more than filler. This time they were silent. So silent Nadia could hear them breathing, and she was certain they could hear her too. She tried to constrict her lungs, to make no sound as she breathed. Starved of air, she now wanted to suck in great, shuddering gasps.

She was helpless. For all she had in her satchel, there was nothing she could do with it now. China, with her husks, had as much power as she needed.

A metallic ticking sound echoed through the beach house. It took Nadia a moment to realize this was laughter: a smug chuckle reverberating from someone who never experienced mirth. China.

"You're here, aren't you?" China said into the house.

The only sound was her voice. The husks had to be completely still, likely waiting for her to give them an order.

"Yes. The false Devin is back. What would you want here? Do you want to be in the movies?" The awful ticking started up again. "I'll put you in the movies. I'll make you a star." She said this last as though she were quoting something, perhaps from some bitter memory.

"Are you going to come out, false Devin? Or are you going to make us look for you?"

Nadia watched her satchel twitch. The lip opened, and Azh slithered out of it, across the slick stone floor to gather himself into a pile.

"I suppose your silence is my answer." China's voice dropped, but with the echoes and the lack of any competing noise, she still made out most of it. China was placing her husks at the exits, hemming Nadia in.

Milena. Nadia thought of her not as a name, but as an impression. Every bit of her, the way she stroked Nadia's head when they were in bed together, the sound of her laugh when they watched television together, the taste of her at the moment of bliss. Every part of the wonderful creature, Milena Franco, and the paralyzing fear she would never see her again.

As the husks moved, scuffling across the floor, Nadia moved as well. She slinked through the kitchen area, leaving Azh behind—he knew what he was after—and toward the wing of the house she had never explored. Farther from China's bedroom and the probable location of the last portion of the curse.

Nadia slinked along the floor, below the counters, and into the hall beyond. The scent of chlorine found her here, bleeding up from another room. She caught a bit of movement in the house beyond, the husks moving into position. One was coming her way.

She watched him step into the place she had been, his blank eyes peering toward her present hiding place. Whether he saw anything was a mystery.

Azh struck.

The big rattlesnake gave no warning. He lashed out, his daggerlike fangs sinking into the husk's ankles and released. Then the dragon was slithering away, into a cabinet hanging slightly open. When the last bonelike rattle had vanished, he was likely gone, back to wherever he went when Nadia did not see him.

The husk dropped and convulsed, his face turning purple. His flailing limbs kicked the cabinet doors, rattling dishes and pots. China came running, trailed by two of her husks. One of them was Devin.

Nadia faded back into the dark, heading deeper into the hallway and leaving the kitchen behind. She found a gym with a wide window looking out onto the Pacific. Another room led to a sauna. A third opened into a lap pool, tiled in deep blue. There was only one other place a door to the outside could be, and she poked her head into the hallway, ready to find it.

Devin was in the hall.

She ducked back into the room with the lap pool and cursed. Had he seen her? She prayed that he hadn't, but there was no one to pray to. Her only option was helping herself. Spit another drink into his face, if such a thing would work a second time.

Devin's footsteps came down the hall. He hadn't called out. There was still hope. Hope for what, Nadia wasn't certain. The simple hope there had to be something of China somewhere in this house. Something to bring the malign energies of the curse to bear. Every moment she was not found was another she could search.

She held her breath as Devin approached. He did not slow, did not prepare to turn. He had to be going somewhere else.

She let the breath out just as he turned and caught her around the neck, one strong hand clamping her airways shut. He walked them both into the pool room and slammed her against the wall. She expected his eyes to be blank, but they were not. A tear shimmered in the corner of one of them.

Nadia reached for her razor, but her boot was too far away.

Black curled in from the edges of her vision. She felt her face ready to pop. Flashbulbs exploded in her brain, then winked out, one by one.

She fought the urge to claw at Devin's hand. He was much too strong, and she did not have the breath to fight such a losing battle. The black had already eaten up too much of her sight. She was looking at him down the end of a long, dark hallway. Every second and he was farther and farther away. The rush of her blood going tinny and quiet.

Her hand dipped into the satchel and closed around something circular and hard.

The DVD. China's movie. Nadia brought it up. She could barely see Devin's face anymore. He was miles away. Couldn't run to him. Not for ages, not with this vise closing her neck shut. She reached out and felt resistance, pushing back against her hand. Her hand? It felt like someone else's. Someone she scarcely knew.

She felt a shudder, a snap, and then she was released. She fell to the floor, slipped on the tiles, and landed hard on her ass. Air flooded into her tortured lungs. She looked up, still helpless, clutching at her brutalized neck.

Devin stood in front of her, faintly confused. The DVD had snapped in half, and now a crescent was buried in his eye. blood dripped from his face to the blue ties, along with a viscous, gelatinous liquid.

"She's here. She's in here." Devin was shouting, but there was no emotion, no pain behind his voice.

Nadia kicked, slamming her instep into his knee. Devin fell backward, and with a loud splash, disappeared momentarily under the acrid water of the lap pool.

It was too late; his warning had already been heard. The sounds of the other husks running filled the air. She was fucked, even worse than before.

Devin surfaced, his gasping the first remotely human thing he had done. She stared at him, barely registering what she saw on his sweater: a single blonde hair slithering across it like a snake, somehow still clinging to it after falling into the pool. Calling to her. It had to be China's. No one else got that close. Salvation, or dooming someone else, someone entirely innocent. Nadia was desperate enough. She crawled to the edge of the pool, reaching for him. Her muscles were screaming, begging for oxygen. Her throat was raw from the squeeze, protesting the breaths she needed. She snatched the hair from Devin's sweater, praying she would not lose it. So easy to go floating away. He grabbed for her, but she struck so fast, he was left groping for air.

Her hand flickered out a second time and tore the DVD from his eye. Devin made no sound. There was not a great spill of blood. There was hardly any at all. She thought of the corpses upstairs, of Angie dead on the slab, of the one she had mutilated. Now her throat burned again, agony flaring anew.

The husks were getting closer. China shouted behind them, ranting about something. The first of them burst into the room.

Nadia threw herself backward, scooting away across the tile. The husks slowed, now fanning out around the pool, hemming her in like pack hunters. China came into the room last. She looked down at Devin, standing in the pool. The stuff coming from his eye was almost like bloody saliva.

"What did you do?" she said to Nadia. "You took his eye."

Nadia did not respond. Couldn't. She was wrapping the bloody shard of the DVD in the single strand of hair. The bit of China's movie, Devin's blood, the act of violence, and the hair. It had to be enough. Had to call the power for her.

China looked up at Nadia for the first time. "You are a girl. Thought I'd imagined that," she said at last.

Nadia did not respond. She wrapped the hair over and over, getting it into Devin's blood. All around, the husks moved closer.

"I've seen you before," China decided. "I like your look. It's unconventional. So I'm giving you the chance to be in my movies." She nodded to herself. She wanted it, so shall it be.

Nadia wound the last of the hair around the shard.

The husks stopped.

"Go on, get her," China said. Then, louder, "Get. Her."

The husks turned on China. Their expressions did not change from the vacuous emptiness, nor did their postures tense. Yet, there was a chance. Even Devin emerged from the pool with the implacability of some ancient monster, awoken by humanity's hubris. His eye was gone, running down his cheek in two glabrous pieces on tears of blood.

He grabbed China's left arm. The other husks were upon her next. She screamed, fighting against them, but there were too many. They slipped on the slick tiles and tumbled into the pool. After that, there was little Nadia could see. It was a shark attack, frothy white water dyed red, a multitude of flailing limbs. It wasn't until she saw China's arm, the one Devin had grabbed, floating away from the rushing scrum, severed at the shoulder. Pulled off the woman like the limb of an insect.

Nadia stood, picking her razor off the floor where it had fallen. She watched for a few moments, then tossed the shard of DVD into the water. There was much to do, and it was spent.

She went through the house again, leaving the husks behind in the lap pool. She left the bodies behind the screening room alone. After China's awful death in the lap pool, she couldn't stomach more butchery. Dripping with chlorinated water, Nadia searched China's room, the screening room, and everywhere else she could think to find. She found talismans. China's makeup. A large collection of movies. More cameras. All of these went into the satchel until it was bulging and could carry no more.

Out of curiosity, she searched the bathroom. She found wads of hair in the drain along with more of the black sludge and plasticky nails in the garbage. More than enough. The toilet was coated in a translucent greenish-brown gel, the stench of burned rubber billowing from it.

She went to the back door, ready to leave, but paused.

Devin.

He had tried to kill her, and the thought made the finger-shaped bruises over her trachea throb. She couldn't swallow without agony, and breathing was still difficult. Devin had not tried to kill her. He was merely the weapon. China had wielded him. And according to Angie, Devin had been a good guy before China got her claws into him.

Nadia owed her friend. She returned to the lap pool.

The husks stood in the waist-deep water, staring at nothing, faces blank. Around them, the water was pink with China's blood, parts of her body bobbing like discarded pool toys.

Devin stood by one of the edges of the pool. The blood had washed from his face, and the eye socket was no longer bleeding. The plasticky flesh gaped.

"Devin?" Nadia said.

He turned. There was no recognition.

"Would you like me to take you home?"

"Sure," he said.

The others laughed, as though she had told a good joke, then fell silent.

"Come out of the pool, Devin."

He obeyed. With a little difficulty, she got him to follow her out onto the beach. The wind cut through her wet clothes. She shivered, hugging her thin body. Devin did not appear to notice the cold. When she got him in the car, she turned the heat up and drove into the city.

She realized she had no idea where he lived. "Where do you want to go, Devin?"

"Where you're going," he said.

So she brought him to Milena's. He walked around the side of the guest house, where the private yard was shielded from the main house. There he stopped and would not move. He looked, to Nadia, more or less happy.

She went inside, stripping off her damp clothes and joined Milena in bed. Milena let out a happy groan. "I was worried."

"Shh. Sleep now."

***

Milena was grateful to have Nadia back in one piece. The great, unexamined swaths of their relationship were troubling: Nadia had no job, she was dependent on her parents, and they somehow did not know their butch daughter was gay. Yet, for now, Milena could let it all go. What mattered was Nadia, and their time together.

She got up, leaving the peacefully slumbering Nadia in their bed. Their bed. Felt good to think of it in that way. She put on the coffee and used the bathroom. She wondered if she would get a full report of what Nadia had done the previous night or even if she wanted one. Nadia was mysterious, powerful, dangerous. Those three qualities helped flooded Milena's body with blood, and abruptly she wanted to awaken Nadia with the most intimate of kisses.

Until she registered the silhouette of a man standing just on the other side of the frosted glass window. She yelped and crept into the living room, looking for some kind of weapon, when Nadia came out of the bedroom, rubbing her eyes. "What?"

"There's a man outside," Milena hissed. "In the yard."

"That's Devin," Nadia said, yawning. Then she winced, touching her throat. It was discolored, dark and purple.

"Who the fuck is Devin?"

"Kind of a friend of a friend. Do you want to meet him?"

Milena pulled her robe tighter and retied the belt. Finally, she nodded. Nadia picked up a pair of boxer briefs from her drawer and wandered outside. "Nadia. You might want a shirt."

Nadia, paused just outside the doorway, looking in the direction of the bedroom, and Milena could see her mentally calculating the distance. Finally she shrugged and continued outside.

Milena followed.

Sure enough, a man stood by the side of the house, amongst a few California poppies and a large hibiscus bush.

"Devin, Milena, Milena, Devin."

The man, who was good looking in a very generic sort of way, turned. Milena put a hand over her mouth. One of his eyes was missing. It was an old wound, having long ago scarred over, and didn't appear to cause him any trouble. "It's a pleasure to meet you, Milena."

"Uh... likewise." She turned to Nadia. "What is this?"

Nadia's eyes were still heavily lidded, but Milena could see the whites had turned red. In the bright daylight, the hideous, hand-shaped bruise over Nadia's throat was a bright memory of violence. "Good god, what happened to you?"

"There was a fight," Nadia said, wincing. "Devin is... I owed Angie. So I brought him where he wanted to be."

"You know what? I don't care. You're safe." Milena drew Nadia into her arms. Devin stared in their direction, but it was through them. He didn't seem to know they were there. Milena brought Nadia inside. Over the next few months, she got used to the man-shaped silhouette outside.

Even as it started to change.

Mercy

In the month since China Jennings was torn apart in her lap pool, life had returned to normal. The bruise around Nadia's neck had faded away and it no longer hurt to swallow. The whites of her eyes had returned to being white, though a small smudge of brown persisted, making the iris of her right eye look larger than the left. And Devin Kassir was still standing in his place outside the window.

A housekeeper had found the grisly scene at the Jennings house. The tabloids made a meal of it. A fixture in the Hollywood social scene murdered in such a bizarre fashion in her own home. Five members of her entourage were arrested for the crime and were presently awaiting trial. The sixth was dead in the kitchen of an apparent rattlesnake bite. The seventh was still at large, though he hadn't been found. He never would be.

The police also found realistic dolls in the basement used for some kind of sex games. One had been mutilated in a particularly odd way. When Nadia heard this detail, the guilt stabbed her, and her attention went to the jar of leavings. All four of the sex dolls were nearly exact copies of existing missing persons. Some of the articles mentioned the names of the missing and asked for any news about them, unaware that the missing had been found. Nadia wished she could explain to Silvia Alcala what had happened to Angie, but that would be impossible. The woman never would get closure on her daughter, because closure was too weird, too awful in this case.

Nadia wondered what had been done with the bodies. Had they been retained as evidence or disposed of? Was Angie's transformed corpse in a landfill or burned in an unintentional mass cremation or waiting in police storage to bolster a case that would never be tried? Nadia did her best not to think of it, but more than one night she awoke from a dream in which she was in the white room again, Angie, burning, sitting up, and beginning to speak. Before Angie could get a recognizable word from her rubbery lips, Nadia snapped to wakefulness.

No one had connected Nadia Eskandarian to China at all. She had been to China's house for a party, but so had half of Los Angeles. There were far more pressing suspects, she imagined, including even her superstar father, mourning very obviously around town. If a cop came in, and identified the things on Nadia's table of talismans, he would know he found the real murderer.

Nadia had to live with the term. No matter what she would do with the rest of her life, she was a murderer. What about Karo? her mind liked to point out. No proof he's dead, and besides, that was self-defense. No such excuses for China. It had been revenge all the way, executed with a cold brutality Nadia hadn't known lurked within her. No matter what else she did in her life, whatever appellations she earned, murderer would always be one of them.

Had she always been this way, or was this something imparted to her by the change? Had the Simcoe Killer slimed off onto her soul, transforming her into this ruthless machine?

She was living in the aftermath of it. Her happy ending. Angie avenged, and China dead. The final step was interring Angie in the only way she knew how. The only way Angie ever would be. Nadia was not certain she believed in anything like a soul, but she knew people could make a mark upon the world persisting after death. Regardless, the funeral was for her. She needed to say goodbye to Angie.

She went to their secret place in the middle of the day. The snakes were everywhere when she arrived, piles of scales and rattles, ready to strike. None of them twitched as Nadia stepped between them, clutching the rabbit charm in her fist. She stopped in front of Azh, who waited in a coil beneath a large elderberry tree. He slithered away as she approached, and she dug a shallow hole in the earth with her hands.

"Angie, I wish I could have done more for you. I know I let you down, and I'd give anything to go back and change things. I hope you know, if you're still anywhere, I hope you know what I did to China Jennings. You were my friend, and that's a powerful and special thing. Thank you for being better to me than I could be to you."

She brushed the dirt over the rabbit charm and stood, her throat abruptly tight, tears stinging her eyes. She went inside and fetched a glass of water. The house where she had grown up felt alien now. There was nothing of Milena in it, so it could not truly be home. This was the mundane domicile of Nadia before her change. Before her becoming.

She heard the front door open, and the beep of someone entering the security code.

"Hi, I'm here," she called out to avoid scaring whoever it was.

"Nadia?" It was Siranush. She came into the room, her hair and nails glowing from the salon. "What are you doing here?"

"I just wanted to pick some things up."

"You don't have to move out of your room. We have enough space."

"I know, I just needed some stuff."

"Nadia, I've been wanting to talk to you. I don't know if you think it is because we pay your bills, but if you want, I can take you shopping. We can get your hair done so you don't look like... whatever this is."

"I like the way I look, mom."

"The tattoos... they can remove those now. Don't worry. It will take some time. I don't know what you were thinking trying to look like a lizard."

"Snake, mom."

"Lizard, snake. You'll regret it soon."

"Yeah, I can't wait."

"Expensive to do. Just throwing your money away. Our money away." Siranush shook her head. "You are so pretty. Skinny, maybe, and flat-chested, but the models are flat-chested and no one cares. If you just wore some makeup and grew your hair..."

As soon as Siranush launched into it, Nadia was already chugging her water, and putting the empty glass in the sink. "No offense, mom, but you're kind of the last person I want to be pretty for."

"Don't be disgusting, Nadia," Siranush snapped, following her daughter to the door.

"Goodbye, mom."

They hugged, but it was fragile, and Nadia returned home, trying to forget the awkwardness of the visit. It happened every time she went to see her parents, as though the universe knew. It wasn't just her mother, either. A child on the street asking their parents if Nadia was a boy or girl, a confused look from an old person, the dance of recognition as a straight person realized she was a woman. This was Hollywood, supposedly a place comfortable with someone like her, and this was where she felt it the most.

The best revenge was living well, she supposed, and she was doing that. She lived with her gorgeous girlfriend in their own house. On the Saturday morning a month after China's death, they were in the midst of having a lazy breakfast before Milena got ready for her evening shift, and Nadia went to hunt the city for more talismans.

When her phone buzzed and she saw her brother's name on the caller ID, she was shocked. "I'm in the neighborhood. Mind if I stop by?"

She'd said yes numbly. She was not frightened about Lex, but she was not looking forward to word getting back to her parents she was living with a woman. She couldn't help but think this was Siranush sending him on some kind of half-assed spy mission after the confrontation the other day. They had not cut her off, and though Nadia's pride made her almost wish they would, she was a realist. If they knew, they would cease supporting her, and she would get to find out how much her master's degree was truly worth.

"M? My brother's coming over."

Milena was making breakfast, filling the small house with savory scents. "Should I make him something? I'm not sure we have enough."

The milk had been going bad very quickly. The refrigerator seemed to be functioning normally, but within hours of putting food in, it changed. Milk turned. Vegetables sprouted. Meat spoiled. Neither Milena nor Nadia talked about it other than to remark on the waste, but Nadia knew the truth. It was her. Whatever forces she tapped in had put some aura around her.

"I think he's fine." Nadia tried to keep the tension out of her voice. No need to get Milena nervous. A few minutes later, a knock sounded at the door, and Nadia's "I'll get it" sounded hideously fake to her.

She opened the door to her brother. He broke into a broad grin and hugged her. "You move out then you never see me again?"

She muttered something into her brother's chest. He loosened the grip and she coughed. "Come over to give me mom's guilt trip?"

"Nah, I just miss my little sis is all." He left the part about Odette unspoken, but she heard it in the faint melancholy of the word "sis."

Milena stepped into the doorway, holding her hand out. "Hi, I'm Milena."

"Lex." He released Nadia and shook Milena's hand.

"We were just about to have breakfast. I could make you something or—"

"I ate. If there's coffee, though."

"There's coffee."

Milena turned around and went back into the kitchen. Lex nudged Nadia with his elbow. She looked up at him and saw he was grinning down at her. "Nice," he said.

She gaped while Lex followed Milena to the kitchen counter. He climbed onto the stool and Milena poured him a cup. They started talking like old friends, and Nadia could not quite believe what she was watching. Her brother didn't make a single crass comment. It dawned on her that he was treating Milena like one of his friends' girlfriends.

She took a seat next to her brother, and the three of them had a pleasant morning. When it came time for Lex to leave, Nadia walked him out to the driveway.

"Hey Lex, if you could—"

"Not tell mom and dad you're gay? Yeah, no problem."

"How did you know?"

"C'mon, Shorty. I'm not stupid."

"No. No, you're not. Sorry I thought you were."

"It's fine. I like your lady. She taking good care of you?"

"I think so."

"Okay. Then I'm happy. Now don't wait so long to talk to me, okay?"

"Yeah, yeah. And mom and dad?"

"Get to hear you're living alone." He paused. "What's with the tats?"

She shrugged. "I just like them is all."

"It's a change," he said.

"Good change?"

"You tell me."

Lex gave her a kiss and left. Nadia sighed. Both in relief for having Lex, and the fact he never noticed Devin. Nadia went around the corner to check on the other man. He was standing where she had left him. A chalky, barky substance had grown over his feet and up to his ankles. He did not respond to her, though he looked more or less content. She left him to his place.

***

Nadia was at Midway, sitting in what she had come to think of as her seat. It was there when she wanted it, and for as long as she saw fit to keep it. Milena was in doing her fortuneteller thing, while Nadia enjoyed a drink with Keegan and another friend, Lincoln. Lincoln did the geek act under the stage name Missing Linc. He could eat anything he liked, though light bulbs were the usual showstoppers. He popped them between his teeth like oversized grapes, crunched the glass between his large, flat teeth, and gulped it all down. He was an oddly-built man, with a great round belly, but powerful and bowed arms and legs. He cultivated wild hair and a thick beard to help with the savage image. Old sailor tattoos covered his body and massive gauges distended his earlobes.

He looked scary, and occasionally he would use it, but he was as gentle as a lamb.

Lincoln had just finished a set, where he had eaten a string of Christmas lights, half a bicycle, and a license plate. He should have looked at least mildly queasy, but he was as content as a Buddha statue. Keegan was waiting for Bekah to arrive so they could go onstage, fully dressed in her saloon girl outfit she would strip out of as cloth was replaced with stapled money. Her bra featured a pair of elephants, their trunks intertwined between her small breasts in a bow. While they waited, the three of them were enjoying their free drinks and good conversation.

Keegan was in the midst of a rant about Bekah's chronic lateness, when Nadia heard a tentative murmur behind her. "Excuse me. Nadia?"

She turned around in the stool and instantly stiffened. She had a flash of the speaker, standing by the mouth of an alley while Karo brought his foot down on her leg, then blinding pain. She must have gasped.

Lincoln slid off his stool. The goon was a head taller than him, but Linc wasn't afraid. "Can we help you with something?"

"I'm here to talk to Nadia."

Linc looked to Nadia. She nodded. "So talk," she said to the goon in Armenian.

The goon did not react, though there was fear in his eyes. He responded in Armenian. "Karo Minasian sent me."

She fought to keep the fear from her posture. If this had been a hit, it would have been more subtle than this. "What does Karo want?"

He reached into his coat and withdrew a piece of paper. He held it between forefinger and thumb, like it was something disgusting. "This is for you."

Nadia accepted it. One corner looked to have been dipped in wine. No, blood. She looked up to talk to him, but he was moving back through the crowd. She was fairly certain it would be the last she would see of him. Probably the last Karo would see of him as well. She opened up the paper, and found it was a note, written in Armenian and spotted with blood.

Nadia. I am sorry for what I did. Please come to my house so I can apologize in person. I will do whatever you want. Just take this curse off of me. I will pay you any amount. I will give you anything. Please.

She stared through the note. Milena had mentioned Karo wanted to see her and she had ignored it. But that was before China. Before she saw how far she could go.

"Is that blood?" Linc asked.

"Sure as shit that's blood," came Keegan's expert opinion.

Nadia started and folded up the note. She had briefly forgotten her friends where there. "Yeah, it's blood."

"What does it say?"

"Who sends a note covered in blood?" Linc wanted to know.

"I've sent bloody notes."

"Other than people like us."

"Gangsters," Nadia said.

They both stared. "I thought he looked like a gangster. I didn't think he was one," Linc managed.

"I need to go," Nadia said, sliding from her stool.

"You sure?"

"Yeah. Don't worry about me. I'll be fine."

She hoped she was correct. If not, those would be very brave words for her friends to remember her by. She drove to Karo's house. Perhaps he had suffered enough. She wondered if it really was for her to decide, but apparently it was. She was the one with the power to both start and stop his pain, so it was in her. He had suffered enough then, she decided. It was time to set him free.

She would make him grovel first. Make him promise everything she wanted. He was a gangster. There was little honor to be had in his word, but she would find honor in his fear.

Nadia arrived at the gate and buzzed the intercom. "Hello?" Karo's voice was weak, diminished. She was suddenly smiling.

"It's Nadia Eskandarian."

"Nadia! Thank you for coming!" He was excited, but his voice was still pathetically weak. The gate opened.

She went to the door and found it open. The sounds of hobbling approached, and Karo appeared at the top of the stairs, leaning heavily on a wooden cane. The handle was carved into the shape of a sitting chimpanzee.

The once-powerful mafioso was a skeleton with a little skin on it. She could see his arteries pumping blood through his wasted frame. His skin was pockmarked with scars and with fresh sores, weeping blood creamy with pus. More stains were scattered around the house, on the walls and floors. He had bled a great deal of his life away.

What have I done? she thought. *What could I do?*

When Nadia had created her curse, she hadn't been certain it would work. Deep in her bones, she doubted, thinking it was a flight of fancy, granting her power she never would have. Looking at Karo Minasian, she saw what she was capable of. China had been a desperation tactic, a one time orgy of violence. This had stolen a man's health, had given him over to a lingering death.

He hobbled down the stairs and met her in the front hall. A sore on his cheek dribbled with pinkish pus. "Nadia, thank you for coming. Bless you, sweet mother, bless you." He had switched to Armenian. Nadia wondered if he did it consciously, or if the desperation had caused him to revert to their mother tongue.

"You're welcome," she responded in Armenian.

"Please, I was wrong to hurt you. I understand that now. I was stupid. I was weak. I've learned what you were kind enough to teach me. Please, lift your curse, and you will never have to see me again."

He was broken. Mad too, probably. The desperate gleam in his eyes was that of a loyal slave trying to keep the master from beating him. Knowing he had little to no way to stop it should the whim take her.

Nadia would not do it yet. Not without hearing the words.

"And?"

He was ready. "Milena's debt is forgiven. I'll pay you too. Name your price. Anything you want, if I can pay, I will give it. You want cars? A house? You want my club?"

"Forgive Milena's debt, and we never see you again."

"Done! Thank you, bless you! May God give you all his blessings. May God give you everything you want!"

Nadia held a hand up.

"Is it off?" he asked, desperate, eager.

"No. I have to get the hex jar. I buried it by the side of your house."

His countenance darkened for a moment. A flash of rage hinting this would not be over when he said it would. "By my house?"

"Yes," she said, challenging him to say something else.

The anger vanished, and he was back to his toadying. "Then let's go. Go! Please!"

Nadia went out the front door. She heard Karo hobbling after her on his cane. She found the spot, knelt by the dirt, and began to dig. She would never forget where she buried the jar and she had not buried it deep. Yet it was not there. She dug another hole. Then another. Maybe it was closer to the corner. Maybe she was remembering wrong. She wasn't. It was gone.

"Are you done? Is it finished?"

Nadia turned, still on her knees, hands filthy to the wrists. "It's not there." The hex jar had vanished. She wanted to think it had been dug up by a gardener. Thrown out in confusion. She knew the truth. The curse itself had consumed it. Gone from its physical representation to the force rotting Karo to the bone.

"It's not there? What's not there?"

"The curse. The physical part. The hex jar. It's gone."

"That's good, right?"

Nadia stood, brushing the dirt from her hands. "I can't help you."

"What?"

She said it again.

Karo's face went slack. The words wormed into him. Then, his face shriveled in rage. "You can't help me? You can't help me?"

The curse was out. Once she released it, there was no way to take it back. It was a vicious beast she had taken off the leash and it would destroy who she set it on. No matter how much she wanted to chain it up, it would not vanish until it had taken the life it had been charged to.

"I'm sorry," she said.

This was enough for Karo. He lunged. The curse had made him weak and slow, and he was nothing compared to China Jennings and her husks. The razor was in Nadia's hand, blade flipped open. She stepped away as he reached for her, opening his right wrist. Karo howled, the blood dropping from his veins as though it had been waiting. Anything to get out of the diseased body.

"You can't go! You can't leave me like this!"

She strode to the gate as he called her every filthy name he could think of, in Armenian, English, and even in Spanish. Nadia stepped through, and turned once, fixing him with a gaze halfway between contempt and pity. He was clutching his wrist and had fallen to his knees. "Goodbye, Karo," she said.

Karo Minasian was found dead on the floor of his front room a few days later. The coroner blamed it on the disease ravaging his wasted body. Nadia found the obituary tucked in a corner of the *LA Times* website.

The curse had been lifted.

***

Hernán Gaff only remembered bits and pieces of his old life. The pain of his transformation had been far too great. Pain, though, that heralded the other great changes in him. Now, pain was a distant memory, a sensation he could never again recapture. He missed it from time to time, occasionally trying to find new ways to bring it back to himself.

Every such attempt had failed.

Immunity to pain had enabled him to sculpt his body into perfection. Though he missed the joy of agony, he did not miss what it had done to him. He no longer wanted to remember the tiny, weak, and dying man he had been.

This was not to say he was pleased with she who had changed him. She had not intended to produce what she had. She was merely testing limits. What she found in Gaff was what lay beyond. How much a body could take before it was no longer precisely human. Before it was better.

His only regret was that he had not had the chance to kill his creator. He would have done it slowly, paid her back for what she visited on him. Not too slow, though. He wanted her to die, not to reshape her the way she had done. He still savored the crime scene pictures Dagmar had shown him. The twisted metal, the fluids spilled over the blacktop.

He trusted she had felt at least a fraction of the terror and agony he had.

Now he existed in a similar state. His mind no longer quite functioned. He saw things through a caul. Even his vision was smudged by the glass sealing off his eye sockets. When Dagmar was not giving him his new tasks, he comforted himself with the even clack of his weights, like a glass heartbeat. Waiting for his next order, the task he would be set upon. He owed Dagmar everything.

***

"So, you decided to shave your head?" Zach asked, the ink gun buzzing.

"Mmm hmm." Nadia was lying. Her hair had been steadily falling out for months. It was gone now, including her eyebrows. She had started to replace those with piercings, giving her the full range of expression again. Keegan had volunteered to do those, drawing on a wealth of experience for simple body modification.

"Any particular reason?"

"I was looking to have you continue the line from my back all the way up over my head."

Zach didn't pause from his work on her right arm. The serpents there were nearly finished. "I can do that."

Zach's work had been beyond good. Her scales gave the sense of motion, of the diamond-clad snakes sliding over one another. Her true skin had been revealed and was continuing to be so. When this was finished, she might not be Nadia sapiens, but she would look like her.

Of this she was certain.

"Nadia?" Zach's voice was suddenly tentative, the buzzing of the tattoo gun falling silent.

"What's up?" She paused, watching the emotions war on his face. "It's all right. You can tell me."

"Not telling, so much as asking. This is just hard to say, you know? Even with someone I know doesn't judge or think I'm weird." He took a deep breath. "I don't have medical insurance. You probably worked that out. I was on my parents', but when I started my transition, that went away. I've been getting my T okay, but there's a problem."

"What kind of problem?"

Zach shrugged. "The surgery. If I'm going to transition all the way, it costs like five to eight grand. That's money I don't have. Money I don't know I'll ever have. And... I know I'm not going to feel right in my own skin until I do."

"Shit."

"And I was thinking you could do something." Zach's eyes were clear.

"What do you think I can do?"

"I don't know exactly. Something. Come on, Nadia... I know you have something up your scaly sleeves."

She had to smile at that. "Do you trust me?"

Zach nodded, too quickly.

"Wait. I'm asking because I'm going to request some strange things, and you have to figure out a way to get them."

"Strange things like what?"

"Well, for one thing, one of your clownfish."

He frowned. "Okay."

"And I need an old picture of you. Childhood. Preferably with long hair and a dress. Can you get one of those?"

"My parents have a ton. They loved their daughter. Not the biggest fans of their son."

"But can you get one?"

"I think so."

"Call me when you have it."

"Nadia? What are you going to do?"

"I'm going to turn you inside out."

***

Dagmar thought about her new toy Richard quite often. When her period came, she stayed indoors, certain he would seek her out. She spent a good deal of time on the small balcony outside her bedroom window, peering into the wooded parts of her expansive backyard. She could not be certain if she was right or wrong, but she swore she saw blond movement. She thought of telling Gaff to do something, but then what? One or both of her tools would be killed. If it really was Vorspan and not her overheated brain playing tricks, better to let him prowl around out there.

When it came harvest time, she drove to the psychiatric hospital. She didn't bother to make an appointment, trusting Vorspan to remember the standing one. She was correct. The side door was open, and Vorspan was outside, nervously smoking and pacing in short, stuttering steps.

She parked and strode out past him, her shoes clicking on the asphalt. "Hello, Richard," she said. "I thought you quit."

Vorspan stubbed the cigarette out self-consciously. "I am. I mean, I did." He opened the door for her and followed her in.

Dagmar did not speak to Vorspan on the way to the basement level. She had nothing to say and preferred to let him stew in his own cowardice. It was sweeter that way. They didn't even speak when they arrived at their destination; an unmarked door in the maximum security section of the hospital.

Vorspan unlocked this and opened it for Dagmar.

Stella Mortimer was bound to the cot. The restraints were largely ornamental, not that Dagmar told Richard this. The true restraints were the lines of Stella's own hair, straightened and tied around her wrists. Small bulbs, taken from flashlights, lined the inner parts of the restraints within the fleece, secured with torn sections of bandanna. This hex was the reason Stella Mortimer could not get out. Otherwise, she would have already disappeared like a ghost.

In the beginning of her confinement, Stella had glared at Dagmar. Then, the bound woman's eyes had changed. They were black now, covered in points of light like stars. In them, Dagmar could see the boundless hatred of the universe. An idea so inimical to life it could only be in the eyes of the Angel of Death.

Now, Stella didn't acknowledge her captor. She stared up at the ceiling where the cobwebs had taken root. On the strands of inky darkness, the spiders scuttled around. Never catching anything except each other, savage cannibalism their only form of sustenance.

Dagmar knelt, and looked under the bed. The largest of the spiders lurked there, some the side of her fist. She caught some of these. They always fought, tried to bite her with their black fangs, but they were helpless. She collected as many as she thought she would need, putting each in its own wooden box.

She stood up and looked down at Stella. There was no pity in Dagmar for the killer. She had become the perfect source of talismans. Finally, her life had some meaning.

***

Stella Mortimer felt Dagmar come and go. Like everything else, it occurred in a dreamlike haze. Whereas once Dagmar had been a figure of incandescent hate, and every one of Stella's conscious moments had revolved around her plans for vengeance, now she was just another ghost who came and went at will.

It was as though Dagmar were already dead. Already part of the legion Stella had sent to the other side in the process of her becoming.

Stella had no way of knowing how long she had spent in Dagmar's web. The only way to reckon time was the price it took on the faces of Dagmar and her little doctor. Dagmar's skin grew tighter, her hair shorter, the lines in her face deeper. She was holding time at bay far better than the doctor, whose body looked as though it were in the process of systemic organ failure. Stella felt a distant and predatory pity for the man. She would kill him, but the true torments would belong to Dagmar.

The truth of it, though, was that anger no longer truly motivated Stella. At one time it had been rage against the theft of her freedom, the burning shame of having been beaten by the witch. Now it had been replaced by a bone deep need. Stella needed to kill. The victim scarcely mattered, and in her nights of hunting, she had been quite free with her choices.

The act of killing was what mattered. What separated her from human.

At least the powers were still there. She felt them in her tissues. When her body first gave up its claim on solidity, it felt as though her arms had been submerged in water, albeit water that was both cool and dry. After that, she was formed of pure night. Night could go wherever it liked.

Until Dagmar, the witch, had found a way to imprison the night. Stella had grown up with the stories of local witches. The women who could take care of a pregnancy you didn't want. Who would make a wayward man come home spilling regrets. Who could keep another kind of man from raising a hand to anyone or anything. She'd never believed. Not truly.

Then this white woman, the picture of the bloodless aristocracy, had all of nature dancing to her whims.

Stella moved her right hand. The cuff was looser here, the bulbs cracked and faded. It was not off her wrist, but it wouldn't stay on forever. She no longer felt the need to smile, but the sensation was similar. The night could be imprisoned, but it could not be locked away forever. Stella Mortimer would be free.

***

Nadia checked on Devin. When he first arrived, she checked on him daily. Then it was every other day. Now it was closer to weekly. He didn't need anything, and he still hadn't moved. The white bark-like substance had grown over his feet and now reached his knees. His clothing was filthy and damp from the sprinklers the main house insisted on using on the dense garden in the back.

Mushrooms had started to grow on his feet.

The empty eye socket never bled, and Devin still maintained the same beatific expression he'd had when she found him.

"Devin?"

"Yes?"

"Do you want to go home?"

"I don't understand."

She said the words almost like ritual. He would offer no other responses. Odds were he couldn't. Anything more was entirely beyond him. She thought this was all there was for Devin, but he was safe, and apparently content.

Nadia knelt on the ground and picked the mushrooms. They were whitish, speckled with green. Poisonous, she imagined, and definitely talismans. A full jar of them sat on her desk already, between the jar of fingers and eyes, and the berries. Nadia had as many mushrooms as she would ever need. Milena had asked a few questions when she saw the fingers, and Nadia answered them as best she could. Milena had seemed to believe her.

Nadia went back inside, placing the half-full jar next to the others. Her collection had grown large. Yet not large enough. She saw them in her mind's eye dwindling away with every use. She had scarcely used them, but she needed more. From somewhere.

Milena reclined on the couch, engrossed in Nadia's old copy of *The World for World is Forest*. Milena had embraced LeGuin on Nadia's recommendation and was plowing through the complete collection. When she was finished, Nadia wanted to start her on Tiptree.

Nadia went into the kitchen for some water when her phone buzzed.

Zach. *I got it.*

OK, Nadia texted back. *I'm on my way.*

"What's up?" Milena asked, the book open across her chest.

"Zach. I'm helping him."

"Good." Milena picked the book back up and continued to read. Nadia gathered her things, a jar of each. She had a vague idea of what she would use but wanted everything on hand. Zach was important, and this was important for him. A final transformation he was entrusting to her.

Zach let her into his apartment. He was small, nervous, like he was about to touch a new girlfriend. "Here," he said almost immediately, holding out a photo, eager to get it out of his hands.

Nadia took it, and could not stop herself from looking, though it felt disrespectful. She was viewing Zach through the lens his parents had placed upon him, a mask he had never wanted. The little girl in the photo looked very much like Zach, baring her teeth in a feral smile.

Zach hugged his body. He was shirtless, and Nadia thought there was something defiant in the act. Her eyes went to the scars under his pecs, the removal of his most obviously feminine traits. He had decorated the scars with detailed tattoos, a pair of moray eels gliding over his chest. Like his other work, they glistened with life.

"Are you ready?" she asked.

"I was born ready," he said, then barked a short and brittle laugh. "What are you going to do exactly?"

"I'm going to finish the change in you. Unless..." Her gaze went involuntarily to the bulge in his pants.

Zach followed her eyes, reached into his pants, and pulled out a rubber cock, complete with a set of balls. "This is, you know, for appearances. I can piss through it, though."

"What?"

"Yeah, it's called a Peecock."

Nadia snorted, then chuckled, then laughed. After a moment, Zach joined her. "Holy shit, that's genius," Nadia gasped.

"It kind of is."

"Let's get started then."

Nadia went into the kitchen and put her satchel on the counter. She removed the jar of mushrooms. Change, considering what happened to Devin. Then there was the shape of the mushroom itself; she couldn't help but attach significance to that. Everything was important. Everything mattered.

"Do you have any T left?"

"A little bit."

"Could you get it?"

"Nadia, it's—"

"When we're finished, you won't need it."

Zach slowly nodded. "Okay. All right." He returned from the bathroom with a syringe and a nearly empty bottle, putting them both on the counter. Nadia went through the cupboards until she found a metal bowl and a knife with a heavy handle.

Nadia put a few mushrooms into the bowl, opened the bottle and dumped the testosterone over them. Zach made a little noise of dismay. "Now I need some of your blood."

"What?"

She opened the razor. It glittered in the yellow light of the kitchen. "Not much, but I need your blood to tell this where to go."

She could see the thought process on Zach's face. He'd already come this far. She took his hand in hers and he winced.

"Does it have to be my palm?"

"Yes. Sorry."

He nodded. "Okay. Do it."

She drew the razor over his palm lightly. The blade parted his flesh with barely any resistance. He hissed, his hand quivering as she held it in place over the bowl. Fat drops of blood, dark and starving for oxygen, pattered into the bowl. When she thought she had enough, she released his hand. Zach cradled it against his chest. Absently, she removed a first aid kit from her satchel and slid it over to him.

"Last, I need one of your clownfish."

"What are you going to do with it?"

"Kill it."

"Nadia, this gets worse and—"

"There's no change without sacrifice. I'm sorry, but I'll make it quick." She didn't tell him what would be done with the fish after it was dead.

A moment later, he returned from the front room holding a blue aquarium net out. Inside, the white and orange fish flopped and struggled against its doom. Nadia nodded to the bowl, and Zach dumped the fish inside.

He turned away as she killed it with a stroke of the knife. A dry heave wracked him when he heard the crack of bones. She was mashing everything up, the clownfish, the testosterone, the blood, and the mushrooms, forming a thin offal. She thought it should turn her stomach, but it didn't. She saw only the change forming inside it, the engine ready to power her desires.

She held the bowl out to Zach. "Eat."

"You've got to be fucking kidding me."

"I'm not. Eat."

"If this is the world's most elaborate practical joke…"

"It's not and you know it's not. You called me here because you already know, on some level, what I can do. Now you're seeing it. Eat."

Zach ate, gagging with each finger he scraped along the bowl and brought to his mouth. He ate until the bowl itself was clean, then retched, holding his stomach. Nothing came back up.

"Now, give it time," Nadia told him.

***

A week had gone by since the hex for Zach. Nadia and Milena were home together, each absorbed in a book. Milena stretched over the couch, her feet in Nadia's lap, while Nadia leaned back, occasionally sipping from her beer. Her phone buzzed. She frowned, pulling it from her pocket. The frown deepened when she saw the caller ID.

Dagmar Eichel.

Who calls anymore? was Nadia's first thought. The second was about Dagmar. The other one like her. After it had been so long since they'd met, Nadia thought they were finished with one another. They knew of each other, and that was all it would ever be, content to dwell in their own ponds.

Until this moment.

Nadia answered the phone, thinking it must be a prank. "Hello?"

"Hello, this is Dagmar Eichel. Am I speaking to Nadia?"

"This is she," Nadia said, and winced when she realized that was a line she got from her mother.

"Nadia, it's lovely to hear your voice. I was hoping you would be available to have dinner sometime."

"Uh, sure?"

"Wonderful! Please do bring your lovely girlfriend. Are you still seeing Miss Franco?"

"Yes?"

"Oh, delightful." Dagmar made plans with them for that weekend, inviting them both to her home. When Nadia ended the call, Milena was staring at her. "What? You look like you just burped up a moth."

"That was Dagmar Eichel."

"Oh?" Milena's voice was high, a caricature of unconcern.

"Yeah, she invited us for dinner at her place. It sounded like a dinner party."

"Dinner party?"

"Yeah, like... formal."

"Do you own anything formal?"

"I had a prom dress."

Milena burst out laughing. "A prom dress? I can't imagine you in anything like that."

"Yeah, me neither. It was sort of the last gasp of fitting in. My mom would have had an aneurysm if I'd come downstairs in a tux."

"I cannot tell you how hot you'd look in a tux. We're going shopping."

Milena dressed them both. For herself, she picked one of her '30s style gowns, jade, with black and white striped stockings. She pinned her rich, curly hair up beneath a pearled snood. For Nadia, they found a three piece suit, fitted and pinstriped. She refused the hat but agreed when Milena suggested a pocket watch. Along with a new pair of shoes, it was perfect. Nadia looked at the both of them in the mirror the night they were to leave.

"We look... elegant," Nadia said with amazement.

"Good. That's what I was going for."

Nadia liked the suit. It felt much more like her, even down to the navy blue tie. As night fell, they drove to the west side, Milena's GPS guiding them to the right spot. Dagmar lived in ritzy Brentwood, in an odd geometric house looming out of the thick trees. The two of them approached the front door, and Nadia did her best not to betray the fear bubbling in her belly. This could be some kind of trap. She did not want to fight anyone, though she was ready for it. Her razor was in the breast pocket of her jacket, and she carried a tiny jar of pool water in her pants pocket.

Milena knocked on the door. It opened a few moments later, revealing Dagmar on the other side. The older woman never looked less than incredible. Her effortless grace was intimidating, even to Nadia. While the overtly feminine aspects did not impress her, Dagmar's unconscious predatory nature did. Dagmar was used to being in charge, and she projected that with every word, every gesture, every look.

"Nadia and Milena. Thank you so much for accepting my invitation." She leaned in to both for a slight kiss on the cheek. "Please, come in. Follow me to the dining room."

They stepped into the foyer. The house was warmly lit, and the hints of savory scents on the air drew them in. They passed down a hall and through a doorway. Nadia was not precisely certain what she was looking at was tasteful or not. She thought it must be. Her family had always been fans of ostentatious displays of wealth, but in a very clean way. Light, immaculate colors were markers of money. Here, everything was stained wood, and paintings, and knickknacks. The table in the dining room looked like something that should have knights lined up on either side. Silver candelabras blazed on its surface. Empty plates and folded napkins waited for diners.

French doors opened up onto a balcony, the heavy drapes drawn back to let in the glittering cityscape. A small, jittery man sipping from a glass of white wine stood by the window. His hair was mostly white, as was his thick beard. He wore a pair of wire-framed glasses.

He looked pale and drawn, perhaps like he had just lost a good deal of weight, as his suit hung off him in lank folds.

"Nadia, Milena, this is my friend, Dr. Richard Vorspan. Richard, these are Nadia Eskandarian and Milena Franco."

The little man started and plastered a strained smile on his face. "How do you do?" he managed.

"Hi," Nadia said, shaking his hand. He was wearing a thick silver bracelet, fitted snugly against his bony wrist, an odd affectation.

Dagmar went to the bar and filled two wine glasses, bringing them to Nadia and Milena. Nadia didn't have the energy to explain that all white wine tasted like vinegar to her. She sipped it and put on her best face. The question still lingered in the air.

"Thank you for coming," Dagmar was saying. "I thought it had been too long since we'd met."

"I thought you had forgotten about me," Nadia said.

"Oh no," Dagmar said, completely missing Nadia's teasing. "I've been rather busy. I imagine it has been the same for you."

"A bit," Nadia said, shrugging. She was not going to go into her battles against Karo or China.

"We can change that. I think our association with one another could be mutually advantageous. I also think we could be great friends, the three of us."

Vorspan did not speak, and he was only barely aware of the conversation at all. He certainly missed the fact that he was not included amongst "the three of us."

"Were you thinking of... trading?" Nadia blurted the final word out, unsure of how to phrase it.

Dagmar laughed like the tinkling of chimes. "It had crossed my mind. I'm pleased it's on yours as well. For the time being, I wanted to enjoy the company of one who is almost me."

The clang made Nadia jump. Vorspan had shaken so violently, his ring had hit the glass, sending out a clear, sharp note, and sloshing the bulk of his wine on the carpet. He muttered an apology.

"Shame to waste good wine," Dagmar said, taking the glass from him. "Although it appears Nadia does not like hers?"

"I'm more of a whiskey drinker."

"Why didn't you say so? I have a lovely selection. I was planning to dip into them after dinner, along with the cigars, if you've a mind for them."

Nadia raised an eyebrow. The gold jewelry through it jingled. "I can wait."

"Let me get you a red then. White is not to everyone's taste."

Dagmar served dinner shortly thereafter. She was an incredible cook, easily the equal of any one of the better restaurants in town. The conversation was light, and Vorspan continued to offer nothing. Nadia was content to eat Dagmar's food and see what she wanted. Throughout the meal the candle flames danced, pulling toward Dagmar and Nadia at turns.

***

Gaff watched the entire meal from hiding. Sitting by the bank of security monitors, he could stand sentry over the whole property. On a normal night, he would be checking the outdoor feeds for the dim movement of a mountain lion in the deep brush. Tonight, the lion was inside, and wearing his false skin. Gaff felt certain he would kill Vorspan before long, but for now, he was Dagmar's toy.

The dinner ended and adjourned onto the balcony. The women had cocktails, and Gaff saw the faint listing in all of their postures that said they were drunk. Soon, they were puffing on fat cigars, taking in the night. Vorspan had not moved from the dining room, sipping his wine.

At one point, Milena went inside, heading for the rest room. Dagmar followed shortly thereafter. Gaff did not bother to track them. He was more concerned with Nadia.

As certain as he was that he would kill Vorspan, he was equally sure he would be called upon for one or both of Nadia or Milena. He only wondered which.

*** *

Milena emerged from the bathroom. She was pleasantly buzzed and surprised at how much she was enjoying the evening. Even the cigars were a satisfying counterpoint to the liquor. She knew she was going to have to wash the smoke out of her hair, but that could wait for now. She was hoping she could find her way back out to the balcony.

Dagmar stepped out into the hallway. "There you are," she said. Her voice was low, nearly a purr.

Milena felt a tightening through her body, a familiar syrupy feeling throughout her. She grinned, and before she could stop herself, said, "Here I am."

Dagmar crossed the short distance, and Milena was acutely aware of two things. The first was that her girlfriend was waiting out on the balcony. The second was that Dagmar's dress hugged every inch of her. Milena's fingers tingled with the urge to touch the other woman.

"I am so pleased you could come as well. I know Nadia and I have far more in common, but you... you're a fascinating woman, Milena."

"Thank you." *Walk away,* her rational mind screamed at her. *You don't need this. She's right in the other room. And that shouldn't even matter.*

"You will have to tell me someday how you discovered your power."

Milena swallowed. "I will."

"Good." Dagmar rested a light hand on Milena's hip. "I look forward to it."

Milena nodded. Now. Done. Walk away. But she couldn't.

Dagmar leaned forward and placed a soft kiss on Milena's mouth. Only the light brush of a gentle tongue over Milena's lips. Then Dagmar withdrew. "I think we should rejoin Nadia."

Dagmar led the way while Milena mentally chastised herself. *What the hell am I doing?*

***

It was late into the night when Nadia and Milena finally left. The dishes were undisturbed on the table, holding the remains of the meal. Dagmar would investigate them fully before removing them, as this had been the entire purpose of the party.

She sat in Nadia's seat, looking over the plate, the napkin, the chair. Next she would go out to the balcony, where they had been drinking and smoking.

Gaff walked in. Now he had the run of the house, after Vorspan had been tucked away in the locked room. He wasn't due for a transformation, but Dagmar would not take chances. Gaff looked over the room and settled on Dagmar.

"What are you doing?" he asked. His curiosity could be childlike.

"There is not a single hair here."

"Hair?"

"She shaved her head. I had not been expecting that. She also has no eyebrows or eyelashes." Dagmar shook her head. "Perhaps it is some kind of fashion statement."

"I don't understand."

Dagmar looked up at her servant. The ghostlike flesh of Gaff's upper body rippled and bunched over his prodigious muscles. "Hair, from Nadia."

"You wish to curse her?"

"Oh no. But one does not enter into associations with dangerous people without assurances. If she were smarter, she would be doing the same with me right now." Dagmar let out a low chuckle. "It would be far easier for her. I have hair." And eyebrows, and eyelashes, and so on.

"What about her cups? Her saliva?"

"If she were someone else, perhaps. If I wanted a little curse to hound her for a day. If I wanted to inconvenience her. These connections will fade quickly and be gone. I need something to stay with me."

"Hair," Gaff said, running a hand over his bald cranium. She could practically read the thoughts on his face.

She got up, smiling, and went to him, one of her hands stroking his flat belly. She stopped at the glass growing from it, to worry around the edges. "Yes, this is why you are beyond my power."

Gaff shook his head. "Don't tease. You have far more hold over me."

Dagmar patted the cool, dry flesh. "You've always been loyal."

"And I always will be."

Now, if only I could catch Milena Franco so thoroughly.

Knowledge

Nadia sat on Dagmar's balcony, enjoying a cocktail. Dagmar reclined next to her, large sunglasses hiding her eyes and an expanse of her cheekbones. The two of them looked out over the city, pausing their conversation only long enough for sips.

In the weeks since the dinner party, she and Dagmar had been seeing more of each other. They had been primarily social calls, though every now and again, they would talk shop. Today, though, Dagmar was explaining. Everything.

"I call them the Matchless," she said.

She was referring to those people Nadia had already found, those like China Jennings and the Simcoe Killer. Dagmar had found her own as well, spoken of in generalities, no doubt as cagey as Nadia about her sources. They were artists and killers, makers of things and breakers of ideas.

"I had nothing to call them. I knew they were out there, I knew they could do things."

"They start out as humans, but they make themselves into something greater. Genius, insanity, both are ingredients. Something, perhaps, in the middle that doesn't yet have a name. The Matchless harness this and change themselves. Their change projects a wake, like a boat moving through the water. Those people, places, things, the wake touches, those things important to the Matchless and her journey, these become repositories for the same power that changes them. Like your cards, so on."

Other than the terminology, Nadia had come to the same conclusions. "Have you met many of them?"

"One or two. I've read about more. Once you begin to recognize the patterns, you can find others, in the past, through careful research and the like. It is very rare to actually catch one in the wild."

"Why so?"

"The curse of the Matchless. What they do upsets the natural order, and the human mind can't take it. They go mad by any sensible definition of the word and destroy themselves. Oftentimes they take quite a lot of others with them. In many cases, they don't even want to hurt anyone, but can't help it. All of those around them suffer."

Dagmar took a long drink. Nadia did not speak. She wanted the other woman to come to it on her own. "The Shadowed are the most changed."

Nadia thought of the berries. Not as powerful as the pond water, but stronger than the cards, a place in the middle. Created on the spot where the Simcoe Killer's victims were laid out on the killing ground. "What changes them?"

"The Matchless, caught in that wake I referred to earlier. Most of the time it is unintentional. A side effect of the personal transformation. This will, or madness, or what-have-you, boils over. Or perhaps it is something like physics. Every action having an equal and opposite reaction, and so on. You cannot change one person without changing another in as dramatic, yet opposite, way. But since you're dealing with supernature rather than nature, the reaction can seem mad. The Shadowed burn themselves out even quicker than the Matchless, because they do not have the willpower to function in their new transformed state. The Matchless might not have been consciously trying to become something else, but they were, in their way, prepared. The Shadowed are victims."

"They also make talismans."

"Indeed they do, but not as powerful as the ones from the Matchless."

"And the Kissed?"

"Like your Milena." Nadia did not like the emphasis Dagmar put on "your," but allowed it to pass. "Some kind of connection with the Matchless changes them. It is not so dramatic as the Shadowed. Their abilities are relatively minor, though they still produce talismans. The Kissed are valuable to us because they are by far the most stable. They can be harvested with very little risk and are much less likely to self-destruct. Sadly, their talismans are also the weakest."

Dagmar took a sip of her drink, then fixed Nadia with a look she felt even through the sunglasses. "You are harvesting your Milena, are you not?"

"Yes." Her voice was tight.

"Good. I would be worried if you were not."

"Do you have Kissed you're harvesting?"

"Kissed? No."

Nadia caught the humor there but did not ask for elaboration. She sensed she was getting everything she was going to get. She thought of Zach, who had been tattooing her real skin over her for quite some time, a work now finished. She had not seen him since the hex to bring his true shape out. She wondered if he were in his apartment, inside a cocoon, ready to emerge.

Regardless, a tattooist who put the real skin on a Matchless would be changed, and Zach's tattoos were far more vibrant than they had any right to be. She had already felt the power humming within the tattoo gun.

"Are we Matchless?" Nadia asked, knowing the answer.

"No." Dagmar's answer was quick, and definite. Nadia allowed it to lie.

"And our curses?"

"What about them?

"I found the formula. The power, the effect, the target."

"I guessed you had," Dagmar said, nodding. "The one thing to be aware of is that it is never a perfect formula. Because something worked once is no guarantee it will work again. In fact, I have noticed a sort of... backlash if you try the same trick too many times."

"Backlash?"

"The world does not like you. Food will spoil in your presence. Mirrors will show the wrong reflections. And stay away from pregnant people or animals. The result can be... unpleasant."

Nadia didn't ask for elaboration. Instead, she returned to another idea. "The hex changes based on the Matchless who gives the power."

"Good, good," Dagmar said, the smile in her voice. "Yes, talismans have their own desires, based on the being who brought them into existence. Due to the nature of the Matchless, it is far easier to harm than it is to heal."

"And what about gods?"

"Who needs them? I suspect gods, or loa, or spirits, were Matchless or Shadowed or Kissed originally. They gained a cult and have persisted. I have yet to see anything to disabuse me of this notion. And there were always legends about people like us, who harness the power of the spirit world for our own ends."

"I suppose there were." Nadia sipped her drink. The liquor was sweet on the way down. "And souls?"

"I don't know. I have never seen one. I've never seen any evidence of consciousness after death. Matchless and their ilk often leave talismans behind at the site of their deaths, but there is never any sign their minds linger. Emotions, certainly. These stay on even from normal humans. The items they produce can be used in curses as well, though not to power them."

"What do you mean?"

"Imagine a handkerchief a mother cried into upon hearing about the death of her child."

Nadia's heart leapt and she was momentarily horrified at her instinctive reaction. "I can see how that would be valuable."

"For the effect, to borrow your term. It would not power anything, but it could help tell the hex what it was to become. Any location with strong emotions can produce this sort of thing. A mass grave, a hospital, and so on. Many carry associations with death as this is the shortest route to strong feelings."

"It just needs to carry the correct association."

"And a strong enough one, yes. Depending on what you're trying to do."

"How do you find Matchless?"

"They find us. We are like magnets to one another. They are not common, but they are out there, and we inevitably cross paths. Some of this is because you will come to know the signs. You will sniff them out. Some of this is because we move in similar circles. They hear the same rumors and find them just as tantalizing as you."

"How many have you found?"

"Living? Three of them."

"Are they still alive?"

Dagmar paused. She swallowed and glanced to the other side of the balcony. When she spoke again, she was quiet. "One."

Nadia felt the moment of trust for what it was and mentally pledged not to follow up with more invasive questions. Instead, she merely nodded and continued to listen to Dagmar. Their alliance might be a fragile one, but it was strengthening.

***

That night, when Nadia was up at the Jellyfish Pool, Dagmar's words were with her. Nadia's skin was dry and tight from the day in the heat, now mercifully bare against the night sky. She looked more and more like a desert reptile, with only parts of her torso and head unmarked by the tattooist's needle. Azh slithered beside her, once again in his original domain.

She noticed, with some dread, there were no more berries. They had not been replenished. There were plenty at her home, bright and red as they day they were picked, but the harvest was done.

She thought of what Dagmar had said about harvesting. She thought of China, torn apart in her lap pool. If China had been kept alive, she could have produced an unlimited amount of talismans.

If.

The price was the pile of plastic corpses growing in China's macabre trophy room. China was far too dangerous, far too unstable to last long. And besides, she had it coming for what she did to Angie.

Nadia was left with Milena and Devin as renewable resources. As Devin's clothing rotted off him, more of his skin was covered in the white bark. The mushrooms bloomed across him with greater frequency. Milena altered whatever deck of cards she used, though the longer she used a deck the stronger it became. These were two resources, a Kissed and a Shadowed (Nadia guessed) for use.

They're also people, she reminded herself. In these moments, when she was alone with her talismans, it was hard to think of them that way. They were means to an end—not even an end, but a pathway. Power itself was the end, but there was no end to power.

She padded across the patio, her bare feet light on the stone. The dim rush of the city came up over the hills, but the loudest sound was the faint thudthud thudthud thudthud of her heart. She found her satchel where she left it by the side of the pool. A few jars, already filled with pool water, were among the bunched folds of the satchel. She squatted by it and placed the empty jars that had been for the berries next to them.

It was sheer luck she saw the movement.

The shape was so large, for a moment, her mind did not recognize it. A coyote, she thought, one of the night's choir who sang through the hills. Too big. A muscular streak of blond in the dark of the patio.

It was a mountain lion, hunched over, its green eyes focused on her, its prey. The drought-desiccated yellow of the leaves hid its coat nearly perfectly. It slinked along the edge of the patio, moving out from the side of the pool.

Nadia rocked back on her heels, careful not to move more than necessary. The lion continued to stalk, unconcerned that its prey was now entirely aware of its imminent demise. Her heart was louder now, beating a terrified tattoo in her ears. She would not show fear. Soon as she did, the creature would charge, cover the short distance in seconds, unsheathing white teeth and black claws.

Without breaking eye contact with the monster, she reached for the folds of canvas of her open satchel. Her fingers played along the surface and curled around a tube. China's lipstick, a shimmery pink, the color of shuddering femininity.

She unscrewed it, the wet finger of pink extending. The act of opening lipstick, even in such a desperate context, felt wrong to her.

The mountain lion charged. She had seen the precise motions on a house cat, loping from cover to savage a toy, but now she was the toy, and the cat was almost one hundred fifty pounds of killing muscle.

Nadia scraped the lipstick over the bricks in a circle, only big enough for her. She snatched her satchel from the outside and stood, dropping the now spent talisman. The tube clattered across the brick and rolled away.

The lion broke off, the charge turning, the massive creature now pacing, staring at its naked prey. It sniffed the air, pacing, never getting closer than a few yards from Nadia. The creature wore a radio collar around its neck; a wild animal marked and owned by humanity.

She realized she was clutching her satchel in front of her naked body. A weak posture, suited for a surprised woman out of the shower. She was the queen of this place, baptized by the dragon. She would act like it. She set the satchel down by her feet, and stood before the mountain lion, wearing only the wind.

The mountain lion hissed, then hopped up, holding its paw off the ground. It took a step, stumbled, then crashed to the earth. A snake uncoiled, its brownish diamonds perfectly hidden on the patio's bricks, and slithered farther onto the patio, only to gather itself up in strong spirals.

Snakes covered the patio, unseen before, but now were everywhere, from the edge of the bricks to the burned out manor house. As one, they rattled, the sound growing louder and louder, reverberating off the hills behind to spill out over the city. Piles of scales, oily in the moonlight, the arrow-shaped heads tracking the dying mountain lion. The cat struggled, yowling in pain, slowly succumbing to the venom pumping through its veins.

Nadia stepped from the circle, and as soon as her bare foot touched the bricks, the rattles stopped. The snakes were silent and still for a moment, and then they uncoiled. There was only the faint hiss of their scales rubbing together as they moved toward the edge of the patio. Nadia walked past them, her bare legs marked with the same diamonds. The snakes let her pass.

She butchered the mountain lion as best she could with her razor. A killer, destroyed by her snakes. And they were hers. She took its eyes, its claws and teeth, a swatch of its fur. When she stood, Azh slithered past. He was huge now, the monster she had seen the first time she beheld him. He opened his mouth, and she thought she could fit perfectly on the cotton-white flesh. Azh began the process of swallowing the mountain lion, and Nadia left him to it.

She found her clothing at the top of the stairs where she had undressed. Above her, the dragon continued his meal.

***

"Nadia. It worked. It fucking worked." The voice was familiar, though without his name and picture on the caller ID, she might have asked who it was.

"Zach?"

"Come over. We have a lot to celebrate."

Nadia headed over to Zach's apartment, and he let her in at the first knock. The differences were astounding. He was still recognizably Zach, with the same kind face and slender proportions, but he had changed in striking, subtle ways. Reddish stubble covered his chin. His shoulders were broader, hips narrower, his jaw a touch squarer. He was even a couple inches taller.

"It worked!" The unabashed glee in his voice made Nadia smile. When he talked, a new Adam's apple bobbed up and down.

"I'm glad to hear it."

"No, you don't understand, Nadia." He began to unbuckle his pants.

"Let me stop you right there."

"Nadia, I fucking... I have a dick. Do you understand what I'm saying?"

"I do. I'm happy for you. I'm just good with not actually seeing it. Besides, I can see the other changes from here."

"Oh shit, I've been having to replace my wardrobe. Thank god for Goodwill."

"Sorry about that."

"Are you kidding? It's awesome. But seriously, I gotta get out of here, or I'm going to jerk this cock right the fuck off my body. Do you know how awesome it is to masturbate right?"

"Yes. Although I don't have the same context."

He burst out laughing and went in for a hug. She held him, and after a moment of stillness, his shoulders began to shake. She parted, and he was rubbing the tears from his eyes.

"You okay?"

"I'm better than okay, Nadia. I'm me. I'm fucking me!"

"Yeah, you are."

"Thank you. Anything you need, ever. I'll cover you in snakeskin."

She rubbed her bald head, picturing the strips of scales she wanted coming up and over her from her spine to her head. "Thank you. I'm going to take you up on it. There's something else I want."

"Anything."

"Your tattoo gun."

"You want to make tattoos?"

"No. I want the gun you use. Every couple of months, I want the one you've been using."

He frowned. "Why?"

"I'm changing you, Zach. You make power from your existence. It will bleed into the tools of your trade. Those things most important to you."

"Yes. Of course. It's all yours. But first, I need to go outside as me with my friend and buy her all the drinks."

"Fuck that. Where we're going, we drink for free."

Milena was at the Midway, and that was good enough for Nadia. Zach had been there once or twice before. He had developed a bit of a crush on Bekah, but had been too shy to ask her out, despite her obviously throwing more than a few signals his way.

Nadia and Zach found a place at the bar, then moved to a table as their group grew and grew. At first, it was just the two of them. Then Linc, fresh off his show, joined them, knocking back his first zombie of the evening. He lit up when he found out Zach was a tattooist, and practically exploded when he learned Zach had made Nadia's snakeskin.

"Holy shit, that's you? I'm due for some touch-ups." Linc was dressed in his usual costume of a simple loincloth—according to Keegan, getting Linc to wear anything more was a challenge—and he showed Zach his copious collection of ink.

Zach, eyes already a bit glassy from his drinks, looked them over. "Happy to."

Soon afterwards, Keegan and Bekah joined them from the show. Bekah was flirting pretty hard with Zach, though it looked like he might miss it all. Then Dave went on break and headed over to the table for another drink. Finally, Milena, on a break from her game, turned the corner and burst out laughing as she saw the drunken revelry.

Whenever Linc needed a new drink, Zach finished the rest of his and ordered another.

Eventually he did tell them while they were celebrating, and they all wanted to have a look. Bekah dragged him into the bathroom and they returned five minutes later, both looking extremely pleased with themselves. After that, Zach's arm was around the elephant girl.

Nadia raised a glass to Zach. He looked like he could barely believe his luck. Nadia wanted to stay with the revelry, but her mind kept wandering. She wanted to do some research online, to see if any of the rumors she heard would lead her to another Matchless. Her belly bubbled with the thought of it, the illicit thrill of a new drug.

She was almost ready to stand up, to make some kind of excuse when she heard, "Nadia Eskandarian?"

The voice was not threatening. It was, in fact, friendly. It belonged to a heavyset man with a close-cropped beard and shaved head. He wore a tailored suit, fashionably tight over his husky frame. His olive skin, dark brown eyes, and black hair implied he was Armenian. A friend of Karo's most likely. Conversation at the table stopped, and six pairs of eyes went to the new arrival.

Nadia tensed. "Who's asking?"

"My name is Savak Krikorian. Sav," he said, holding his hands out where she could see them. A gold ring glittered on one pudgy pinkie. "I'm sorry to interrupt your party. I'm not here to start anything."

"What do you want?"

"I was hoping we could have a word over drinks."

"You're not my type." Nadia put a hand on Milena's thigh.

"Nothing like that, either. Please, I promise, on my honor, you have nothing to worry about from me."

"She's got nothing to worry about in here," Linc said.

Sav held up his pudgy hands. "Believe me. I am not here to hurt or threaten."

A few scars on his face said he'd fought, but they were all old. Nadia had a feeling of danger from him, though not directed at her. Finally, she said, "All right. One drink."

"You sure, Nadia?" Linc asked.

"Linc, if you'd come along please."

"No problem," he said, cracking his lumpy knuckles.

Sav gave Linc a worried glance but did not comment on it. "Thank you. Really," Sav said.

Nadia led him half a room away to a small, semi-private booth. Here Nadia and Linc were the normal ones, and it was Sav, in his stylish suit and manicured appearance, that drew the distrusting looks. The Midway was Nadia's place of power, Sav was going to have to talk to her on her terms. He squeezed himself on the other side of the booth, while Linc stayed standing, looming close by. Dave brought Nadia a fresh Sazerac and took a beer order from Sav. Even the small act of getting Nadia her usual drink showed Sav where she stood in this place.

Sav was keeping Linc in his peripheral vision, slightly distracted and off guard by the strange man. Good.

"Do you mind if we speak Armenian?" Sav asked her.

"Go ahead."

They switched tracks on language. Neither of them had an accent in English, and both could hear their American roots in their ancestral tongue. "You've guessed I'm one of Karo Minasian's associates."

"A gangster."

Sav opened his mouth, reconsidered, and said, "Yes," with a small smile.

"Then why aren't you here to kill me?"

"Because I am not a stupid man."

Dave returned with a full pint of beer and a fresh cocktail. He paused long enough for Nadia to give him a slight nod, and only then did he move off. Milena and Keegan were watching from across the room as well. Nadia was as safe as she could possibly be.

"You didn't like Karo."

Sav shrugged, nodding a thank you to the waitress. "Not especially, though this is hardly a factor in my decision. Would you like to hear a story?"

"Sure," Nadia said. She had not relaxed, but Sav still hadn't done anything overtly hostile. She saw no one else like him in the crowd, but they could be out there hiding. In a blink, she saw Karo's foot coming down on her leg, the blinding crack of her bone. She covered the momentary wince with a sip of her drink. No one would do that to her. Never again.

"A few months ago, I start hearing rumors. Karo Minasian is sick. Sick how? I want to know, but no one can tell me. No one has seen Karo in weeks, or maybe it is months. He was fine, he was earning. Everyone was happy. So I start looking around, and eventually I find his man, Hakop. We call him Jack. You know Jack. Large man, always at Karo's side."

Nadia got a flash of the man standing against the side of the alley while Karo broke her leg. Then another flash of the same man looking diminished and terrified, handing her a note. She nodded.

"And from Jack, I hear about a girl. She is a small thing. Skin and bones, he says. Not much hair on her head, and Armenian like us. She wanted to talk to Karo about one of his girls, an escort and fortuneteller who works at a bar in Hollywood. Karo hurts her."

Sav looked at his beer, as though he could see Karo within it. "A little while later, Karo develops a sore on his cheek. Weeping. Blood and pus. And this is when he tells Jack this is not the first one."

Sav shuddered and drank.

"There were more after that. They bled Karo's life from him, one disgusting hole at a time. Jack told me he could barely stand to look at Karo, and he loves... loved... that man like a brother. Karo says he offended a witch, so she placed a curse on him."

Sav was silent now, waiting.

"Yes."

"Then you confirm this? You killed Karo Minasian?"

Nadia tensed. The razor was in her boot. She could get it with a reach. Linc was right there, and a word would have his freaky strong arms on Sav. Dave was close too, in the middle of one of his fire-eating routines. Azh might be around as well, somewhere hidden in the bottom of her satchel. Sometimes he was there, sometimes not.

She thought of Sav trying violence on her, and she was surprised to find she hoped he would. *Try it in this place. See what happens. See what I do to you.*

"Yes," she told him.

Sav merely nodded, sipping his beer. "This is why I don't want to kill you."

"I don't understand." Relief, but also disappointment, flooded her.

"You did this to Karo because he didn't do what you wished. He kept his escort. He broke your leg. You showed him the price of such arrogance. I don't know how you did what you did, but you placed a curse on Karo, and it killed him. There were some of Karo's associates who thought to take you to task for what you did. I tried to speak to them reasonably. To kill you would, at best, kill you."

"And I'm too valuable."

"Your friendship is too valuable," Sav clarified. "Revenge killing is only good for business when it prevents others from murdering your employees. In this case, who would believe a witch placed a curse on us? No, they would think we were insane."

Now Nadia relaxed, taking a deep drink. "But you believe. I can see it in your eyes."

Sav's eyes widened for a split second, the first crack in his cool façade. "Yes."

"What do you want from my friendship?"

"I want you to make me bulletproof," he said, tapping the center of his forehead.

Nadia frowned. Her mind was already forming the necessary hex without her consciously working on it. This was becoming second nature. "I would need some of your blood, preferably shed by a bullet. And some bullets as well."

"And your price?"

"Fifty thousand. And a few bullets dug out of a dead man's brain."

Sav broke into a broad grin and raised his glass. "Done."

***

Dagmar was at home, flipping through a paperback without much interest when her phone buzzed on the table next to her. She picked it up. Richard Vorspan calling.

"Richard. What can I do for you?"

"She's escaped."

The words he said were the ones she had never imagined would ever be spoken. Her trap had been too perfect. Her cage had been unbreakable. There was no way out. Disbelief, though, did not dull the blade of chilled fear running through her heart.

She raged at him through the phone. He had to be involved. That foolish conscience of his. There was no way for her to get out. No possible way. The hexes were ironclad. Reinforced with mundane security. Stella Mortimer could scarcely move, let alone escape. Vorspan kept insisting, even as his voice quavered in naked terror, that she had escaped. She was gone.

This was all Dagmar needed before she was running to her car and speeding to the hospital. She didn't even check on Gaff, but it was Gaff she was most worried about. She had escaped. She was running loose. The deception could be laid bare. Gaff would know, and his rage would be boundless. Gaff was more dangerous than Mortimer. Rage was one thing, but betrayal cut so much closer to the bone.

She found Vorspan outside, pacing. The sun was setting, and though he was not due to transform, Dagmar felt a little thrill at the sight of him. Vorspan might be a broken man in the daytime, but for several nights each month, he was the perfect killer. All due to her. She should not be frightened of this escape, not when she could work such terrible wonders. But she was, and she could not control it. Perhaps salvation lived within Vorspan. Send one perfect killer to catch the other.

She got out of her car and strode across the parking lot. She projected her unflappable aura, even as she was screaming inside. "How?" was all she said.

"I don't know!" Vorspan nodded, the fight against total panic on his face. "She's not in her room. She's out!"

"You did something to her bonds. You forgot the chemical restraints. You broke one of the lines of hair, one of the light bulbs."

"No, I swear. I kept everything up. Except..."

"Except what, Richard?"

"Except when you had me. When I was in the... room. When you... changed me."

Dagmar swallowed. Had she really caused this? She took Stella's jailer away, and those moments of lucidity when Vorspan wasn't filling her veins with opiates could have been enough. No, the wards were still in place. Still as strong as she could have made them. The mundane stuff was just for back up.

"What do you know then?" she snapped, covering her sudden guilt with annoyance.

"I checked on her today, and the room was empty."

"Show me."

"Miss Eichel... we need to get ready. She's going to start killing again, and it's not much of a guess to figure out where she's going to start."

"What would you have us do, Richard? Call the police? I am certain they would be very interested in how we've been keeping her for fifteen years." She left the rest of her sneering response unspoken. The police would be helpless against Stella Mortimer. Her time in captivity had only sunk her deeper into madness, and as she had descended, so too had she continued to change. When Dagmar had caught her, Stella had already been far too powerful for any mortal to deal with. Now she was something else.

"We could hire someone. Bounty hunters. Mercenaries. Private contractors!"

"You're being hysterical," she said. Vorspan's panic would normally help calm her, but not now. She kept searching his face for a sign of change. Of his beard going from gray to blond, or his eyes from brown to green. Dagmar measured the distance to the car and to the door of the hospital. If he changed, could she make it inside? His form was holding steady.

"I'm not hysterical! I'm reacting rationally to the fact that Stella Mortimer is free!" He hissed her name, as though that would keep it from the ears of an eavesdropper.

"I caught her once," Dagmar snarled. "Now show me her room, Richard. I don't want to ask again."

The threat brought him back down. *That's right. Fear me more than you fear her*, Dagmar thought at him. In his fear, she would find some sort of comfort.

Vorspan nodded, opened up the back door with his key, and led the way down. The back hallways of the hospital were empty, quiet. Stella's escape had done more than take her, it had deadened the prison on top of her. It was a foolish thought, but Dagmar had it regardless.

Vorpsan unlocked the door to Stella's room carelessly. "See for yourself," he said.

She almost wanted to explain to him what she was actually doing, to cut his snotty tone off at the base. She didn't; there was no need to explain oneself to one's subordinates.

She stepped into the room and saw immediately that Vorspan was right. Stella Mortimer was gone. The cot was still there, and the restraints were still buckled, as though she had turned to smoke suddenly. A few of the shadow spiders cavorted in the dark places, those Dagmar had not yet harvested. She made a mental note to get them later—as soon as possible—as her finest source of talismans had just vanished.

A flare of rage nearly made her stand and put a palm across Vorspan's face. How could he be so stupid? She could not know how Stella got out, but the responsibility lay with him somehow. Even if it had been when she took him, she had only done that because of his ill-conceived rebellion. His foolishness had released a dangerous enemy into the wild, but worse, it diminished her stores of power.

No, she needed to solve this mystery in the simplest way. She needed to find something of Stella, something to link her. Fifteen years, and she had all of Stella she could have wanted. Hair, urine, blood, skin, fingernails. She had taken none of it, because she never had to target Stella with anything. She had been inexcusably arrogant.

Dagmar could not send Gaff after her, which was unfortunate. Gaff might be able to take her alive, but he would never forgive the fact that she was alive. No, she would be sending her cat after him. Vorspan, quaking and shivering, would be the one to bring the corpse back to her. She hoped there would be enough left to use.

There was nothing. She thought of Nadia's frequent visits to her home. Every time, she hoped for something. Hair, skin, blood. She left needles in Nadia's napkins, in the hopes she would prick herself. Thus far, the other witch had been careful.

Now too with Stella Mortimer. She'd had a wild mass of kinky hair, yet there was not a single strand on the pillow. There had been injections, and in the early days of incarceration, self-harm, but there was no blood. Even the cot had no real link to Stella—it seemed the Matchless had never formed the slightest emotional attachment to it, either positive or negative. It had merely been there and had never grown sympathetic to its occupant.

The spiders were no link either, produced by Stella's own changes. They were of her, yet no way to anchor a curse. Using them in such a manner would cause the hex to explode.

Dagmar stood, fear and anger warring for supremacy. How had she left nothing? Stella had been changing through her life. Had she managed to complete the last phase of it? Emerge from her pupa into her final form? Dagmar shivered. If she had, then there was no wonder she escaped, no wonder she had left nothing behind.

Dagmar emerged from the cell. Vorspan's face was pale, ghastly. She had a second, stronger urge to slap him. "You see? She's gone!" He sounded almost triumphant.

"I do see," Dagmar said. "And I will return for what is mine."

She left the hospital. She was several blocks away before she had to pull over. Her body would not stop shaking. Stella Mortimer was out there, and she was coming.

***

Bekah had known about this place. Since the evening at the Midway, she had become Zach's girlfriend. Nadia knew Keegan far better, and she found Bekah to be both similar and vastly different from her foul-mouthed partner. Zach had wanted to do a double-date kind of thing, and Nadia thought it might be fun to try it. A witch, two carnies, and a tattooist. They were definitely a flashy group.

Nadia was enjoying the new lines of snakeskin over her skull. It had hurt going on, the vibrations burrowing into her bones, but they had been worth it. She had finished her physical transformation, and she was at ease. These tattoos healed even more quickly, scarcely abrading her scalp. Zach gave her the tattoo care lecture out of habit, then started to laugh. "There's no guidebook for people like you."

"Like us," she'd said to him.

Bekah took them to a restaurant not far from Leo Carrillo beach, where the outdoor patio overlooked the glittering Pacific. The four of them, Nadia, Milena, Zach, and Bekah, ate tacos and drank beer and enjoyed the companionship.

Bekah spent most of her time talking to Milena. The two of them were good friends from work, and both had exacting taste in clothes and style. Bekah skewed more modern than Milena, sporting a shaved temple and prominent piercings, but both were firm believers in the power of dresses and heels.

As Nadia finished yet another taco, she realized was happy. This was not an unfamiliar feeling for her, but the accompanying contentment was. The sense there was not something looming over the horizon, not another shoe about to drop. Nadia was with three people who knew, to varying degrees, who and what she was. This was a precious thing.

The purpose of the celebration was manifold. The final completion of Nadia's tattoos, for one. Enough hours to more accurately be called days, and she was content with the results. Her shirt was sleeveless, showing off the impressive work, the cool ocean wind delicious on her bare skin. Her head was uncovered as well, displaying the three strips of snakeskin going to temples and widow's peak. She drew second looks in plenty. At first, she began to turtle inward, withering under the attention. Then she realized, she had sculpted herself into this. She was Nadia sapiens, the final version of herself. With each look, she felt strength.

Nadia's phone buzzed. It was her brother. She excused herself and walked out of the patio area, and down a few stairs. Now she was on stacked volcanic rock, separating the sandy beach from the short rise to the road. "Yeah, Lex?" she said into the phone.

"Hey, Nadia." She heard the worry in his tone clearly.

"What's up? You don't sound great."

"I heard some rumors."

"About me?"

"Yeah."

She waited, letting him expand on what he'd heard.

"I heard you were running around with a tough crowd," he said.

"A tough crowd?" She laughed. "I'm out with my girlfriend and some friends. We're having fish tacos, which for once is not a euphemism."

"No, Nadia. I think you know what I'm talking about."

"Sav Krikorian?"

"Yeah."

"Well, I don't want to point out the irony here, Lex, but if you heard about it, that must mean you have some of the same connections I do."

"I know the vultures around dad's business. I also know not to make any deals with them."

"Is that what you heard? I'm making deals?"

"Are you?"

"Lex, this is none of your business."

"Just be careful, Nadia. You don't know these guys. If you get in bed with them, they own you."

"Believe me, I know exactly what they'll take," she said. *And I know what will happen to them should they try.*

***

Dagmar's journey to consciousness was slow until it suddenly wasn't. In her dream, she was running through her house, but it was much too large to be her house and looked more like the mental hospital. Growling thundered behind her, and periodically, she would look about and see a flash of a great cat slinking along the hallway. She was being hunted.

Then she was in her bed, a billowing, dream version of it. The windows open, though not out into her balcony, but onto burning star fields. Her things were gone as well; the room was empty save for the bed and the gauzy curtains wafting on the breeze.

Bandages covered her body. The weight of them squeezed her flesh. Though when she looked, she saw nothing at all, just her body. Then, a dimple in the bed. More weight, a presence, attention, looming beside her. Icy fingers closed over her arm, and they were far to real, too definite, to be part of the dream. The touch bridged the gap between worlds, and she crossed it, wakefulness splashing over her face as she sucked in a deep breath from the real.

She opened her eyes, and for a moment, thought she was still in her dream. The door out to the balcony was open, the breeze rustled her light curtains. She looked down at herself, and found she was wearing her nightshirt, and there were no bandages on her. Yet she still felt them, on her inner left elbow.

She turned her head and found it heavy, sleep still clinging to her like cobwebs.

Someone was sitting on her bed.

The weight had not been a dream. Neither had the touch. She felt cool, dry hands on her arm, then the silver stab of a needle. She gasped.

The shape turned. Dagmar could not make out features, save for dim pinpricks of light where the eyes perhaps should be. They regarded her, and Dagmar quailed under the strength of the gaze. It was not hate but rather a detached interest in what the worm at the end of the hook was doing. How would it wriggle away from its doom.

The shape made a hideous sucking sound, and a moment later, placed a strip of duct tape over Dagmar's mouth. She struggled, and that was when she found she could not move at all. She had been tied to the posters of her bed, wrists and ankles at each point. She screamed into the tape at her lips.

The shape spoke. "Hello," it said. The voice was creaky, whispery, rusty. From fifteen years of disuse, perhaps, though Dagmar still recognized it. It could belong to no one else.

She made a noise.

"In time," Stella Mortimer said.

Stella was not much more than a shadow. Dagmar wondered what would happen if she flicked on a light. If she pinioned Stella with some kind of high-powered flood lamp. Would she vanish into a scream and a settling of sooty dust? Or was the change more of an illusion?

She was solid enough in the dark. She could touch and be touched. Dagmar felt strips of medical tape on her arms, securing something in place.

An IV. Stella had hooked her up to an IV. It could be nothing else. She had killed in so many ways, but her favorite had always been poison. It had been plentiful in her hospital. After all, poison is, in many cases, simply too much medicine. Stella had proven there was little in the hospital she couldn't take a life with, but it had always come back to this. It was why there was no clear accounting of her kills; so many had died from a little too much morphine, not quite enough antibiotics.

Once the changes truly took hold, Stella had other ways of killing. Dagmar watched one now. The shadow woman held the end of the tube, where another needle protruded, shining in the dim light. Dagmar shook her head, pleading. She couldn't die like this. For Stella, this would be the only way to murder her tormentor.

Stella rolled up her sleeve. The gloom parted only enough to reveal the brown skin of her arm. It looked so mundane, so unlike what the angel of death should look like. Just an arm, nothing to see here. A vein bulged against the surface of her skin and shuddered. The blood itself wanted to get out. Wanted to work its strange magic.

Stella punctured her vein and held the IV against it. Soon the blood, black as oil in the night air, flowed into the tube. Dagmar's eyes widened, her muffled screams growing more hysterical, as the blood progressed through the artificial circulatory system to her veins, where it would consume her whole. And then a part of her looked at the blood with naked avarice. What could she do with such a powerful talisman? What could she destroy with the blood of Stella Mortimer?

"Miss Eichel?"

Dagmar turned her head, so heavy in the deep night. Gaff loomed in the doorway, his bare skin shining like a ghost. She wanted to call to him, for a moment not even considering what he was seeing.

Stella leapt upward, the IV tearing loose from her arm. Dagmar watched, fear crystalizing the world, the droplets of black blood spraying out over her bedroom.

Gaff stared across the room at Stella. Then: "You."

"And you," Stella whispered.

Gaff roared and charged. Stella was not ready, and the massive man hit her and carried her into the wall, both of them crashing to the floor. A moment later, and Gaff was alone, Stella out on the balcony. Another moment and she was gone from there as well, all without moving.

Gaff stood, breathing heavily, searching for his enemy. As an afterthought, he reached over and sliced the rope binding Dagmar's right wrist to the bed with his glassy fingernails. Then he stopped, focusing in on his absent prey, a black rage over him.

"That was Stella Mortimer," Gaff said.

Dagmar almost lied. It was such a reflex, a good way to keep Gaff on his leash. The lie did not come to her lips. "Yes."

"She was dead. You said she was dead."

"She's still alive."

Gaff screamed. His agonized wail echoed through the house and out over the sleeping city. "Why? You said you killed her. You said she was gone forever."

"You have to listen to me. She was locked up. She was far more valuable to us than just your revenge."

Gaff turned on her. The tears on his cheeks were indistinguishable from the glass shards. "She needs to die for what she did."

"I know. I made a mistake."

"For fifteen years!"

"A mistake." Dagmar realized she was no longer merely worried about Gaff pursuing. The fingernails he had used to cut her ropes were sharp enough to slash her throat as well.

"This was no mistake. This was malice, pure and simple."

"No. She was useful to me. To us."

"She is a killer who wants you dead. And now she is free to do just that." Gaff took a few steps toward her, his fingers curled into claws, glass nails glittering.

"Please," she said.

Gaff stopped, turned on his heel, and ran.

Dagmar freed herself a short while later. Even with one hand unbound, it was difficult, as she was shaking quite badly. She searched the house, convinced Stella would materialize from the shadows, or else Gaff would think twice about leaving and come barreling through the door. It was completely quiet. Empty.

She ran to her cabinet of reserves. They were still there. Every piece she had collected. But there would never be any more. The ones she was harvesting, Stella and Gaff, were gone. Now her supply looked meager indeed.

***

Nadia got the call in the middle of the night. She was still awake, though alone in the small guesthouse. She had just finished tending to Devin, who no longer spoke or registered her presence. He was mostly covered in the white bark now, his surface sprouting mushrooms. Nadia watered him, unsure if this was what she was supposed to do and collected a few more of the mushrooms.

Inside, Azh was on the desk, his powerful coils between the various jars of talismans. He tasted the air languidly, unafraid of anyone within this place.

When Nadia's phone buzzed, it made her jump. A,mundane intrusion into her late night. It was Dagmar calling.

"Yeah?"

"Nadia? It's Dagmar." Her voice was soft, brittle.

"Are you okay?"

"Yes, yes I'm fine. I'm glad you're awake."

"I'm sort of a night owl."

"Yes, I remember, or I wouldn't have called. Are you available to come over?"

It was one in the morning. Milena wasn't getting off for another couple of hours, but Nadia had been planning to be asleep in bed by then. "I suppose?"

"Oh good. Please, come as soon as you can. I'll be up."

Nadia got in her car and took the drive over. This late, and the freeways were as clear as they ever were. There were always other cars, and Nadia could not help but wonder if they were all on similar errands. If each one of them was the hero in their own bizarre drama.

She barely had to knock on Dagmar's door before it was thrown open, and Dagmar, for the first time looking haggard and drawn, was on the other side. "Come in."

She had not put on makeup, and the bags under her eyes were heavy. Her crow's feet and laugh lines showed stark against the golden complexion. She wore a simple nightshirt over yoga pants, and her hair was mussed from sleep. It was the first time Nadia had ever seen her less than immaculately put together. The first time Dagmar had appeared vulnerable.

Dagmar led Nadia into the dining room. The table was largely bare, and when Dagmar sat at the head of it, she managed to look more defeated than ever. Nadia settled into the chair nearby and waited for Dagmar to speak.

Dagmar slowly straightened in her chair, putting on the familiar mask. "I need a little help," she finally said. She almost looked like she believed it was so minor.

Nadia glanced out the window at the night sky. "Help with what?"

"Subduing a Matchless."

"Oh."

"It would not be so difficult, but I have nothing to track her."

"Have you gone to her house? Hairbrushes, shower drains, bathroom wastebaskets, those are good—"

"She doesn't have anything like that."

Nadia frowned. The obvious question was who doesn't have that who would suddenly go missing?

Then, the horrible answer dawned on her. All the pieces where there, waiting to be put together. "Where did she escape from?"

"It hardly matters. She's gone, and she left nothing behind. She changed more than I had thought." Dagmar fixed Nadia with her gaze. There was the old Dagmar, the edifice of strength. "Will you help me?"

Whatever Dagmar had done, the Matchless were dangerous. Judging from Dagmar's near hysteria, this one was worse than most. Maybe getting revenge. Revenge she's deserved. Despite the voice in her head urging her to stay out, Nadia nodded. "I'll help in any way I can."

Understanding

Nadia returned home shortly after making her pledge to Dagmar, relieved to get away from Dagmar's weird cube-house. It had always felt like a museum to Nadia, less a place where one lived and more of a location to show off money well spent. Now it was hollow like a toothless mouth.

Nadia's mind spent time conjuring the pit Dagmar had placed her Matchless in. Something below the house, maybe. A cellar like in *Silence of the Lambs*. A literal pit dug into the center with weeping dirt walls. She could lower a bucket filled with food, and the Matchless would replace the food with talismans. Feeding your pet almost-human.

The image didn't jibe with Dagmar. No, a pit with her would have to be done in brick, with Greek statuary on the rim. Or perhaps some kind of old style French Revolution jail. Not a jail but a *gaol*. An iron mask for the prisoner and thick steel gauntlets to keep her abilities at bay. The kind of place people were thrown into with no intention of ever being let out.

Or maybe it would be a thoroughly modern facility. Chemical restraints along with the physical, so bland and indistinct so as to be invisible. Institutional mint green walls. The kind of place where, until recently, they would have thrown Nadia. No one around would know the glory of the prisoner within.

Nadia had trouble picturing a Matchless so helpless. She had only experienced one directly, but China Jennings never would quail fearfully at the bottom of some pit. She would use her abilities to get out, to wreak vengeance.

Then again, her abilities had not saved her from Nadia's wrath.

Perhaps this one had done just that. Dagmar never said how long her prisoner had been held, merely that she had been. She might have foolishly taken one alive, kept her for a week, and found out this was impossible. Dagmar had said it herself; the Matchless were dangerous and tended to burn themselves out.

But the way Dagmar was reacting, it sounded like the prisoner had been held longer than a few mere weeks.

Nadia could not quite wrap her brain around the horror of holding someone and harvesting them for... how long was it? A year? Five? More? What did it take to do that to someone? Was this what Dagmar had in mind for Milena? Or Zach, if she knew of him? Or even Nadia herself? She shuddered again.

Now Dagmar realized her error. The Matchless escaped and Dagmar needed Nadia's help to kill her. Even if the Matchless was entirely justified, she would be too dangerous to allow to remain free. Dagmar might be the first victim, but she'd never be the last. Nadia would not be responsible for the actions of another China Jennings or Simcoe Killer.

She parked on her street and made her way up the drive. Milena's car waited at the end. Nadia hoped

Milena would still be awake for a little while longer, but the house was dark. She let herself in and heard stirring in the bedroom.

"Nadia?" Milena's voice, thickening with sleep, though still aware.

"Yeah," she said, pulling her boots off.

"Come to bed."

Nadia slipped off her clothes and into bed. Milena held the covers up, the heat from her body drawing Nadia in. There was no need for awkward seduction or conversation. The two of them fell into each other quite naturally. And when they were finished, slicked and scented in the other, Nadia held Milena's soft body close, pillowing her head in Milena's fragrant hair.

"Were you up at your secret place?" Milena asked into the darkness.

Nadia stroked the smooth skin at Milena's hip. Her secret place was Simcoe Manor, though there were less and less reasons to go. Now it was only the pool water, and she could see the levels slowly but surely dropping away as she harvested. "I was at Dagmar's. She called me over."

Milena rolled over to look at Nadia. "That's sort of late."

"It was. An emergency."

"What kind of emergency?"

Nadia toyed with a strand of Milena's curls. "Someone she was harvesting escaped."

"Harvesting?"

Nadia explained the concept, even as her belly began to roil.

"Like you're doing to me," Milena said.

Nadia shut her eyes. "Yes."

She felt Milena's hand settle over her heart. "Nadia. It's okay. If I can help you, I want to. I love you."

Nadia put her hands over Milena's. "I love you."

"So it's okay, then. I know you're here no matter what." Then, in the dark, she smirked. "If mind-blowing sex can't keep you here..."

Nadia laughed and kissed her nose. "Then nothing will."

"I take it Dagmar's version of harvesting isn't like what we have? Or like what you're doing with Devin?"

Nadia involuntarily glanced in Devin's direction, as though she could see through the walls between her and the planted man. "I don't know what I'm doing with Devin. But he seems happy." *Or he did when I could still see his face.* The white bark had swallowed it. Now Devin looked like an uncannily humanoid tree with a fungus problem.

"This one wasn't?"

"I got that impression." Nadia shook her head, then told Milena her fears.

"You think Dagmar would do that to someone?"

Milena's disbelief gave Nadia the familiar jab of jealousy. She tried to be rational—she had just finished bringing Milena to an extremely vocal orgasm, while Dagmar was alone in her house. "All I know for certain is that she had someone very dangerous imprisoned, and now she's escaped."

"Yeah, that certainly sounds like it. It sounds like you sympathize more with the person she had locked up?"

"A little. I mean, that's wrong. But then I've seen what people like this do. China. The man who killed my sister. These are monsters, and if one of them is out, she should be, I don't know... dealt with."

"Killed."

"Yeah."

"Dagmar didn't kill this one the first time."

"No. She wanted to harvest her."

"And you kind of understand why."

Nadia found herself nodding.

"If you could have kept China alive and locked up, would you have?"

"No," Nadia said, but that was not the entire truth. Milena could hear it as well, but thankfully, she did not challenge it.

"The two of you are going to curse her then?"

"We would like to, but she's changed, I guess. There was no hair or fingernails or anything else left at wherever Dagmar was holding her."

Milena ran her clever fingers over Nadia's bald scalp. "Yeah, you tend to have an uneasy relationship with hair."

"I guess I'm not the only one." Nadia smiled, though her mind was hung up on what Milena had just implied.

"What about the talismans?" Milena blurted.

"What do you mean?"

"Those are pretty strong links, right? Whatever this person produces and leaves behind has to be connected to her somehow."

"I think it's dangerous. I can't quite explain it, but it's like putting nuclear fuel in your car. It'll work, but it might also explode."

"If you have no other options..."

"Yeah. You might be right."

***

Dagmar had the look on her face Nadia was expecting when she shared the idea.

"That's an irresponsible waste," Dagmar sneered.

It was the following night. Nadia and Milena had slept deep into the following day. Milena left that evening for one of her games, Nadia called Dagmar. The call was answered so quickly, Nadia did not think the other woman had slept at all. When she arrived, she was certain of it.

Dagmar had cleaned up, had styled herself in her usual way, though cracks showed through. Probably invisible to anyone who didn't know her well. Her makeup was not as neat as it usually was. Her dress bunched on her thin frame. Her body was stiff, her eyes dark. For someone who spent as much time and effort on her impressions, this would have been like a normal person answering the door in a ketchup-covered undershirt.

Dagmar's attitude did not improve with Nadia's presentation. Unlike every other time Nadia had seen her—Friend? Ally? Mentor?—in the evening, Dagmar had gone for wine or cocktails. Here she had brewed coffee that was closer to caffeinated sludge. Nadia asked for a cup and immediately regretted it, sipping it with exaggerated care and knowing she would be jittery for the full night afterwards.

And then there was the presentation. A difficult sale under the best circumstances, this was far away from the best. Dagmar did Nadia the courtesy of listening, but before she was even finished, Dagmar was already shaking her head.

"Don't think of it as a waste. We have no good options, so all we're left with are the bad," Nadia said.

"Did you miss the most important part of what we're doing? She's gone. I can't replenish my stores. You're asking me to spend talismans just to direct a curse."

"Yes."

"Have you ever done that?"

"No."

"It's dangerous. Very, very dangerous. Throwing raw power into the mix at two places in the process is liable to create side effects, or just blow up in our faces."

"I realize that."

"And yet you came to me with it."

"It was the only option I could think of. If I thought there was another option, I would have come to you with it. You asked for my help. This is it. If you have another way, I'm all ears."

Dagmar seethed, then sipped her coffee. "All right. I'll get what we need. Stay here."

Nadia did not move from the table. Following Dagmar to her stash would have been the height of rudeness. Even in a culture numbering at two, there were certain inviolate rules she knew instinctively. Still, hearing Dagmar's heels disappear upstairs, a thrill shivered up Nadia's spine, bringing with it the temptation to creep along. *It's upstairs somewhere,* her mind told her. *Narrow it down further.* She wasn't even planning to steal from Dagmar but knowing where it was could be important. Somehow. Sometime.

Dagmar returned with a collection of things. She laid a map of the city over the table. It was a cheesy one, folded, and refolded, with a few movie star homes picked out in ink. Nadia wondered when Dagmar had bought it. Probably late last night or early in the morning, anticipating a breakthrough.

She laid down an empty syringe. It buzzed without Nadia even needing to touch it. A talisman from this missing Matchless, whoever she was.

Last was an inkwell. The ink was a deep, dark red.

"What's this?" Nadia said, gesturing to it.

"Blood from her victims. She was a poisoner." Nadia's reaction must have shown on her face. "Yes, I did not call you lightly. This one is a monster and needs to be put down."

"What's last?" Nadia asked. They were missing a catalyst.

"Something from you. I should not be the only one risking my stores."

Nadia did not comment that the only reason she was here was for Dagmar. Griping would solve nothing. Instead, she put a jar on the table. Dagmar uttered a tiny gasp at the sight of the cleanly severed fingers and sightless eyes within. Nadia unscrewed the jar and extracted one of the eyes, then returned the jar to the satchel at her feet.

Dagmar scowled at the eye, then picked up the syringe. Using it on the inkwell, she extracted a few ccs of blood. "Nadia, if you would hold your..."

Nadia smirked inwardly at the other woman's squeamishness. She picked up the eye and held it out. Dagmar, her mouth in a disgusted moue, injected the eye with the blood. The white turned pink, then scarlet, then nearly black. Nadia placed it on the surface of the map, out in the middle of the Pacific Ocean. The color paled, vanished, absorbed into the once biological tissue.

The eye was still for a moment, wobbling uncertainly on its irregular curve. Then, it began to roll across the paper surface. At first uncertain, a couple revolutions, then a pause, then a few more, always teetering, swaying. It looked as though it was reacting to the surface beneath moving, like one of those wooden mazes the players tilt to guide a metal ball without dropping it through a hole. But no one touched the eyeball. It moved of its own accord.

It wound its way over the blue Pacific, then paused when the city was beneath its iris.

"It's working," Dagmar whispered.

Nadia did not speak, for fear of jinxing it. But it was working. She could feel it in her bones, trilling the same frequency as the eye itself. The eyeball was at the end of a tether, Nadia and Dagmar at the other end, waiting for the inevitable.

The eyeball moved north, rolling for the rich areas of west LA. Pacific Palisades, Brentwood, where they were now, Beverly Hills, and the like. Close. It would make sense; the Matchless hadn't gone far.

The eyeball rattled to a pause over Brentwood, shimmying, ready to pick a new direction to move off into, perhaps somewhere north, maybe moving into the west. Nadia held her breath.

The eyeball never moved again. There was a pop, and a blaze. Nadia saw only white, her reflexes propelling her backward. The chair she was sitting in tipped over, and she found herself looking up at the ceiling, her face hot. Dagmar was still sitting in the chair, her arms up to protect herself.

Black snowflakes fell about the room. Where they hit, they blazed, some of them starting white fires like magnesium, others sputtering. Out of these fires came scuttling shapes, racing into the dark corners of the room. One of these snowflakes alighted on Nadia's arm and she yelped in pain as it flared up. She felt the scuttling thing trying to tear into her. She brushed it away, her arm searing with phantom flame.

She got to her feet, cradling the burn.

On the table, the map was largely consumed. The center was a crispy, black-edged hole. The border was still mostly intact, but everything that had been on the table, from the talismans to the candelabras, was gone.

Fear seized Nadia and she went to her satchel, sitting on the floor, right next to where her chair used to be. Her jars were intact. Only then did she inspect her injury. The skin was livid, and already turning white and peeling away. She felt a momentary rage for the damage of her tattoo, then covered it with her hand.

"You see?" Dagmar hissed. "You see?" The second was more of a shriek.

"Dagmar, I—"

"You think you can come to me and tell me things I don't know. Tell me to use my resources on this. Why?

Why? Are you trying to weaken me? Exhaust my stores?"

"Of course not."

"No. You're just stupid. Stupid, and inept, and now we're no closer to knowing where she is hiding."

"The eye got close. It was poised right around here. Maybe on your house."

"It was tracking us! Or the rest of the talismans! We designed it poorly and instead of learning something useful, you set a fire in my house!"

The fires were guttering now. Having blazed brightly, they only consumed what was closest to them and had turned into black ash as soon as they were made.

"Dagmar—" Nadia tried again.

"Get out. Get out of my house this instant. I can't stand to look at you."

Nadia knew it was futile to argue. She picked up her satchel and went out the door. When she was outside, she looked at the wound again.

The skin had peeled back. What it revealed were scales.

***

Gaff watched from his position in the deep green surrounding Dagmar's house. The demand for privacy had been without truly considering precisely what that meant. In this case, it meant Gaff could quite easily watch his betrayer without her knowledge, using her as she was meant to be used: bait.

With the way he looked, he could not participate in the world as others did. He could not rent an apartment, or open a bank account, or even turn up at a homeless shelter. They would see the glass in him, the mirrored teeth, the lenses over his eyes, and they would know he was no longer human.

All because of Stella Mortimer.

Who was still alive.

Meaning Dagmar had lied. He pictured her coming to him in the hospital, when the change was still overtaking him. He was in agony, despite the sedation. The glass snowflake in his body was growing, or so he pictured it. No one had been inside of him since Stella, and he healed up nice and tight.

None of the doctors knew quite what to make of him. He was due for exploratory surgery in the morning. Anything to silence the screams. They didn't know Stella Mortimer would make certain the orders were lost and Gaff was transferred to another ward. Keep him moving and hidden until she could take him home. For whatever reasons she had for creating him in the first place.

Then Dagmar Eichel entered his room. She looked like the kind of woman who didn't exist anywhere but on television shows about rich and beautiful women. She was in her early thirties then, and she did not quite have the unflappable confidence she displayed now. The victory against Stella gave her the swagger. What Gaff assumed to be the culmination of a brutal curse.

Dagmar spirited him out of the hospital and hid him in her home. She did not complain at his howls of agony. No, she only showed him love. She comforted him, cared for him. She brought him food, and water, and the most precious gift: photos of the blood on the asphalt, of the twisted hunk of metal that had been Stella's car, and the pulped bodies within. Stella was dead. For fifteen years, he had believed it, believed it even more because had she been alive, he had no doubt she would come for him.

She had been in Dagmar's room. Older, grayer, but still obviously her. He could not imagine where she had been all that time. He still wasn't certain what he could do with Dagmar. Trust was broken, but there were still years of love, affection, and service. It was difficult to wrap his brain around both truths.

In the meantime, he was watching.

Stella would return. He was not anticipating when or how.

He watched as a spiderlike shape crawled from one of the attic windows. Gaff frowned, his shrouded eyes tracking the shape as it scuttled down the wall. Stella, of course. She had changed a great deal. Gone feral maybe, mad in whatever prison Dagmar threw her into. She crawled to a window and slipped inside, though there was not enough room for a full body.

Stella had not gone anywhere. She had been hiding in Dagmar's place. Stella loved fear—Gaff remembered the relish she'd taken in his pleading—and had likely been waiting for the perfect time to strike. That was now. Gaff stood, shedding the blanket from his bare torso, his pale flesh glowing in the moonlight.

The only question he had was whether he would kill one or both of them.

***

Nadia returned home. The whole way she picked at her wound. There was no pain. The scales beneath were hard and dry, her blood beating under them. The design worked flawlessly into the tattoo, visible only where the scar tissue receded. She wondered if she was head to toe in this. Wearing a suit of armor beneath her skin. Would there be serpents as well? Would she unearth their hissing heads, their raspy rattles?

While still driving, she lifted her shirt, where her belly was still unmarked. Her skin was taut, the muscles clearly delineated beneath it. She touched the flesh, probing for the scales beneath. She felt nothing, but she had felt nothing before. How far had she changed? What was she becoming?

The clouds gathered on the ride home, eclipsing the sky with apocalyptic suddenness. Nadia went inside as the first rumble of thunder announced this would be a storm. Relief from the drought maybe, fleeting and momentary. She let herself in and found Milena watching TV. Nadia settled in next to her, and tried to get lost in it, but could not stop thinking about the failed hex at Dagmar's.

"What?" Milena asked her.

Nadia shook her head. "I was at Dagmar's."

"You go there a lot."

"We're both... you know."

"Gay?"

"This is about that... person... she was harvesting. She wanted help tracking her down."

"You... cast a spell?" Milena's tone carried awe, but also a bit of fear.

"Yes. We tried. There was nothing to link to her. No way to target it, except for the talismans."

The sky broke. Rain rattled on the roof like a million pebbles. Nadia leapt off the couch and started to pace. For no reason she could name, the rain was chattering over her nerves.

Milena leaned over the back of the sofa, frowning. "I thought you said—"

"That's how it's supposed to work. Talismans are catalysts. Batteries. But if you have nothing else, they should link to whoever created them."

"My cards?"

Nadia turned. "They carry your scent, yes."

Milena jumped. Nadia heard her own words and tried to keep a poker face, even as she worried the area around her scales.

"You took a risk," Milena said.

"A stupid risk." The guest house was stuffy. The air was heavy, wet. Nadia needed air. She opened the front, wanting the clean scent of rain to wash the sticky heat off her skin. It did not smell like rain. It smelled like fresh organ meat, washed in subtle sandalwood.

The rain hitting the cracked cement outside the house was thick, like snot, slopping about in fatty clumps. It no longer sounded like pebbles. It sounded like spoiled milk poured over the city. Nadia stared at it in mute rage.

"What's that smell?" Milena asked, joining Nadia at the door.

The masses had spots on them, one per mass. Like the great storm of Jupiter, or the nucleus of an amoeba. These stretched and distorted as the gelatinous blobs spread out and melted to water.

"Angel tears," Milena said in amazement.

"What?"

"This stuff supposedly falls from the sky... like blood, or like fish. But this is supposed to be the tears of angels."

Nadia stared at it. She knew the real reason it was falling. It was a punishment. A taunt maybe. The hex had failed and reality itself was saying what it thought of arrogant witches who tried to change it. Angel tears. Perfect.

"What is it?" Milena asked.

Nadia opened her mouth to answer, watching more clumps of the stuff hit the earth and spread out. Was anyone else noticing this, or was this a show for her and her alone? No, this would be falling at Dagmar's house as well. Had to punish both of the will-workers involved.

The house where the eyeball had stopped. Right before the map exploded and revealed Nadia's true skin. She scratched at the border of the wound, beginning to feel a little give there.

Right over Dagmar's house.

The hex had not failed. It had worked exactly as planned.

Nadia ran to her car, the angels crying over her shoulders, and drove hard through the slick LA streets.

***

It was not surprising to find that Vorspan's tastes had changed somewhat. He had never kept kosher, though he avoided some of the worst violations. Tonight he was devouring his bacon-wrapped liver with relish. Dagmar watched with faint amusement, wondering if the changes extended to his innards, even when he was in his human form.

Keeping Vorspan as protection was perhaps foolish. He should be bound from hurting her, though there was no way she was going to actually test it. He was not due for a change this evening, either. He was the human equivalent of a security blanket. Well, mostly human.

This domestic pantomime made it easier to ignore the angel of death out there somewhere. Dagmar could only hope Stella's urges would not be contained. The first body she dropped would put Dagmar on her trail. Precise victims had never mattered to Stella before, and her years of captivity wouldn't have given her a greater reason to value human life. In the meantime, there was nothing to do but wait, and hope Stella decided to save Dagmar for last.

At least she could savor her meal. Cooking was something she had always enjoyed. Now even more so. The greater meaning was inescapable. As with her hexes, every meal had a variance. She could not precisely control the quality of the ingredients. She could not precisely measure the seasonings down to the atom. Although, unlike the other, there were certain recipes she had perfected and could return to at will. Try to do that with a hex, and things went very, very bad indeed.

She luxuriated in her liver, alternating bites with the water chestnut salad. The full-bodied Malbec paired perfectly, unlocking the richer, meatier flavors of both liver and nut. Vorspan hardly cared. His salad lay untouched on the plate, and he was helping himself to his third serving of liver. He hardly looked up, and when he did, it was furtively, never making eye contact with Dagmar. Some bodyguard.

The only other option was Nadia Eskandarian. She was far more intent on wasting talismans, though Dagmar chalked that up to foolish inexperience rather than outright malice. In any case, there was little Nadia could do that Dagmar could not do better and more efficiently. Dagmar knew the enemy, and when Stella was unmasked, Nadia's brute strength could be used.

The little witch was impressive for her raw power. She seemed to delight in distancing herself from the normal mores. There was going to be some divergence expected for a lesbian, but Nadia took it to an extreme. The shaved head and eyebrows, the relentless snake tattoos, the lines of gold rings at her brows. Add to that her strong Middle Eastern features, and she looked like a reincarnation of an Arabian snake goddess.

Maybe she was onto something after all. Dagmar had always felt it was best to use the prevailing aesthetics. Own them. For a woman like Nadia, with her hawkish nose and boyish figure, that hadn't been an option. Maybe there was power to be found in the other direction.

Maybe more power.

She frowned. A faint metallic, almost gasoline taste underneath the liver gnawed at her tongue. She would not have noticed it without the wine worrying at her taste buds, opening them up to inhale the subtleties of the food. She put down her fork, staring at the morsel of liver on the end, as though it could tell her what impurity had crept in. What mistake she had managed to make in the preparation to give it that taste?

This taste was familiar. She'd had it once, fifteen years ago, and had nearly died as a result.

The crash came swiftly thereafter. At the other end of the table, and Vorspan had fallen unconscious, his head resting in a savory pool of red grease. Dagmar stood up, knocking her own chair behind her.

Then the whispering began. Words at the edge of hearing, chased by the mad chuckling of the dark. The dining room, with its French doors opening onto the balcony and wide windows, was suddenly gloomy. Shadows pressed in on all sides, like vision at the moment of sleep. Dagmar picked up a fork and jabbed it into the back of her hand.

The pain was white, but the darkness did not get pushed back. It was not the poison in the food doing this. It was actually getting darker in the room. The lights of the world turned down in this place, giving it over to the night.

And still, the whispering. It was not in the room with her. It scuttled in from both inner doors and the one on the balcony, as well as the windows, from all around. Through one was the kitchen, through the other, the living room. Outside, the balcony went all around three sides of the house.

This could only herald one thing: the arrival of Stella Mortimer. She was here, sooner than expected, and the master poisoner had taken out the one being between her and her prey. Dagmar could have laughed; in his present state, poisoned or not, Vorspan was less than useless.

She looked to the potential four exits. The whispers played up and down the hairs on her neck. No matter where she turned, Stella was right behind.

Dagmar ran two steps, her heels clicking loudly on the floor. She kicked them off and into the corner, her bare feet finding traction easily on both carpets and hardwood. She tried to fight the blinding fear, the urge screaming at her to *run just run*, knowing this was no solution. Stella wanted her to lose reason; she liked her prey simmering in terror.

Dagmar paused at the door, peeking into the living room. Two large sofas and several fat chairs were arrayed around a low coffee table and a fireplace. Plenty of places to hide. *Bait*, panic hissed in her mind, *exactly where Stella is waiting for you.*

Maybe. Dagmar peered into the shadows, hunting for the telltale shape. The last time Stella had stalked her was fifteen years ago. Then, even when her form slipped away into tenebrous strands, there was a human silhouette. Something for the eye to latch onto. She had changed in her isolation, though Dagmar had to hope there were still limits. If not, no amount of hiding would do much good.

She ran to the back of the sofa, mashing herself in a darkened corner, beside an end table and amongst the hanging limbs of a spider plant. There she waited, doing her best not to breathe.

What's the next step, her rational mind demanded. *Get out? Call for help?*

The police would be helpless, but they might scare Stella off. The poison—Stella's blood—lingered on her tongue. She resisted the urge to frantically spit. There had not been enough to hurt her. If there had been, she would already be unconscious or dying.

The best thing to do would be wait, even as Stella's sibilant voice grew louder, yet still betrayed no direction. It surrounded Dagmar, even bleeding through the wall behind her and the vent at her feet. She wanted to scream at the voice to stop. She clamped her mouth shut and stayed put, willing herself to become part of the sofa, part of the shadows, part of the plant.

Upstairs. Get to her talismans. She might be able to craft something, and there was some of Stella's blood still on her tongue. There was some in the food. Enough? Enough to try, certainly, in this desperate place.

She tensed, ready to lunge back for the dining room, to scoop up the morsels of liver, and bring them with her to her stores, her mind already working with the symbolism to craft a nasty curse for the invader. Right as she was about to seize the moment and make her run, movement pinioned her to the spot.

The shape glided across the living room like smoke toward the dining room. Stella was barely a shadow, but a three-dimensional one, existing without being thrown against the wall. The whispers were loud enough to understand.

"Dagmar... Daaaaaagmaaaaar. I've missed you so much. Where are you? Why are you hiding? Daaaaagmaaaar."

Her name, drawn out in a vicious taunt, a sign of who had the power. After fifteen years of captivity, of being reduced to a milk cow, the tables were turned. Said all in the mocking vowels of her own name.

Stella drifted, an ethereal presence, toward the dining room. Dagmar did not move. Could not. A single twitch would draw the eye sure as a gunshot. She had to stay there, her head partially exposed, her eyes glittering. It was impossible to determine which way Stella was facing, either. No features broke the darkness of her shape, or if there were, the gloom had scrubbed them from her. The only way to track was the steady movement toward the dining room.

When the shadow went through the door, Dagmar ran for the stairs.

"Daaaaaagmaaaaaar," came the voice. "I can hear you."

***

Nadia pulled up in front of Dagmar's house. The lights were off. The door was closed. It could have been empty, Dagmar out at one of the society parties Nadia imagined she attended. But Nadia knew Dagmar was home. She had to be.

It had not rained here. Nadia did not dwell on this distinction, but later, she would wonder why this happened. It should have rained in both places. Should did not always matter when it came to what she was.

Nadia knocked on the door, loudly. There was no answer. She tried it. Locked.

She went around the side of the house. The plants were thicker here, likely to discourage this very thing. The balcony wrapping around three sides of the house began here, a scant five or so feet from level ground as the terrain took a precarious dip into the shallow canyon below. A copse of banana trees grew here, the waxy, segmented trunks being almost impossible to climb, and making a running start difficult. Nadia looked down the slope and sighed. She might be taking a tumble.

She secured her satchel close to her, the jars tinkling about inside. Azh had been in there before, but he was not now. He might return, though she never liked to depend entirely on him. At least he wouldn't have to take this trip.

She backed up a few steps, ran, juking around the banana trees but trying to hold onto her forward momentum. She jumped, hitting the railing of the balcony with her chest, and her breath exploded out of her in a sprained gust. She hung on, breathing as deeply as she could before hoisting herself up and over.

Up ahead, the French doors yawned open, the white curtains billowing out into the still night. The entrance to the dining room. No other lights betrayed anyone inside.

Nadia moved along the wall, wincing whenever the jars in her satchel clinked together. She arrived at the edge of the doorway and peeked in. She was not certain what she would see, but years of horror movies told her to expect something terrible. For a flash, she saw Karo Minasian standing in the center of the room, his wrists cut, his body covered in sores, but he was gone, a mere phantasm to beguile her.

The dining room table was set, and on the other side, a balding man collapsed on his plate. It took her a second look to recognize this man as Richard Vorspan, Dagmar's nervous guest at dinner. At the time, she hadn't known what to make of him. Now, with the information about this other prisoner, Nadia wondered what horrors Dagmar had subjected this man to. Or was he as big a monster as China? Did he deserve his torments?

It wasn't for her to judge. She entered the house with the intention of rushing to his side, but she was stopped in her tracks.

The Matchless was in the house.

Nadia could not pinpoint precisely how she knew this. The house was quiet and dark. Other than Vorspan, who might have been knocked out and abandoned, it could have been empty. But it wasn't. Whoever this escapee was, she was somewhere in the house.

If she was there, Dagmar was as well. Likely still alive and being hunted.

Nadia checked Vorspan's pulse. It fluttered against her fingers like a dying bird. She pulled him up and back, slumped against the chair, his mouth open. His face was covered in a thin film of grease. A bit of bacon stuck to his beard. She dropped to her knees, shrugging off the satchel. She was working on pure instinct.

She extracted a berry from a jar and the razor from her boot. The blade opened up her finger in a line of fire. The blood was thick and flowed readily. She swore as a few drops hit Dagmar's white tablecloth. She grabbed the berry with her bloody finger, along with a few water chestnuts from Vorspan's plate, and jammed both into the man's mouth, forcing food and blood into his throat. Vorspan made a snoring sound.

Nadia took her hand away and moved Vorspan's jaw to chew up berry and chestnut. After a few passes, he was chewing on his own, though still unconscious. The mass made its way down his throat. A moment later, he started coughing. His eyes were still closed as he vomited up a thick black fluid onto his plate. Then, he leaned back, and he was breathing easily. Nadia checked his pulse again, it was strong and steady. She picked up her satchel and a cloth napkin, holding it in her balled fist to get the blood to stop flowing.

Then she stood in the dining room, alone in a house with a killer. Find Dagmar first, she thought, and nodded to herself. That seemed like a good start. She crept to the doorway and paused.

She had no idea what to expect. She had come into contact with two of these, and both China Jennings and the Simcoe Killer were vastly different creatures.

Difficult to prepare for any of them and add the fact she had no way to target a curse.

Not unless she found Dagmar's talismans.

The idea pulled at her. Dagmar's talismans would have untold power, undreamed of versatility. She had been harvesting these people for decades, experience Nadia couldn't touch. Who knew the dizzying variety of Matchless, Shadowed, and Kissed Dagmar had met over her time?

All that remained was navigating the darkened house without running into the killer.

Nadia crept into the living room, expecting at any moment to be discovered. She kept going, and opened the door to the bathroom. It was empty. She continued into the dark section of the house, her eyes drinking in the meager light. Shapes loomed from the darkness. She avoided these—furniture, as it turned out—and checked one door after another.

She found rooms she was not expecting. Dagmar's house was huge, far more than one person could ever need. When she lived with her parents, she never would have noticed the ostentatious waste; now it was obvious.

When Nadia found a small bedroom that had obviously been occupied recently, she realized Dagmar might not live alone after all. The bed was unmade, and the bedclothes were pale sheets with some kind of pattern. Nadia knelt by the bed, wondering who this person could be. The pattern wasn't a pattern. It was drops of blood, smeared, spattered, and streaked. The product of a thousand tiny wounds. The sheets carried a clean chemical smell, almost like Windex.

A few books leaned on a bookcase—self-help texts and workout guides—as well as a pair of fifty pound dumbbells.

Nadia left the room, wondering who this houseguest or roommate was, and went out into the hall. The next room she entered stopped her. That Dagmar should have a home gym was not surprising. A woman her age who had such a sleek, polished appearance would have to have easy access. The surprising part was the weights. This was a place for a dedicated bodybuilder, down to the mirrors lining both walls, and spinning Nadia's reflections out to infinity.

She crept to the end of the room, where the glass doors opened up onto the balcony. Beyond, lights of the other rich houses twinkled in the night. The ones who had no idea something so strange and awful was going on inside the stacked-cube house.

"It's you."

The voice chilled her. It carried the menace and surety of one who has held a life in its hands. It was soft, neither precisely masculine or feminine, an odd accent beneath. Nadia turned slowly, smoothly. She would not betray fear. Fear in front of a predator led to attack.

The man standing in the doorway was a couple inches over six feet tall. His torso was entirely bare, and every muscle and vein picked out against ghostly white flesh. His head was angular and strangely shaped, shaved or perhaps as naturally bald as she. The eyebrows were makeup or maybe tattoos, simple inverted Vs making him look almost like a cartoon character. Patches of his skin glittered like diamonds. He watched her with a simple curiosity.

"It's me," she said. She had never seen this man before, but he had seen her.

Her brain clicked over the puzzle, snapping the pieces into place. The Matchless was female; this was a man. A bodybuilder. Dagmar's houseguest. He must have been lurking about, and Dagmar hadn't mentioned him. Because he was someone to be harvested, or was she planning to use him as an instrument of murder? *Again*, her overheated brain added.

"The other witch."

"And you are?"

"You don't get in my way," he said, taking a step forward. Nadia tensed. She could easily picture this monster tearing her apart with his bare hands.

"I'm not here for you."

"You're here for Dagmar's secrets, hmm? You can't trust her. Fitting she can't trust you either."

"I'm not—"

"Shh..." He held his index finger to his lips. His fingernail shone. "She keeps her talismans upstairs. There is a room off her closet. Take whatever you like."

Nadia fought the quaver in her voice. "What are you here for?"

"I am here for the angel."

"Angel. Dagmar?"

He shook his head. "I am here to kill the angel. I might kill Dagmar too... I'll kill you if you get in my way."

"I won't—"

He nodded. "I know, I know. You want to get home to that pretty plump girl of yours. Sleep in a warm bed and forget about the house of monsters. This is what I want as well, but my body is a house of monsters. I can't wake up."

"I'm sorry."

"You did nothing to me, Nadia the witch. You and I are picking over the same carcass."

The ghost-man turned, his broad back like a sheet. Then he was out the door, hunting whoever else was in this place. Nadia stood still, catching her breath. She felt lucky—she got the impression not many people had survived the man with the ghost skin.

She went to the doorway, pressing herself against the wall, and peeking out into the hallway. He was gone. She keeps her talismans upstairs. The promise from a demon. A good one. Dagmar might be upstairs, close to her center of power, her mind told her. Yes, that was why she was going. Not to raid Dagmar's stores. To help the woman herself.

Nadia went down the hall. The ghost man had vanished, along with whoever else. The Angel.

The stairs uttered a creak when Nadia put her boot on the bottom step. Her heart iced over, and she waited for the inevitable descent. All three of them to one spot, ready to kill whoever made the sound. No one came.

Nadia took the stairs one at a time, setting her feet down before slowly transferring her weight. She walked by the wall, where the wood wouldn't make as much of a strain. A lesson she learned in Angie's old wooden house in the more working class section of Hollywood. Angie, dead, but still guiding her.

She made her way up the stairs, and found wider, open hallways. A double door at the top of the stairs said the master bedroom. She went to it and put her hand on the knob. She didn't want to turn it. Going in meant the allure of the talismans was what was truly driving her. Do that and she was little more than a thief, little better than people like China or Karo.

Dagmar first.

Nadia crept along the hallway and opened the first door and ducked inside. The room was brighter than most. It would be the front of the house, the closed window getting a little bit of illumination from the close street. Nadia's eyes drank in the light and found a guest room. This one looked like it was being used for that purpose, with the usual immaculate but inoffensive decor.

She realized then she wasn't alone.

It wasn't quite a sound, nor was it the sight of a shadow on the wall. She felt as though she were being watched, a sudden weight on her body, a prickling on her hackles. She froze, then recovered, continuing to move as though she were unaware of this new danger. Whatever was out there needed to think she was helpless.

She walked around the far side of the bed, and that was when she saw who was looking at her.

Dagmar huddled in the corner of the room. So far from the untouchable patrician Nadia had been used to. She was wide-eyed, haggard, pale. Feet bare like a child. She hugged her knees to her chest, pulling herself into the smallest ball possible.

Nadia dropped to her knees next to Dagmar. The other woman flinched, drawing in a ragged breath.

"Dagmar! It's me. It's Nadia!" she whispered.

"Nadia?" Dagmar's voice was almost swallowed.

"She's in the house, isn't she? Where?"

Dagmar nodded. "I don't know. She's out there. Can't you hear her?"

Nadia cocked her head. All she could hear was Dagmar's shallow breathing and the blood pumping in her own ears. "No."

"She's everywhere," Dagmar said.

"We need to find her," Nadia said. "The two of us together can do something."

"No. You don't understand. We have no way to put the curse on her. No way to prepare."

"That's bullshit. We're better than that." She opened the razor. It glittered it the moonlight. "I'll open her up myself, and we'll have more blood than we know what to do with."

"Blood? Some of her blood is downstairs. She poisoned us with it... in the liver!"

"That's what happened to Vorspan?"

Dagmar nodded again.

"Great. Come on. We don't need any of that, then. We'll use my stuff. I have enough. Her blood, Dagmar, that Angel will wish she was back in your jail. Come on!"

"No, Nadia! You can't go out there. You don't understand. She's a killer... she's a murderer."

"I do know. One of these killed my sister."

"That's it. That's where you found out. Where you got your first talismans."

Nadia hesitated, then offered one curt nod.

"Then you know. We can't do anything against her. Not when she's out there, ready to kill us."

"Jesus fucking Christ, pull yourself together."

Nadia did not mistake the flash of hatred in Dagmar's eyes, but the return of her paralyzed fear washed it away. Dagmar shook her head, huddling farther into the corner.

"Fine. I'll deal with her myself."

Nadia left Dagmar for the hall. She felt eyes on her again, and at first she thought it was residual from Dagmar's terrified attention. It was not. Something else was in the hallway.

Nadia paused, turning slowly. She knew it wasn't the ghost man. This was the other, the Angel.

Darkness swallowed the end of the hall. Far more suddenly than it should have. Even in the dim light making its way into the house, Nadia should have been able to see shapes, but it was as though the end had been bitten off entirely, leaving nothing but a void.

Not a void. Eyes.

They were no longer human. Black, save for a bright light in the center of each. The shape moved forward, and the darkness came with it, lingering behind. Soon the eyes were given a face, and dimly, hair, arms, but nothing else. No torso, no legs; these were lost in the gloom.

The face was smooth, artificial, with few wrinkles in the skin. The hair was a wild explosion of curls, growing vague, like ink dropped into water. The hands were open, relaxed, the fingers strong and lean.

It was difficult to think of this as a person, but it was. She was. She had been entirely human once, but something had changed her. Maybe the act of murder was the key. Both China and the Simcoe Killer were multiple murderers. But with them, the murders felt incidental. China was an artist, the Simcoe Killer a parasite.

The Angel was death, pure and simple. Whatever she sought was found in the deaths of others. And now she was staring right at Nadia.

"Who are you?" she whispered. The words came from all around.

Nadia did not answer. She burst through the master bedroom door, desperately looking for anything to save her.

Dagmar had a full body mirror, antique, on a rotating stand taking up a corner of her large bedroom. Nadia pulled a jar from the satchel, feeling it slosh around inside. She hawked saliva into her mouth, then filled the rest with the gritty pool water. She spat the entire mouthful on the mirror. Her reflection distorted and ran like wax.

Nadia turned—there was no sound, merely what her brain supplied. The Angel was as quiet as the night. She took up the entire double doorway, her shadows as integral to her body as the few swatches of flesh amongst the black.

She moved toward Nadia and the mirror. She did not step, nor did she quite fly. It was a smooth, steady advancing, with none of the twitches and motion that made a creature feel alive.

The Angel stopped a few inches from Nadia. The wet mirror carried her image, running and broken by the water and Nadia's spit. The Angel squinted her alien eyes, peering through the room. Nadia stood there, motionless, as this new creature hunted for her, though she was right in the open. Nadia did not move. She did not breathe. Her face, inches from the cold dark of the Angel.

She found herself praying. Not to the god of her parents. Not to any of the other spirits or pagan goddesses she'd flirted with in college. She found herself praying to Milena, or the larger being that Kissed her. The source of her power. *Please. Let me come back to her.*

The Angel made no sound. No sudden inhalations, or any muttering. She merely stopped looking.

It looked like a plume of silt coming from the bottom of the pool, absorbing her face, then she was out the door. Nadia sighed.

"Stella." The voice, out in the hall, belonged to the ghost man.

Nadia ran to the doorway in time to see a pale form streak past her and into the mass of darkness. The glass in the ghost man's skin caught the light, blazing brighter somehow as he closed with the monster of darkness. He barreled into her, and Nadia turned from the flash coming from each individual point on his skin.

There was a slamming sound, and Dagmar screamed.

Nadia turned back to find Angel and demon on the floor, fighting in the now open doorway of the room Dagmar was hiding in. Nadia could not see much, as the darkness covered most of the ghost man in a tattered sheet. The diamonds sparkled in quick glimpses. Dagmar was standing on the other side of the room, hand over her mouth, eyes wide as the two once-human creatures fought.

Nadia advanced into the hallway, flicking the razor open in one hand. She did not know what she was going to do, but she would be ready.

The ghost man's fingernails flickered, cutting into the center of the shadow. A wet sound came from the mass, and greenish black slop splashed against the ghost man's torso. He grinned, but it was short lived. The shadows wrapped around his neck, and the head of the Angel was poised above him. She opened her mouth, and more of this—blood, it's her blood—spilled from her mouth into his. The ghost man coughed and sputtered, his body seizing up, his eyes bulging from his skull.

This was Nadia's chance. There would not be another. Nadia jumped into the scrum and reached for the ghost man's chest. Her hand slipped on the blood, stinging her skin where it touched. The glass bit into her finger, and she could not recoil. She pried it out of the ghost man's body, even as he was shuddering in his death throes.

The Angel turned, her eyes narrowing. "You. You vanished."

Nadia did not have time to speak. Her razor flickered outward, slicing a line down the left side of the Angel's face. More of the caustic blood flowed. Nadia crabbed backward across the floor, leaving black blood handprints behind her. The carpet sizzled where the blood clung.

The Angel flowed off of the dead man on the floor. She had changed even more. Now she was an animate storm, a serpentine line of greasy black. Nadia opened an empty jar, brought just in case, as she told herself, and dropped the shard of glass inside. It clattered on the bottom, the Angel's blood dusting the side. Nadia smeared more along the rim of it, clotting surface to surface.

The Angel was gone. The room seemed to inhale.

Nadia stood, holding the jar in her hand. Dagmar was across the room, eyes wide. Nadia held the jar in front of her. She could swear she saw the smoky darkness in the tiny shard of glass. Then again, maybe it was the green-black blood of the Angel.

It didn't matter. She dropped the jar to the floor and crunched it under her boot.

The wail echoing through the house was no dream.

***

Dagmar watched in mute horror as Stella Mortimer murdered Gaff, then was hexed into a jar and killed herself. *Maybe she's still alive*, her optimism begged. Dagmar knew Stella was dead, though. She felt the curse in her bones, vibrating with the sick energy of radiation. Nadia had harnessed something terrible.

Her face was flushed in victory, breath heaving, eyes alight. Dagmar wanted nothing more than to wipe that look from her face.

"Help him!" she screamed instead, running to Gaff's side.

His skin was cold. It was always cold. His chest was covered in Stella's green-black ichor. His eyes were cloudy beneath their lenses.

Nadia shook her triumph off and fell to her knees next to Gaff. She pressed a pair of fingers into his neck. "He's dead, Dagmar."

"He can't be dead."

"Who is he? What is he?"

"He's Shadowed! He won't die easily."

Dagmar saw the doubt in Nadia's eyes, but the younger woman shook it off. "Okay. Okay, I'll try."

She rummaged in her satchel. Nadia's secrets tinkled together in their jelly jars. Dagmar wanted to grab them and run. Fair price for killing her two best sources for talismans.

Nadia pulled a jar of berries from the satchel and unscrewed the top. She had used a straight razor on Stella, and this was still open, stained with black blood. Nadia scraped this off with her finger and spooned it into the lid of the jar. She took a little more from Gaff's chest. She spat into the mixture, adding berries and smashing it up with the handle of the razor. When it was a paste, she applied it to Gaff's lips.

She rocked back on her knees.

Dagmar lightly slapped Gaff's cheeks. There was no response. His chest wasn't moving. He had consumed a lot of Stella's blood, more than she had ever seen anyone drink. There was no way out. But he was her Shadowed, her loyal man, her enforcer, and the source of her precious glass.

The dim shape of her hand under Gaff's neck resolved itself, first a shadow, then growing in detail, adding color and detail. She wiggled her fingers. Gaff was going transparent. "No. No, this can't be happening."

He continued to fade. Soon, he was crystal. Only the dimmest shadows showed his features. Stella's blood sluiced off of him, no longer having enough friction to stay put. The cracks came shortly afterwards, running through Gaff's form, and he shattered, falling to the floor in a collection of tiny shards.

"Oh god. Dagmar, I'm so sorry," Nadia said.

"Sorry?" Dagmar looked up and found Nadia wobbly and indistinct. "What did you do?"

"I tried to heal him!"

"You failed!"

"I know! I'm sorry."

"How could you be so stupid?"

"I saved your friend downstairs. What's his name... Vorspan. He was dying when I came in. I saved his life!"

"Fuck him!" Dagmar shut her eyes. No matter how stupid Nadia had been, how incompetent, this was neither the time nor the place. She took a deep breath. "I'm sorry. I didn't mean that." She opened her eyes and found Nadia watching her warily, clutching the now closed razor in her hands.

"Are you sure?"

"Yes. I'm sorry. This was... a stressful evening."

"I guess you could call it that."

"And this man was my friend. My dear friend."

A frown flickered over Nadia's face, but it was gone just as quickly.

"Thank you, Nadia. I think you should be going, though. I need to clean up a little before I call anyone."

"Who will you call?"

"There are no bodies. Nothing anyone will recognize as blood. I am going to call a professional cleaning service."

A chuckle bubbled out of Nadia. "I guess you're right."

Dagmar got to her feet. She nearly stumbled but fought it. No more weakness in front of the younger woman. Too much of that already. "Let me show you out."

Only when Nadia went out the front door did Dagmar collapse against the despair.

***

Nadia returned home. Her finger burned where she cut it, and the places the Angel's blood touched itched like a healing sunburn. The rage Dagmar had shown was no act. There was much more to what had happened than Nadia knew. Look no further than Dagmar calling the ghost man her friend when he was still deciding whether to kill her.

Friends like these.

Nadia returned to the darkened guest house. She could not quite face Milena yet. Not after the prayer had come true. She went to the backyard, where Devin had rooted. He was entirely unrecognizable as anything other than a slightly man-shaped plant, though one lacking leaves. The mushrooms grew rampant over his skin.

China's Shadowed, turned into the only thing she had left of them. Had Angie survived, Nadia would be visiting her now, harvesting her for talismans.

Nadia stroked the paper-like bark, considering. Then she went inside and found her relieved girlfriend.

Wisdom

"**P**ower is what truly matters," Dagmar was saying. She stood in the dining room, sipping from a slender glass of red wine. Nadia sat nearby, her own cocktail in hand. It had been more than a month since the battle in Dagmar's home. Of the fight, and of the destructive hex, there was no sign. Whoever had cleaned had done their job quite well.

For the first couple weeks, Nadia did not hear from Dagmar at all. She had been expecting a period of silence, a time for the rage to work itself out, if it would. Had Dagmar chosen to end their relationship, Nadia would not have been overly surprised. The loss of a Matchless and Shadowed would have hurt, even if keeping them alive was wholly unrealistic. Dagmar seemed to Nadia the kind of person who got their wishes, no matter how unlikely.

Dagmar reached out with a phone call in the fourth week. Now, a few days later, they were having the drink Dagmar had suggested they have.

Her poise had entirely returned. Her short blonde hair was freshly cut, her makeup was subtle and effortlessly highlighted her aristocratic features. Her dress was as tight as ever, her jewelry as tasteful and expensive. Gone was the terrified prey animal of that awful night.

Nadia had spent the month worrying the edges of her wound, widening it, revealing more of her scales. The cut on her finger had not precisely healed. It revealed long, slender scales—scutes—like those found on a snake's belly. She wondered what her fingers really looked like now, denuded of troubling humanity.

Dagmar had welcomed her in and placed a Sazerac in her hand. A good hostess knows her guest's drink, she said with a fragile smile. Other than that, Dagmar had not had much use for preamble. She launched into what felt like a prepared speech, coming to the line: "Power is what truly matters."

Nadia could have taken it at face value, but she knew Dagmar really meant talismans. "Harvesting," Nadia prompted.

Dagmar turned, and looked at Nadia for what felt like the first time, her strident voice softening. "Exactly."

"They don't seem very common," said Nadia.

"They're not, in the scheme of things. In a city as big as this one, they are nearly inevitable."

"I suppose so. I'll keep an eye out, I guess."

"As will I. I can tell you know this isn't why I called you."

Nadia blanched. "That easy to read, am I?"

"We've known each other for a time. Seen each other at our best and worst."

"I suppose we have." Nadia did not mention that Dagmar had only seen one of those extremes in her, but she was not sure which.

"And we're both still here. That means something, I think."

"What did you have in mind?"

"Cultivation. In some sort of organized manner."

"Matchless?"

"And Shadowed and Kissed. They all have value, though some more than others."

"And?"

"When we find one, the two of us work together. We trap the person and can harvest as much as we like."

Nadia's stomach tightened. "Dagmar... they're insane. The one who was here was completely unreasonable, and, I'm sorry, but your friend didn't seem much better. Before we really started hanging out, I ran into another Matchless, and she was just as crazy."

"And you killed her?"

Nadia nodded. "I had to."

Dagmar hesitated. Then: "I'm certain you did. Like it or not, we depend on them for our power. With them, we can do anything. Without them, we are nothing. This means you and I need to treat this logically. You can shear a sheep as many times as you like, but you can only eat it once."

"Most sheep don't have superpowers and homicidal tendencies."

Dagmar waved the point aside. "Nadia, you and I are of a kind. The only two I know of. I am certain there are others, scattered over the globe. As good or better than us, with access to talismans we can't dream of. Together we are much stronger than we are alone."

"I agree with that."

"Good. And if someone were to threaten us, we should deal with them."

Nadia let the burn of the liquor comfort her. "Yeah. I guess I've already done that."

Dagmar fixed her with a gaze. "And if they were to threaten our supply of talismans, we would have to move against them as well."

Nadia watched Dagmar for a long moment. Then, she nodded. "Yes."

Dagmar relaxed. "I'm glad we're in agreement, Nadia." She returned to the bar and poured herself another glass of meaty red.

***

Nadia met Sav in one of the Midway's back rooms. Missing Linc stood at the doorway, scowling at the next room. He looked the part of enforcer, and as long as no one knew he sobbed at every Pixar movie, that illusion would stay intact.

"Private party," she heard Linc say to a patron. The angry muttering followed, but obediently moved off.

Sav had some of his men with him, but Nadia insisted they remain in the bar area. Sav had merely gestured to them, and they obeyed the request. He followed her into one of the back rooms, Linc in tow.

The room was decorated like the interior of a car, with clown pictures lining the walls. All the famous ones, from Bozo, to John Wayne Gacy, to Koko, to Georgie Giggles. The table they sat around was a booth set up like facing car seats. Sav had a bit of difficulty fitting, but after some sliding, was more or less comfortable behind it.

"Thank you for seeing me," he said.

She nodded.

"I have what you asked for." He put a bowling bag on the table and opened it. "First, your payment." He removed an envelope bulging with money and slid it over to her. She put it in her satchel without bothering to count it. Next, Sav placed a Ziploc bag on the table, containing several mashed bits of coppery metal. Bullets. Used ones. Nadia accepted these as well and placed them alongside her money.

"Then, the other." Sav lined three unfired bullets like soldiers in front of them. Then he put a vial next to it, filled halfway with blood.

Nadia picked it up. "Shed with gunshots?"

He nodded. "Hurt like a bitch."

"The pain is a sacrifice," she said.

"I see."

She wondered if he bought that part. It sounded good to her. She placed the jar of fingers she had harvested from one of China's victims along with a small leather bag embroidered with a beaded snake. She shook a single finger out in front of her and returned the jar to her satchel. Sav raised an eyebrow at the sight but did not comment.

She washed the used bullets in Sav's blood and put them in the bag. Her hands were slick now. With the razor, she sliced the severed finger into steaks, the rubbery bone giving way easily. She washed the slices in Sav's blood and it joined the rest in the bag. She tightened the drawstring, and tied it off, his blood scabbing on her fingers.

She tossed him the bag. It bounced off his chest and he caught the rebound. "Wear that on you, wherever you go."

Sav tied the long leather cords around his neck and tucked the bag into his shirt. "Thank you," he said to her, sliding from the booth with the exaggerated care of the hefty. He nodded respectfully to her and left the room.

Nadia went to the door, headed for the bathroom to wash Sav's blood from her fingers. Linc stood at the door, his tattoos hiding his expression in a false vision of a savage. Keegan loitered outside with him. Fresh off a show, she was dressed in little more than a lacy bra and panties, her skin covered in tiny pinpricks, like she had just been attacked by a swarm of miniature vampires.

"Who the fuck was that guy?" Keegan wanted to know.

"An associate."

"Are you in the mob now?"

"Sure. Linc here's my enforcer."

"I don't like to fight, Nadia."

"Yeah, but you look scary."

"Fuck this. Let's get something to drink. If I'm going to sweat, I'd rather it smell like bourbon," Keegan said.

Nadia ducked into the bathroom, washed her hands, then joined her friends at the bar.

"Seriously, what was that?" Keegan asked when they'd had their drinks.

"Man wanted a favor. Paid pretty good."

"Did you have sex with him?" Linc asked, horrified. Linc was drinking a zombie, and the thing looked like a Tiki party against the subdued cocktails she and Keegan preferred.

"God no. Gay, remember?"

"Oh yeah. Sorry, I forget what we all are sometimes."

"Thanks, Linc. That's sweet."

"Come on, you fucking tease, spill." Keegan hopped up on a barstool and demurely crossed her legs. She was drawing many looks and enjoying every second.

"Well, he's in the Armenian mob."

"I fucking knew it."

"And I'm not."

"I'm a little disappointed. Not gonna lie."

"He wanted a charm. To make him bulletproof."

Keegan and Linc stared at her, waiting for the punchline.

"That's the end of the story."

"And you gave him one?"

"Yes."

Linc considered it, his geologic thought processes finally getting him to a point. "You cheated him?"

"No. If he keeps it on him, he should be pretty much immune to bullets. I don't know if they'll stop or if they'll just not hit him, but he won't be killed by a bullet."

"You're serious," Keegan said.

"Yes."

"You're a witch."

"I guess I am."

Linc stretched out. The tattoos over his shirtless shoulders danced. "Okay," he said.

Nadia blinked. "Okay?"

"Linc's just saying okay. As in, 'Okay, what else you got?'" Keegan sipped her drink. "Goes for me too."

"You don't think I'm crazy?"

"Didn't say that. Look, I haven't known you that long, but we spend a lot of time together. Fact is, I sniffed weird shit off you from day one. Did you know that your shadow goes the wrong way?"

Nadia looked at the bar. With the light in the room, she didn't properly have a shadow, only a thin film of black stretching in all directions. "What?"

"Goes toward the light, dear. Not the only part, either. On the nights we share a drink, I wake up the next morning and all my staple cuts are healed."

"And no matter what I ate, I don't get the squirts," Linc said.

Keegan burst out laughing. "On the job hazards."

"So you're saying..."

"I'm saying you're something. You tell me you're a witch. You tell me you can make some gangster bulletproof, I say okay."

"That sounds right," Linc said, sipping on his zombie. He looked up at the clock. "Oh shit. I gotta eat a bicycle in like five minutes." He chugged the rest of his drink and wandered off toward the geek room.

Nadia looked over at her friend. "Thanks, K."

Keegan hugged her. "Don't worry about it, sweetie. We freaks have to stick together."

***

Nadia spent Saturday morning on the couch. After the craziness of her life, it was nice to have a day to relax. She read, she napped. She watched the shadows on the other side of the wall. She thought about what she'd done, and whether she was okay with it.

Two now. First China, and then the Angel. Both of them were killers. The only difference was that Nadia didn't wait for the Angel to kill one of her friends to finish her off. Sav was a killer too, and she'd helped him. Helped him for fifty grand, and some ingredients she couldn't get otherwise. He killed someone for those bullets. Someone he would have killed anyway. At least the death would have some kind of meaning. Strengthening the man who did it.

There were others out there like Sav. Others who might want a witch. They couldn't pay in money like him, but maybe they could pay in information. Talismans were worth more than money. Even rumors could have value. Her friends at the Midway—Keegan, Linc, Dave, Bekah and the others—might have heard something. They all moved in strange circles. The life of the professional prodigy in the 21st Century.

Her phone buzzed and she picked it up. "Hi, mom," she said, wondering if there was going to be a lecture.

"Nadia! I'm in your neighborhood. I wanted to see this place of yours and give you a housewarming present."

Nadia sat upright. "Um... it's okay, mom. The house is plenty warm." She'd been there for months at this point. Why now? That was Siranush, an urge crystallized in her head, and suddenly became of vital importance.

"Don't be silly," and just like that Nadia gave Siranush the address. She was up and pacing afterwards, glancing around the apartment at all the things that were obviously not hers. She shut the door to the bedroom, where a few of Milena's dresses were drying on hangers. The knickknacks weren't quite Nadia yet, but maybe Siranush would concentrate more on the yellowing stacks of paperbacks by the wall.

Milena had gone to a morning game to win a little extra money. She wouldn't be back until the evening. Nadia couldn't quite imagine the look on her mother's face to be confronted with the relationship. Maybe she could get her in and out the door nice and quickly before she said anything too awful.

When the knock came at the door, it was barely louder than her heart.

Nadia opened it up and put a brave smile on her face. "Hi, mom."

Siranush was heavily made up and perfumed, leaving scented after-images wherever she went. She held a spider plant in her hands, and Nadia remembered seeing them in Dagmar's living room. She didn't want to touch it, out of superstitious dread.

"So small!" her mother said, coming in.

"It's as big as I need."

"I suppose so. I got you this," she said, holding out the spider plant.

Nadia hesitated, but took it, her skin crawling. She set it down on a table quickly.

"Is that where you work?" she asked, nodding to the desk.

"Uh, yeah."

"A novelist in the family. Your father does not approve, but we both know once it is out of your system, you will come around. Write something we can sell for you."

"I don't think that's how it works," Nadia said. She thought about correcting the idea that she was a novelist, but it was difficult to explain her current job.

Siranush took off her sunglasses and looked Nadia over, shaking her head. "Are those tattoos on your head? Oh, Nadia. Why do you insist on looking so ugly?"

"My girlfriend likes it." The words were out before she could stop them, poised on the fraying edge of her nerves, to be severed entirely by Siranush's last comment.

Nadia stunned herself, and she saw her own feelings echoed in her mother's face. Siranush recovered quickly and decided to mishear. "It's well and good for your friends, but if you want to attract a husband, you should grow out your long and pretty hair. Wear makeup. Removing those tattoos will be expensive, but we can afford it."

Nadia was not certain why she bulled ahead. Ignoring her was somehow worse. See me, she wanted to say to her mother. The tattoos, the rings in her eyebrows, everything. Her appearance was not an accident.

"No, mom. My girlfriend. The woman I'm living with."

Siranush's face hardened. "Nadia, I know you went to college, and they do things there, but this is the real world—"

"I'm gay."

"Nadia! Stop trying to make me angry."

Nadia's shoulders slumped. "I'm not, mom. I'm just tired of not telling you. I'm a lesbian. I'm living with a woman. I'm pretty damn happy about it. She loves me, mom. I love her. We're good for each other."

"Are you listening to yourself?"

"I'm not the one here having trouble listening."

"Odette never would have humiliated us like this."

"Odette? For one thing, Odette was straight. For another, she did humiliate you. Remember how crazy you got when she moved in with Tyrone? They weren't married, and he was black. You and dad, doing everything you could to get her back home, married off to a good Armenian boy. I heard you telling her about how I would never do something like that to you. Of course, this was back when I had long hair and looked like someone else entirely. And what's worse, you never got a chance to meet Ty, either. He was good for Odette, and he was sweet to me. But he and Odette were murdered, and as soon as that happened, you forgot all about Ty, and Odette got fitted for a halo."

Siranush slapped her. The hit didn't even burn. It was a vindication.

"That's what I thought," Nadia said.

"I don't know who you are, but you're not my Nadia."

"No, I'm not. I'm something so much more."

Siranush stood there, small and weak, her breath coming in gasps. Her hand fluttered at her side. Nadia dared her to let it fly again, staring hard into her mother's eyes until the other woman broke contact, and fled for the door. She tore it open and Milena was on the other side, hat and sunglasses hiding her from the sun.

"Hi," Milena said, the question in her voice.

Siranush pushed past her and down the driveway.

"The hell was that?" Milena asked.

"My mom," Nadia said. "I think she just cut me off."

Milena came in, shedding sunglasses, hat, and purse, and putting her arms around Nadia. "Are you okay?"

"Yeah. I think I am, actually."

Milena watched her, then broke into a smile. "Well, good."

"I thought you were at a game until this evening."

"I was. But sometimes you get the perfect hand, the perfect marks, and the perfect pot. I quit early." She laced Nadia's hands around her back. Nadia loved the feel of Milena's lovely soft curves. "I thought we could use a trip, and now I know it for sure. We're not a secret to anyone, and I think that calls for a celebration."

"Where?"

"A little town a couple hundred miles north of here. Now get your stuff together."

"Are you serious?"

"As a heart attack. I already called your brother to come over and water the plants. Now pack a bag."

Nadia laughed and did as she was told. Twenty minutes later they were in Milena's car, heading north. The murmuring of Milena's podcasts put Nadia out, and when she woke up, it was nearing sunset, and they were pulling into a motel across the street from crashing waves. "Where are we?" Nadia muttered.

"Vacation."

They spent the next few says in that paradise, not doing much more than eating, relaxing, and loving. Their cares were far, far away.

***

Dagmar held the swatch of cloth in the palm of her hand. A tiny white square with frayed edges, unremarkable to anyone except her. She had cut it from her tablecloth as soon as she saw it and verified the precious treasure it carried in the fibers.

The two red drops were blood.

Gaff had not bled downstairs. Stella's blood was not red. She checked Vorspan and found no wounds on him. The blood could only belong to one person. Nadia.

She turned the swatch over in her hand. Before that night, she might have held off. Kept the cloth in the hopes of never using it. A trump, should Nadia ever be foolish enough to go against her.

Not anymore.

Nadia was too dangerous to keep around. Not to Dagmar, but to the talismans. She had been willing to kill Stella, had failed to save Gaff, and then had admitted she'd killed another Matchless. Dagmar couldn't imagine how many talismans she had pissed away in that act of violence. They could have grabbed this other one Nadia destroyed and locked her away. Now this Matchless was gone. Her talismans vanished from the earth. Forever.

There would be others, and with Nadia on the loose, there was no telling how many she would murder. Dagmar had even asked her what should be done with someone who threatened their supply. Nadia had admitted it: they kill that person. She had given Dagmar her permission, her blessing, to do what had to be done.

The decision had been made. The intervening time had been spent gathering what she needed for the curse. Now, she had to craft it, and she found herself hesitating. Nadia was an ally. Almost a friend. She had risked her life to rescue Dagmar from Stella, and though she had been stupid and reckless, she had done it.

Dagmar stared at the ingredients on the table. They were a murder weapon, when assembled correctly. It had to be now or wait another month. She was scheduled soon, the cramps telling her she was right on time. Revenge would be tonight.

She placed the swatch of cloth on the table. Inside, she put a few shards of bloody glass, taken from Gaff's body. She smeared a bit of the paste Nadia had used to save him on it as well. There was no true energy in it but called to mind the ultimate fate of the man who held it on his blue lips. Last, she added the claw of a mountain lion, purchased from the same man who sold her the last one. He had not done more than raise an eyebrow at her request, but the money was good, and he did not object.

She gathered the square around the curse and tied it into a bag using a few of her own hairs as a string. It was heavy in her hand. A loaded gun.

Dagmar placed it in her bag and drove to the small guest house where Nadia and Milena lived. It had been easy to find; all that was required was a peek at Milena Franco's records at the Midway, something the boss had been happy to allow Dagmar to do for another bribe.

She came up the driveway brazenly. If anyone was home, she would play it off. Act like she belonged, say she was a friend. No objection came from the main house or the small structure in the back. Dagmar paused at the end of the driveway. It was a cute place. Small. Cozy, probably. She wondered if she would be able to get Milena to move into her place once Nadia was gone, or if the card player would insist on staying here.

Or if something more extreme would be required. Milena would not be nearly so hard to corral as Stella had been.

Dagmar went around the side, looking for soft earth to bury the bag.

Right around the side of the house, shielded from the front by a robust hibiscus bush, was a strange whitish tree. She cocked her head, staring at it. It was vaguely man-shaped, down to two separate trunks sprouting from the earth and joining together in the middle. A few mushrooms grew along the tops of its "shoulders." She touched one and felt the comforting buzz of a talisman. She allowed herself a smile. This would be hers soon enough. She forced her quivering hand away from the talismans. She could not harvest. Nadia would know someone had been there. Someone with eyes to see.

The tree stood in the soft earth of a flowerbed. Perfect.

Dagmar took a few steps, and nearly tripped. She looked down, and found a thin wire stretched across the lawn. She frowned, and then felt a stabbing on her ankle. Like someone had jabbed a fork into the flesh just above the bone in her ankle. She toppled over.

Only then did the snake rattle.

A curse. A fucking curse in the backyard. A tripwire calling Nadia's little friends.

Dagmar pulled herself away from the snake, rattling and readying itself for another strike. Its tongue flickered in and out. Her ankle was filled to bursting, sloshing around inside, burning wherever the venom washed up against. She pulled her leg away and nearly cried out.

Then, the snake was gone, as though it had never been there. Was it flesh and blood, or was Nadia's presence creating them from the earth? Dagmar could not imagine such power. Perhaps a reward for resculpting herself into an oddity.

No time to ponder. Dagmar reached over and slammed the bag into the dirt. She didn't bother putting it deep. There might not be time.

She hauled herself to one foot. Weight on her wounded leg sent fire up and down her body. The ankle was turning blue, swelling up around the twin punctures of the snake wounds. More of these tripwires stretched from fence to tree, or house to bush, a spiderweb of security. Trip one and the reward was a snake.

Looking at the pattern, it was a minor miracle she hadn't tripped one earlier. One more would likely kill her. At the very least, it would take the working leg from her, and she couldn't crawl out. She needed a hospital.

Dagmar limped from the yard, biting back a scream whenever she put too much weight on her wounded leg. It felt at once asleep and in terrible pain. At the hospital, they shot her full of antivenin after she described the snake to them—a Western Diamondback, she learned— and she spent the night in a hospital bed. She learned later the pins-and-needles feeling in her ankle was nerve damage and would never completely go away.

Small price for removing Nadia.

***

Vorspan was home alone. Dagmar was never far from his mind, but at that moment, she was as far from it as she ever got, shielded by the desperate mundanity of his day-to-day. He was in the midst of his routine, fetching his low-calorie meal from the freezer— vegetarian lasagna, he noted with weary good humor— when the pain hit.

It was a spike extending from his anus, up through his guts, chest, and throat. Like a red-hot wire, igniting his spine and radiating outward to the tips of his fingers and toes. The box of lasagna fell from his seizing hands to clatter on the floor. There he would find it the following day, lukewarm and blue-black with flies.

That this pain was not the worst he had ever felt was somehow worse than it coming from nowhere.

Because he had felt it before. Once a month, give or take a day or so.

He felt his body realigning itself. No longer his, it would change, reshape, and take on a form pleasing to its true master: Dagmar.

His bones creaked. Some lengthened, others shortened. His muscles bulged and stretched over the new frame, crawling to different positions before throwing down roots of vein and sinew. His mouth exploded in agony. He tasted blood on his suddenly flattened tongue as his teeth grew, shrank, and shifted. His spine cracked like a whip, throwing him to the floor. He caught himself with his hands, and saw they weren't hands anymore.

Conscious thought was gone from him after that. He had dim memories of what came next, filtered through the twilight red haze of the animal sight. He perceived so much more, but his brain was unused to such stimuli. He would try to parse them when true thought returned to him the next morning, when the unfamiliar tastes infected his tongue. He would get flashes of images, of scents, of sounds, his nighted human senses could never perceive. Unraveling their mysteries were impossible; he was an alien to his own mind.

He had the vague sense that he prowled the wilder areas to the north somewhere. Where they foliage grew dense and there were rabbits and deer and coyotes to hunt and kill. There was never the sense of direction, of will.

Until now.

Tonight, there was a target. He remembered the underbrush whipping past his face. He stayed away from the wide roads as much as he could, never crossing when he saw the headlights splashing over the blacktop. He had no way of calculating or even understanding time. He only knew he ran a long distance, through the wild areas, but he never tired. He was being pulled, the scent of blood in his nose beckoning him across the wide planes of the city.

These things: car, city, he only understood in abstract. They all became danger. He knew to stay to the darkness, where the plants grew their wildest.

The scent was familiar, though not. It sparked no memory in him. It gave the concept of prey, a bright, hot, arterial thought, spraying over his mind.

He arrived at the place he was called to. A small house, though this too was a concept scrubbed from his mind. The prey lived within. He could smell it, all around. The prey was not there now.

The cat that was Vorspan padded around the side of the house and settled into the dense hibiscus, his green eyes probing the dark. Waiting.

Some time later—and he did not know how long—a person came up the driveway. Walking quickly, and making sounds—talking, his mind said, as though this meant something. The person approached the door, fished a key from beneath the mat, and went inside.

Vorspan sniffed the air. The person carried a scent of the prey. It was not perfect, though it was quite close. Vorspan lacked any ability to make a decision; it was made when he lunged from the bush and slinked inside. The person was by the sink, upending water over some pants.

The person had time to scream once before Vorspan brought him down.

Vorspan regained consciousness much later. He lay on his couch, nude. The taste of blood was metallic on his tongue. The memories came flooding back to him. The feel of the flesh parting under his claws. The taste blooming over his mouth. He'd eaten. Oh god, he'd eaten.

Vorspan curled up on the floor and wept.

"Are you done?"

He didn't look up. He had not known Dagmar was there until she spoke, though he was not surprised. He could picture her in his mind's eye, sitting aristocratically in his best chair, watching him sob. Her toy. Her little toy.

The tears burned, his throat swelling shut. He willed it to close, to choke off his cursed life. Maybe he would stop tasting the blood. Blood he was still swallowing at each moment, reliving his act of cannibalism, again and again.

"I take it she's dead?" Dagmar asked.

Vorspan fought the flooding images, focused as they were on the meat and the blood. The taste, the divine taste, and the way he had gorged himself on the viscera of the dead person. And the worst: he craved another taste, praying Dagmar would send him on another task. He managed a nod through his sobs.

"And that was all? You only killed one?"

Vorpsan nodded again.

"Good. If you had killed Milena Franco too, I would have been rather angry."

Vorspan opened his eyes, wiping them with a balled fist. Dagmar was standing, and she looked drawn and harried. She saw him looking and put a smile on her face.

"But I am not."

No, Vorspan could read her better than that.

***

Nadia spent the drive down listening to Milena sing softly along to the Cure, gazing out the window at the ocean. The vacation had lasted forever and ended too quickly. Was this life now? It felt like nothing could penetrate the bliss she had taken from it. Even the looks she received around the small central coast town were of the curious rather than hostile variety. The strange young woman who turned herself into art.

And besides, what could they do against her?

She first knew something was wrong when they turned down the driveway and Milena uttered murmur of dismay. Nadia perked up and saw the door was partially open.

"That would be perfect," Milena sighed.

"Did you leave the door open?"

"I don't think so."

"Oh god. It was probably Lex. When he stopped by, he must have forgot."

"Or, someone broke in. Most thieves can pick a lock."

"Who's stealing from us? Unless they're really into old sci-fi paperbacks."

The car came to a silent stop a few feet from the door. Both women got out. Nadia stared at the door in distrust as though it had something to do with the betrayal. It gaped hollowly, the dark beyond containing its secrets only barely.

Milena went to the door and paused. Nadia was right next to her. She reached out and held Milena's hand — the house had been hers, and the bulk of the things within belonged to her. Nadia's only worry was for the talismans on her desk, but most of those appeared to be relatively useless items, with only some of China's old camera equipment carrying any monetary value.

Nadia nudged the door open and regretted it immediately. A smear of blood ran through the apartment, going from the kitchen area, out from behind the island, forming a hideous welcoming carpet. Flies had found it, feasting on the larger collections. They broke off in a wave as Nadia approached, mesmerized, leaving behind their white and wriggling offspring.

She wanted to stop herself from going around the island to see the source, but she could not. It pulled her in. Even as she knew, there could only be one person behind there, she had to look. Had to know.

She stepped around it, and a scream tore its bloody way from her throat. It was a scream of the likes she hadn't heard come from herself since she was small. Since the kinds of things that could be so cruel still lived in the shadows of her life.

Her brother lay on the kitchen floor. He had been torn apart, and large parts of him were simply gone. She knew it was him, because half of his face, some of it visible under a coating of flies, stared sightlessly at the ceiling. She did not remember much afterwards, only she was on the couch, sobbing helplessly.

She dimly saw Milena talking to the police, and she tried to answer the few questions they posed to her. Milena sat with her, rubbing her back and holding her whenever she had a spare moment. Nadia wondered how she was going to tell her parents.

She got the basic information from Milena. There was no murder investigation. It was a wild animal attack, and later, analysis of the wounds found the culprit to be a mountain lion. While no mountain lions had been seen in Echo Park, it was not too far from Griffith Park in the scheme of things. The evidence fit. A freak accident.

Nadia called her parents the same day. She was darkly relieved to get her father on the line. He was gruff, though not unkind, and when she gave him the news, he was stoic. She heard him tell Siranush, and the horrible, gut wrenching cry that followed. The tension in Vartan's voice was obvious. He thought he had already done the worst thing a parent would have to do when he buried Odette. Now he was putting Lex right beside her.

His only child left was the freak daughter. The one he couldn't understand, who made her mother cry.

Milena did her best to shield Nadia in the following days. Reporters eagerly buzzed around—after all, this was the kind of weird segment the news loved. There were even curiosity seekers out on the street, though few braved the long driveway to the guest house.

Nadia had to buy a black suit for the funeral. Milena was lovely and strong in her black veil and dress. The remaining Eskandarian family was all there, battered and bruised by this fresh tragedy. There were others, though Nadia scarcely saw them. Everyone circled the grieving parents. Nadia was largely ignored, she suspected because she looked nothing like the mousy, long-haired girl they'd known.

They returned to the Eskandarian house and Nadia ate food she couldn't taste and kept thinking about her brother. Milena was never far away.

She went to her mother once, needing to say something, but having no idea what to say. She was the last remaining child. She hoped this would mean her mother could accept what she'd learned, that they could put it behind her. Nadia hugged Siranush, and her mother hugged back, a hard reflex. She was about to return to Milena and grief, when her mother muttered something just out of the edge of hearing.

"What?" Nadia asked, regretting it as soon as she did.

"I said, 'What was Lex doing at that place?'"

"We asked him to water the plants. We were going on vacation."

"We? Who is we?"

"Milena and I. Mom, please don't do this."

"All because you want... this... unnatural thing, your brother has to die."

The words hit with the force of a punch. Nadia had only enough air to squeak something almost like "have," but the word had no meeting.

"You heard me," Siranush said to her daughter, throwing Nadia's words back.

Nadia stared dumbly at her mother, then glanced at her father, who was pointedly looking away. Nadia resisted the urge to flee. She staggered, stiff-legged, back to where she had left Milena, who was watching the exchange out of earshot.

"We have to go right now," Nadia said.

"Okay, yeah, of course." Milena put aside her plate and held Nadia as they walked out. Nadia leaned on Milena, grateful for the strength of the other woman.

***

Milena hated leaving Nadia in the house. They had spent the last few days at a motel. Nadia's friends had been concerned, calling condolences when they heard what happened. Nadia wanted to spend her time with Milena and Milena alone.

Reality ensued. Milena couldn't lose her job at the Midway, and she was due for a shift. Most of the remains had been cleaned out of the kitchen, but big splotches of blood stained the linoleum. She told Nadia to stay away from it, not to think about it, promising herself she would scrub until her fingers bled if that's what it took. Nadia had nodded, but Milena knew Nadia would do whatever popped into her mind to do.

Milena arrived for her shift, and Dave the bartender stopped her on the way back to ask about Nadia, wanting to know if there was anything he could do. She thanked him and made it back to the room. Before long, Keegan, Bekah, Linc, and a few others checked in, all asking after about Nadia. Milena hoped her girlfriend knew how much her friends cared for her.

She settled into the game, pushing her worry as far from her mind as she could. She put on her character of the Fortuneteller like a veil. Give those who came to the Midway their thrill, see what the cards had to say. They were not speaking much, but she had gotten good enough to lie when that was happening. Make a prediction vague or universal enough and it wouldn't kill her reputation. In the meantime, she was going to win a good chunk of rent off the marks.

Several hours in, she had given a single true prediction (the thief was her cousin), and a host of false ones. The mask was on perfectly. The air in the room was thick with awe, and Milena felt truly at peace. The customers kept coming in, and she skipped her normal break, though when Tasha the waitress checked in on her, Milena did not have her customary cocktail.

Milena did not react when the empty chair on the other end of the table slid out, and a gold-clad shape creeped in on the edge of her vision. She dealt, giving the newcomer a hand like everyone else at the table. She dropped her ante in the center of the table—someone else's money, she noted with a sense of pride—and looked up.

Dagmar Eichel was the newcomer. She hadn't picked up her cards, her graceful hand resting just above the surface of the table, her long fingers lightly stroking the green felt surface. The dress was a scoop neck, showing off curving neck and swelling breasts, highlighting the drop necklace resting between her clavicles. Her makeup was similarly metallic. She had truly become a golden woman, excising the few remaining islands of humanity in her persona. Only her eyes, the feline jade, flashed at Milena.

"Hello," she said. Hell, she nearly purred.

Oh shit, Milena thought. She hasn't heard.

"Good evening," Milena said. She was doing her voice and was glad she'd never tried an accent. She was a quarter Hungarian, but that was as close as her bloodline got to eastern Europe. Too far from her real persona. It would have slipped.

She played the hand quickly, giving the other two people at the table their fake fortunes and scraping in the pot.

Dagmar watched the two of them leave the table out of the corner of her eyes, her grin stretching wider. "Can I buy you a drink?"

"Yeah, sure. We should talk somewhere private."

Dagmar looked around the small room. "This is private enough."

Milena swallowed. Not quite this private. "Customers will keep coming in. I don't have a sign or anything to keep them out."

"All right."

Milena led Dagmar into the clown car room. A moment later, Tasha came and took their orders. The room was far from empty, but it was a place for subdued conversations. They got their drinks quickly, Tasha dropping off an old fashioned for Milena and an Americano for Dagmar.

Dagmar brought the cocktail to her lips and swallowed a caramel mouthful. She fished the orange peel from the glass, and sucked the liquor from it, appraising Milena.

Milena inwardly quailed under the look. Nadia was at home with the blood of her brother. "I am glad you were willing to see me," Dagmar said.

"You are a friend."

"I am." She continued to toy with the orange peel. Milena found her throat closing up. Drinking her cocktail would be impossible. "I wanted to tell you I was sorry about what happened."

Milena blinked. Oh, of course. She read it online somewhere. The story had been picked up for listicles and other weird items. A man getting eaten by a mountain lion while inside a house was bound to attract the morbidly curious. "Thank you."

Dagmar reached across the table and took Milena's hand. It felt hot and brittle, like it had been left in the sun too long. "I wanted you to know I'm here for you. Anything you could need."

Milena let her hand lie there, limp, Dagmar's clutching at it. "It's not me who needs it. You should call Nadia."

"Nadia?" Dagmar leaned back in shock, losing contact.

"Yeah, Nadia. It was her brother. I mean, I knew Lex. He was a good guy, but Nadia was the one who lost her brother." On top of losing her sister a few years ago.

"Her brother? Her brother was killed?"

"Yeah? Isn't that why you're here?"

"Yes. Yes, of course. I'm so sorry, Milena. I should go. Please, give Nadia my condolences." Dagmar stood up in shock and tottered out, suddenly graceless in her high heels. Milena watched her go.

Tasha came by the table to pick up the half-empty Americano. "What was that about?"

"I'm not sure." She held a hand over the Americano. "Wait." She plucked the orange peel from it and wrapped it in a napkin.

"Okay," Tasha said, walking out with the remains of the drink.

***

When Milena left for the Midway, Nadia tried to sleep. She retreated to the bedroom and lay in hers and Milena's bed. The bedroom door hung open, the meaty scent of blood washing over her.

It was insane, of course. There was no scent of it anymore. Industrial cleaners had cut it to nothing. Turned it to acid. It was just a stain that would take some time to get out.

Nadia found herself on her knees, scrubbing at the remainder, the white soap foam turning pink with each pass. She tried to pretend it was nothing but a stubborn stain. She couldn't. This was her brother, the parts of him that made his body move, that animated him, that made him what he was.

And there was so much.

The creature had torn him apart. The arterial spray reached the ceiling. Covered the fronts of the cabinets. Pooled in the cracks and lingered. The best the crime scene cleaners had managed was soaking up the deepest pools, leaving wide streak marks over everything. Nadia would see the blood as it was for the rest of her life.

Her back and knees ached. Her fingers burned with the caustic cleaning agents. It felt like the blood of the Angel, and the pain comforted her.

The blood of the Angel. Had she not killed that creature herself, she might think this was somehow her doing. A mountain lion coming into a house might fly with the official investigation, but Nadia knew there was more to it. There had to be. She had crossed a great deal of powerful people, had discovered a netherworld of the mad gifted, and now it had come home.

She gagged, spilling her meager breakfast onto the floor in front of her. More heaves, and then it was just a little more she had to clean up, and she did.

Murder? Was she truly thinking murder? Lex intimated he had connections to men like Sav Krikorian.

It could be a hit. Or perhaps one of them had decided to take out the little witch who killed Karo Minasian. Or maybe it was a new Matchless who was getting tired of her hunting them down, a new kind of Matchless with a sense of pride and community.

Regardless, if there was a murder, there was a murderer. The police weren't looking for him, and they would not have the ability to punish him properly. Not like Nadia could.

She went outside into the dark areas around her house. A flashlight traced the lawn, picking up the tripwires she strung all over. Here, alone with Nadia, the snakes were obvious, coiled in muscular piles over the lawn, ready to strike. She stepped amongst them, checking wire after wire. One had been torn. Someone, or something, had tripped it.

Frowning, she paused, and stood up, playing her beam over Devin. He was only a tree now. The mushrooms were whitish splotches against the bone-bright bark. He did not appear to have any bare patches of mushrooms. Had it been Dagmar, she couldn't have resisted.

But who else?

Who else knew her? Knew her home? Could wield an animal like a weapon?

She stopped herself. She couldn't imagine it would be Dagmar. Why kill Lex? He was innocent. If Dagmar wanted someone dead, it would be her, over the matter of the dead Matchless. Killing Lex accomplished nothing.

There would be a way to find the killer. The inspiration was clear and true, a note rung from crystal.

Nadia went inside, pulling a knife from the block on the counter, and kneeling by one of the seams in the linoleum where Lex's blood had pooled. She pulled it out in flakes and chunks, breathing shallowly to avoid scattering it, scooping it up into a small bowl.

She brought it over to her desk and located one of China's cameras. A sharp blow from a hammer dislodged the lens. The camera was no longer a talisman, its energy transferred in the act of freeing the lens. She put it aside, with the murder bullets Sav had given her. Perhaps good for an effect later on.

She brushed the flaked blood into the concave lens, then picked Azh up from where he was sleeping by the window. The dragon fluttered his tongue sleepily, content in her touch. She squeezed the sides of his head and the shocking white mouth, like raw chicken, opened wide, the two fangs flicking outward.

Azh did not struggle. Two beads of venom gathered at the tips of the fangs and dripped into the lens. She set Azh down, and he slithered away to disappear. She went into the bedroom and selected a needle from Milena's sewing kit. She used it to stir the venom and blood until the flakes dissolved in the faintly amber liquid.

Then she wiped the needle off and set it on the surface of the liquid, blobby chunks of liquid membrane holding the needle horizontally. It spun slowly, but with purpose, turned and pointed roughly west.

Nadia set it down and fetched her satchel. Azh was inside, wrapped around the talisman jars. He knew he was needed, or at the very least wanted.

She placed the lens on a bed of handkerchiefs and secured it in the cup holder of her car. She was going to have to drive steadily so as not to spill, periodically checking the needle to see which way it was pointing.

As she drove, she determined it was indicating one direction resolutely. It was not guiding her step-by-step, but rather showing her the ultimate destination. The location of Lex's murderer. The one who shed the blood now holding the needle. She followed the streets as closely as she could, and soon realized she was heading into the rich territory of West LA. Dagmar was close by in Brentwood—she cut the thought off. Wait to see who it was before throwing blame.

She imagined a gangster with some kind of outside zoo. Maybe it had been a freak accident, and she was going up into the hills after a predatory cat. Maybe a Matchless had some control over animals. Maybe. Maybe.

Anything but the truth.

By the end of the trip, she was moving around in a tightening spiral. Every turn made the needle spin crazily until it shuddered to a stop, indicating an entirely new direction. Eventually, Nadia found what it was pointing at: a brick townhouse in Westwood. Not huge, but certainly large enough. It said money, though not the kind of money she would expect out of a gangster. More than Karo, she thought in a flash of spite.

Not Dagmar's, and that too was a relief.

She left her compass in the car, grabbing the satchel. It was still heavy with the snake. She peeked in and found him coiled, head and rattle out. Ready to strike.

Nadia knocked on the front door. There was no question in her mind. When the murderer answered, she would let Azh incapacitate him. Then, if she wanted, she could save his life. Give him more pain than he had thought possible. Show him what he had done to her, to Lex, to her family as a whole.

The door opened, revealing Richard Vorspan. Her stomach turned inside out again, but all that made it into her throat was a burning column of acid. Her hands shook, tears blurring her eyes.

"You?" she heard Vorspan say. The shape, now little more than that, stumbled back into the hall.

Nadia straightened, spitting out the bit of bile. She wiped her eyes and stalked inside.

Vorspan was the murderer. Somehow. This mousy little man. He had seemed unstable; maybe that was it. She had saved his life. She had made it possible. She should have let him die. Let the poison eat him from the inside.

The hallway was dark, and Vorspan was at the other end, terrified hands up. "No! Please, I didn't want to kill you!"

Nadia paused, cocking her head.

Vorspan fell to his knees, cradling his hands, weeping. Nadia had never seen anything quite so pathetic. It stayed her. She felt pity, despite what he had done. Her satchel was heavy on her shoulder, Azh shifting and slithering inside of it, wanting to come out. *Do I give you to my snake?*

She crouched next to Vorspan, putting a hand on his shaking shoulder. Azh struggled. She would not be able to keep him in the satchel for long, and when he emerged, it would be to kill Vorspan.

The terrified man shrank from the touch. "I'm so sorry. I'm so sorry. I didn't want to kill you."

She put a hand under his chin and guided it up. His eyes were wide, unfocused, hopelessly mad. The scraps of a man she had seen before were now entirely gone. All that remained was this quivering husk. No more present than one of China's slaves.

"Why did you kill me?"

"She told me to. She wanted it done. I can't say no. I can't."

Dagmar. Dagmar had made him do it. Somehow.

She pictured Dagmar planting a hex jar by the side of the house and tripping one of Nadia's wires. She hoped the venom burned.

Vorspan was disconsolate, not even really looking at her anymore. All that was left for him was his hopeless crying. Nadia peered into his eyes. Deep in them, she saw a flash of green. She might be tempted to call it her imagination, but she knew it was more than that. His inhumanity obvious even now.

Nadia left him there, driving home, numb. How long had Vorspan been transformed? Before the dinner party most likely. Dagmar had broken him, but he had not truly been shattered until she used him. Or until he saw what he thought was a ghost coming to wreak vengeance. Confronted by flesh and blood guilt.

Killing Vorspan was pointless. Whatever he had done had been punished. No, he was little more than a knife or a gun.

She arrived home shortly afterwards, putting her things aside and finding Azh had vanished from the satchel. She had not been keeping track, but she imagined the instant she chose not to kill Vorspan was the moment Azh had vanished, returning to wherever it was dragons went.

Nadia was lost in thought when the door opened up and Milena came in. Nadia glanced at the clock. Midnight, meaning Milena had rushed out after her shift without sticking around for a drink with any of her coworkers.

"How are you?" was Milena's first sentence as Nadia came through the door.

Nadia nodded. There were no words for precisely how she was feeling.

Milena glanced at the section of kitchen where Lex had lain, now scrubbed clean. "Something really weird happened at work today." She paused, waiting for Nadia's nonverbal consent to continue. "Dagmar came in and she was hitting on me. She seemed to think you were dead."

It was not a shock to Nadia in the slightest. It fit everything she knew. Only one moment slid into her chest like a shard of ice. The conversation with Dagmar.

If anyone threatens our talismans, they would have to be dealt with as well. Nadia had agreed.

Dagmar had been asking permission to kill her.

And Nadia had granted it.

"I'm going to need to kill Dagmar," Nadia said. Her tone was so reasonable, so neutral, she could have been ordering brunch.

Milena placed an orange peel on the table. "She was sucking on that."

Nadia got to her feet. Though her limbs felt very far away, she was straight and steady. "I need to get something."

Milena followed Nadia out to the street, and the two of them got in Nadia's car. They prowled the streets of East LA. Nadia knew what she was looking for, and Milena never asked. The streets were as dark as they ever got, the cars fewer and fewer as they hunted through the streets and freeways.

Nadia finally saw what she wanted in the middle of the intersection at Sunset and Lucile. A car turning left up a hill had been broadsided by an SUV. The police and ambulance were already on the scene. One person was pinioned to a spinal board, being loaded into the back of the ambulance while a man pressed a bandage to his bloody forehead.

Nadia pulled over. Milena was still silent. That time of night, there weren't many cars out, but one of the police had taken to waving the people around the twisted hunks of metal at the intersection.

When the crosswalk showed the walking man, Nadia started purposefully toward the other side. When she hit the center, when the largest parts of the wreck were between her and the cops, she made a right turn for them. At a glance, it looked like the SUV was the one hitting, while the crumpled Honda was the one that had gotten hit. Nadia rushed to it and knelt by the front bumper. She wanted the exact spot of impact, where the SUV put all of its mass into the heart of the car.

"Hey. What are you doing?"

She peered into the place where the two cars met. The bumpers were hopelessly snarled, mostly obliterated in the impact. She found a good chunk and yanked it off the front, shoving it into the satchel.

Then she leaned into the SUV, and with her razor, cut off a swatch of material from the airbag.

"Some guy is looking around the wreck!" the voice called.

"Sir, I need you to get back to your vehicle." Nadia wasn't certain if it was directed at her, but she moved anyway. She made it to the opposite side of the street, where Milena joined her. The people milling by the accident site had already forgotten she was ever there. They had more important things to worry about.

Nadia and Milena returned to the car and went home. Nadia laid out what she was going to use.

"Why the car?" Milena asked. It was the first thing she had said since they left the house hours ago.

"Irony," Nadia said.

The curse wouldn't be identical, but it should do roughly the same thing as the one Dagmar used on the Angel. Nadia wondered if she would appreciate that on a professional level. Maybe for a moment just before she died.

"I need a hammer."

Milena brought her one, and Nadia prepared the hex. She took one of China's movies, one prominently featuring a car chase, and placed it with the orange peel and the section of bumper. She hammered these into oblivion. When they were dust, she wrapped them up in the piece of airbag, then sewed them shut with venom-soaked thread.

Then she slept. When she woke up, she drove to Dagmar's, parking several blocks away. She wore a knit cap over her skull and long sleeves covering her tattoos. She walked quickly the few blocks, expecting Dagmar to emerge from the house, full of false apologies. None were forthcoming.

Nadia went to the side, where the old banana tree marked the spot where she could make the jump onto the balcony. She did it quickly and went to the side door. She peered into the dining room and saw nothing. Not even Vorspan, somehow where she left him, only this time dead from the Angel's blood. The carpet had been replaced, and the burn marks in the floor gone or covered.

Nadia circled the house, trying windows and doors and finding all of them locked. Dagmar was not home.

Fine. Nadia went to the side of the house, where the brush was the thickest. She was shielded from all sides here, with the perfect view to Dagmar's driveway.

Someone else had been here. A camp, maybe for a homeless person, but the equipment was too new for that. A designer bag, and the kinds of camping food found at upscale places. The ghost man. It had to be him. Where he had waited for his revenge. Now Nadia had taken it over, a spot for all the people who had been betrayed by Dagmar.

She waited for hours, perking up with the occasional car passing down the quiet street. Nadia thought she was imagining it when the white BMW turned the corner, something provided by a starved mind inventing things to entertain it. The car slowed at Dagmar's driveway as the automatic garage door opened. Nadia saw the aristocratic face of her enemy behind the wheel.

The car drifted forward. The driver's view was blocked by the edge of the garage.

Nadia broke cover and sprinted. She dropped to a crouch around the passenger side, then to the floor. The garage door rumbled downward. Dagmar's door thunked open. Nadia, lying on the concrete floor of the garage, watched Dagmar's high heels click down onto the floor. She held her breath as Dagmar moved around on the other side of the car.

Nadia had to keep track of Dagmar by her feet, contorted into shape by her punishing shoes. The other woman was taking her time. Nadia started wondering. Had she been seen? Was this another game by Dagmar? Get her in this position and spring another bizarre enforcer on her, a cousin of Vorspan or the demon.

Then Dagmar clicked away, the door into the house opening, and then closing. Nadia was alone in the dark.

With a bit of duct tape, she secured the bag to the bottom of the car. She waited until well after nightfall and sneaked out through the house. Dagmar was upstairs sleeping while her murder was attached to the car. Nadia slipped out through the dining room, jumped from the balcony to the front, and found her car. She'd gotten her revenge, though no one knew it yet.

***

Since Dagmar learned Nadia was still alive she was forced to reconsider. Her first instinct had been to bitterly curse Vorspan. It had been his fault, after all. This was foolish, and she knew it even as she was mentally insulting him. He had no will in the matter. He was but a tool.

Then, she cursed the idea of blood. She had thought it would be the most ironclad of links to her prey, overlooking the importance of the way families were said to share blood. Due to the nature of the curse, the nature of the actor, now it looked inevitable that it should fail in such manner. Everything looked inevitable in hindsight.

Then, she cursed herself.

Nadia had been stupid and wasteful. She'd killed two Matchless and allowed Gaff to die. Yet she'd had the best of intentions in all situations. What she needed was guidance, not judgment. There would be others and Nadia had already found some. More efficiently than even Dagmar herself. It had been Dagmar who had gotten lazy, entrusting too much of her stores to Stella and Gaff, when a single incident could easily rob her of both.

Nadia would never know Dagmar had been the one to kill her brother. It was useless information. Water under the bridge as it were. Nothing was going to bring the brother back, and Dagmar's anger—regrettable though it was—had been spent. She could make it up to Nadia by becoming the mentor she always should have been.

She got into her car. Today would be a few errands. Nothing terribly heavy. Not with her ankle still troubling her. When she returned, she could call Nadia, invite her and Milena over for drinks, conversation, and making up.

Beforehand, Dagmar could do a little preliminary research. There had to be stories. Urban legends. Whispers about a person with inexplicable powers, or the paranormal phenomena that inevitably followed in the wake of the Matchless. Bring that information to Nadia when they were enjoying their drinks. The alliance would truly become ironclad when they stalked their first source of talismans together.

And, when Nadia saw how humane the incarceration in Vorspan's hospital was, she would drop her silly protestations against harvesting. After all, she couldn't seduce every one of her sources. Although that was wise; Dagmar had done the same with Gaff. She had to admit though, Milena was far more appealing.

The decision made, Dagmar started the car and backed out onto her street. Only a few cars were parked along the curbs, and none were driving. The radio played muted music from the oldies station: songs she remembered from high school. Everyone got old, she supposed. One day Nadia would be hearing songs from her formative years, have the same stark realization, and then wonder what to do with it. The answer was the same as it ever was; move forward. If Nadia was lucky, she too might have found an apprentice of sorts.

She was distracted when she entered the first big intersection. The light was green and her path was open. Movement, or more precisely something growing, in the corner of her eye made her turn her head.

A pickup had barreled through the intersection right for the passenger side of her car, already dwarfing the sky. Dagmar had time to do one thing, and it would determine whether she lived or died. She floored the accelerator. Instead of bisecting the car, the pickup clipped the back end of the BMW, spinning her around.

Dagmar didn't scream. Her entire body tensed—she found this out later, when every one of her muscle groups ached—but she did not scream.

The car spun around and around, tires shrieking on the asphalt. She saw the other car only as a stuttered image, first far away, then much, much closer. She had time to think, in the most terribly rational way, that car is going to hit me. And it did, hard. The front end of the BMW crumpled. It was only the angle that sent the engine block toward the passenger side and did not crush her legs.

The airbag punched her in the face. The bright flash turned to scarlet. Her broken nose, fountaining blood over the white surface of the bag.

The car was still, the sound of dripping and ticking in her ears.

You have to get out. She heard it as another voice, comforting, in her ear. It was her voice, though she only recognized it later, using the same tone she would use with Vorspan or someone else who needed hand-holding to understand the wisdom of her action. *You have to get out of the car.*

Her vision swam in front of her, her breakfast of fruit and oatmeal ready to burst up and out of her. *Can't move,* she told her mind. Someone will call an ambulance.

This doesn't seem familiar to you? This isn't a coincidence. Two cars hit you. There are more on the way. You did this to Stella Mortimer once, and now another witch is doing it to you.

Stella Mortimer survived.

Because she got out of the car.

Dagmar felt like she was swimming up through spinal fluid. Her mouth was filled with a chemical meat taste. She knew the voice—she, herself—was right. There would be more cars. She had to move now. The next one would obliterate whatever was left of her vehicle, with her inside.

She reached over with shaking hands and clicked the button of her seatbelt. It zipped away, catching on the deflated airbag for a moment before retracting. She rolled to the side and heard someone speaking through jelly. "Stay still, ma'am! I called an ambulance!"

She couldn't explain to him; There were more cars coming.

She rolled out of the car and spilled onto the asphalt. She had lost a shoe somewhere along the way. Pain stabbed through one ankle—the same one scarred by snake fangs, she reminded herself—and she stumbled to all fours.

"Oh shit!" She didn't know if it was the same speaker or someone else.

She looked up. Her vision was wobbly, and she didn't know why. She only saw a shadow, and it was eclipsing her at a terrifying rate.

Time to move, the voice said in its faintly disapproving tone.

She tried to stand, but the ground swayed under her feet and threw her back to her hands and knees. When she moved, leaving behind streaks from sliced palms behind her, she did it in a hobbling, skittering crawl. She did not know where she was going. She tried to pick a single direction and go in it as fast as possible, praying there would be a sidewalk there. A place away from the death at the intersection.

The impact was deafening, somehow worse than the two previous. She felt a muscular rush of wind and threw herself down blindly. The apocalyptic smash was followed by a clatter and tumble, the parts of her car, she learned later, scattered on the road, raining down around her.

She was no longer able to swim to the surface to catch her breath. She sank down through the mint-green waters into the depths.

***

Dagmar regained consciousness when the paramedic was examining her by the side of the road. She left reality as quickly as she came and emerged later at the hospital. She quickly learned that, while she had a litany of injuries, she was not in any immediate danger. She had a broken ankle, several ribs, her nose, and in a bit of an insult, big toe. She had numerous superficial injuries, the most severe being a slice along her left temple requiring fifteen stitches and half her head being shaved.

The worst injury was the concussion, though the whiplash caused a lot more pain over the next few days.

No one came to visit her. She didn't wallow. In fact, she barely noticed. She spent her time enjoying the pain medication and thinking about what she was going to do to Nadia.

She had to admit, using a similar curse to the one Dagmar used on Stella had a bit of style. While this wasn't enough to make Dagmar not kill Nadia, she had to give respect to where it was due. She would have to craft something as suitably ironic. It was a shame she never learned how Nadia killed the other Matchless. She could try what Nadia had done to Stella, but she suspected that had only been possible due to the extent of how much Stella's body had changed.

The idea occurred to Dagmar one night while the hospital was as quiet as it ever got. She emerged from the fog of her medicine long enough to be inspired.

Dagmar was released when she was no longer in agony. She was well and truly on the mend, though she was going to be getting around on crutches, then likely a cane. Her doctor had clucked a bit over her age but was quite relieved when there was only a bit of nerve damage, and the joint damage was minor as these things went.

Nadia had failed.

Dagmar started by checking on her weapon. Her car was still being taken care of with insurance. She had acquired a rental, though she hesitated getting behind the wheel. She kept hearing the smash behind her, the one before consciousness showed mercy. It was not the truck hammering into her back, nor the car crushing her the second time. It was the one she had escaped.

Because she kept placing herself in the wreck. She kept imagining herself a second slower. A second more arguing with herself. So many ways could have put her in the car for the fatal blow, and she would have been little more than liquid on the street.

She forced herself behind the wheel. She was stronger than this foolishness. She was the master of her mind.

She drove to Vorspan's at least ten miles below the posted limit. She waited at intersections long enough to get a few honks behind her. She signaled, looked, hesitated, looked again, before doing anything on the road. The drive took four times longer than it should have, but when she arrived, she let out a long, relieved breath and found her hands needed to be massaged away from the white knuckle rictus she had placed them in.

Dagmar went to Vorspan's door. She knocked, but there was no response. She found the spare in the fake rock by the door but didn't need it. The door was unlocked.

The house was in chaos. Furniture had been tipped over. Books were scattered over the floor, pages town out. Feces had been rubbed over the walls.

Dagmar found Vorspan in his bathtub, nude and covered in filth, shivering in fear. He recognized her, but the sounds he was making were hardly human anymore. She sighed. In the hospital, she had done a little research and learned Nadia's brother Alexander had been the one to die. That failure had apparently sent Vorspan down the spiral of madness where he found himself now.

Dagmar hobbled off and found a sheet in the linen closet. She wrapped Vorspan up in it. He was still as she swaddled him like a baby, watching her with blank, mad eyes.

They turned green. A sudden bloom of color beneath the brown. She started, nearly dropping him. It was daylight, and she was not due for a little over a week.

The green fled from his eyes, and they went back to the terrified blankness. She wrapped his naked body in the sheet and piled him into the car. She took him home, and he barely seemed to notice when she locked him in the same room he had undergone his first change. There was a certain symmetry in that.

Vorspan wasn't to be her instrument against Nadia. That was not enough of an insult for what Nadia had tried to do with her car accidents. No. This had to be perfect.

The flag she was able to buy online and sprang for next day delivery. She didn't want to wait.

She got the anti-psychotics from the hospital. She didn't even need Vorspan to escort her; she had been seen with him enough for the staff to know she had the run of the place. The bottle's absence would be missed, but it would never be linked to her.

The final ingredient was the most difficult.

Finding the Eskandarian family had been easy. Once Dagmar made the connection, she realized she was acquaintances with friends of Vartan and Siranush Eskandarian. Small world, she thought with some amusement. Their home on the lip of Mulholland was an institution, and it was far more remarkable that Dagmar had not been there. Fortunate too, as they would not know her face.

The drive there was more harrowing than the one to Vorspan's. It was farther for one, and along a serpentine ridge running along the Santa Monicas. The houses contributed to this illusion, clinging, cantilevered structures poised to tumble down the slopes, daring the Big One to play a modern Joshua.

Dagmar instantly dismissed the Eskandarian home as gauche. They were, after all, pretenders. Playing at the upper class, but with one of the class or taste that position implied. Their daughter proved that, from her increasingly bizarre appearance to her attempted murder. Dagmar put her own practiced, patrician smile—sunny without being warm, pretty without being flashy—on her face and knocked on the door.

The woman who answered was shorter than Nadia. Rude adjectives like "squat" popped through Dagmar's head, but she dismissed them. Think well, speak well. She saw Nadia in the woman's face, from the prominent hooked nose, and the keen brown eyes. The woman's hair was dyed a vibrant burgundy with a slash of blonde through it. It seemed the urge to alter oneself in unnatural ways was not unique to the daughter. She was dressed in black, and her makeup did not quite hide the sleepless nights under her eyes.

"Mrs. Eskandarian?"

"Yes?"

"I'm sorry to drop in like this. My name is Dana Eick, and I work for admissions at Harvard Graduate School."

Siranush's eyebrows shot up. "What is this about?"

"Your daughter, Nadia. May I come in?"

"Of course." Siranush stepped aside and Dagmar hobbled up onto the step. "Are you all right? What happened?"

"Minor fender bender," Dagmar said with false bravery.

"Oh, I'm sorry. Please, come to the living room."

The Eskandarian house was the opposite of Dagmar's. Whereas hers was cluttered with antiques with a dark maple light, this place was open and white. Huge windows looked out over the canyon, and the city could be seen glittering off into the distance. It was not a place to mourn, but it was uneasily being used for it.

The mantel held two pictures, both of which looked to be high school senior photos. One was of a handsome, if swarthy, young man. He had a short beard and equally short hair, intelligent eyes looking from dark brows. He wore a collar and tie poking from his robes. The other picture was a beautiful young woman. Her hair and makeup looked maybe a decade out of date, but they still complimented her face. She had Siranush's strong features, but they had softened just enough to make her more of a conventional beauty. With her olive skin, mahogany eyes, and long, black hair, she was gorgeous.

Dagmar had done enough research to know these were the two dead children, Odette and Alexander. One family, having to bury two children. It was misfortune most could scarcely comprehend, and the Eskandarians had to do it twice.

Dagmar would have them do it a third time.

Nadia's picture was on a table, far away from the mantel. A position of relative ignominy. She only barely recognized Nadia in the pretty, long-haired girl in the picture. This girl's smile was false, and the makeup a mask. Dagmar knew the real Nadia was a snake and had been slowly turning herself into one. Not this sweet faced little thing, still with baby fat in her cheeks.

"That was Nadia in high school," Siranush said, coming in.

"She is very pretty."

"She does not look like that anymore. You should know that."

"We don't base admissions on appearance."

Siranush sighed. "That's good. I didn't know she applied."

"She did." Dagmar had gotten sparse information from Nadia in their many conversations out on the balcony. She knew Nadia had a Master's in English, and she had to imagine the parents would be proud of such a thing. In brighter times, Dagmar had hoped Nadia would return for her Ph.D. Misplaced pride, perhaps, no less strong for their differences.

"Finish her Ph.D, for all of the good it will do. No offense."

"None taken." Dagmar's smile was no more brittle than any of the others since she arrived. "I am sorry, but the drive up here was longer than I expected. Might I freshen up?"

"First door down that hallway," Siranush said. "Can I get you something to drink?"

"Yes, please. No alcohol, though. It reacts with the medication."

"You won't mind if I have wine?"

"Of course not."

Dagmar opened and shut the bathroom door loudly, then went down the hall, quietly opening and closing doors. She was nearly ready to give up, when she opened the door at the end of the hall.

This room could only belong to Nadia. Though it had been straightened up, it was exactly the sort of place she would have imagined a girl like Nadia to live in. The posters of pretty pop stars on the walls, the toys that looked more appropriate for boys than girls, and a largely empty bookcase with only a few books left behind. Nearly any of these would link directly to Nadia.

Dagmar wanted something special. She went through the other door in Nadia's room and found a small bathroom. It had clearly gone unused, and the lip of the tub was still jostling with toiletries. With unerring confidence, she picked up a bottle. Shaving soap.

The first ingredient in Nadia's ultimate transformation. There would be nothing stronger. She slipped it into her purse and sneaked out.

She spent some time talking to Siranush, ostensibly interviewing her about Nadia, and then quietly excused herself.

The following day, when her package arrived, she opened it and set the rainbow flag on the table. She cut a swatch off of it and wrapped up both the anti-psychotics and a bit of the shaving soap. These she smashed into a paste inside the piece of the flag. When it came time to seal it, she unspooled a VCR copy of *Fill Me With Moonlight*, the mad cartoon by a Matchless from the '30s. The cartoon depicted a woman being pursued by various incarnations of a monster, each trying a different tactic to make her his own. Dagmar tied the bag up with the film, and she had her curse.

She was able to plant it beneath Nadia's front step a day later.

***

Nadia saw Dagmar place the curse. She saw it the evening after it had happened, when she reviewed the digital recordings on her laptop. After Lex was killed, Nadia was not going to risk being blindsided again.

She noted with dark amusement that Dagmar had not risked the side lawn. She pulled up the front stoop, a narrow slab of concrete alive with tiny centipedes and rolypolies, placing the hex beneath it. Nadia could not see precisely what it was, though its physical form hardly mattered when measured against its power. Dagmar had also chosen the one place it was impractical for Nadia to place one of her tripwires, though it had been in plain view of two of the security cameras she'd since installed. Mundane security in addition to her hex traps.

As soon as she saw it, she went out and lifted the block up. On the cracked earth, amongst the dirt-covered strands of spiderwebs and enameled bits of exoskeleton, she could see a dim shape. It was smudged, like a painting someone had drawn a thumb over. It had mass, and presumably weight, but it was not fully there.

She reached for it, and a bolt of agony shot through her fingertips. She had not felt pain like that since Azh had placed his blessing in her. She recoiled, watching as the hex, whatever it was, vanished. It did not go all at once, but in between her blinks, until it was easy to believe it had not been there at all.

Nadia knew Dagmar survived her curse. She had several Google alerts set up, for accidents and for Dagmar specifically. Eventually, she had tripped both. Nadia's curse had injured Dagmar, though the single article was coy on how much. This left Nadia to prepare. Dagmar would be coming back, Nadia would be ready.

Dagmar's house was effectively impossible to break into. She could smash a window if she liked, and Dagmar's expensive security would there in moments. No, the best way in was as she had done before, which could not be done until she knew Dagmar was home. With the planting of the hex, Nadia knew for certain it was time to strike. Break Dagmar, perhaps she could break the hex.

An emotional paradox confronted her. Would she become a murderer?

She already was. This had been decided. China, Karo, and the Angel had all met their ends at her hands, and with each, an escalation. China was a monster who died for what she did to Angie. Karo had been murdered from ignorance, then finished off with a modicum of mercy. The Angel was a monster who Nadia dispatched with cold efficiency. Ironically enough, in Dagmar's defense.

Nadia could hide behind self-defense. Dagmar clearly hadn't tried to kill Lex. She had come after Nadia and failed and would obviously try again. Yet this wasn't a comfort. Dagmar had been a friend, and in some ways a mentor. Dagmar was not a ravening monster like China. Not a vicious thug like Karo. Not a bloodthirsty murderer like the Angel.

She was more like Nadia than anyone else in the world.

She was a danger, yes, but she was a danger to Nadia alone. Other Matchless as well but look at them. Killers, monsters, bogeymen.

Just like her fears when Sav Krikorian came from the woodwork. She thought he was out for revenge for a symbolic brother, when in reality he had been a shrewd businessman looking to make a beneficial deal. Dagmar had the same shrewdness, turned against Nadia.

Was she truly killing Dagmar out of self-defense? Or was this revenge for Lex? Was one more excusable than the other?

She and Dagmar had been close. It had been Dagmar who fired the first shot, practically tying Nadia's hands. It didn't make the retaliation any easier to take.

Dagmar fired her final shot, and Nadia needed time. She did not need more pool water from Simcoe Manor, but she needed to go anyway. The act of collection would calm her, focus her. Prepare her for the final battle ahead. Fill her limbs with steel.

Nadia walked out to her car, trying to come to peace with her new identity. It was just after nightfall, when murderers went about their tasks. She had noticed she was growing more jittery over her reserves, paranoid someone might find her reservoir. It was in her best interests, therefore, to get the rest of it before anyone else could. She wouldn't get it all now, but another jar should keep the demons at bay for a bit longer.

She wasn't quite certain when it started. As she drove from Echo Park toward the Hollywood Hills, she began to see faces. Gray splotches at first, at the corner of her vision. When she finally looked, she found them staring back at her. People on the street. People of the city. From street corners, from other cars. Most disturbingly, pedestrians would pause mid-stride, turn and stare at the car as she passed by.

These stares were the ones she feared, not the ones she had grown to relish. Since she transformed herself, the stares were curious, wondering. She decided why they existed. Look at the freak with the snakeskin and gold eyebrows. Look at Nadia sapiens. Look and wonder.

No, these were the stares she felt when she had first started to claim her identity, the ones she saw when she closed her eyes and woke her in panic. These were glares of pure hatred, following her with narrowed eyes, lips rippling over teeth. She had seen this kind of loathing, but it was thankfully the exception rather than the rule.

Tonight, it was everyone, and it was an expression of universal, homicidal rage.

She wanted to think she was imagining it, but block after block, with more and more people looking, she could not pretend it was not happening.

She turned on the street that dead-ended into the dirt road. Simcoe Manor would be waiting for her in the hills, a short walk away. This had to be the curse. Make her a pariah, turn her identity against it. Fucking Dagmar, probably doesn't even know what she's really done. Every last one of Nadia's fears was tied up in this. The withering look in her mother's eye, the belittling comment from a straight guy, the question about her gender from a child. She got out of the car.

When she turned around, she saw she was not alone.

It was late, so it was not quite a mob. There were five of them, and they were not of a type. A homeless man in stinking clothes. A pair of hipsters on a date. A tired-eyed woman in hospital scrubs. A young man in a natty suit. They were charging up the hill toward her, snarling like animals.

Nadia hesitated only a moment before jumping back into her car. The people thumped into it, screaming and shaking it, slamming their fists against the windows, their faces contorted in rabid hate.

Nadia started the car and spun it in a quick U-turn. The man in the suit and one of the hipsters went sprawling. The others recovered easily and were up and chasing her. She hit the gas and saw with horror more people were coming up the street, charging her. She swerved around them and onto the street. A few slapped her car as she went by, shouting terrible things after her, but she was free.

The mob followed along for a block, howling its rage. The farther she went, the more of them drifted off, back to the sides of the streets. Some cast baleful looks after her, but others seemed to forget she even existed. As she drove, she noticed she was shivering.

Worst of all, the faces were still glaring as she drove past, plotting their revenge.

The streets were nearly empty, and she gave thanks for that, thanks for her habit of harvesting after dark. When she made it to Milena's street, only one man, walking his dogs, was outside. She passed him and parked, sprinting up the driveway. She heard him calling after her, the dogs barking. She made it through the front door.

A moment later, he was right outside shouting, pounding at the door.

She closed her eyes. If the landlords heard... if more of these people heard... they would descend on her, pull her apart.

He screamed. This time it was a startled yelp of pain. Then, a dog did the same.

Nadia opened the door. Immediately, she had a wet retriever nose in her hand. She whined, trying to get Nadia's attention. Now Nadia was a friend, a helpful human who could sort out whatever problem had befallen her. The anger her master had shown was forgotten.

Nadia stepped out onto the porch and looked up the driveway. There night was still. The lights in the front house were out. They must not be home, she decided.

She stepped around the side of the house, to the little yard. She saw the other dog first, some kind of pit bull mix, lying still in the grass, body beginning to bloat.

The man was still alive. His flesh had turned purple. His eyes bulged from his skull. Rattlesnakes surrounded him, some coiled, others slithering. Periodically, one would strike again, injecting more venom into his rapidly swelling body.

He was dying. Fast.

When he saw Nadia, he croaked, "You bitch. You're gonna die."

She went completely still. The dog wanted to go to her master, wanted to comfort him, but the snakes warned her off with a shake of a rattle. She danced and whined at the edge of the lawn, periodically looking back at Nadia, begging her to do something.

Nadia could only watch. The man was trying to crawl over the lawn toward Nadia, still cursing her. "Gonna rape you, gonna kill you, gonna burn you up." Like a litany. The venom was eating him. He was dying in a hellish fire. It did nothing to quench his limitless rage.

She knelt, opening her satchel. Azh had not been in there before, but he was there now. The massive rattler spilled outward. The dog yelped again, but Azh had no attention for her. He wrapped himself up in a coil.

The man's promises were no longer words. They were just a hateful mush falling from rapidly numbing lips.

Azh never rattled. He struck. Too fast to see. One moment, he was in a coil then a blur, then the twin fang marks on the man's jugular vein. Azh, his work done, went to the pit bull and bit the corpse once as well, then disappeared into the undergrowth.

The bodies, both of them, swelled even further. They burst quickly afterwards around their bellies, the smell caustic but sweet. The extremities turned to earth, or else the earth took them. Nadia was not sure. She only remembered the end of it, and it felt as though it had always been that way. The meat rotted quickly, the bones turning brown and cracked.

Nadia watched both of them become little more than dirt spread over the dying grass of her lawn.

The surviving retriever whined, then bolted for the mouth of the driveway. Nadia went inside, and found she was still shivering.

She texted Milena. *Dagmar cursed me. Trying to figure out what to do.*

Nadia almost had to admire Dagmar's hex. A curse of terrifying power, especially in this arena. Surrounded by potential murderers in the largest city in the world.

Nadia would have to craft a curse to finish this. First, though, way across town. Take with her the bulk of a curse to destroy Dagmar in the most painful way she could imagine.

Nadia lay on the couch, watching the ceiling, as she thought about it. Sounds from outside, even the most innocuous of city white noise—cars shushing down the street, a dog barking—made her freeze, certain the mob had found her, grown larger, and was bearing down.

She had an absurd moment of terror when she heard the faint electric hum of Milena's car, accompanied by the headlights shining through the bedroom window. Milena. She hopped up, relieved to have Milena home, forgetting for a moment the curse.

The door opened, and Milena's tired face was locked in an expression of worry. "Hey, sweetie, what happ—"

Then Milena's eyes darkened. Her face contorted. "You fucking bitch," she snarled. "You're gonna die now."

374

The Crown

The worst parts were the sounds. Milena had spent the first several hours screaming like an animal. Now, her voice was gone, and in Nadia's mind, hanging in ragged strips from her ruptured throat. Now, the only noise came from the clawing at the bathroom door, growing steadily harsher as the time passed.

Nadia was in the bathtub. She was finished crying, and her eyes and throat burned with shed tears. The sun had risen, and Milena's maddening scratching had not ceased. Each scratch put a new furrow in Nadia's heart. Milena, homicidal. Milena, a weapon.

Despair was Nadia's closest companion in the cramped bathroom. She didn't know why she had just assumed Milena would be immune to Dagmar's curse. Love, she guessed. Love was supposed to transcend everything.

Turned out there were things far more powerful than mere love.

She had spent too much time grieving. It was time to do something. Some way to get out of this. Some way to make this all okay. In a stroke of luck, she'd grabbed her satchel when Milena lunged. Milena fell over the couch, and Nadia bolted for the bathroom, the only place she could hide. Milena slammed herself into the locked door several times before settling into the scratching. Nadia preferred the mad violence to the soft, eerie scratching.

Like scratching on the inside of a coffin lid.

Nadia had her things. A collection of talismans, and even a few of her harder-to-find ingredients like Sav's bullets. She felt a strange sense of relief as she noted Azh's absence. Azh wasn't here to kill Milena. Nadia didn't know what she would do if she watched his venom rot the woman she loved into dirt.

Nadia had already tried to open the window to get out. Devin was in the way, growing too close to the house for even little Nadia to squeeze past. Milena had howled when she heard the window, cursing Nadia. Slinging hateful, homophobic filth through the shut door. Hearing those words in Milena's sweet voice, even ripped with rage, was what brought tears to Nadia's eyes.

She kept looking at the mirror. Something similar to what she had done before, but not identical. Never identical. Dagmar had warned her of that, and the one time Nadia had tried it, the ghost man had died. The warning had come long ago, in a different time. Nadia rose, taking the toothbrush holder off the sink. She hefted it, the metal and porcelain heavy in her hand. She threw it into the mirror, which shattered, spilling glass into the sink. She selected a shard, thinking of the ghost man's teeth as she did so.

She opened her veins. The jagged glass made the wounds burn, but her painless razor wouldn't do. She needed to link the mirror to the act itself. To the blood. She took the gore from her wrists and mixed it with pool water, painting her face with the grimy, gritty product.

She put the rusty streaks over and under her eyes, around her mouth and chin. Old lines, calling to mind those women who had done these kinds of things in the past. Warpaint. Ritual mask. Her new identity.

She bandaged her wrists only when it was done, and soon the gauze was soaked through.

Then she opened the door.

And nearly cried out. She stuffed it back into her mouth, her eyes growing wide, tears blurring her vision. Superstitious, maybe, but she was in the edge of superstition. Hidden within the secret madness in the corners of reality.

Milena was lying against the door, the sudden opening startling her from her trance. That was not what made Nadia gasp in horror.

The skin from Milena's fingers was gone. White bone poked from the ruined tips. The door was gory with her blood, the scarred wood filled with scabbing crimson.

Milena got to her feet. There was no wince of pain. No sense she was aware of the damage she'd done to herself. She stared into the bathroom with consuming hate, her fingers curling, the awful bone-claws ready to tear apart her quarry. Her quarry; the woman she loved more than anyone.

Nadia stayed silent, her shoulders shaking with unshed sobs. She watched, without blinking as Milena took two steps into the room, hunting for someone who was no longer there. She looked through Nadia once, then twice.

"Nadia," she said to Nadia. "Where is she? Where is that bitch?"

"I don't know," Nadia whispered.

Only then did Milena collapse, cradling her broken hands and weeping in agony.

Nadia wanted nothing more than to comfort her but knew she could not. If she stayed with Milena, the rage would return. Her own curse, this invisibility of sorts, would be breached. Just as China had done it, so too would Milena.

Nadia slipped from the house. She swallowed her pain, swallowed the grief, the guilt of leaving Milena behind. There was room only for rage. Dagmar had done this, and Dagmar would suffer. Outside, the mounds that had once been man and dog were open. Nestled inside, Nadia found a clutch of eggs. Snake eggs, glistening and oblong. A gift, as sure as any.

In her car, she nearly called an ambulance. Her finger poised over the call button. Would they amputate? If they did, Nadia was terrified she could not do anything. No, she had to leave Milena there, in agony, until she could return and heal her. Hope the curse would be broken by then. Use her powers to salvage what she could of Milena's hands.

She focused on preparing the last bit of the curse. She mashed the eggs up with a few of Devin's mushrooms. These went into a small golden bag with one of Sav's bullets. It was still missing one last bit, but she was going where there was as much as she would ever need.

She drove to Dagmar's.

The front door opened as soon as Nadia pulled up in front. Dagmar stood in the doorway, a glass of red wine in her hand. "Nadia. What a pleasant surprise." She leaned on a cane, her ankle in a cast. A tight smile rippled over Nadia's face as she saw this.

"Hello, Dagmar."

"Please, join me in the dining room."

Dagmar turned and went down the hall. Nadia stepped up to the doorway. Her rational mind reminded her this could be a trap, but she knew there was no trap.

That would have been rude. Against the arcane rules Dagmar delineated inside her mind, the same ones compelling her to ask Nadia's permission before the attempted murder. She would let her curse run its course. This was how friends behaved.

Dagmar lingered by the bar, mixing a drink, when Nadia walked in. "Sazerac," Dagmar said with some pleasure, handing the drink over. Their fingers touched over the glass.

Nadia accepted it, raised it in toast and took a sip.

"I was worried you would think I would poison you," Dagmar said.

"No."

"No," she agreed. "Interesting choice of makeup. Was that how you made it over?"

Nadia nodded.

"You are so resourceful." Dagmar sipped her wine. "I am glad you're here. We need to talk."

"Do we?"

"Things have gotten a bit... out of hand, I think."

"You killed my brother."

"I did not mean to kill him. It was a mistake. One I regret, not that this matters very much. No matter how many tears I shed, he will not come back."

"I'm sure you cried your fucking eyes out."

"Nadia," Dagmar said sternly, "If we are to talk like civilized women, we have to make an effort. I cannot be the only one holding out an olive branch. Or did you forget what you tried to do to me?"

Nadia's eyes darted to the cane now leaning against Dagmar's chair.

"I don't begrudge you that," Dagmar said, her tone softening. "I rather appreciated it. It was difficult to ignore the connection to my own past."

"It's where I got the idea."

"Very good. It nearly did the job, too. You should be very proud of yourself."

"You didn't think I could do it."

"I didn't think you would do it. There is a difference."

"Not after I saved your life?"

"You killed my sources of talismans." Dagmar held up a hand and blanched. "I am sorry. Comments like that aren't what I meant about moving on."

"What do you want from me, Dagmar?"

The older woman considered, staring into the purple-red depths of her wine. "Friendship."

"Friendship?"

"There are only two of us, Nadia. Until I met you, there was only one."

"There are more of us. There have to be. You know what we are. There are names for us all over the world, and they all mean 'witch.' We must have lived throughout history, and every one of us that there are stories about, well, there had to be more who never came out of the shadows."

"Perhaps."

"Not perhaps. All we needed were Matchless. What do you think people like Jesus, or Hercules, or any hero, messiah, or monster were? Stories about Matchless, Shadowed, and Kissed. Where they lived, there had to be those who understood how the things they left behind still contained power. Hell, the Catholic Church collects bones from saints... I bet there's more than one of us in their past as well."

"What are you saying?"

"I am saying, you believe we're alone because you never looked. Now you're latching onto me. You don't want my friendship. You just want my talismans. You want to harvest Milena, and you want to know what else

I have. Who else I've found. I don't even know if you believe in this friendship bullshit or not."

"I'm sorry to hear you say that," Dagmar said, rising and leaning heavily on her cane.

"You were dead the minute you hurt Lex. The minute you hurt Milena."

"Milena? What's happened?"

"Worried you'd hurt a good talisman source?"

Dagmar turned away.

"This is a holding pattern, Dagmar. I'm here to kill you, and you're here to die."

"I see."

Dagmar opened the door leading into the living room. A mountain lion padded in, his golden coat burnished in the soft light. His green eyes locked on Nadia as he approached. There was no hurry in his movement, but there was menace.

"Vorspan," Nadia said.

"He gave up on his human form not long ago. Seems the mind was gone." Dagmar shrugged. "He is far more useful as a cat."

Nadia tensed as the lion closed. A wild animal in Dagmar's dining room, amongst the tasteful antiques. The creature was hunting Nadia, though there was none of the stealth of the one up at Simcoe Manor. This creature might look natural, despite the silver on its wrists, but it was nothing of the sort. In marrying man and beast, it was the darkest part of both. Murderous intent of a man, the killing tools of the cat. It paused scarcely an arm's length away, tail twitching back and forth at the tip.

Only then did he bare his teeth. Nadia saw the same expression on Milena, the inhuman anger, now in the feline face. She briefly wondered if the tiny bits of sentience flashing in Vorspan's brain were reacting to

Dagmar's curse, spurring him to violence. Was there hate in the gesture, or simple animal hunger?

She barely had time to brace herself when the creature pounced. She collapsed beneath the sudden impossibly heavy weight. Her skull bounced off the floor, and the room swam for an instant. She sucked in air to scream when her throat was closed in a wet vice. The creature's breath was hot against her skin.

She felt it in slow motion, her brain giving her a chance to savor her moment of dying.

The teeth dimpled her neck, the crushing force driving inward. The head was an implacable presence too close to fight. She only saw the side of one ear, flattened against the cat's skull. She felt her skin open, and the hot blood spurt upward from the wound.

But it wasn't wet.

There was no feeling of it splashing and running. It moved, but it was smooth and dry. It undulated down the side of her neck, and several discrete thumps came from the carpeted floor. Her brain, in the throes of death, panicked? Perception divorced from reality in the moment of dying. She reached up, thinking to find the lion's eyes, gouge them with her fingers, maybe get it to let go. The creature's head too close, its sharp, animal scent filling her nose.

Then the rattling started. It came from all around, the hissing beads spun over and about madly, echoing in her ears, reverberating in her mind. The blood had not stopped flowing. More of it spilled out over the rug, still dry, still tickling.

The agony of the cat's teeth was kept at bay. Shock, her rational mind reminded her. At any moment, the tide would recede, and she would feel what it was to have her neck torn open from the front.

The cat released her, and yelped, hissed, and yelped again. She heard it stumbling away, tripping over its powerful legs, the rattling never ceasing.

Nadia sat upright and was surprised to find she could. Her hands went to her ruined throat, and she found it wasn't blood dripping through her hands.

It was snakes.

Hundreds of baby rattlesnakes, each with only a nub or two of a rattle fell between her fingers to slither away on the floor. Some bunched up into coils, others fled for the dark corners of the room.

Vorspan, the lion, could no longer get up. The snakes kept striking. Some pursued him, others merely surrounded Nadia and warned him away with a shake of their tails. The great cat was panicked, his green eyes rolling in his skull, desperately searching for a way out. There was none.

The snakes bit, retreated, each adding another shot of venom into the animal who used to be a man.

Nadia stood. She felt the snakes wriggling through her fingers. She opened her mouth to speak, but blinding pain stopped her. Dagmar watched with mute horror, going from Nadia's rebirth to the death of her most loyal servant.

Nadia wished she could explain this last part to Dagmar. The other woman had never truly understood. She placed herself above, never knowing they were all parts of a larger whole.

They were Matchless, and Vorspan was her Shadowed. The Shadowed were always linked to their creators, through a bond stronger than blood. Nadia walked to the dying lion, the snakes slithering away from her steps. When she took her hand from her throat, more snakes fell to the carpet, their rattles joining the cacophony on the floor.

Nadia knelt by Vorspan, looking down into his dying eyes, the snakes from her wound dripping onto him. She sliced his forehead with her razor and soaked the golden bag in it. She held it up for Dagmar to see.

"Nadia, please. We don't have to go down this road."

Nadia tried to speak, but all that came out was a hiss.

She dropped the bag onto the table.

The snakes converged. They did not bite Dagmar. They climbed her, covering every inch of her body in writhing scales. She screamed, but one forced itself down her throat. She fell, trying to clutch at anything, but there was no way around the moving, hissing, lashing serpents. The pulsing mass continued to move around her, and soon, there was no difference between the individual snakes. Heads and tails were visible in the mass, but they were everywhere, free of any kind of structure. It was merely a mass of all the things that could be called "snake," a shimmering collection of golden brown and white diamonds, utterly obliterating any remnant of what had been Dagmar.

When Nadia finally left, her satchel was stuffed with new talismans. She exited the room, even as the Dagmar-mass split open ripely, displaying a perfectly undamaged clutch of serpent eggs.

***

Hector Solano had not slept in three days. Three days to finish the symphony to truly unlock the hidden patterns of the mind and body. To unite it all in a single sound. And, he had learned what could happen when he tore the notes.

Three days. He was living in a realm of waking dreams. He could not return to his house. Not after what he had done. Because, he knew, as soon as he entered that place, he would fall back into the symphony. The notes would take over, and he would make something else. Something terrible and sublime.

He did not know precisely how he found himself in this place. It was a room out behind a sports bar, paneled, with phony cages in front of fake ticket kiosks. The room felt much larger than it actually was, even the man with the impressive mustache, lounging at the other end, felt yards and yards away.

"Can I help you?" he asked.

Hector chuckled to himself. "I'm running away from home."

"In that case, welcome," the man said, kicking a panel in a wall, which threw open a door. He revealed an antique wonderland, all gold light and canvas walls. The pictures ranged from black and white to the washed out earth tones of the '70s. All were of circuses, circus performers, marquees, and animals.

Hector blinked, thinking this must be his mind giving him the dreams he had missed. Beautiful women in clown makeup passed him, holding trays of drinks. A dapper white guy behind the bar swallowed a burning brand then belched a fireball over the cheering heads of the patrons. Hector flinched.

"...and she'll tell your fortune."

Hector blinked, turned to the speaker. A couple of hipsters, whispering at a table. They looked at him in ill-disguised fear. He could imagine how he looked; wild hair, unshaven, sweaty. "Tell my fortune?"

"Yeah, in the back. The fortuneteller here is legit. Like, real powers."

Hector staggered away, going through other rooms, each decorated for some theme in the circus. He poked his head into a room decorated with a tattooed man biting the head off a chicken. On stage a caveman covered in old sailor ink and wearing nothing more than a loincloth was in the midst of eating a bicycle. In another room, two gorgeous girls were getting paper money stapled to their nearly-naked bodies.

Hector finally found the fortuneteller. It was a small room, and a poker game was going on. She looked like an old painting, rounded and lovely. Her brown eyes were surrounded in a thick layer of dark makeup. She wore cream-colored gloves to her elbows, and her fingers were uncomfortably slender.

Hector fell into a chair and slid money across the table. The fortuneteller dealt him in. After one hand, which he lost, badly, the fortuneteller looked up at him in surprise. He saw it in her face: she knew. Knew what he was. Knew what he could do.

And she was unafraid.

A grin rippled her lips. "Follow me, please. There is someone who has been wanting to meet you."

Hector thought about running. This kind of thing sounded bad. Very bad. He nearly chuckled. Why run? There was nothing else for him. Find out what this fortuneteller wanted really. What she could tell him.

He followed the woman, trying not to focus on her ample backside. The room she led him to was tucked off the main branch, and it looked to be like the others with live acts. The picture on the wall was of a half-naked carny woman entwined with a boa constrictor.

One of the elephant girls leaned by the door, her skin wet with perspiration and blood, the paper money decorating her like feathers. She turned to the fortuneteller and smiled, showing off a mouth full of large teeth, topped with impressive canines. "Who's this?"

"Who we've been waiting for."

Hector looked from woman to woman. He knew he was being stupid. Letting himself be lulled by two beautiful women. "Who wants to meet me?"

"Her," said the fortuneteller, pointing to the other end of the room, where the gloomy shadows were only partially held at bay. A table sat on the stage, and two people were huddled around it. Hector could not make out features on them, but he caught flashes of gold on the face of the one facing the door.

A few flickering lamps gave off fitful light. Whatever show happened in this place was not happening at the moment. The walls were lined with more pictures—as he leaned closer he saw a black and white shot of sixty tribesmen somewhere in South America lined up behind a colossal snake—and terrariums. Inside the terrariums were rattlesnakes.

They watched him with their keen eyes and flickering tongues.

The person facing the door handed a bag to the other.

"This will cure it?" the other person said, her voice high, whispery.

The other nodded.

"Here's your money," she said, putting an envelope on the table. "And what you wanted. The nurse at my hospital. She knows things. What you really are. One look, and she knows for certain. Her name's in the envelope as well. Is that what you wanted to know?"

The other nodded.

The one whose back was to the door stood, and for the first time saw the three people in the doorway. She flinched in surprise but softened when she looked at the fortuneteller and the elephant girl. The visitor was painfully thin, her bald head partly hidden under a bandanna. She made her way out, and the elephant girl kindly took her elbow to help.

The snakes began to rattle, their bonelike tails twisting in a tattoo. They persisted for several seconds, then, as one, stopped.

"This is who you've been looking for," the fortuneteller said.

Now Hector could see the strange shape on the other side of the table. She sat in a large and ornate chair, leaning forward, into the light.

Her body shifted and moved in strange ways, until Hector realized, snakes were all over her and the chair, languidly slithering on their reptilian errands. Rattlesnakes, every one of them, their heads like arrows and their rattles held aloft.

The snake woman was slender, her face all hard angles. Her eyebrows were a strip of irregular golden hoops. Her head was shaved, and three prongs of snakeskin came from her collar to her head. As she moved, her sinuous arms caught the light and showed more of the diamondback tattoos.

Hector took another step forward and gasped.

Her throat was little more than a mass of scar tissue. Nearly concave, he wondered how she could be missing that much and still be alive. In answer, she made a sound. A hiss.

"She says hello," the fortuneteller said.

Hector turned. In the doorway, the fortuneteller had been rejoined by the elephant girl, along with the caveman-like geek, his belly distended from his metallic meal. They watched him with gleeful interest. The three of them came into the room, the fortuneteller taking her place beside the snake woman, the elephant girl lounging in a chair, and beginning to pluck the bills from her punished flesh, and the geek becoming an intimidating presence at the door.

"What is this?" Hector asked.

"We've been searching for you," the fortuneteller said. "And we would like to offer you a deal."

Hector looked at the snake woman. No matter who spoke, she was the one in charge. And the way the light reflected around her head, he could swear she was wearing a crown.

About Your Author

Much like film noir, Justin Robinson was born and raised in Los Angeles. He splits his time between editing comic books, writing prose, and wondering what that disgusting smell is. Degrees in Anthropology and History prepared him for unemployment, but an obsession with horror fiction and a laundry list of phobias provided a more attractive option. He is the author of more than 10 novels in a variety of genres including detective, humor, urban fantasy, and horror. Most of them are pretty good.

Other HellBound Books Titles
Available at: www.hellboundbookspublishing.com

The Other Side of the Mirror

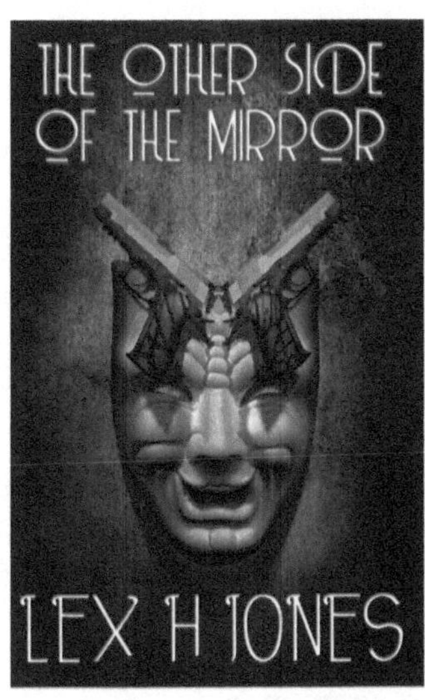

Carl Duggan has worked as a Detective in the City for a long time. The kind of 'long' where you've seen everything, and seen it twice. With that in mind, it comes as no surprise to him when a pregnant nineteen year-old girl washes up on the banks of the Styx. But something about this one is different, and before Carl gets any answers, two more bodies join the pile; a corrupt Judge and a big-shot lawyer. Carl's gut tells him there's a connection, the little things, the tiny details that others would ignore.

The bodies keep on coming when a second case rears its head; three young men with nothing in common except their sexuality, each murdered in their own home. Gaining little assistance from his fellow officers, Carl goes it alone into the darker regions of the City. Along the way he makes acquaintances and enemies of the City's more colourful residents, including the beautiful sister of the first dead girl, a Catholic hit man dubbed "His Holiness", and a shady casino owner named Dice. The closer he gets to the truth the more Carl's life is put in danger, forcing him to move further and further away from the rule of law. Never once does he suspect that the two cases are so intimately linked, or that the truth could be so close to home.

Satanic Panic

An incredible homage to 1980's horror!

Satanic Panic, a mass hysteria created in the nineteen eighties, has returned to a small college town in the Midwest.

Ritualistic murders and the presence of the occult have bled below the surface of the town in the form of icy accidents and other coincidences.

And when three lifelong friends find themselves on the radar of a killer—and leader of a satanic cult—they must fight for what's good without being seduced by the evil that possesses their campus.

The Dead Room

A week before Christmas, terrorists detonate dozens of dirty bombs throughout Britain and release a man-made contagion, leading Nicola Allen to begin a frantic hunt for her husband and daughter while a nation burns.

Fleeing from a horrendous event she refuses to speak of and desperate to find shelter in a dying country, Nicola's sister-in-law Cate takes cover in a partly destroyed hospital.

Terrorised by visions of mutilated bodies and the screams of phantom children, Cate joins with a group of survivors, all of whom are under attack by ruthless scavengers and looters.

If Nicola is to have any chance of finding her family and if Cate is to escape from the siege, they must reunite and then descend into the belly of the ruined hospital where the horrific truth of what truly connects the two women is waiting for them.

Waiting for them down in the dead room.

Deadly Nightshade

Thirteen years ago: summer's end. A final night of vacation at New Mexico's Gila Cliff Dwellings. A picnic under the moonlight for high school sweethearts meets a deadly end...

Things will never be quite the same again.

After eloping, newlywed Virginia Campbell's bright future grows dim. Eerie night visions begin to haunt her. Are they real or imagined? Her husband's sudden aloofness raises suspicions of an affair. Unable to sleep, doubts torment her—doubts about her marriage, her unborn child, her sanity. Then, there is blood. She awakens to blood-soaked sheets.

Is it too late to save her unborn child? Her only hope is her charming doctor for whom she is falling. Can he save her from this living nightmare?

Ten-year-old Kyle also suffers from insomnia and eerie night visions. Something, or someone, sinister has brought them together... waiting for the moment to strike.

Three years later: Mother's Day.

The nightmare is not over.

A surprise visitor greets Virginia with a gift one morning. What begins as a day of celebration is twisted into a violent, bloody confrontation as festering wounds reopen.

Shopping List 3

By popular demand, the third volume in our bestselling anthology series, twenty-one spine-chilling, terrifyingly creepy tales of terror by a bunch of the best independent horror authors writing today!

Featuring horror stories – and shopping lists – from: Richard Raven, Dhinoj Dings, Jeremy Thompson, Jeremy Wagner, Nick Manzolillo, Steve Stark, Jeff C. Stevenson, Kevin McHugh, James Watts, D.W. Jones, Nick Swain, Mark Thomas, Brian McGowan, Jason Gehlert, Mark Deloy, Richard Barber, Sergio Palumbo, Megan E. Morales, Alizure Indigo, JN Cameron, and David Simon

Schlock! Horror!

An anthology of short stories based upon/inspired by

and in loving homage to all of those great gorefest movies and books of the 1980's (not necessarily base in that era, although some do ride that wave of nostalgia!), the golden age when horror well and truly came kicking, screaming and spraying blood, gore & body parts out from the shadows...
This exemplary 80's themed/inspired tales of terror has been adjudicated and compiled by one Mr Bret McCormick, himself a writer, producer and director of many a schlock classic, including *Bio-Tech Warrior*, *Time Tracers*, *The Abomination*, *Ozone: The Attack of the Redneck Mutants* and the inimitable *Repligator*.

Featuring stories from: Todd Sullivan, Timothy C Hobbs, Mark Thomas, Andrew Post, James B. Pepe, Thomas Vaughn, Edward Karpp, Jaap Boekestein, Lisa Alfano, L. C. Holt, John Adam Gosham, Brandon Cracraft, M. Earl Smith, Sarah Cannavo, James Gardner, Bret McCormick, and James H. Longmore.

**A HellBound Books LLC
Publication**

http://www.hellboundbookspublishing.com

Printed in the United States of America

www.ingramcontent.com/pod-product-compliance
Lightning Source LLC
Chambersburg PA
CBHW032201180726

48284CB00001B/135